It was ~~NOV 0 1 2008~~ then, just as ~~DEC 2 4 2008~~ Good Girl fantasy about what would ~~on~~ on that night, the date took a very sharp, downward-plunging turn into nightmare dating hell.

"You're ... you're *thirty*?" Ted asked, his voice strained and incredulous.

"Well, not quite. I'm turning thirty in January. The first. I was a New Year's baby," I gabbled, the way I tend to do when uncomfortable.

And then, unbelievably, he said, "I thought you were older."

What? "What?"

"I thought you were older than that."

Oh. My. God. "How old did you think I was?" I asked, incredulous, and yet panicked at the same time. I knew I was prematurely wrinkling. It must be worse than I'd originally thought. I must have skin like beef jerky.

"Mid-thirties," he said.

Thirty-two? Thirty-three? I hoped fervently.

"Thirty-eight or -nine," Ted continued.

I was silent. This was terrible. Horrible. Unbearably bad. I knew it. My crow's-feet were worse than I'd thought—my date had actually judged me to be nearly a decade older than I actually was.

PUSHING 30

Whitney Gaskell

BANTAM BOOKS

PUSHING 30
A Bantam Book / October 2003

Published by
Bantam Dell
A Division of Random House, Inc.
New York, New York

Book design by Glen Edelstein

Library of Congress Cataloging-in-Publication Data
Gaskell, Whitney.
Pushing 30 / Whitney Gaskell.
p.   cm.
ISBN 0-553-38224-1
1. Single women—Fiction. 2. Women dog owners—Fiction. 3. Middle aged men—Fiction. 4. Television news anchors—Fiction. I. Title: Pushing thirty. II. Title.
PS3607.A7854P87 2003
813'.6—dc21   2003048016

Manufactured in the United States of America
Published simultaneously in Canada

RRH   10 9 8 7 6 5 4 3 2 1

For George, with love

Chapter 1

The one thing you should know about me is this: I'm the consummate Good Girl. I wash my makeup off every night, no matter how tired I am. I mail out my Christmas cards every Thanksgiving weekend without fail, and thank-you notes are written and posted within three days of receipt of any gift. I've only called into work sick once when it wasn't really true, and even then I spent the entire day too racked with guilt to enjoy it. I'm an extremely loyal and dependable friend, and have never cheated on a boyfriend or tried to steal a man away from another woman. And I never, ever say yes when a friend asks me if she looks fat, particularly if in the throes of a heartbreak she's been hitting the Häagen-Dazs pretty hard, because girlfriends should stick together and not make each other feel self-conscious about their weight. But the problem with being a Good Girl is this—I'm terrible at conflict. Absolutely hate it, am terrified of it, will do anything to avoid it. When it comes to the fight-or-flight phenomenon, my fight is nonexistent, as wimpy as Popeye pre-spinach. Luckily, I am a world-class sprinter when it comes to running away from everything having to do with anything that even remotely resembles strife.

Which is why, as I sat in the wood-paneled bar of McCormick & Schmick's on K Street nursing a glass of merlot, I was dreading the arrival of my soon-to-be ex-boyfriend, Eric Leahy. After weeks of dodging his phone calls, I was resolved to finally end the relationship. And unlike every other breakup I had ever muddled with my pathetic timidity, this time I had a plan: I would tell Eric gently, but firmly, that it was over, and at all costs preserve our dignity. I was a career woman, an attorney (a career you might—as my friends do—find amusing for me to have stumbled into, considering my above-mentioned aversion to conflict), and there was no reason why I couldn't end this relationship gracefully. No matter what, there would *not* be a messy emotional scene, nor would I allow myself to be guilted into giving it a second chance or entering into couples counseling. I had let this relationship drag on for far too long, and just like with a Band-Aid, it's better to rip it off all at once. Of course, as I sat there, hunched up on a hard wooden chair that was putting my butt to sleep, while dipping pieces of pita into a pot of lemony hummus, I didn't feel cool or dignified; I felt sick to my stomach.

I'd come to the bar directly from the office, and I had that end-of-the-workday feel—grimy and sweaty, my feet tired from walking the five blocks to the bar from my office in my three-inch stacked loafers, the waistband of my favorite black pantsuit digging into my skin. It was August, and far too hot to be wearing a suit, even one made out of lightweight wool crepe that was supposed to be "seasonless," but which felt as heavy as a mink coat in the city heat. I'd tried to perk up the otherwise dull, buttoned-up look with a hot-pink shell which I had thought looked great that morning, but as soon as I got to my office I dribbled some iced mochacchino on it, leaving brown spots splattered all over my top, and was forced to button my jacket up over the stain. I hadn't sweltered in my office, which was kept year-round at just above freezing, but as soon as I ventured back out into the damp heat of Washington, D.C., in August, I began to melt. My foundation dripped from my face, my mascara was smeared around my eyes, and my wavy hair, normally beaten into submission with a vast battery of anti-frizz products, had rebelled, and began wisping up into a Brillo-pad mess. I didn't feel elegant and composed; I was sticky and weary, and dreading what was sure to be an unavoidably messy scene.

Eric arrived. I caught sight of his affable, smiling face as he waved at me and headed toward the table I claimed, cutting through the after-work crowd of yuppies gathered in the bar. He collapsed in the empty chair I'd been fighting to keep for him, and kissed me on the cheek.

"Ellie," he said. "You look beautiful." Considering how grubby I both looked and felt, I knew he was lying. But as far as lies go, it was a sweet one. And Eric was always saying things like that—heaping compliments on me, telling me how wonderful he thought I was. It was a very appealing trait in a man, one that had kept me from breaking up with him before.

It wasn't that Eric was unattractive—he had glossy black hair, ruddy cheeks, and bright blue eyes, and looked sort of like a pudgy J.Crew model. And while he was a little chunky, and dressed in stodgy three-piece suits and shirts with cufflinks (both of which looked pretentious on a thirty-two-year-old man), he was gentle and thoughtful. Not funny exactly—well, no, not funny at all. He tried to crack jokes now and again, but they were always the kind that had obvious punch lines, and he usually mangled the telling of the joke so badly you couldn't even laugh at the sheer silliness of it. But he was a good man. A kind man. Exactly the kind of boyfriend the Good Girl aspires to, and nearly identical in appearance and personality to my last four boyfriends. We even had cutsie, matching names—Ellie and Eric, E & E.

But, just like my previous four boyfriends—Alec, Peter, Winston, and Jeremy—Eric bored me to tears. All he wanted to talk about was his job—something having to do with international finance (although I still wasn't exactly sure what, even though he'd explained it to me more times than I cared to recount)—or whatever football/basketball/baseball/cricket game ESPN had broadcast the night before. I'm not one of those women who pretend to like sports in order to snag a guy; in fact, I'm pretty up-front about how I couldn't care less about grown men cavorting around on fake grass in short pants with a ball tucked under one arm. But despite explaining my lack of interest to Eric pretty much every time he started a conversation with "You wouldn't believe what happened in the game last night," he persisted in boring me to tears with a play-by-play analysis. Spending dinner with him was pleasant as long as I could coax him into talking about something else, and the sex was tolerable, if not predictable. But just the idea of something more permanent, of lying beside him in bed every night and waking up to his face every morning, made me feel like I was being buried alive.

And besides, Eric just didn't smell right. It wasn't that he had b.o., or that funky ripe odor some men get when they're sweaty. He was very clean and deodorized, but there was something about the way he smelled when I wrapped my arms around him and breathed in deeply that was just ... off. And his cologne—Polo, just as Winston and Alec had worn (Peter wore Drakkar Noir, and Jeremy, who had spent a semester studying in Paris, wore Hermès)—which he practically showered in, was overpowering and artificial smelling. Surely the man I was meant to spend my life with would smell sexy and good and safe, and not like a cheesy club promoter.

"I'm so glad you called," Eric said, after ordering a martini.

Why is everyone in my generation always ordering martinis? Is it a desperate attempt to try to return the world to the days before the Boomers came along and wrecked everything with their self-indulgent Me Generation crap? As though a single cocktail can undo the sixties, I thought, forgetting about the impending breakup just long enough to get annoyed by Eric, who had a tendency to be pompous, and then promptly feeling a flood of guilt when I remembered what I was there to do.

"I've been wanting to talk to you about something," he said, stirring his drink, and spearing the olive on a toothpick.

Oh, good, I thought, relieved. He's probably sick of the way I've been acting—ducking his phone calls, avoiding sex, snapping at him when he launches into one of his insufferably long diatribes about the yen—and wants to dump *me*. It will make this *so* much easier. He'll try to let me down easy, and I'll try to look a little stricken, but say of course, I understand, I've been so caught up at work (ha ha!) that I haven't devoted enough time to the relationship. A dignified, understanding split, and I'd be mercifully spared from having to do it myself.

"Oh?" I said, and smiled at him encouragingly. "I've been wanting to talk to you, too."

"Okay. What about?"

"No, you go first."

"Well . . ." Eric said, and then ducked his head shyly, a nervous smile playing on his thin lips. "I want you to move in with me."

What? Move in. With him. As in *not* breaking up. As

in living together. I thought I was going to be sick. No, no, no, this can't be happening, I thought. This is the part where he's supposed to say something like "I never meant to hurt you," or "We've been growing apart for a long time."

Eric—obviously misreading my hesitation—said, "I don't mean without other plans. We could get engaged first. Maybe over Labor Day weekend we could take the train to Manhattan, go ring shopping, maybe see *The Lion King*—" and then, seeing my stricken face, "What is it? What's wrong?"

"It's just ... um ... is the air conditioner working in here?" I asked.

The bar had become so hot and stuffy I could barely breathe, much less think clearly. Eric's words— "engagement," "plans," "move in together"—were jumbling around my brain. A minute ago I thought we were nicely on our way to a collegial breakup, and now all of a sudden he wanted to live together forever, buy a house in the suburbs and have babies and minivans. What was it with men, anyway? Why is it that when the woman wants a commitment, they panic and flee the jurisdiction, but grow a little distant and suddenly they're out shopping for diamond solitaires and monogrammed guest towels?

"What were you going to say?" he asked.

"God, it's hot in here. Do you think it's hot in here? I'm burning up," I blathered, and chugged a glass of ice water.

"No, it feels fine to me. Are you okay?"

"Oh. Yes, yes. Just hot," I said gaily, shrugging off my jacket, no longer caring about the stain on my top.

Eric had a strange look on his face. "What were you going to say?" he asked again.

"I was going to say ... well, I *don't* think we should move in together," I said weakly.

"You don't? Why not?"

Why not indeed. If I had been incapable of a brisk "It's over. Let's be friends," before, now, in the face of his proposal, I had no idea where to start. "Well ... I was thinking that maybe we should think about, well, you know ... maybe think about taking it a little more slowly."

"Slowly. But I thought this is what you wanted, to get engaged, to move forward. I thought you'd be happy," Eric said.

"Um," I said.

"What do you mean by taking it slower? I mean, you still want to see each other, don't you?" he continued.

"Er," I said.

"You don't want to see other people, do you?" he asked, in an incredulous tone.

This was just the break I was looking for. I nodded eagerly, and said, "Well, yes, we could do that. See other people. That might be a good idea," I said, as though it was his idea, and I was just going along with it. Encouraging his sound judgment.

But I don't think Eric bought it. Instead, he looked startled, with that deer-in-the-headlights expression people always talk about (although since I don't commune with nature, I've never come that close to running over Bambi).

"See other people," he repeated, and as he absorbed my words his face fell like a child who's just been told that there's no such thing as Santa. "You mean, instead of being exclusive. But you don't want to break up, do you? Not entirely? I mean, you still want us to see each other, right?"

Again, typical male reaction—complete and utter shock at the very suggestion that they somehow fall short of your ideal. And it's not just the smart, handsome, successful, rich men—the stupid, ugly, losers are equally flabbergasted that a woman could find them anything less than highly desirable. But when a woman gets dumped, she immediately starts moaning about how if only her thighs were thinner or if she had only been more willing to engage in nightly fellatio, if she could only have been more perfect, then he wouldn't have left. This is a universal female reaction, no matter how brilliant and smart and wonderful the woman in question happens to be, nor how much of a reject the boyfriend is.

"Oh, no. No. Well, I mean, we could see each other," I hastened to say, and then, remembering my resolve about Band-Aids, whispered, "As friends."

Eric just sat there, holding his martini, his head bowed forward. He looked . . . sick. I felt sick. This wasn't going well at all. Why did I do this? Why hadn't I gone first, said my piece, and avoided the whole engagement/move-in-together thing? Why? *Why?*

Eric still didn't say anything. He just got all droopy, and sniffly, and for a horrible moment I thought he was going to cry. He looked at me with wide, wet, dog-being-dumped-in-the-country-because-he's-no-longer-a-cute-fluffy-puppy eyes. And I felt dreadful, worse than a dog deserter—more like a monster who'd just finished gleefully decapitating a nest of fuzzy baby bunnies.

I couldn't bear the silence any longer. "I'm so sorry. I had no idea that you thought . . . that you'd been thinking . . . I didn't know," I finished lamely.

"I noticed that you'd been distant. At first I thought it was just your work or something, but then you never wanted to get together, so then I thought that you were getting annoyed that we weren't making plans for the future. I thought that you wanted a commitment. But I guess that wasn't it at all," Eric said, shooting me another reproachful, teary look. "I thought that we were in love."

And just like that, my resolve wavered. He thought

that I loved him. It was such a terrible, terrible thing to tell someone who thinks that he is loved that no, sorry, you aren't. I didn't want to be that person, the one who takes what's all warm and cozy—winter afternoon mugs of cocoa, Saturday night video rentals, Sunday morning crossword puzzles over pancakes—and rips it to shreds. And the part of me that didn't want to be the heartbreaker was pulling way ahead of the side of me that wanted to shake Eric out of my life. I couldn't stand his desolate, reproachful gaze. I was willing to do anything—maybe even go ring shopping—to make it end.

"Oh, Eric," I said, my will collapsing. If at that moment he had said one more word about love, or wanting to give it another try, I would have done it. Knowing all the while that five years later when we'd married and had babies, and I was having lustful fantasies about the neighbor's teenage son who cut our grass, we'd be able to trace all of the marital discord right back to this very moment.

But thankfully, it didn't come to that. Eric pulled himself together. He took a deep breath, drew his shoulders up and his chest out, lifted his chin, and moved from lovelorn victim to Gloria Gaynor singing "I Will Survive." He smiled bravely and stood up, thrusting his balled-up fists into the pockets of his wool Brooks Brothers suit pants with a certain resolute dignity, and stood for a minute at the edge of the table.

"Well. Bye. Maybe I'll call you later?" he asked.

I nodded encouragingly and said, "Oh, yes, please do," while my conscience was screaming, *No! Tell him not to call! Like the Band-Aid! Tell him about ripping off the Band-Aid, and how even if it seems worse now it's actually much, much better in the long run.*

After Eric left, I sat in the bar and finished my wine, which felt like battery acid churning around in my stomach. When I was sure that he'd had enough time to get a taxi, so I wouldn't have to bump into him on the street, I dug my cell phone out of my bag and called my best friend, Nina, and asked her if I could come over.

"I need to talk. It's an emergency," I said.

And then, before leaving McCormick & Schmick's, I went to the ladies' room and managed to make it to a stall just before I puked up all of the hummus and pita bread.

It was exactly five months until my thirtieth birthday.

Chapter 2

A few nights after the botched breakup, I turned my hair pink. Not on purpose, but rather in a desperate attempt to avoid paying the ridiculous amount my stylist, Gino, charges for highlights. Of course, every time I attempt home coloring, I end up turning my hair red, or pink, or even ink black once, and end up at the salon anyway, only now paying for color correction, for which Gino—well aware of what a pink-haired woman desperate to return to her normal mousy brown color will pay—charges what's surely equal to a house down payment in less-populated areas of the country. Nina always tells me to call her when I'm contemplating home color, promising she'll talk me down from it, and if necessary come over and show me old photos of me with bad hair color. But despite these dire experiences, I went ahead and started to slap the color on, cheerfully forgetting all of my past bad experiences with home bleaching kits. It was a little like drinking too much—you have a vague memory that it's something you might later regret, and yet it seems like such a good idea at the time you uncork the bottle.

This time the hair disaster was my mother's fault. I

had no sooner pulled my hair through the highlighting cap—a plastic bonnet reminiscent of the fifties, with chin straps and a visor—and dumped the bleach on my head, when the phone rang. My mother. Crap. The one time I pick the phone up on the first ring instead of screening through my answering machine, and there was Gloria on the other end. With a sigh, I slumped onto the closed toilet seat and braced myself for the onslaught of maternal guilt.

"Ellie? Is that you?" she asked. As though still unsure of my voice after nearly thirty years of acquaintance. And as though anyone else would be in my apartment answering my phone.

"Mother," I said wearily. "Of course it's me."

"Daddy and I are going to one of those boring fundraisers they insist the judges attend, and I was going to wear my black dress made out of that stretchy material, but then I was thinking that maybe I should wear my red silk suit instead. What do you think?"

"I have no idea. I've never seen you in either outfit," I said, breathing deeply and counting to five.

"Well, just imagine what they look like. The black one is long and formfitting, and the red suit is short-sleeved, very tailored, but with a sexy short skirt," she said.

"Hmmmm," I said.

"What do you think?"

"The black dress," I said, mainly because it sounded like something I would wear, whereas I wouldn't be caught dead in a red silk dinner suit that likely had big gold buttons running down the front and enormous, 1985-era shoulder pads.

"But the red one shows off my legs, which you have to admit are pretty sexy, especially for a woman my age.

Buddy Johnson was just telling me the other day how sexy he thought they were, and that he wished Mary had kept her figure like I have," Mother preened.

"Mom, I can't really talk now," I began, already tiring of the conversation and its familiar "aren't I the most beautiful, intelligent, and sexy woman in the world" theme.

"And Dr. Patel patted me on the ankle the other day during my checkup, which was of course flattering, but then again, probably not very professional. And you know he always feels my breasts every time I go in," Mother continued, completely oblivious to me.

"He's a gynecologist," I pointed out. "They always check your breasts. For lumps. To make sure you don't have breast cancer."

"Not every time," my mother insisted.

"Yes. Every single time," I said, exasperated.

"Don't be silly. Dr. Patel is the only doctor I have who touches my breasts. I'm not saying he's hitting on me, but I think it's obvious that he finds me attractive. You just find it hard to view your mother as a sexual creature. So, what day are you coming home?" she asked, smoothly transitioning the conversation.

I know that not everyone's mother drives them crazy. I know women—seemingly sane, happy women—who purport to be on the best of terms with their mothers. They go shopping together, and have high tea at ritzy hotels, and sometimes even vacation together, and proclaim with healthy, nondysfunctional gaiety that their mother is their best friend. I am not one of those women. Whenever I'm around my mother, I revert to a sullen fifteen-year-old girl, slouching, snapping my gum, and rolling my eyes skyward and groaning, "Moth-errrr." My mother is one of those moms who, when you're growing up, your friends think is cool. They loved her hip clothes, that she would confide in them as if they were her adult contemporaries, and the way she would shimmy around the kitchen, her hips gyrating, to our modern, eighties pop music. I did not love any of these traits. Nor did I appreciate her off-the-wall sense of humor (for example, telling my tenth-grade math teacher that he looked like a penis—although there was a certain unmistakable bald-bulb-headedness about him), her narcissistic preening, nor her screaming confrontations with my bewildered father, who, as he does whenever facing anything remotely personally messy, would retreat to the solitude of his office.

I have also never appreciated her blatant emotional manipulation of me. She doesn't just push my buttons— she installed each and every one of them, and operates me with the slick ease of a seasoned pro.

"You are coming home for Daddy's birthday, aren't you? Your brothers are coming, and we're going out to the lake for the weekend. And you didn't come last year," she said accusingly. "Your father was crushed."

The blatant guilt trip had its immediate and intended effect on me. Even though I knew my father probably still hadn't noticed I moved out of the house twelve years ago to go to college, I still felt terrible for not wanting to go home to the crazy house. But knowing that she was just manipulating me, I tried to fight the feeling of guilt bubbling up inside me. "I don't think I can," I said, with forced nonchalance.

"I told Nana that you were coming," Mother said triumphantly, thrusting her secret weapon—a dagger of grand-maternal guilt—through my heart. It worked: I felt horrible for having neglected my poor father and cranky grandmother, and pissed off at my mother for imposing it all on me.

"Well, ah, that commercial storage case is going to trial in September, and my boss pretty much said not to make too many plans between now and then," I fibbed wildly.

My mother paused and lit a cigarette, her lighter making the familiar clicking sound. I could hear a long exhale, and imagined the cloud of smoke exiting through her nostrils, dragon style. "But your brothers are coming home," Mother said. I sensed a note of defeat in her voice. The only thing she'd concede was more important than enduring another family get-together nightmare was my job. Mom, who'd always been bitter about never living out her fantasy of having a high-powered career, loved that I was an attorney working for a successful D.C. law firm. Unlike my friends, she didn't see any incongruity between my aversion to conflict and my career as a litigator. Or else she was too consumed with her illusion of me as a glamorous career woman to care that my profession made me miserable.

It wasn't as though I had set out to be a litigator—hell, I hadn't set out to be an attorney. Law school just seemed to be a highly appropriate next step for a poli-sci major—not to mention that my father is a judge, and was heartbroken when neither of my older brothers chose to go to law school—and I am nothing if not appropriate. I'd signed on with the Snow & Druthers litigation section after graduation because I wanted to live in the District, and it was the only firm that extended me an offer. Frankly, I hated my job. It was dull work, and I spent most days going blind on a mountain of boring contracts. But my mother thinks that she missed out on something by being a part-time stay-at-home mom, part-time teacher, and had a lot invested in my living out her fantasy of black Dior power suits and Chanel red lipstick, striding around the office in Prada heels and snapping orders at terrified paralegals. Every once in a while I make an attempt to enlighten her on the reality of an associate's life—long hours, decent but by no means the extraordinary pay needed to buy designer clothes, and a lot of groveling to shitty partners whom, if they were accidentally run over by a car, I wouldn't spill tears over. But Gloria would hear none of it—she rarely lets reality interfere with her fantasies.

"Well, Mark and Brian both live in Syracuse, and so all they have to do is drive for ten minutes to visit you. I have an eight-hour car ride or a six-hour train ride. It's not really the same," I reminded her. As I had over and over again before. It was like convincing her that I wasn't actually ever awake at 5:30 A.M., and that every time she called that early for one of her little chats, she was in fact waking me up.

"Well, I suppose you can see everyone at Thanksgiving," she said, feinting and then throwing a surprise punch. Damn, how did she do that? Stealing my victory of avoiding Dad's birthday by sentencing me to a horrific four-day weekend with them. But one of the key characteristics of any Good Girl is a knack for repressing resentment and putting on a happy face.

"Great," I said without much enthusiasm. "Thanksgiving."

"Did you hear that Beth is getting married?"

Oh, crap. I'd forgotten about Beth's wedding. It was probably a mental block against seeing the last of my single high school friends married. Leaving me as the last one standing. The old maid. Even worse, I was going to have to go home for the wedding anyway, and now Thanksgiving, too. Shit, shit, double shit.

"Of course, Mother. She's one of my oldest friends. I got an invitation in the mail yesterday." I sighed in defeat.

"Her fiancé is an orthodontist," Mother said approvingly. "Maybe he has a friend he can set you up with."

"I don't need to be set up with anyone," I said, trying to keep my voice pleasant through gritted teeth. Beth's fiancé, Seth, was prematurely bald and—according to her—during sex poked at her clitoris like it was a button on the television remote. He was one of those people whom you look at and immediately know what he'll be like in forty years—his eyebrows will thicken and his jowls will droop, his belly will expand over his golf pants, and he'll give dirty looks to the teenagers necking in the back of the movie theater.

"Of course you don't. You have Eric. You'll bring him home for Thanksgiving and Christmas, of course," my mother said smoothly, thus neatly doubling the holidays my presence would be required for without a chance for contradiction.

"Eric and I broke up."

My mother actually gasped, and I pictured her on the other end of the line swooning, grasping the butcher-block kitchen island for support. "He dumped you!" she cried.

Irritation pricked at me, and I had to take a few long breaths so as not to snap. My mother read my hesitation as sorrow. "It will be all right, honey. Maybe you can talk to him, get him to go to counseling with you. Are you exercising, keeping yourself trim? You know what happened to you in college when you were eating that greasy food all the time, and put on all that weight and your skin broke out. You didn't have a boyfriend for *two years*."

"Mom! God! I'm not overweight, and my complexion is fine. And I broke up with Eric, not the other way around," I grumped.

"What happened?" she demanded, and wasn't satisfied until I relayed the entire story to her, omitting the part about the strange, artificial way Eric smelled, since

I knew that in a million years she wouldn't understand that. By the time I assured her that yes, I had done the right thing, and no, it wasn't too late for me to get married at some point, and yes, I was very sure that Eric was not The One, and *finally* hung up the phone, I realized that the bleach on my hair had passed the lovely medium-beige blonde stage and turned into a color that was dirty and faded, but unmistakably pink.

"Oh, fuck," I said to my reflection.

I stared at my head in the mirror, willing the straggles of hair peeking up through the plastic hat to go back to lovely beige-blonde, or even its original boring light brown, anything other than strawberry pink. All the while trying hard not to think about the $300 Gino had charged me for a color correction the last time I turned my hair pink. Why did I do this over and over? Why not just pay the $150 he charged for highlights and emerge from the salon with tasteful, elegant, Jodi Foster–colored hair, rather than paying twice as much for the bland brownish color he would have to turn me into just to cover the pink? Why? It was like a kind of amnesia, the way I continued to forget, time and time again, that the drugstore stuff never worked.

Ah, but maybe I could fix it. If I went to the twenty-four-hour drugstore, picked up a box of the ultra-lightening super-blonde bleach, I could at least bleach the pink to colorless white. It would be a little more drastic than I had planned, but what else could I do? It was Saturday, the salon wouldn't open until Tuesday, and I couldn't go to work Monday with pink hair.

The larger problem was how was I going to get to the drugstore with the highlighting cap on my head? The oft-colored hair was segregated from the rest of my head by the cap, and if I took it off, I would never be able to target the pink strands with the super bleach. I would have to bleach all of my hair, and end up looking like I should live in a West Texas trucking town, slopping plates of lumpy chili in front of road-weary truckers. I dug through my closet for a hat. The only one I could find was one Nina had given me as a joke that had the word "Cocks" embroidered across the top in scarlet letters (short for "Gamecocks," the mascot for the University of South Carolina). I shoved it on my head and did the best I could to tuck the chin straps of the highlighting cap up under the baseball cap. The sides were still barely visible, but there was nothing I could do, save tie a big woolen scarf around my head, and since it was August, that would look stranger than the highlighting cap. I said a little prayer that I wouldn't see anyone I knew, hooked up my churlish pug, Sally, in her halter and leash (and was growled at for my trouble—Sally has a strong sense of what she does and does not like, and taking walks definitely falls into the latter category), and we headed out the door.

The drugstore was only two blocks away from my postage-stamp-sized Dupont Circle apartment. I walked as fast as I could, dragging Sally, who was moaning about the forced exercise, behind me. The drugstore was within sight, its blue fluorescent sign blinking in the night, when a flash of something white darted by, scampered around us, and then threw itself on top of Sally. It was a dog—a scrappy mix of some sort, and it was happily humping at Sally with the enthusiasm of a horny frat boy. Sally, not one to tolerate anything she finds unpleasant, and who possesses no fear of letting her feelings be known—really, she's a role model to me—let out a high-pitched shriek, bit her would-be suitor on the nose, and then threw herself into my arms, panting dramatically at her ordeal. I was more concerned about the canine Romeo, who despite a clear set of fang marks on his tender nose, looked as cheerful and interested in Sally as ever. In fact, more so now that she had let him know he wasn't fit for butt sniffing. Men, they're all the same, I thought, bending over and petting the little fellow. Sally simultaneously growled at the masher and swooned in my arms, practically throwing one paw over her brow like a silent film actress.

"Oscar!" A shout, followed by quickly approaching footsteps. "There you are. Have you been bothering this lady? Come here."

It was a man. An older man, tall with graying yet still full hair. His features were terribly handsome, yet not perfect—the nose a little crooked, the green eyes a little squinty, the narrow lips unforgiving—in a perfect way. He had a lean, athletic body that was still substantial, particularly through his broad shoulders, and he was beautifully dressed. I know just enough about men's clothes to recognize that you couldn't buy such a perfectly tailored shirt and trousers at the local Gap. I guessed that they were custom-made, and with expensive fabrics. I wondered if he was a politician—he had that well-groomed, appealing look—although as he cuffed the energetic Oscar and hooked him back on his leash, there was something sardonic about his expression that most slick, successful politicians would be careful to hide.

"I hope he didn't scare you," the man said.

"Oh, no, of course not. Although I don't know if Sally here is going to get over it," I said, lifting the pug slightly so he could see her. She was still in wounded victim mode, although she perked up once she saw the handsome stranger. Sally has a thing for men—whenever she gets near one, she throws herself on her back, all four legs splayed apart, and presents her belly for stroking. She's something of a pug slut.

"Well, let's hope she makes a full recovery," the man said, and then he was reaching toward me, and for a confused second I wondered if he was trying to grab me, or maybe even kiss me—why I thought this, I don't know, maybe I'd spent too many hours luxuriating in bubble baths with romance novels—but instead he just stroked Sally on her silky, wrinkled forehead, while she preened. "She's very pretty."

"As she well knows," I said, and nodded toward Oscar. "And Oscar here is an appealing little guy. Is he a terrier? Or a beagle?"

"Yes and yes, I think, although his origins are unknown. He just showed up on my doorstep one day, and adopted me," he said, looking down at Oscar. I thought he sounded a little embarrassed to admit to such a sentimental gesture.

Stories like this always make me feel guilty. Instead of adopting a pathetic yet deserving canine bundle from the local SPCA who would forever thank me for the gesture by years of faithful friendship, I had shelled out four hundred dollars for Sally. Four hundred dollars to enslave myself to a twenty-pound dictator, who let me know at all times that my care of her—gourmet pet food, bottled water, a faux-fur leopardskin bed and a fetching plaid coat from Coach—did not meet her expectations. I wondered whether Sally might be the reincarnation of Pol Pot, that is if there was such a thing as reincarnation, and if there was a chance that a brutal dictator could come back as a spoiled, pampered lap dog, and not a cockroach or slug.

"So. Well. I suppose Oscar and I should get home. I'm Ted Langston, by the way," he said.

"Ellie. Ellie Winters," I said, and smiled at him.

He smiled back, and I felt a ping in my stomach, a warm tightening that I hadn't felt in a long time. A long, long time. I'd certainly never felt it for Eric. There was something about this man, this Ted Langston. He was certainly attractive, and although there was no doubt that he was quite a bit older, he had a quality of strength and virility that gave me a heightened awareness of just how close we were standing to each other. As Ted looked my way, his green eyes sharp and appraising, I wondered if he was feeling the same attraction.

"Um. I think that ... Oh. Well," he said.

Was he about to ask me for a cup of coffee? Or for my phone number? I wondered hopefully. I returned his smile, in what I hoped was a flirty, open way. But then, ever so tactfully, he pointed at my head.

"There's something stuck to your hat," he said, and I reached up to pat the "Cocks" cap.

Oh. Fucking. Shit. The highlighting cap had popped out of one side of the baseball cap, and the chin strap was flapping in the hot summer breeze. I had no doubt that it looked exactly like a plastic version of the tinfoil hats that crazy people wear to prevent aliens from sending mind-controlling radiation signals to them. Here I was imagining that this elegant, impressive man might be interested in me, while I was dressed in the stretched-out and faded gray sweat suit I always wear when coloring my hair, had no makeup on, and was wearing a plastic highlighting bonnet under a crass baseball hat. I was lucky that he wasn't trying to track down the police to haul me off to the nearest loony bin. I flushed bright red, and fervently wished that the ground would open up and swallow me into it. When the earth failed to move beneath my feet, I took the only other course of action I could—I ran.

"Nice to meet you," I mumbled, and fled, dragging Sally, now on the ground again, grumpily behind me. I could hardly believe my bad luck. The first non-Eric—and for that matter, non-Alec, non-Peter, non-Winston, and non-Jeremy—man I had met in forever, and I was in the middle of a freaky pink-haired crisis. Lovely.

Chapter 3

Ted Langston. *Mmmmm.* I couldn't stop thinking about him. His face was so interesting, so compelling. Sort of like Russell Crowe, not that he looked anything like the actor, but he had the same sort of attractive intensity and gleaming, crinkled eyes. And his physique, all lean and rangy, yet substantial through those wide shoulders and broad chest. I wondered if it would look as good unclothed, or if he had one of those Cary Grant bodies that looks great in clothes, but ends up being sort of puny and concave-chested. *Ted Langston naked,* I thought dreamily, and then laughed out loud at how silly I was being. He was probably married, I told myself, and it's both pointless and pathetic to get a crush on a married man. And even if he wasn't married, after the highlighting-cap incident, he undoubtedly thinks I'm deranged. But still ... *Mmmmm.*

Even more pathetic than fantasizing about a man I hardly knew, I was sitting in my office trying to pretend that I wasn't actually at work, but maybe the star of a sitcom whose character was an attorney, but would be saved from having to do any real work just as soon as David Spade walked in and started cracking jokes. Unfortunately, television shows like *Ally McBeal,* with all of the zany, interesting characters prosecuting zany, interesting cases, are about as far from the reality of a law practice as you can get. Likewise with *The Practice, L.A. Law,* and all of the John Grisham novels. The reality of law—and in particular litigation—is that it's a dull exercise in paper pushing and obstruction, and has very little to do with any noble causes or worthy clients.

Which is why the first thing I do every morning when I get to work is go online and search the employment classifieds for new jobs. All of the jobs advertised sound so much more interesting than mine—head of this oversight committee, or president of such-and-such university. I used to send resumés in for every job listing, but stopped once I could no longer bear getting back the stiffly worded rejection letters wishing me good luck, but, sadly, they were only interviewing competent and qualified candidates. It was too depressing, especially since it was further evidence that life is not at all like the movies. In the celluloid world, the young ingenue always gets the glamour job she's inherently unqualified for, only to rise to the occasion and surprise everyone with her cunning business sense. Like Melanie Griffith in *Working Girl.* The ingenue does not stay in a thankless job being slave-driven by heartless employers who view her with vague hostility should she need to take an afternoon off to donate a kidney or give birth to a child.

"Well, if you absolutely have to," they say, shaking their heads and wondering why they hired such a shirker.

My boss is like this. Howard Shearer—a fat, pompous, balding blowhard—always looks surprised when I take the odd Saturday or Christmas Day off from the litigation hamster wheel. He's fond of saying things like "When I was an associate, I billed twenty-five hundred hours a year. This new generation of lawyers always talking about their 'quality of life' seem to think they can glide through without paying their dues." He's also the kind of person who simulates his quotes with bunny ears, waggling his index and middle fingers in the air as he says things like "quality of life." I hate him.

So, I was in my office, playing solitaire—how does anyone get any work done now that they have computer games and the Internet on their office computer? Am I the only one who spends 90 percent of her time surfing the gossip sheets and shopping online catalogs, and the other 10 percent working like a demon to make up for all the time spent diddling around?—when Shearer the Shit came trundling into my office, clearing his throat and adjusting his testicles. This was another of his disgusting habits, the constant ball arranging, often performed just before offering his hand to shake.

"Winters," he boomed. I think he thinks calling me by my last name will make him look nonsexist, in a hardy-har-har, you're-just-one-of-the-boys, don't-sue-me-for-gender-discrimination sort of way. "Clear your calendar for tonight."

My heart sank. *No, don't make me work tonight,* I begged silently. There was a new episode of *Buffy the Vampire Slayer* on, and I was planning a night of vicarious undead butt-kicking, a take-out deep-dish pizza, and a bottle of merlot. But, of course, I didn't *say* any of this. Good Girls are always willing to work late. Without complaint. Yes, sir, of course, sir, whatever you say, sir.

"What's up?" I asked, making a mental note to update my resumé. Just that morning I'd seen an employment ad for a webmaster of an Internet start-up, and wondered if I needed to know more than point-and-click computer skills to qualify for the job.

"The firm's got an invite to Senator Lawton's fundraising party tonight. Need you to go and represent our interests."

"What interests are those?"

"You know, shmooze and politic. I'd go myself, but the wife's expecting me home," he said vaguely, and looked pleased with himself. "The wife" was his third, and used to be a paralegal at the firm before she dislodged the second Mrs. Shearer the Shit from their Alexandria McMansion and took up residence. He tossed the invite on my desk and departed, murmuring under his breath "Good, good," as he always does. Shearer walks through life affirming his existence.

This was so typical. I was being forced to go to what would surely be a horrible party full of boring, self-important windbags, none of whom I'd know, with no idea whom I was expected to "shmooze" and "politic," and apparently because I'm single and don't have a spouse waiting at home for me, Shearer thinks that I'm always free to drop everything at the last minute. I had no doubt that the partnership had asked him to attend the party, or he'd volunteered, and was only now punting the thankless job to me. At least, according to the engraved invitation on ivory linen paper, there would be an open bar, and there was always a spread at these things. Free dinner and free drinks. Maybe it wouldn't be so bad after all.

I decided to go to the party straight from work, hoping that I could pop in, make a few brilliant remarks to all the right people, and then make it home in time for *Buffy*. I'd played with the idea of ditching the party altogether—how would Shearer find out, after all?—but I saw two problems with that plan. One, I might not be the only one from the firm going, and two, I'm horrible at lying. Whenever I try to tell even the smallest fib, I turn pink, stammer, giggle nervously, and everything I'm lying about sounds flat and fake. So if Shearer asked me tomorrow how it had gone, I'd probably dissolve in a fit of high-pitched squeals and say that I'd talked to someone who would turn out to be dead.

Since I was planning to keep my appearance brief, I didn't have time to go home first and change out of my work clothes. If only stupid Shearer had given me the invitation yesterday, I could have planned ahead and worn my gorgeous new black wool gabardine skirt suit that makes me look much thinner and more stylish than I actually am. As it was, I was wearing my old navy pant-suit, which was comfortable but a little frumpy, with its pleated front pants and pilling sleeves. This is probably why beauty magazines advise you to keep a slinky tank top, kitten-heel sandals, and a tube of red lip gloss in your desk drawer, so that you can pull off these last minute parties by transforming from worker bee to party babe. Unfortunately, all I had in my desk drawer was a dog-eared paperback novel, a pack of gum, and a pink gel-inked pen with pink feathers on one end. No doubt some beauty editor would be able to pluck the feathers from the pen and glue them to her shoes using correction fluid and a stapler, turning them into knock-off Jimmy Choos, but that was a little out of my league. All I could do was duck into the ladies' room before leaving the office to powder my nose and slick on some sheer berry lipstick. I didn't look my best, but I supposed good enough to attend a party where I wouldn't know anyone.

I am overall an average-looking person—five feet five inches tall, neither slim nor fat, shoulder-length blonde hair, a nose larger than I'd like (but certainly not Cyrano-like)—although even "average" is a subjective description. Probably most people consider themselves average looking, the way everyone always describes themselves as middle-class, even if they have four houses, a staff of servants, and a jet on call, or, conversely, live in a one-room shack without any power or indoor plumbing. In Los Angeles, where all of the women shriek in horror if they eat an extra Tic Tac and balloon into a size four, and receive plastic surgery gift certificates for their sweet sixteen birthdays, I would be regarded as a fat, schlumpy Quasimodo, while in those trailer parks where everyone looks like Roseanne Barr pre–plastic surgery and dresses in Wal-Mart–purchased polyester pantsuits, I would comparatively be seen as a Michelle Pfeiffer–like goddess.

I've always been reconciled to my average girl-next-door looks. But suddenly, while leaning forward a few inches from the mirror in order to apply my lipstick with laser precision, I saw something in the mirror that made my blood run cold and goose bumps spread over my arms. *Wrinkles*. There, at the corner of my eyes, still faint and yet ... there. Surely I was too young! Who gets wrinkles in their twenties? And yet there they were, squiggling insidiously out from the corners of my eyes, harbingers of what the next decade of my life was to hold for me. It was too unfair. I still had a spray of pimples running along my jawline—what kind of a hellish universe would make it possible to have wrinkles and pimples at the same time? And why had I spent so many hours as a teenager lying out in the sun, smugly rubbing my golden skin with only baby oil? Why had I shunned hats and SPF 40? Was it too late? Oh, God, why did I have to turn thirty? Why? Why?

And why do I have to go to this horrible party, I thought miserably. It was so unfair. All I wanted to do was put a bag over my head, go home, put on my most comfortable pajamas and eat a pint of Dulce de Leche Häagen-Dazs straight from the container.

*   *   *

The party was in a posh, private club with lots of wood paneling and expensive flower arrangements. There was already a full house of suits present—male and female—laughing their best shmoozey, fake laughs. If Manhattan excels at being a town of aggressively chic fashionistas, D.C. is the capital of dorks, filled with the kind of people who were Phi Beta Kappas and on law review, and who now wear horn-rimmed glasses, conservative navy suits, and unflattering, mushroom-shaped bobs.

I didn't see a single familiar face, so I headed to the bar for a gin and tonic, and then scooped a few cheese puffs and onion tartlets off the buffet table. I stood to one side of the buffet and looked around at the crowd, wondering just who it was I was supposed to be sucking up to. There were a few familiar faces, but I couldn't tell if they were clients of the firm or local politicians. I'm probably the only person living in the District who can't name the Labor Department under-secretary or the assistant to the Assistant Attorney General, much less someone obvious, like the majority leader of the Senate. Everyone there seemed to consider themselves a Very Important Person, but who knows if they lived up to their own press? For all I knew, they were all law firm associates, forced into attendance by horrid, slave-driving partner bosses.

After a while, I gave up trying to identify anyone, and my thoughts began to wander: *God, my pants feel tight. I knew I shouldn't have eaten all of those nachos the other night. I wonder if it's water retention from the salt in the tortilla chips, or actual fat gain. That's it, I'm going to start the protein diet again. Even if in the past carbohydrate deprivation has made me so insane I actually debated swiping jelly donuts off of a coworker's desk. I probably just didn't drink enough water, that's all. Hmmm ... what should I get Nina for her birthday? She was hinting about wanting a new purse the other night, but for a starving artist, she has expensive taste. She probably wouldn't want a Nine West bag on sale at Macy's. Oh my God, I wonder how noticeable my wrinkles are? I knew I should have been using alpha hydroxy lotion, although didn't I read something in the new* Allure *about a new cream that—*

"Are you standing over here to horde food, or are you hiding?"

I was startled. Oh. My. God. It was Ted Langston. And here I was wearing a scruffy suit and stuffing my face with hors d'oeuvres. On the bright side of things, I wasn't wearing a highlighting cap and obscene baseball hat, and after the pink hair crisis, I had managed to coax my hair into lemony-blonde highlights. A bit on the whitish side, but better than the muddy pink color. While I still didn't look my best, I also didn't look crazy. A definite improvement over our last meeting.

"Hmph," I replied, since I had just stuffed a whole pea pod–wrapped shrimp in my mouth a moment earlier. I chewed and chewed for what seemed an eternity—damn that shrimp!—and by the time I had finally swallowed the crustacean, I was red with embarrassment. "Sorry," I muttered.

But he just smiled his sexy smile. He was as attractive as I remembered, with green eyes that crinkled at the edges. It's so unfair that wrinkles look sexy and distinguished on men, but aging on women. He held out a hand to me. "Ellie, right?" he said.

"Yes," I said. "How's Oscar? Still pining away for Sally?"

Ted laughed. "He's up to no good, I'm sure. He's learned how to pry the top off the garbage can, and likes to go through the trash while I'm at work."

"What is it that you do?" I asked.

He looked a little surprised. I hoped he wasn't a famous senator or something.

"I'm in the news," he said.

"How so?" I asked, now curious at his oblique answer. What did he mean by "in the news"? Did he mean that he had recently been written up in the newspapers for killing his wife? Wouldn't that just be my luck, getting a crush on a serial killer. Although it would of course mean that he was no longer married. Argh! I shouldn't be thinking such horrible thoughts. Why don't I follow the news? Honestly, all I ever do is work—well, work, sleep, sloth, and drink. How could anyone expect me to find the time to read newspapers and take note of Very Important People doing Very Important Things?

"I'm the news director of Gold News. And I have a daily political news show that airs weekdays at 5 P.M.," he said.

Gold News was an all-news network, and its main competition was CNN and Fox News. Ah. Well. He's head honcho of a major cable news network. I probably should have known that, I thought, coloring even more.

"Oh. Um, I don't usually get home from work until almost seven, so . . ." I said, tapering off apologetically.

"So you're not a fan?" he said, but not in a vain way, since he laughed as he said it. "Where do you work?"

"I'm an associate at Snow & Druthers. In the litigation department."

"Do you like that?" he asked.

"Sure," I lied, keeping my voice bright. Luckily, I can lie when it's just polite social chitchat. It's a necessary Good Girl accessory, on par with owning a Coach bag and monogrammed note cards. "It's a great firm."

Why was this conversation sounding an awful lot like I was talking to one of my parents' friends? I couldn't get a read on him. Normally when a man who is not a work colleague seeks me out at a party, there's at least a chance he's interested in me. Unless the party was dreadfully boring—like this one—and there's no one else to talk to. Like this one. At least, there certainly wasn't anyone else *I* was more interested in talking to, although I had spent a good part of the day wondering what Ted Langston looked like naked, so maybe I was a little biased. But the important question was still there—was he interested in me? He didn't move away—in fact, as someone passed by, he stepped closer to me to get out of her way, and then didn't move back—and he kept his eye contact with me as he talked. But then again, he was a reporter, so certainly he was trained to look intently at the person he was talking to. I wondered if he was married, and quickly checked his left hand. No ring. But not everyone from his generation wears rings. Of course, weren't most men his age divorced?

"Ted!"

"Darling!"

A middle-aged couple with matching toothy smiles, crepe skin, and a loud, blustering way of talking swooped in, the woman snatching Ted into a hug, while the older man clapped him on the arm. They crowded around, edging me to the side, so that the man's back was to me.

"I was *hoping* you'd be here. I was just *saying* to Dolly the other day that we haven't seen you in *ages,* and *must* invite you to dinner, and *here* you are," the man blustered.

At the same time, the woman trilled, "You're looking so wonderful, so fit. Now, you just have to do me a favor." She leaned closer to him, as though she were going to impart a confidence, yet kept her voice at a loud, high-pitched squeal. "I'm cochairing a fund-raiser for adult computer literacy, and you just *have* to come speak at our luncheon. I just won't take no for an answer!"

Her husband continued, raising his voice slightly to be heard over his wife. "I saw your *piece* about that Mideastern conference, and I had so much to *say* on the subject, I was talking *back* to you on the television, if you'll believe that. As you know, I've traveled *extensively* to the Mideast—at least three separate times—and I know quite a lot about their customs, and particularly how they treat Americans traveling there. People say the French are rude to foreigners, but they are a *charming* people in comparison. I think you should have me on your show, as an expert of sorts."

His wife was now yelling to be heard over him. "It's on the nineteenth of September, so I'll put you down on the guest list. You'll have a *wonderful* time, all of the ladies on the committee are just dying to meet you," she screeched, and then—amazingly—began to bat her eyelashes coquettishly at Ted.

Ted took my hand in his, firmly said, "Please excuse us," to the couple, and guided me away. Together, hand in hand, we walked from the room out into a black-and-white-tiled foyer. A tuxedo-clad waiter passed by with a silver tray full of champagne glasses in his hand, and he stopped so Ted could retrieve two flutes, dropping my hand so that he could pass a glass to me.

"Are they following us?" he asked softly, his mouth only a few inches from my ear, the warm breath reverberating deliciously against the fine hairs inside my ear. I shivered, and goose bumps covered my arms.

I looked back and saw the couple had turned their attention to tag-teaming a prominent congresswoman—even I knew who she was—and she stood between them looking helplessly back and forth as they took turns yipping at her.

"No, I think they've found another victim," I said, laughing, and then clapped a hand over my mouth. "They

PUSHING 30

33

weren't friends of yours, were they?" I asked apologetically.

"God, no. I don't have any idea who they are," Ted said.

"That must happen to you a lot."

He grimaced. "More than I care to think. It's why I hate coming to these parties."

"So why did you come?" I asked.

"Just part of the job, although undoubtedly my least favorite part. I'm expected to come to a certain number of these. Rub elbows and all that. My show is relatively new, and we're trying to build up a respectable list of political commentators. Are you a supporter of Roger Lawton?"

"Who's that?" I asked, crinkling my nose in confusion. The name sounded familiar, but I couldn't place it.

"The senior senator from Missouri who's hosting this party," Ted said patiently. "I guess not. You know, you could do a pretty good job of devastating most of the people in that room, just by not knowing who they are. Their egos couldn't take it."

I flushed pink. He must think I'm an idiot, not knowing where he worked or who Senator what's-his-name was—I suddenly remembered his name sounded familiar because it was on the invitation—or for that matter, anyone else in there. "I'm only here because one of my partners made me ... I mean, one of my partners was invited, and couldn't come, so he asked me to come in his place."

"Well then, let's get out of here," Ted said, putting his glass down and reaching for my hand again. His hand was strong and soft, and large enough to make me feel like I had dainty little hands, which I don't. I felt a warm, bubbly feeling in my tummy, a mixture of the champagne and the innocent yet erotic feeling of his hand clasping mine.

"I think there's a pizza shop on the corner. I could go for a slice. How about you?" he said.

"That sounds great," I said brightly, trying not to think about how I hadn't shaved my legs in the past five days, which meant that under no circumstances could I end up back at his place *in flagrante delicto*. Although, according to *The Rules*, and every other book on dating ever sold, you should never sleep with someone you're really interested in on the first date. And there was one thing I was completely sure of—I was very, very interested in Ted Langston. Interested enough to regret not having shaved my legs.

Chapter 4

What do you think of older men?" I asked Nina and Harmony. We'd met at Pizza Paradiso for lunch and were all munching on chicken Caesar salads.

"I love them. They're incredible in bed," Nina said. Nina had been my college roommate, and has the exact opposite personality from mine. She's brash, brutally honest, occasionally foul-tempered, and incredibly open about sex. She sleeps with whomever she wants whenever she wants, without any of the Good Girl angst I suffer from. In fact, we're like photo negatives of each other. She continued: "And they're much more appreciative of blow jobs. Guys our age think that it's their God-given right, and start pushing your head in their lap on the second date. Older men—especially married older men—have done without it for so long they think you're a goddess for blowing them. In fact, lack of oral sex is the number one reason married men have affairs."

"It is not," Harmony said. "The main reason married men cheat is lack of communication with their spouses. There was an article about it in *Newsweek* just the other day."

Harmony's hippie parents cursed her with an incense-and-peace-symbol name, and so, of course, she turned into a very serious tax attorney with a six-figure income and a lovely townhouse in Georgetown. Harmony shared none of my misgivings about the law as a career—she decided to be a tax attorney at about age six, had charted a course toward that target, and was now as happy as a lark muddling through the kind of paperwork that drives the entire country collectively bug nuts every April 15th.

"I'm speaking from personal experience. Older men like getting head," Nina insisted.

"Really?" I asked, intrigued. "When did you date an older man?"

"In high school," Nina said, nonchalantly chewing on a piece of focaccia.

"High school!" Harmony exclaimed.

"Yes, high school. The father of the kids I baby-sat for. Don't look at me like that, Ellie, it's not like it doesn't happen all the time. He would drive me home after I sat for their kids, and pull the car over to the side of the road, and we would mess around, and then he'd drop me off," she said.

"Didn't his wife suspect something when it took him so long to drive you home?" I asked, scandalized. This was a common occurrence? The most titillating thing that had ever happened to me after a baby-sitting gig was when Mr. Bastrop drove me home after one too many glasses of wine, and I'd sat in the passenger seat clutching at the door handle in terror as he nearly sideswiped a parked car and then briefly veered over into the lane of oncoming traffic. The idea of Mr. Bastrop pulling the car over to the side of the road and sticking his hand up my skirt was disgusting—he was a fat, hairy little man, with a round head and Dumbo ears.

"Don't know." Nina shrugged, and then she smiled and

37

cocked one eyebrow up. "But he made me come for the first time. Well, besides masturbating, I mean. He did this thing with his fingers where …"

Harmony rolled her eyes and cut her off, as we often have to do with Nina before she starts offending everyone at surrounding tables. "I had an affair with an older man once. An unmarried older man, though," Harmony said. "He was my professor in college for an American poetry course. I used to have to sneak into his apartment, because he wasn't tenured and was terrified that if someone found out about us he'd get in trouble."

"What happened?" I asked, fascinated.

"How was the sex?" Nina added.

Harmony answered me, ignoring Nina. "I thought he cared about me, but he was just in it for the sex. So I dumped him and changed my major to business."

I had never dreamed that it was so common for women my age to be with older men. Sure, you hear about the Donald Trumps and Hugh Hefners of the world, but since they were both vulgar and sexually unattractive, I'd always thought that it was just a money thing. And the other older men I knew—my father's friends, Shearer, etc.—were even more disgusting. Just the thought of them naked … ick, no. Too gross.

I told them about meeting Ted at the party, and how we'd gone out together after. We'd eaten pizza, sitting for a long time on the high, plastic padded stools of the pizzeria, talking about nothing and everything. Afterwards, before putting me in a cab, he'd asked me to have dinner with him on Friday night. And he'd paused and looked at me for a minute in which I thought he might kiss me, but instead he just smiled and patted my arm.

Nina and Harmony both knew who Ted was—they were obviously more tuned into the D.C. political scene than I was.

"He's *very* sexy," Harmony said, obviously impressed. "And very successful."

"So you don't think it's crazy? For me to go out with an older man?" I asked.

"It's not like he's the kind of older man that shuffles around in a cardigan with leather knot buttons and smells like Vicks VapoRub. He's sexy older. Like Sean Connery," Harmony said.

"There are a ton of movie romances with older men and younger women—Gwyneth Paltrow and Michael Douglas in *A Perfect Murder*," Nina began.

"He tried to have her killed in that movie," I exclaimed.

"That's not the only one. There's also that movie with Winona Ryder and Richard Gere, although I think that ended badly, too. I don't know, it was so terrible I turned it off early. And then look at Michael Douglas and Catherine Zeta-Jones in real life. They're considered very hip, and there's a huge age difference between them," Nina continued.

"I think it's sexist how movies always show older men with younger women, but never vice versa—unless it's for shock effect like in *Harold and Maude*, or tragic, like Susan Sarandon and James Spader in *White Palace*," Harmony said.

"You're right! When I'm in my fifties, I'm going to seduce as many twenty-something young studs as I can. It'll probably turn me into a feminist icon," Nina said, which made both Harmony and me laugh. "Oh, and I forgot. What about Monica and Tom Selleck's character on *Friends*? They had a really normal relationship."

"But they didn't work out because of their age differences. She wanted babies, and he wanted to drive sports cars and smoke cigars," I said. "That's exactly what I'm worried about."

"I don't think you should worry about that quite yet. You barely know him. This dinner you have planned is really your first date. See how that goes before you start stressing over whether he'll want to have babies with you," Harmony said sensibly.

It was an amazing first date. A perfect first date. There was the usual basic information exchange—I learned that Ted was indeed divorced, about a year ago, no kids, and apparently worked an inhuman number of hours, although that seemed to be by choice. When he talked about his work, Ted's eyes gleamed like a child's on Christmas morning, and I was struck by the combination of confusion and jealousy I always experience when someone tells me that they actually love—or in Ted's case, *live for*—their job. I'm one of those people who map out the life they're going to lead after they win the lottery, and suffice it to say, those plans do not include continuing to work in the coal mines of civil litigation. Ted was less forthcoming about his personal life, ducking even the most gentle questioning on the subject, but he seemed more uncomfortable than secretive. In any event, I found his self-restraint refreshing—most of the men I've dated would grasp any opportunity to blather on endlessly about themselves.

I told him that I'd grown up in Syracuse, had always loved the District, and moved here to take the job with Snow & Druthers. Ted asked me how I'd chosen litigation as a field, since he'd heard from many attorneys that it wasn't the most rewarding practice, but I tried to brush off the questioning. The last thing a Good Girl does is complain, and everyone knows that you should stay as upbeat and positive as possible on a first date. Since we didn't have any friends in common, we moved to light gossip. He told me about a young, handsome senator planning to run for president who was having an affair with his male aide, and I told him about a federal judge who'd been caught trying on ladies' underwear at Barney's.

And there was just enough eye holding and hand brushing to add the electric excitement of potential future sex. For my part, I was in the process of developing a very big crush on Ted Langston. He did this crooked smile thing, where one corner of his mouth turned up. Every time he did it, I got a fluttery feeling in my stomach. I was very glad I had taken the time to shave my legs, exfoliate and moisturize the rest of my body, and wear my very best black lacy push-up bra and panties set from Victoria's Secret. I had agonized over my underwear choices before dinner, torn between the push-up bra that makes my boobs look perky, and an incredibly sexy silk camisole and tap pants, finally opting for the former, as it allowed me to wear a formfitting top. I knew that if I was really interested in him, there was no way I should be thinking about sex this early on, but there was just so much delicious sexual tension between us I couldn't help it. After all of the Good Boys I'd been dating, with their bland personalities, soft bodies, and low sex drives (with the exception of Jeremy, whom I broke up with after he asked me if we could have a threesome with one of my girlfriends), it had been a long time since I'd met someone I wanted to jump into bed with four or five dates shy of the requisite six.

But then, just as I was having a dirty, non–Good Girl fantasy about what would happen later on that night, the date took a very sharp, downward-plunging turn into nightmare dating hell. Ted was telling me about a trip to London he'd recently taken to interview Tony Blair.

"Is he as nice as he seems on television?" I asked, very

impressed that he had met England's personable young prime minister.

"Yes, he's very nice. Of course, he's a politician. Most of them are well practiced at being nice," Ted said. "Even Richard Nixon was charming in person."

"You met Nixon?" I exclaimed. Nixon was president the year I was born.

"I've interviewed every president from Nixon right on down," Ted said, and I tried to do the math to figure out how old it would make him. At what age did reporters typically get to interview presidents? I would have guessed around forty years old, but that would make Ted almost seventy, and I didn't think he was a day over fifty. He must have been a gifted and ambitious young reporter. Mmmm, that made him even more sexy, at least to me. I've never been preoccupied with those brooding, poor, communist men who spend all their time talking about existential angst and suffering, and then sponge dinner off you.

"Did you get a chance to do any sightseeing while you were in London?" I asked.

Ted looked a little surprised, as if the thought of touring one of the largest, most exciting cities in the world hadn't occurred to him. "No, not this trip. But I've been to London dozens of times for work. I suppose I did do some sightseeing back in the early days," Ted said.

"I wanted to go to London for my thirtieth birthday, as a present to myself. But now I don't know if I will. I don't want to go alone, and my friends either can't afford the cost or can't take the time off work," I said, spreading some butter on a cracked-pepper roll.

Looking stricken, Ted stared at me as though I'd sniffed my armpits and announced that I'd forgotten to put on deodorant. Oh no, I thought—he must think I'm suggesting that he go to London with me in a psycho, Glenn Close-in-*Fatal Attraction* way.

"I didn't mean ... I mean, I wasn't suggesting that you go with me," I hurried to say, but my clumsy words just added to the already palpable uneasiness that had suddenly risen between us. A minute ago we were flirting over the tournedos of beef with the cherry reduction sauce, and now there was just an awkward silence.

"You're ... you're *thirty*?" Ted asked, his voice strained and incredulous.

"Well, not quite. I'm turning thirty in January. The first. I was a New Year's baby," I gabbled, the way I tend to do when uncomfortable.

And then, unbelievably, he said, "I thought you were older."

What? "What?"

"I thought you were older than that."

Oh. My. God. "How old did you think I was?" I asked, incredulous, and yet panicked at the same time. I knew I was prematurely wrinkling. It must be worse than I originally thought. I must have skin like beef jerky.

"Mid-thirties," he said.

Thirty-two? Thirty-three? I hoped fervently.

"Thirty-eight or -nine," Ted continued.

I was silent. This was terrible. Horrible. Unbearably bad. I knew it. My crow's-feet were worse than I thought— my date had actually judged me to be nearly a decade older than I actually was.

"Do you know how old I am?" Ted demanded, his face stormy. He looked cross, as though I'd lied to him. As though I'd arranged to develop prematurely aged, prunelike skin just to deceive him into asking me out to dinner.

"No. And I don't care," I said, defensively crossing

my arms in front of my chest. Actually, I was suddenly seized with worry that my formerly perky breasts were now drooping down like balloons letting out air, thinking that at some point I had stopped paying attention, and suddenly my entire body had, overnight, wrinkled up and pouched out in all the wrong places.

"I'm fifty-two. I'm twenty-two, no, nearly *twenty-three* years older than you," Ted said.

"I don't care," I repeated, aware that I was bleating like a sullen teenager.

"Well, I *do* care. Do you know how ridiculous it looks for a man my age to be dating a woman your age?"

I considered pointing out Michael Douglas and Catherine Zeta-Jones to him, but then thought better of it. "Well, maybe everyone else will think I look a *decade* older than I am, too," I snapped. "Besides, if you thought I was thirty-nine, you'd still be older than me by, er …" I counted in my head.

"Thirteen years. And yes, it would be a difference, but not so wholly inappropriate," Ted said. "I have no intention of being one of those ridiculous men who, after going through a divorce, buys an overpriced sports car and starts dating coeds."

He pushed his half-eaten dinner back, and peered at his watch and then glanced at the door, apparently trying to work out how long it would take him to sprint through it. Unbelievable. First he insults my appearance—even if I do have wrinkles, it's rude to make assumptions of age, and if you have to, you should at least err on the side of *more* youthful, just as a matter of common courtesy—and now he was obviously planning to ditch me halfway through dinner. I sat there shaking with anger and embarrassment, feeling absolutely humiliated. But I did have some pride, and I was not going to let him desert me in a crowded restaurant. Not when I could get out of there first. Even Good Girls have their limits.

I stood, tossing my napkin on the table and shouldering my bag, and said, "I think it would be better if I went. Enjoy the rest of your dinner."

"You can at least finish your meal," Ted said in a horrible, pinched-up way.

"No, thank you," I pronounced dramatically. I turned to leave, but looked back at him over my shoulder. "And I am *not* a coed."

And then I strode out of the restaurant, feeling absolutely fabulous at my bitch-on-heels exit, and terrible at the awful, horrible, disgusting news that I looked a decade older than I was.

The very next morning, I spent $297.42 at the Clarins counter. I made the mistake of confiding to the salesgirl that I wasn't nearly as old as I looked—although my eyes, puffy and red after having spent the rest of the night in tears, didn't exactly help—and while I didn't expect the miracle skin of a preadolescent child, I merely wanted to look my still young, still twenty-something self. She performed a thorough examination of my parched, scaly, shoe-leather skin. Her conclusion: I needed a new cleaning-toning-moisturizing-and-antiaging routine that involved two kinds of cleanser—one for morning, one for night—one mild toner, two moisturizers—again, one for morning, one for night—an AHA cream, a youth serum, and a forty-dollar half-ounce pot of eye cream. She packaged everything up in a posh little bag, dumped a few samples in, and promised me that if I followed the routine meticulously, I would look younger in no time.

On one side of my brain I knew that I'd been had by a

cosmetics con-artist, cashing in on my low self-esteem by selling me duplicative and overpriced products that probably wouldn't do a bit of good. The other part of me—the part that was in charge of my credit card—was immensely grateful to her for supplying me with a plan of attack.

I'd show Ted. The next time he saw me I'd have skin like a baby's bottom, and he'd be full of jealousy and insecurity due to the fact that, in comparison, he was just a shriveled old geezer.

Chapter 5

Harmony and I met for lunch at Trio to do a post-mortem of the Date from Hell. Needless to say, I was still sulking about the apparent fact that I looked a decade older than I actually was, not to mention that I'd had an allergic reaction to the Clarins products I'd spent so much money on. Apparently they have all kinds of plants in them, and I'm allergic to everything that has anything to do with nature. I have a personal rule about never going camping, or sleeping anywhere I can't plug my hair dryer in (it's what kept me from being one of those chic environmental activists while at college). After only a few days on the Clarins products, my skin broke out and turned all red and bumpy. Harmony made a not-so-good attempt to cheer me up.

"It's his loss," Harmony declared.

This is one of those lies that your friends tell you when you get dumped by someone who was out of your league in the first place. Then again, was Ted out of my league? He was gorgeous and famous and smart, but he was ... older. Didn't the bloom of youth tip the dating scales in my favor? Wasn't he fortunate that a twenty-something like myself would give him the time of day?

But then there was the sour reality that he didn't think I was twenty-something. He thought I looked thirty-something—thirty-nine to be exact. Which set the scales firmly back in his favor, especially since age had brought him those distinguished graying temples, and all of that power brought on by career success.

"It's his loss that a handsome, successful man dumped me in the middle of our first date because I looked prematurely aged?"

"You're ridiculous. You look younger than you are, not older. You have the skin of a teenager."

While this sounded supportive, I had a feeling Harmony was referring to the colony of pimples sprouting up on my forehead.

"I don't know why he would tell me he thought I looked older even if he did mean it. It's cruel," I grumbled, while inside, part of me—a large part of me—was screaming, *Why doesn't he want me? What's wrong with me?* "Why do I have to turn thirty? Why? Why can't I stay in my twenties for the rest of forever? Be thin no matter what I eat, and be able to go to work in the morning after clubbing all night? And not have men that I'm trying to seduce mistake me for being a decade older than I am?"

"I don't know what Ted was thinking when he told you that—maybe you were just tired the night he met you. Anyway, I don't see why you're having so much angst about turning thirty. It didn't bother me at all," Harmony said, spearing a leaf of arugula lightly dressed with fat-free balsamic vinaigrette and nibbling on it.

I stared at my cheeseburger and fries and felt a twinge of guilt. Harmony rarely ate anything other than twigs and leaves and air. I will never understand how some women—like Harmony—survive on eating what appears to be little more than nothing. If I consume anything less than two thousand calories a day, my body shifts into starvation survival mode and compels me to wolf down loaves of french bread smothered with butter. But that was another thing about getting older—not so long ago, I could eat pizza, bread, and ice cream smugly content with my God-given high metabolism. Then, at some horrible point, when my mid-twenties gave way to my late twenties, my metabolism slowed down. Now if I even think of indulging in a full-fat latte or one of those glorious chocolate chip cookies the size of a dessert plate, I immediately put five pounds right on my hips. No one mentioned this cruel, hideous fact of life to me before—at least I don't think so. I do have a vague memory of my mother moaning about middle-age spread, but I thought that was something that didn't happen until your forties, or at least until after you'd had a baby or two. Was it really possible that you could hit your thirties sans children and just naturally end up with the same hip-heavy shape? That it isn't having kids that gives you the pear-shaped torso and flabby buttocks, but it's just a natural form of the female aging process? It was too awful to comprehend. No wonder people used to die off at the age of thirty.

"I don't know why it's bothering me so much," I sighed, and began eating my fries one at a time, dipping each in a pile of ketchup first. "I just feel so . . . unaccomplished, I guess."

"Don't be silly. You're an attorney, that's an accomplishment. And if you mean men, well, you've been on the cusp of getting engaged what—four times? Five times?"

"Only three times," I said indignantly. "And I wasn't on the cusp of anything. I've just had boyfriends who've mentioned it."

It was true—three of my past boyfriends—including

Eric—had mentioned marriage. Of course, they only brought it up at the moment I was wobbling out the door, in some sort of a sick power-grabbing mind game with the only rule being that you only want those who don't want you. After months of apathetic dating, with the man in my life giving me those sideways are-you-really-the-best-that-I-can-do glances, the minute I had one foot out the door, suddenly they were tossing me benefits as fast as a politician seeking office. *A diamond ring, is that what you want? Done! What has the little lady won? A ring on her finger, a house in the suburbs, and me!*

Harmony had a more pragmatic take on my serial monogamist past. "Well, there you go. You could be married, if that's what you wanted, but obviously you don't. And it's not uncommon these days for a woman to concentrate on her career and get married later in life. So, really, you've accomplished more than most people have by this age," she said, and put down her fork with a sigh, as though she were stuffed on the three ounces of lettuce she'd just consumed.

I knew Harmony was trying to make me feel better, but it wasn't working. Before, when those boyfriends, staggering under the burden of not being wanted, had proposed, I hadn't thought I wanted to be married—at least I hadn't found anyone I wanted to be married to. But now that the young, ripe years of my twenties were drying up, I wasn't at all sure I wanted to be alone. Not that I was missing Eric. Maybe I was missing the idea of him.

To make matters worse, the wedding of the last of my single high school girlfriends was coming up this weekend, the mark on my calendar causing me the same kind of dread I have when looking forward to my yearly ob-gyn appointment. As the last of my friends from high school to play the single, urban career woman, I was starting to feel like an anachronism. They were all starting families and disappearing into the suburban mist, reemerging only at the holidays to send out pictures of their new families—the parents dressed as Mr. and Mrs. Claus, the children as elves—and those annoying Christmas newsletters that trill on about trips taken to Italy and new houses being built. It was hard to imagine that my contemporaries were already moving out of the starter-house phase, and I was still renting in the city.

And then there was my career, a job that I hated more and more with each passing day, partly because I was a paid combatant—me, the woman who can't stand conflict—and partly because my days were full of dreary depositions and dull motion drafting.

The Big Three-Oh was bearing down on me, like the unstoppable boulder meeting the unmovable post, and what did I have to show for my life to date? A career I hated and a nonexistent love life. And, at the accelerated rate that my skin was aging, I was going to have to decide between plastic surgery and looking like a dried-up raisin. It was all too depressing to contemplate.

Later that night, sitting alone in my apartment and still brooding on the world's worst date, I didn't feel much better about my life. Even taking a super hot lavender-scented bubble bath, accompanied by a glass of ice cold chardonnay and my new issue of *Allure,* didn't make me feel much better. But then a story in the magazine caught my eye. It was about Internet dating. Apparently, there were services on the web where you could list a personal ad and then correspond with the men who answer it by e-mail or in a chat room. You could go on as many of these electronic dates as you wanted before meeting anyone face-to-face, so that you could filter out the freaks from more desirable suitors. At first the idea didn't seem all that appealing to me. The idea of Internet dating seemed even more sad and desperate than personal ad dating, and the men I was bound to meet were going to be of a caliber where they didn't want to risk being seen by their date. Probably lots of thirteen-year-old boys, convicts, and men so enormous they were confined to their rooms and could only be weighed on a postal scale.

But on the other hand, with online dating I wouldn't have to shave my legs before a date. Or wonder how soon was too soon to have sex. Hell, I wouldn't even have to change out of my old, tattered flannel pajamas. And maybe it would give me a chance to meet a different kind of guy than the boring, preppy Nice Guys I had been dating. Maybe that had been Ted's attraction—he was the most different man I'd met recently, and although going out with him had been a huge mistake, there were other types of men out there. But who should I go out with if I wanted to break a Nice Guy habit? A biker with a ZZ Top beard and a preference for women who wear American flag bandanas as shirts? I shuddered at the thought. And certainly not a latex-pants-wearing deviant who enjoys frequenting bars called Whips & Chains. Way, *way* too different. So, what was between boring Mr. Nice Guy and an older celebrity newsman? Someone a little edgier, like a Nice Guy plus a hipper job and maybe a tattoo?

I splashed out of the tub, wrapped myself in my terry cloth robe, and padded over to my laptop. Once I had AOL running, I checked the *Allure* article again to see what sites they recommended, and a minute later I was browsing through hundreds, no *thousands* of personal ads. Women looking for men. Men looking for women. Men looking for plus-sized transvestites. Women looking for bi-curious men comfortable with voyeurism. Every imaginable type of ad, from the sweet (piña coladas and getting caught in the rain) to the gross (handcuffs and black velvet hoods) to the puzzling (couple looking for nanny/cook/plaything). I back-clicked to the search criteria page, and filtered the ads down to just straight men looking for straight women for friendship, but there were still an overwhelming number of lonely hearts.

After scanning a few ads, I decided it would be more expedient to write my own ad. For $9.95, I was allowed five lines and a free e-mail address. I had e-mail through work, but since I'm always paranoid that one of the computer geeks in Systems is monitoring my e-mail, I decided that the new mailbox was definitely worth it. Here's what I wrote:

> Straight, attractive professional woman in the D.C. metro area who is tired of dating preppy guys. Interested in meeting a man, aged 30–45, who has more to offer than a Brooks Brothers wardrobe and stock options. No perverts or Axel Rose wannabes need apply. E-mail groovygirl@sweethearts.com.

And then, before my courage failed me, I clicked the Enter button, and a second later my personal ad was added to the long list of people looking for that special someone. Or, in the case of one twisted subscriber, that special goat. I wasn't expecting much of a response. After all, if I hadn't taken the time to sift through all of the personal ads, who would?

Chapter 6

The heat had broken earlier than usual, and the weatherman was promising a perfect Labor Day weekend—blue skies, low humidity, eighty-degree temperatures. Nina and Harmony were going to Annapolis for the weekend, planning to ogle cute young Navy men and scarf down a few crab cakes. Instead of going with them, I was stuck on a train bound for Syracuse to face the double dread of a weekend with my family and my friend Beth's wedding, which I was attending—horror of horrors—without a date. To make the trip that much more pleasant, Sally, who was stuffed against her will into her hated travel bag, howled the entire ride, while everyone in the train car glared at me with expressions of pure malevolence.

Thankfully it was my brother Mark who picked me up at the station. Nina and I had had a margarita send-off the night before, and my head was throbbing. I wasn't up for my mother just yet.

"Hello, dog breath," Mark said, enfolding me in his arms. "Put on a few pounds?"

"Doofus," I exclaimed, hugging him tightly. My brother was married and did something in banking that I could never understand, other than that it involved foreign markets and constantly weighing the dollar against whatever. But some part of us would always relate on the level we were at when he and my other brother, Brian, tried to shut me into the fold-out couch.

"Mom's in a real twist," Mark warned me as we drove to our childhood home in the suburbs of Syracuse.

"I should have had a career instead of raising you kids? I'm not going to be the Mother of the Bride while I'm still young enough to wear Vera Wang? Are these the legs of a suburban mother of three?" I guessed.

"No, it's a new one. Something about getting in touch with her inner goddess," Mark said, grinning. "She's reading a bunch of astrology books, and keeps wanting to talk about her sexuality. Obviously, I've been avoiding her."

"Oh no," I groaned.

Mark laughed. "I think it might actually be worse than the time she became convinced that she was the daughter of Marilyn Monroe and had been adopted by Nana and Poppy as an infant."

"Oh, I remember! She kept talking in that breathy voice and dyed her hair platinum," I said, annoyed at the memory. "This weekend is going to be even worse than I thought."

"Don't say I didn't warn you."

"So how's Kate?" I asked. Kate was Mark's wife, and I absolutely adored her. She could have been a model—she's five feet ten, 120 pounds, auburn red hair swishing down past her shoulders, flawless features. She's so gorgeous that you don't think you could possibly like her, and yet so down-to-earth and sweet-natured that it's impossible not to love her.

"You know. Kate's Kate," Mark said a little vaguely. I started to ask him if something was wrong, but he changed the topic back to Mother's goddess phase, and how he caught her browsing the Internet, looking at Wiccan websites. It was just beyond disturbing.

When we got to my parents' house, Mother came out of the house waving to us. I was glad Mark had given me the heads-up on her current craziness, or else I would have been really confused by the outfit Mom had on—an Indian sari made out of gold and crimson silk, and gold thong sandals. Her normally sleek blonde hair was loose and frizzy around her face.

"Dar-ling," she trilled, pecking me on the cheek and then spinning around to show off her new look. "What do you think?"

"Very bright," I said, feeling a small stab of pleasure at her dissatisfied face. Mother is a world-class gold digger of compliments, and somehow manages to work every conversation back to why she's so marvelous. Of course, instead of just feeding her the compliments she craves, I usually turn into a sulky teenager in her presence and refuse to indulge her.

I let Sally out of her carrier, and she immediately turned around four times and squatted in Mom's newly planted bed of pansies.

"You brought the dog?"

I sighed. "Her name is Sally, and I told you I was going to. Remember?"

Mother and Sally exchanged an unfriendly look. As both are narcissistic prima donnas, neither is too fond of the other. At their first meeting, Sally had taken an immediate dislike to Mother; since then, whenever she sees her, her smooth coat tufts up in peaks of hostility and she bares her teeth like a bloodthirsty Doberman pinscher. And I've actually seen Mother kick little Sally out of her way, even though later she claimed, "It was just a gentle push, and besides, she was underfoot." I tried to explain that Sally is a small dog and therefore to some extent is always underfoot, but my mother just sniffed, and asserted for the millionth time that she's always preferred cats. It's like they're two Miss America contestants gunning for the crown and roses, and will do whatever they have to to take the other one out. I made a mental note to make sure Sally didn't break into Mother's closet and chew on her Ferragamos, like she did the last time we visited.

"Hi, Dad," I said to my father, who'd appeared at the door.

"Counselor," my dad, the judge, said. He was tall and portly, with distinguished white hair and a bushy beard, and looks exactly like what everyone thinks judges should look like. He always looks out of place dressed in civvies and out of his black robe. "How's work?" he asked.

"Just fine," I lied. I couldn't bear to tell him how much I hated my job. Neither Mark nor Brian had shown any interest in the law, so my father had pinned his hopes on me to continue the family tradition. If he thought for one minute that I wasn't going to follow in his footsteps, a distinguished career at the bar before taking my place at the bench, it would break his heart. And that was the one thing I could bear less than continuing on in litigation.

"Good, good," he said, looking pleased.

I'm glad one of us was.

My oldest brother, Brian—I was the baby of the family, Mark was in the middle—came home for dinner that night, bringing with him a new girlfriend, Becca, obviously counting on my presence to cushion the blow. Brian had previously married and divorced his college sweetheart, Lindsey, a topic that still caused my mother's face to pinch up as though it were threaded by a drawstring that had been pulled tight, even though the divorce had been final for two years. Mom loved Lindsey—I knew for a fact that they still talked on the phone once a week—and was still angry at Brian for leaving her. For his secretary. And then the dog's vet. And then their marriage counselor. Brian has never been the nicest of men, but he'd always been Mom's favorite. Mark and I had both been enjoying his fall from grace.

We sat around the table—Mom, Dad, Brian, Becca, Mark, Kate, and me—noshing on barbequed spareribs and potato salad.

"Why didn't Beth ask you to be a bridesmaid?" Mom asked me. She'd been studiously ignoring Becca, and the poor girl was almost in tears. Becca kept looking at Brian, her face a question mark, obviously wondering what she'd done to give offense.

"We're not that close anymore," I said shortly. And then, "So, Becca. You own a holistic store? I've been thinking of taking up yoga."

Becca nodded eagerly. "Oh, you should, it's wonderful. You'll feel like a new person—"

"But you're one of her oldest friends. You'd think she'd have asked you," Mom continued, as though Becca didn't exist. Apparently, even Becca's potential for contributing to Mom's goddess craze—after all, who better to supply goddess supplies, such as essential oils and herbs and all of that crap, than the owner of a holistic store—didn't make up for the fact that Becca wasn't Lindsey. "After all the times I drove her home from Girl Scouts."

Kate, ever the diplomat, smiled kindly at Becca. "It's hard to have everyone you want in your wedding party. Becca, I'd love to take a yoga class, too. Can you recommend one here in town?"

"Dad, pass the baked beans, will you," Brian said, his sole contribution to the conversation.

My father was worse than Brian. He sat like a mute at the head of the table, lost in his thoughts, and when he did speak he interrupted whoever was speaking to make an off-topic comment. For example, as Becca started to impart advice on the best yoga instructor in Syracuse, Dad boomed out, addressing me, "Have you given any thought to writing that article on the misuse of the Commerce Clause that we were talking about on your last visit?"

"Yeah, genius, how about it?" Mark teased, as Kate elbowed him in the side and shushed him.

"Well, um, no, not yet, Dad. I've been pretty busy at work," I began.

"You should start publishing as soon as possible. I keep telling you, you're never going to get a judicial appointment if you don't have a full body of work behind you," my father, a former law review genius, scolded me.

"Right," I said faintly, and glanced around the table. Everyone had fallen silent—Mother looking annoyed, Brian and Mark focused on their ribs, Becca stricken. Only Kate looked back at me, her face warm and full of sympathy.

I wondered, not for the first time, why she had *chosen* to marry into this family, especially considering all of the other normal families out there with appropriately aged sons. It wasn't like Mark was all that great of a catch, with those ears that stick out and his goofy har-har-har laugh. Okay, so he was a nice man, good-looking, and successful in his career. But still—Kate was one of those women who could have had whomever she wanted, so why did she choose someone whose family was such a dysfunctional mess? I was starting to think that Lindsey had gotten off easy. Maybe her husband had cheated on her, but at least she didn't have to attend these charming little dinners anymore.

*   *   *

There is nothing quite as awful as going to the wedding of an old high school friend—and in Beth's case, she was a friend/enemy, since while we were growing up she was always trying to steal my boyfriends. Not that she'd ever succeeded, I remembered with smug pride, but the very fact that she'd tried made her one of Those Girlfriends, the supercompetitive ones you can't really ever trust, the kind who are always happier and more congenial when your life is going to shit. I had no doubt that in her score-keeping, Beth was counting her getting married before me as being worth huge bonus points, especially since I was the only girl out of the group we were friends with in high school that she'd beaten to the altar. The one thing worse than having to attend the damned wedding was that I was going without a date. The idea of showing up unescorted was so awful I had even considered getting back together with Eric, who was still calling and leaving me mushy messages on my answering machine.

My dad dropped me off at the church, a great white mammoth of a building, and after I waved good-bye to him I felt a nervous flutter in my stomach, followed by a shot of self-loathing. Almost thirty years old and a professional woman, and I was still afraid of making an entrance alone. It was ridiculous, I thought. I held my head up high, sucked in my stomach, and tried to glide gracefully into the church, all the while desperately looking around to see if there was anyone I knew that I could sit with.

"Ellie! Oh my God! Hi-eeee," a voice squealed. I turned toward the pews and saw a hand waving furiously at me. The hand was attached to—oh God. Kristin Goodman. I never could stand her. In high school, Kristin was the kind of girl who always carried her Le Sports Sac to class, instead of leaving it in her locker the way the rest of us did, and dotted the *i*'s in her name with bubbly little hearts. And she was also one of those girls who hides her vicious streak under a simpering, goody-goody facade, masking her cruel digs as chummy confidences, e.g., "I think you should know that Maureen isn't a very good friend to you. She told me that if she had a nose like yours she'd get a nose job. But don't listen to her, I think you're really cute anyway."

Like a mouse cornered by a cat—a stupid, white, fluffy cat—I glanced around desperately looking for somewhere else to sit, while Kristin called out, "Come and sit with us, Ellie."

This was going to be worse than I thought.

"Ellie Winters? Is it still Winters?" a voice behind me said. I turned to see a slim redhead with an open, freckled face beaming at me.

"Molly! How are you? It's been so long," I said, and we exchanged one of those chiffon-light social hugs where you don't touch breasts or bellies. Molly and I had run in different circles in high school—she was what my Mom called an "early developer," meaning she was J. Lo curvy by age fifteen, and had a college-aged boyfriend when the rest of us were still practicing French-kissing on our pillows. We'd always gotten on well, though, and had been lab partners for eleventh-grade chemistry.

"Are you here alone, too? Shall we sit together?" she asked, and I gratefully nodded, silently blessing her for offering me sanctuary from Kristin.

"I'm so glad I'm not the only one here without a date," I confided as we slid onto the smooth, mahogany pew that was draped with ribbon garlands and sprigs of lilac. "Everyone's married now, or engaged, and I just hate coming to these things alone. It makes me feel like such an old maid, and everyone just stares at you wondering what's wrong with you and why you aren't married ... what's wrong?"

To my horror, Molly was blinking rapidly, and her lips trembled. "I'm getting a divorce," she said, her voice breaking on the D-word. "Rod and I ... we just ... that bastard ... left me."

And then she burst into tears—loud, shoulder-racking, hiccupping sobs. People I hadn't seen since high school were turning to look at us, and I smiled at them, recognizing some of the faces. "Hi, Diane! Amy, how are you?" I sang out, patting Molly on the shoulder, while she continued to sob, "... that cheating, limp-dicked bastard."

Luckily the organ music—make that an organ, several trumpets, and an electric guitar—cued up, and moments later, the procession of three flower girls, twelve bridesmaids, and one matron of honor, followed by the bride, who was looking very pleased with herself in a white, flouncy puff of a dress, rolled down the aisle, and Molly struggled to pull herself together, only letting out an occasional hiccup. The ceremony was long and a bit plastic-y. Beth and Seth had singers (two different soloists and a trio of tenors), readers, an intricate candle-lighting presentation that seemed to involve every member of their extended families, and two sets of vows—one traditional, one set written by the bride and groom. From start to finish, it took over an hour for what really boiled down to two people promising not to fool around or desert the other if he/she should become sick, sticking some rings on fingers, and kissing to seal the deal. I don't know if it's Martha Stewart's influence, but suddenly every bride is dead set on turning her wedding day into a huge, overblown production involving planners with headphones, thousands of dollars of out-of-season flowers, and couture dresses that cost as much as a new car.

The reception was even worse. Beth had chosen the theme of "Starry Night" and had twinkle lights hanging from every available surface, including from the branches of a row of fake trees that lined the entrance hall that I think were supposed to make the room look like a forest. Glitter-encrusted stars and moons were suspended from the ceilings, and the tables, dressed in starched white linens with midnight blue chiffon overlays, were scattered with more star-shaped glitter. I didn't even know you were supposed to pick a theme for your wedding reception. In fact, I thought that "We Just Got Married" was pretty much supposed to be the theme of the night.

Molly, who was still weepy but apologizing profusely for the hysterical outbreak, drove me from the church to the hotel where the reception was being held. On the way, she told me her grim story. Two weeks ago, Rod—Rod Glick, I was shocked to hear, who had graduated with us but was a complete dork, and not at all the type of guy I thought that curvy, popular Molly would ever go for—inadvertently had his plane tickets for a purported business trip delivered to his house. Molly had opened the envelope and learned that instead of going to a sales meeting in Orlando, Rod was flying to Fort Lauderdale with the twenty-two-year-old receptionist from his office.

"We're in love," Rod had declared, and moved out of their house that night.

Molly was fluctuating between intense, dark anger ("I think Lorena Bobbitt had the right idea. I should have cut it off when I had the chance.") and heartbroken anguish ("Do you think he'll ever come back to me?").

By the time we arrived at the reception, I was exhausted, not in the mood to celebrate the institution of everlasting love and devotion, and a little freaked out. I hadn't known we'd reached the age where a woman as beautiful and vivacious as Molly would settle for a no-body like Rod Glick, much less get dumped by him for a younger woman. We weren't even thirty yet! Weren't we supposed to *be* the younger women? And just like that, Ted's handsome face popped into my thoughts. *Go away,* I told him, and tried to focus on the Starry Night party.

Luckily, Molly and I weren't seated at the same table. She'd been put at a table of attractive young hipsters, including the only cute guy I had seen so far that didn't have a wispy, silk-sheath-clad girl hanging on his arm. I felt guilty for being happy to be rid of Molly, but I didn't want to hear anything more about Rod, who with Molly's every comment was sounding more and more like she was lucky to be rid of him ("His erect penis is the size of a baby carrot!" "He puts depilatory cream on his back!"). My bubble of happiness was short-lived, however, when I saw who I was seated with.

"Ellie! You're right next to me," Kristin yapped.

"Oh, good," I managed feebly.

"This is my *husband,* Harold," she said, gesturing proudly to the man standing behind her. He was very short, and had a tiny, pin-sized head, and reminded me of Beetlejuice after he'd had his head shrunk. I quickly pretended to scratch the tip of my nose so I could hide my smile.

"You're not married yet, are you? Well, don't worry," Kristin said soothingly. "So why didn't Beth ask you to be in her wedding party? I thought that the two of you were really close. Much closer than she and I ever were, and she said that she wanted to ask me, but her mother black-mailed her into having all of her cousins."

"No, not so much anymore," I said, and then wished I could bite the words back in. Knowing Kristin, as I did too well and could tell she hadn't changed a bit from high school, she would translate my innocuous statement to Beth as "Ellie said that she doesn't think of you as a friend anymore."

Which I didn't, really. But that was beside the point.

The couples began to discuss where they were buying or thinking of buying a house, a conversation that took a decidedly bitter turn when one of the Hale twins announced that she wouldn't be caught dead living in a certain neighborhood, only to have Sondra Matthews clear her throat and announce that she and her husband had just entered into a contract on a house there. There was an ugly silence, and then instead of backpedaling and saying something like "Oh, well, I'm sure your house is lovely, one of the last really good ones available," Cindy Hale—actually, now Cindy Wells, although it was impossible to think of her and her sister Melanie as anything other than the Hale twins—only coughed delicately, and said, "Oh."

Then Kristin smugly announced that she and her husband—who, it turns out, was the son of a wealthy local developer who was only too happy to hand over pots of money to his pinheaded son and smarmy wife, thus proving once and for all that good things happen to bad people no matter how unfair it is—had just purchased a five-bedroom ranch in one of the most expensive neighborhoods in town, and while everyone cooed disingenuous congratulations, Melanie Hale-Travis suddenly blurted out in an I-won't-be-outdone tone of voice that she was pregnant, thus expertly stealing the limelight from a now openly pouting Kristin.

By the time dinner was over, no one really wanted to talk to anyone else, other than sullen whispering between spouses. I excused myself, went to the bar, and literally ran right into my old high school boyfriend, Charlie. It was my fault; I was looking back over my shoulder, noting that Molly was giggling flirtatiously at something Cute Single Guy was saying. How unfair is that? She's single for all of two minutes and already has someone interested in her, I thought, and walked straight into Charlie Owens, who was coming out of the bar with a Scotch on the rocks in his hand.

"Shit," I exclaimed, as the cold Scotch splattered on my cream cashmere cap-sleeved sweater, leaving a large, ugly brown stain on the front. I plucked the sweater away from my chest, but the Scotch had already seeped through the fabric, leaving my skin cold and sticky.

"Ellie. Christ. I didn't know you'd be here," Charlie said. "Sorry about your sweater."

"Hi, Charlie," I said, still holding my sweater out and away from my skin.

It was surreal seeing Charlie—my first love, my first lover—after all these years. I hadn't laid eyes on him since our freshman year in college, when we broke up over Christmas break. It's always weird seeing someone you used to sleep with, the fact that his penis was once in your body making for a particularly awkward conversation. And Charlie was my first. I had lost my virginity to him— and he to me—on the couch in his parents' den after our junior prom. As with all juvenile lovemaking, it was awkward and clumsy, and after humping at me in a frenzied daze, he'd finished in under a minute. It felt strange to even look at him now, for in high school he'd been a skinny beanpole of a kid, and now he was fat, his face round and fleshy.

"I think I should get some mineral water to put on the stain," I said.

Charlie followed me into the hotel bar, got a glass of mineral water from the bartender, and then sat with me while I dabbed at my sweater with a paper cocktail napkin. All I succeeded in doing was making the spot wetter and more noticeable.

"Is it ruined?" Charlie asked.

"No, I don't think so," I lied. "Don't worry about it."

"So, Beth said that you're a lawyer," Charlie said, and we were off, exchanging the stories of our lives—heavily edited, at least on my part, to make it sound better than it actually was—since we had parted. Charlie was also an attorney, and had used his undergraduate background in engineering to specialize in patent law. He worked in Manhattan at a firm impressive enough to make my eyes open wide, and reported that he loved his work and life in the city. I don't know if he, too, was exposing only the glossy-magazine version of his life, but it struck me that he was one of the few attorneys I'd met who seemed genuinely content and happy with his work. But then, Charlie had always had a precise, scientific mind, and it wasn't a stretch to see that he would enjoy the process of bringing order to problems.

Shortly after we sat down, Charlie made a joke about how it would probably be better if he abandoned the Scotch and switched to something less damaging, and retrieved an expensive bottle of chardonnay from the bartender. I don't know if it was just the effect of the wine we were drinking, but Charlie was delightful. So much so that I found myself wondering why we had broken up in the first place—he was the original nice, preppy, and above all else, appropriate boyfriend in my life, and in fact the prototype for Alec, Peter, Winston, Jeremy, and Eric. But, unlike the five increasingly stiff and stuffy boyfriends of my twenties, Charlie actually made me laugh. In fact, as we drank our way through first one bottle of wine and then another, we relived the silliness of our youth, even boldly bringing up the embarrassingly bungled mutual loss of our

Whitney Gaskell

virginity. Through the night, we laughed so hard we were frequently reduced to tears, slapping at the table with open palms and gasping for breath, and never got around to rejoining the reception.

"I don't really know anyone here, other than Beth, of course," Charlie said, as an excuse for why he wasn't in a hurry to return to the increasingly raucous reception, and I wondered why Beth had invited him to the wedding. She'd only known him through me, the boyfriend of a friend, and then only in high school. But I was glad she had. Without him, I would have been stuck sitting at the circular table while Kristin peppered me with nasty, edged questions about why I didn't have a boyfriend, the line of questioning undoubtedly meant to demoralize me because I wasn't married to a rich, pinheaded husband, and being forced to let the other women's husbands take turns pity-dancing with me.

Charlie saved me from this embarrassment, and I was much happier slurping wine with him than dealing with the competitive marrieds. But I am not a good drinker. Not that I become mean-spirited, but after only a few drinks, I quickly lose the ability to talk, walk, or make reasoned decisions. Which is why, after our third bottle of wine, I let Charlie drive me home, and then made out with him like a teenager in my parents' driveway.

If it was surreal to see Charlie as a chunky lawyer, it was even weirder to neck with him twelve years after we'd last dated. His lips felt different, but I remembered the way he smelled, a cozy, homey aroma of wool sweaters wet with snow. For a few minutes, I was transported back to high school, feeling the long-forgotten surge of teenage emotions that were as thrilling as a roller-coaster ride. And with nostalgic randiness, I was suddenly pulling at his sweater and belt, and he at my bra and pantyhose, and I think that had my mother not flicked the outside house lights on, we would have had sex right there in his rented Camry, me sitting astride him with my ass against the steering wheel.

But the outdoor lights did flicker on, saving me from finding out just what I was capable of when drunk, lonely, and depressed to be the last woman of my high school class to still be single.

"Christ," Charlie said, pulling away from me. His lips were pink and raw from having rubbed against mine. "I don't know why, but that still terrifies me. Your father always scared the shit out of me."

"Why?" I asked, surprised. "He isn't the one flickering the lights. It's my mother. Dad never knew when I got home. I don't think he cared."

"Your father, your mother. It's all the same. I feel like I'm sixteen again, and illicitly stealing their daughter's virginity."

"You didn't steal anything," I said, and smiled at him. And then he kissed me again.

"I'm going to call you," he promised.

I walked up to my front door, wondering if I had a hickey on my neck and feeling like a kid again for caring that my mother would see it, not to mention annoyed at her for flickering the lights. I knew Charlie wouldn't call. And that was fine. I'd had a fun time with him; kissing him had been like recapturing my quickly vanishing youth. But it was like going to your high school reunion and dancing to all of the old, eighties New Wave records—it may be fun for a night, but doing it every day would get depressing.

Mom was waiting up for me when I walked in the house. She and Sally were sitting in the front room, Mom in an armchair, Sally on the couch, glaring at each other.

"I tried to move her off the couch, and she bit me," Mother announced.

"Sally bit you?"

"Well, she tried to. She snarled and lunged at me."

"But there was no teeth-to-skin contact?" Mother shook her head sulkily. "Then she didn't bite you. I'm sorry, I should have told you that Sally likes to sleep on the furniture, and she takes it very personally if you try to push her off," I said, scooping up the sausage-shaped pug and cuddling her in my arms. I love coming home to Sally. She bundled herself into my arms, kissing me wildly with her stinky pug breath.

"Well, how was the wedding?" my mother asked as Sally snorted up into my face.

"Awful," I said, and then told my increasingly delighted mother about the tacky theme, the bloated ceremony, how Beth's dress looked like a Hostess Sno-ball, and how her family had crimped costs by serving everyone the smallest portion of chicken and rice pilaf possible. My mother, who's fond of the saying "If you don't have anything nice to say, come sit by me," was thrilled.

"Did you see any of your old friends there?"

"Well, I saw Charlie Owens. Remember him?"

"Of course I do. He was such a sweet boy. What does he do now?"

I hated to tell her. She viewed every one of my ex-boyfriends as a lost chance for grandchildren. "He's a patent attorney in Manhattan."

"Oh," my mother said, drawing the word out into two lugubrious syllables. She looked at me, mournfully. "I always liked him. I'd hoped that you two would end up together. Anyone else?"

"Kristin Goodman. Well, Kristin Janicki, now," I said, and we both shuddered. Mother had never been fond of

Kristin, or her mother, who was a carbon copy of my yappy classmate.

"I got stuck at the reception sitting at a table with Kristin, her hideous husband, the Hale twins and their husbands, and Sondra Matthews and her husband. All of them got into a snit about who lived in the best neighborhood. Complete nightmare. I don't even know why Beth stuck me there, since there was a table of single people who looked like they were having a great time."

"Beth never liked you. She was always very jealous of you," Mother said sagely.

"What? What does that have to do with sitting me at the sucky table?"

"She doesn't want you to meet a nice man and outdo her," my mother said, and I was just wondering if for once she was making sense, when she spoiled it by adding "You should never have broken up with Eric. Do you really think you'll be able to do better than him?"

I took a deep breath. Only twelve hours to go until Sally and I could return home to the relative sanity of D.C.

Chapter 7

I was stuck at the monthly luncheon for the litigation section of my firm. It was an excruciating exercise, where we all sat around the enormous claw-and-ball conference table eating overly mayonnaised finger sandwiches, wilted carrot sticks, and tepid ice tea, and reported on our current caseload. One by one, we took our turn boring each other to tears with braggadocio reports of clients snatched away from other firms, cases settled for inflated amounts, and chest-pounding war stories of deposition antics.

"You wouldn't have believed the look on his face when I asked his client about the billing records. He was so mad, he stood up and challenged me to go outside so we could settle it like men," Phil Duffy droned on about a recent conflict he'd had at a deposition. "I told him sure—if the court reporter was willing to go with us and put it on the record!"

Phil was a partner, so most of the suck-up associates guffawed and congratulated him. I hated Phil, almost as much as I hated Shearer the Shit. At least Shearer had a personality. Phil was more like an automaton. He billed out a ridiculous amount of hours, basically working seventeen hours a day and apparently without ever stopping for food or sleep. I rarely beat him to work in the mornings (his secretary, who as part of her flex-time schedule arrived to work at 7:30 A.M., once told me that he was always there when she got in), and when I left the office, normally at around 7:00 P.M., he was almost always still there.

Duffy finally started to wind down his self-congratulating diatribe on the deposition. Oh, God, it's almost my turn to talk, I thought, desperately trying to think of something to say. Ever since the time I had suggested the firm purchase an espresso/cappuccino machine for the break room, as it would both provide all employees with a drastic improvement in the quality of coffee as well as cut down on wasted time spent making dashes to Starbucks, and everyone stared at me as though I'd suggested we construct a pagan altar in the middle of the lobby on which to sacrifice fluffy puppies, I'd tried to talk as little as possible at these lunches.

"And with that being said, I plan to ask Ellie," I suddenly heard Phil say—oh, God, what was he saying? Why wasn't I listening?—"to be our point person for this new class-action case. Ellie, it will be a lot of hard work, a lot of late nights, but I have absolute faith that you're the right person for the job."

There was a lot of murmuring around the table, and suddenly everyone was staring at me.

"Congratulations, Ellie."

"This is certainly a big step up for you."

"What a great break!"

Argh! What was he talking about? What class action? What? And did he say late nights? I tried to smile, look modest, and say "Thank you," but inside I was churning with resentment. I didn't want some big project hanging around my neck, keeping me at the office late at night and making my life miserable. But then I noticed that Katherine Polk was staring at me with unconcealed jealousy.

Katherine Polk was my archnemesis. We started at the firm at the same time, the fall after we graduated from law school, and hated each other on sight. Katherine is horrible—she's gorgeous, tall, skinny, with white-blonde hair that she wears in a hip, chin-length bob, and looks exactly like what I always imagined the White Witch from *The Lion, the Witch and the Wardrobe* to look like. She also has beautiful clothes, and plays off her pale, creamy skin and ultra-blonde hair with bright red lipstick and a lot of eye makeup—whereas I often get to the office with my suit wrinkled, my hair still wet, and zit cream plastered on my chin. And it's not just that she looks like a model—Katherine is always poaching the best assignments, sucking up to the partners, and backstabbing her fellow associates right and left. So the very fact that the horribly complicated-sounding class action was going to me was causing Katherine's face to pinch up and her delicate little nose to flare, was deliciously gratifying.

"I look forward to working on the case," I declared once it was my turn to talk, and everyone actually applauded a little. I couldn't help throwing a smirk in Katherine's direction.

Later that afternoon, I was passing by Shearer the Shit's office and glanced in. I normally do this to see if Shearer has left early for the day, as he frequently does, which means that I can scoot out of the office at a decent hour guilt-free. But he was still there, slumped behind his desk, making all kinds of strange, throat-clearing sounds. And, ensconced in a brown leather visitor's chair, with her back to the door, was Katherine. I paused, just past the open door, so that neither Shearer nor Katherine could see me, and pretended to look at some case books resting on a nearby shelf.

"But why did Ellie get it?" Katherine was hissing. "You promised that I would be the point man on the next big case we got. I need it if I'm going to make partner early."

"You'll make partner, don't worry," I heard Shearer say in a weird, soothing voice. What? Why is he telling her that? I wondered. We were only fourth-year associates, and partnership was still at least three, if not four or five, years away. And no one, not even associates with a parent on the partnership committee, was guaranteed to make partner.

"I'd better. Unless you want the partnership to find out about us," Katherine snapped.

Us? I had to slap a hand over my own mouth to keep from shrieking. Katherine and Shearer were seeing each other. Immediately—and unfortunately—I conjured up a picture of the two of them in bed, Katherine's slim body rubbing against Shearer's hairy fat, all the while Shearer cried out, "Good, good!" I shuddered with revulsion. Actually, it wasn't all that surprising, considering that I knew Katherine would do anything to make partner. It's just that Katherine is so concerned with image and aesthetics—I was amazed that she could stomach seeing Shearer naked.

"For Christ's sake, either close the door or lower your voice. Someone will hear you," Shearer hissed back.

"I don't care if they do. I'm not the one who's married," Katherine said in a huff.

Shearer's voice dropped down so low, I couldn't hear what he was saying, but his tone was wheedling, as though he were talking to a temperamental child. I hurried back to my office before either of them could see me.

I sat at my desk and just shook my head, dumbfounded at the idea. Shearer and Katherine together. It was too horrible to contemplate, worse than Beauty and the Beast. And how had it started? What would make a man like Shearer—short, hairy, and chubby—think that he could score with a beautiful amazon like Katherine? Or had it been the other way around—had she seduced him? And if so, how? Did she let her fingers casually caress his thick, Porky Pig thighs while preparing for trial? Had she stuck her tongue in his hairy, waxy ear? It made me nauseated just to think about it—how had she ever stomached *doing* it?

But thinking about sex—even gross, perverted sex— reminded me. I hadn't checked my personal ad e-mail since posting the ad the week before. Somehow, between the wedding and work, I'd completely forgotten about it. I clicked onto my web browser on my work computer and then typed in the website address. After I entered my name and password, I sat there, blinking at the screen in disbelief. There were 175 messages in my in-box. It must be a mistake, I thought. It must be 17, or maybe even 75, and an extra number got tacked on. But when I clicked on "Inbox," there were indeed 175 messages listed in a neat, numbered column. I clicked on the first one, written by someone with the handle "Licker," and began to read it: "When you feel my pierced tongue flick against your ..." Ack!

I hit the Delete button and looked around furtively, to make sure no one had sneaked into my office and seen what I was up to. Of course no one had, but I always had an irrational fear that the firm was somehow monitoring me at work like Big Brother, with a camera trained at my desk, and would learn that I was reading lewd e-mails on company time. At first I tried to brush it off as paranoia, but then I saw an episode of the TV news magazine *Date-line* that showed companies beginning to do just that—training cameras on their employees to monitor their work performance, which completely freaked me out. Now I'm convinced that every time I start browsing through the Gap website or the Nordstrom's online shoe catalog—not to mention reading e-mails from perverted freaks—it's being entered into some kind of virtual employer demerit book. I looked back at the screen, where the next message had flashed up: "Looking for a nonjudgmental woman open to new experiences. I'll bring the anal probe, you bring your strap-on."

Strap-on? What did that mean? Anal probe wasn't too hard to figure out (ick!), but a strap-on? I called the only person I could think of who would know.

"Nina, what's a 'strap-on'?" I breathed into the phone, praying that no one in my office would be able to hear me.

She shrieked with laughter. "A strap-on? God, Ellie, I didn't think that was your kind of thing," Nina hooted.

"It's not my thing. It's just I got an e-mail with some-one mentioning it, and I didn't know what it was," I said.

Nina broke into peals of laughter. When she finally explained—and I don't want to repeat what she said—she forced me to tell her the context in which it came up.

"A personal ad," she exclaimed. "I've done that be-fore."

"Did you meet anyone? I mean, other than perverts wanting to dress you in leather?" I asked.

"Oh, yes, please. But no, you don't really meet anyone. Not face-to-face. It's just to find people to have cybersex with. Didn't you know that?"

Cybersex? But the *Allure* article had gone on and on about glamorous workaholics in Manhattan who'd met their billionaire husbands online, as it was the only way they'd had time to date. It hadn't said much of anything about cybersex.

"Er, no," I confessed. "How does that work anyway?"

"Well, you have to be really proficient at typing with one hand," Nina began.

Ah. Now I understood. "Never mind," I hastened. "Bye."

The list of chosen handles displayed in the "From" column on the in-box screen suddenly made a lot more sense—many of them included words such as "dick," "lick," and "pounds." I hit "Delete all," emptied out the in-box, and then canceled my account. Maybe when I was thirty, and truly in the decade in which single women become desperate, I would be reduced to relying on cyber-sex. But it was only the end of September—I still had three months left before it came to that.

Chapter 8

I have only two true talents in life—laser accuracy when applying liquid eyeliner (performing the task in one smooth stroke without lifting brush from lid), and drawing jokey caricatures of friends and enemies alike (the latter easily differentiated from the former, as I delight in putting bulbous noses and protruding ears on the people I hate). It's a great trick; everyone loves it when I whip out sketches of friends at cocktail parties. I also find drawing relaxing, which is why, after being appointed to my first mammoth class-action case, and already starting to have panic attacks at the imminent mountain of paperwork I was facing, I was sitting in a Starbucks café—conveniently located only a few blocks away from my apartment—drawing a short man seated across the room, and playing up his Elmer Fudd features and round, swaying belly. It's a real challenge to draw someone without having him notice that you're staring at him, taking in his furrowed brow, alcohol-reddened nose, and petulant lips. You have to glance at him, taking in as many details as you can, and then look down quickly before he makes eye contact. I'd done this before and had the man I was drawing think that my constant staring and then looking away was a come-on. One even approached me and grabbed my sketchbook, only to see a cartoon of himself, with a caveman forehead and protruding bubble-butt.

I love Starbucks, although Nina always dismisses it as tacky and bourgeois. She objects to the highly polished decor and overpriced coffee, and particularly the modern mural of various famous writers—many of whom weren't alive at the same time, and yet are all depicted as sitting in a café together. Nina insists that it perverts art and writers by turning them into capitalistic currency. I don't mind. I like the soft lighting, the modern-retro ambiance, and the overpriced coffee, and think that the mural is pretty cool. But then, I suppose I'm a capitalist at heart, and not at all offended by corporate attempts to make my life as smooth and hip as a Pottery Barn catalog. God knows I don't have enough time to conquer the legal world, find true love, and expend the necessary time and energy to make my surroundings chic, comfortable, and serene.

As I sat and drew Elmer, memorializing his enormous stomach in my cartoon, the woman next to me began to laugh hysterically. I glanced over at her. She was heavy, and wearing rollers and house slippers, and was reading a paperback copy of Webster's Dictionary. I couldn't tell if she'd come across a particularly funny word worthy of her mirth, or if she was just nuts and likely at any minute to pull a gun out of her plastic shopping bag and turn the coffee shop into a killing field—when you live in a big city, you have to consider these things. I was debating the likelihood of each scenario, watching her under lowered eyelashes, when I saw Ted. He was in line at the café waiting to place his order, and was standing with a handsome woman in her forties. It was the first time I had seen him since our ill-fated dinner back in August.

They're on a date, I thought, noticing how the woman

kept reaching out and touching Ted's arm as though to make a point. This was the oldest dating trick in the book, establishing sex in the relationship through seemingly innocent touching. Ted was not, I happily noted, touching her back. Though he was smiling, and nodding attentively as she gabbed on, her high-pitched laughter echoed through the café, causing the other patrons to shoot her annoyed glances. She was also, I noticed, holding on to Ted's arm as though without it she would fall over sideways.

His date was attractive, I had to admit. She was trim, with dark, well-cut shoulder-length hair and smooth, straight features. Her clothes—a dove gray suit, clutch handbag, and three-inch heels—fit her well and looked very expensive. In fact, she looked like the well-groomed, well-heeled wife of a successful politician. And she was older. Older than me. Probably well within Ted's mandated age range for female companionship. I stared as long as I dared, and just as Ted picked up their paper cups of steaming espresso and turned in my direction, I slouched down—not easy to do in the spare, modern café chair—and lifted my pad in front of me, hiding from his keen reporter's eyes. My heart was beating faster, and I felt like I was in high school again and had spotted the captain of the lacrosse team across the cafeteria. The temptation to stare was intense, but the consequences of being discovered were too horrible to contemplate. Making eye contact as a form of flirting is one thing; staring at the man you went on one disastrous date with but who rejected you midway through dinner is quite another.

Just don't look up, don't make eye contact, I told myself.

"Hello, Ellie."

I nearly jumped out of my seat. Ted had deposited the attractive brunette at a table across the room and was standing over me, looking taller than I remembered him.

Actually, to be perfectly honest, I didn't need to remember anything, since I had started taping his news show every night and watching it when I got home from work (not that I'd ever admit that to Harmony, who doesn't tolerate such juvenile behavior in matters of the heart). But I'd found that it's quite convenient having a crush on someone on television—you can tape him, and replay him, without anyone being the wiser. Of course, it also smacks of having an adolescent crush on a scruffy pop star, memorizing every statistic about him and kissing his poster each night before going to sleep.

"Um, hi. How are you?" I said, and for some reason, I blushed. I have a pale complexion, and unfortunately turn bright red whenever I'm angry or embarrassed or looked at by a sexy man I have a crush on. It's maddening, especially when I'm trying to come off as aloof and mysterious and just end up looking like a stammering love-struck teenager.

"I'm fine, thanks. I saw you sitting over here, and, well . . . I've been meaning to call you," he said.

"You have?" I asked, sounding far more interested than I ought to.

"Yes, I really owe you an apology about that night that we, uh," he glanced at the brunette, who smiled tightly, obviously displeased that he'd abandoned her, "had dinner. I'm sorry for the way I acted. I shouldn't have gotten angry with you."

"Actually, it was less the anger than the insults," I said, and when Ted looked confused, I added, "about my age. Or, more specifically, about how I look ten years older than I actually am."

Ted now looked seriously chastened. "Christ. I don't know what I was thinking. I was angry, and everything I said came out wrong. You don't look that . . . it's just before, at that party, you were in a suit, so I just assumed you were ... especially since you told me you were an attorney and your hair was up, and, well, seeing you sitting here now ..."—I was now wearing jeans and a tan cotton sweater, and my hair was loose and messy, spilling down over my shoulders—"you don't look a day over twenty," he said generously.

"Really?" I asked shyly, but beaming at the compliment.

"Yes," he said, and he broke out one of his slightly crooked grins.

"Thanks. And thanks for the apology. I'm sorry, too. For walking out on you, I mean," I said.

Ted smiled. "What are you drawing?" he asked, and when I showed him the pad, he looked startled. "You drew that? Just now?"

"I just mess around. I'm not that good," I said.

"No, to the contrary, it's excellent. Seely Howard, right?"

"What?"

"Your drawing. It's a cartoon of Representative Seely Howard, isn't it?"

"I don't know who he is. It's a drawing of that man over there," I said, nodding in the direction of Elmer Fudd. Ted looked over, and Elmer practically jumped out of his chair and ran over. I quickly closed the cover of my sketchbook to hide the less-than-flattering caricature from him.

"Ted, good to see you!" Elmer boomed in the loud, articulate voice of a politician, and shook Ted's hand and slapped him on the back. It was exactly the kind of attention that Ted had attracted at the cocktail party. It was annoying that people felt free to barge into our conversations, but still ... there was something to be said about a powerful man. Very sexy.

"Congressman, good to see you," Ted said in that

tone of voice that was deep and serious, yet with a slightly irreverent quality to it. It was the voice of someone who saw the world with cynical eyes, and yet never failed to be amused by it.

"Well, I've been busy, hammering out that new Social Security bill with Wentworth. If you, ahem, would ever like me to come on your show, I'd be delighted to talk with you about it."

Ted just nodded and continued to look faintly amused, and after some more backslapping and shameless self-promoting, Elmer/Seely hustled back to his table, looking very pleased with himself.

I looked at Ted and raised my eyebrows. "Happens all the time," Ted murmured. "There's nothing politicians love more than to get on television."

"Ted," the well-dressed woman called out. She looked at me with the expression of a cat staring down a mouse, ready to unsheath her claws and slice me to shreds, although when Ted glanced back at her, she smiled creamily at him.

"I think she's waiting for you," I said, nodding at the woman. "Your date."

"Well. Yes. She's not my date, though," Ted said. And for just the slightest moment, I thought that he looked a little embarrassed.

Aha! "Oh," I said, keeping my voice light and non-committal.

"I mean ... well, we did have dinner together. But I didn't ask her out. We were ... actually ... a mutual friend set it up," he finished, with a rueful smile. He stuck his hands in his pockets, and rocked back on his heels. He was still standing beside my chair, and I had to tilt my head way back just to see him. "But, I should get back. It was good seeing you again, Ellie," he said, and then returned to his non-date date.

Did he just make a point of telling me that he isn't involved with her? I wondered, hunching back over my drawing and trying not to look at Ted and the brunette and obsess over the fact that she was finding more reasons than humanly possible to reach over and stroke Ted's arm. There was only so much imaginary lint she could pretend to pick off him.

I went back to the Starbucks Café the next night. And the next night. And the night after that. It was in my neighborhood, after all, I reasoned, and plenty of people were regular fixtures there, like the student tip-tapping away on his laptop, and the middle-aged woman with the long silver gray braid reading an Oprah Book Club pick. I hadn't asked Ted where he lived, but since I had met him out walking his dog, and then bumped into him at this coffee shop, which was only a few blocks away from my apartment, I was pretty sure he lived in the area. And if Ted just happened to come in, well, that was just a coincidence.

Ted came into the café on the fifth night. This time, he was alone. As soon as he walked in the door, I could see him scanning the room. When his eyes rested on me, he raised a hand in greeting, and I smiled back foolishly. He went to the counter, retrieved a paper cup of coffee, and then joined me at the small table where I was sitting with my sketchpad.

"I was hoping you'd be here," he said.

"Oh?" I said.

"I wanted to talk to you about your cartoons," he said. "The drawing you made of Seely Howard was priceless. Do you have any more samples of your work?"

I hesitated for a minute. I had my sketchbook with me, sitting on the table, and defensively I put an arm over

85

it. Drawing was a lark for me, a fun way to pass the time. My friends loved my cartoons, but I didn't know if I wanted this near-stranger—whom I'd been having delicious, naughty daydreams about for months—to see it.

"Do you have any more in your sketchbook?" he asked, extracting it from under my arm and flipping through the pages. He nodded, and smiled, and scrutinized a few of the drawings. "These are perfect."

"Perfect for what?"

"The network is developing a political online magazine to increase traffic to the news web page. We're going to carry various syndicated columnists, and want to hire someone to sketch a drawing of each of the columnists and perhaps some of the politicians they're discussing," he said.

"You want to use my drawings?" I asked, completely taken aback.

"I'd like to take them to show Nick Bloomfield. He's the editor of the website, and will have the final say, but I think it's exactly what we're looking for. We'd pay you for them, of course."

"God, I don't know. I mean, well, sure, go ahead and take it," I said, nervously nodding to the sketchpad. The idea that someone would want to buy my sketches was just unbelievable. I'd never fancied myself an artist, although there hadn't really ever been a time when I wasn't sketching and drawing. It made me happy and relaxed me. But I never for a minute thought that I could make any money doing it. Ted's interest in my drawings, treating them as actual artwork, was just incredibly flattering. But perversely, at the same time I was a little let down that it had been my drawings, and not me, that Ted was interested in. When he first sat down and said that he had been hoping I'd be there, I'd thought he meant ... well, I guess he'd made it very clear at dinner that night that he wasn't interested in having a relationship with someone my age. Just because I was having flights of fancy about him didn't mean that he had any of the same feelings for me.

"Will you be here tomorrow night?" Ted asked. "Will you meet me here? I'll bring back your sketchbook and let you know what Nick says."

And even though I knew he wasn't interested in seeing me for anything other than business, a balloon of hope welled inside me. "Sure. Tomorrow night," I said. "At what time? Eight?"

Ted beat me to the café the next night. I got stuck at the office, scanning hundreds of pages of depositions to see if each deponent mentioned a particular name—thrilling work, just like on *Ally McBeal*—and didn't get home until after seven. I raced around my apartment, letting Sally out, changing from my stodgy suit to my favorite Levi's and black turtleneck sweater, then freshening my makeup and brushing out my hair, and was just walking out my door at eight. When I got to Starbucks, Ted was sitting at the same table we'd occupied the night before. I went straight to him, quickly touching his arm in greeting. I never claimed to be above using such tricks.

I was completely aware that I was asking for trouble. It smacked of masochism, this infatuation of mine, like when I was in the seventh grade and developed a searing crush on the young, handsome—and newly married—art teacher, which had the inevitable conclusion of shattering my adolescent heart when I saw him at the movies with his wife, taking her hand in his and stealing a kiss on the back of her neck. Of course, my art teacher had never asked me to meet him for coffee, for business or any other purpose. I had spent the better part of last night tossing in my bed, fluctuating between fantasies about Ted that ran the gamut from sweet (his cupping my face in his hands before kissing me tenderly), to ridiculous (our wedding, posh and filled with Washington elite), to sexual (the tender kiss going quite a bit further), and pondering whether it really was as inappropriate as Ted seemed to think it was for us to date. He was older than me by a little less than a quarter of a century, it was true. For the first two-thirds of my life, it would have been criminal for him to view me as an object of desire. And yet, just like you always start hearing sad songs everywhere you go after you've had your heart broken, I seemed to be hearing for the first time just how many May-December marriages existed: There was Michael Douglas and Catherine Zeta-Jones, for one. Rupert Murdoch married a woman thirty-five years his junior, and they had a baby together. The same for Charlie Chaplin. And then there was Shearer the Shit and Katherine, not that they were a romantic ideal. But they were seeing each other, and had at *least* the same age difference between them as Ted and I did.

But then, there was the ugliness of our first date. Well, of our only date. Ted had not been exactly kind when he learned my true age, and despite my intolerance for my previous boring Nice Guy boyfriends, I did still rate kindness as very high on my list of what to look for in potential mates. Then again, Ted had apologized for his behavior. And it was so easy to dismiss that early mishap—he had been caught by surprise at the differences in our ages, and it had weirded him out.

And now we were meeting for the third time in a week, and by appointment. And as I brushed his arm, and the electricity of this contact sent goose pimples exploding down the tender white flesh of my arms, I saw the look in his eyes. And his eyes were not the impersonal business eyes of Shearer, nor the vaguely patronizing expression of a professorial mentor. They were the eyes that Charlie had fastened on me right before he kissed me in the front seat of his rental car. Curiosity, interest, and hopefulness.

"Hi," I said.

"Hello. I was beginning to think you were going to stand me up."

Stand me up? That was date lingo, I thought. I decided to start keeping track, and that was one point in the date column, and zero in the non-date column. "I'm sorry. I had to work late. I would have called you, but ..." My voice trailed off. I didn't want him to think I was hinting for his cell phone number.

"Can I get you a cup of coffee?" Ted asked.

Buying me a cup of coffee—more date lingo. Safe speak for I'm-not-ready-to-commit-to-dinner, but date lingo nonetheless. Two for date, still zero for non-date.

"Yes, please," I said.

Ted stood and then turned to me. "They don't really sell just coffee here. Do you want a nonfat no-foam latte, or a six-shot espresso, or what?"

I laughed. "A tall café mocha, please," I said. "With whipped cream."

A minute later he was back with my steaming drink—the weather had dipped into the forties for the first time—and sitting in the intimate, comfortable café, sipping hot chocolate laced with espresso, was beginning to feel very datelike indeed. Fearful that I was obsessing, I tried to force myself to think of anything other than whether or not we were either on, or headed toward going on, a date. What should I think about? *Mmmm, Ted looks very sexy in that sweater. I wonder if it's cashmere? He said he was divorced—I wonder what his ex-wife is like. Okay, this isn't exactly off the topic of dating him. What can I think about? Shoes, shopping, the latest episode of* Survivor *... no, nothing is coming to me. Maybe if I ...*

"Ellie?"

I jumped in my seat. I had been so busy trying to concentrate on something other than Ted, I hadn't heard what he said to me. "Hmmm?" I asked, smiling at him, hoping to disguise my inattention as enigmatic, the mysterious female, and all of that.

But Ted had become all brisk and businesslike. "I talked to Nick and showed him your pictures. He thought they were perfect. He wants to meet with you, but I can tell you right now he's ready to offer you the assignment of drawing our columnists, on a freelance basis, of course."

I was speechless. It all seemed so peculiar. They wanted to pay me—me, an attorney, a litigator—to draw? Work was, by definition, tedious. It wasn't supposed to be something that made the time speed by, your heart soar, and your chest fill with quiet contentment.

"Oh," I said.

Ted looked at me, curious. "Aren't you interested? Have you changed your mind?"

"Oh, no, no, no, no," I hastened to say. Very, very interested. Very. "Of course I'm interested. It's just so, well, so overwhelming, I guess."

Ted smiled at me and then played with his paper coffee cup. I noticed that it was empty. "I'll arrange for you and Nick to meet, and he'll work out the business end with you. He knows you're an attorney, and we'll have to work around your schedule, but since the website isn't up and running yet, that shouldn't be a problem."

I nodded and said, "Okay, okay," and wished that I had some idea of how to act. Shocked was not the most sophisticated reaction. Some sort of blasé, of-course-you-want-to-buy-my-drawings-who-wouldn't? facade would have worked, as would businesslike briskness. But all I could do was stare, nod, and wonder what it would be like to kiss his lips. They were thinnish, but firm, and capable of stretching into that wonderful, crooked smile.

"So, should I call you tomorrow at work? Or, maybe I should have Nick call you, and that way you could set up a meeting with him, since he'll be the person you'll be working with," Ted said.

"Oh. Sure, have him call me. Here," I said, pulling out one of my impressively expensive-looking business cards, and scribbled the number of my private office line on the back of it. Better if Nick didn't call me through the receptionist. We were a large law firm, but not immune to gossip, and the partners did not condone moonlighting by their associates. One of the women I used to work with was fired when the partnership learned that she was drafting criminal appeals on the side and making a cool forty thousand a year in addition to her salary.

Ted nodded, and I expected him to stand up and make a brisk exit, crumpling up his empty paper cup and tossing it overhand into the garbage can as he had the night before. But he continued to sit and look at me.

"How have you been?" he asked, in a way that sounded like he really did want to hear my answer.

"Good. Work's been a little hectic recently. I've had more to do recently, but otherwise good. Any more trips to England?" I asked.

"No, I've been traveling for work, although I'm hoping to cut it back. I'd really like to spend more time in town, focusing on building up the network," Ted said.

"It sounds amazing to me, getting to go to exotic places, but I guess it must get tiring," I said.

For the next hour we chatted about our jobs and lives. Ted had recently accompanied the president on a trip to India, although he again denied having done any sightseeing.

"I think the network would have been a bit put out with me if I had missed the president's joint press conference with the prime minister of India because I was busy touring the Taj Mahal," he said. "You said that your work has picked up?"

"Yeah. My two bosses head the litigation section. They appointed me to take over this big class-action lawsuit. It's sort of a big deal, I guess," I said lamely. I lacked all of Katherine's skills of tossing my hair, bragging about my resumé, and making every assignment sound fascinating. Especially to a man who was a top anchor for a major news network.

"Congratulations. They must think very highly of your work there," Ted said.

"Well, I guess," I said doubtfully. Did Shearer the Shit and his cohorts think highly of me? Somehow, I doubted it. My antipathy toward the law, and litigation in particular, had surely spilled into my work. Not caring about your work—hating your work, to be precise—was not exactly conducive to doing a bang-up job. I was never eager to go the extra mile at work—coming in on Saturdays without whining, lobbying for more responsibility, nor (thinking of Katherine) giving the boss a blow job.

Ted looked at me expectantly. "You don't think you have a future there? They wouldn't give you one of their biggest cases if they weren't grooming you for advancement. Surely they want you to make partner."

"Oh, God, I hope not," I blurted out, without thinking. How had I started down this path? I hated litigation, hated the boring, painstaking work, hated the constant conflict of it all. I could barely sleep some nights, spending the entire night dreading having to go in to work the next morning. The idea of making partner, of committing to litigation and the firm for the rest of my life, of working even longer hours than I was now, toiling late into the night—the very thought made me sick. I didn't want to make partner, and I didn't want the stupid case, and wished they had given it to Katherine, or anyone else but me.

"What is it?" Ted asked gently.

"Nothing," I sighed. "Just job stuff."

"Tell me."

"I don't want to bore you," I insisted.

"I wouldn't ask if I weren't interested. Tell me what's going on," Ted said.

And so I told him. All of it. And he sat and listened to me. No, he didn't sweep me into his arms, wipe the tears tenderly from my cheeks, and press his lips against mine, like an old Hollywood movie. Nor did he purse his lips and impart saccharine platitudes like "Everything happens for a reason," or "It will all work out in the end." Instead, he just listened to me. Attentively.

"Why did you go to law school in the first place?" Ted asked when I finished.

"For my father. He's a judge, and he really wanted my brother—well, both of my brothers—to follow in his footsteps, and when they didn't, I thought that it would make him really happy if I did. And I was always an 'A' student, and majored in history, so what else was I really going to do? So I applied around, and got into a good law school, and it just all seemed to work out so well. It made sense, it made everyone happy and relieved that I was working toward a career ..." I lifted my hands in the air and shrugged.

"But you didn't like it."

"Well, I didn't know. Not until I got to law school anyway. Then I figured it out pretty quickly, when a professor of mine—a real egomaniacal asshole who thought he was John Houseman from *Paper Chase*—made me cry on the first day of Civil Procedure class. You know, sliced me down with one of those 'Go call your mother and tell her you'll never be a lawyer' insults. Not that exactly, but close. And it didn't get any better," I said. I realized that I was babbling, and blushed. "I'm sorry. Do you have to go?"

Ted waved his hand, annoyed at either my apology or hesitation, I'm not sure which. "Then why didn't you drop out?"

"And do what?"

"Well, drawing, for starters. You're very talented. I can't believe no one's ever told you that before."

"It's not the kind of thing you can make a living at," I pointed out.

"We're willing to pay you for it," Ted said.

I shrugged and smiled. "That's wonderful, of course, but what were the odds of you hiring me? A million to one? And what are the odds that I'll get any other work, much less enough to support myself?"

"Pretty good, I think," Ted said. "I think that you should at least try."

"I don't know," I said.

"I do," Ted said.

He smiled at me, and there was something about the steady, optimistic gleam in his eyes that made me wonder if it was just possible that he could be right.

Chapter 9

I t's not a date," I said. "At least, I don't think so."

"You're having lunch with him," Nina pointed out. "You've had coffee together twice, and now he's asked you to go to lunch. How is that not a date?"

We were power-walking around the Mall, up one side of the reflecting pool, past the Lincoln Memorial, and then down the other side of the pool toward the Washington Memorial. It was the most beautiful part of the city, and what I loved most about living in the District. Almost anywhere you go in the city, you're privy to incredible views of regal monuments and gorgeous buildings. The District has a majestic quality unique in a country where most of the cities are full of ugly self-important skyscrapers and cookie-cutter apartment buildings.

"Because the coffees weren't dates—that was business. To discuss my, er, doing that freelance work," I said. I didn't want to go into too many details of the drawings that Gold News had commissioned from me—fifteen in total, at five hundred dollars apiece—because Nina was a Real Artist, a painter, and might be a little sensitive about my dabbling in her world. "And he said he wanted to take me to lunch to celebrate my getting the commission.

I think he's doing it as more of a mentor than anything else. Besides, lunch isn't a date meal."

"Yeah, right," Nina snorted. "Like single men ever ask out hot young chicks just to mentor them. This is just like that episode of *Seinfeld,* where that guy kept asking out Elaine, but pretended to do it as friends so he wouldn't feel stupid if she said no. That's what Ted's doing. He's dating you under the guise of business. Or mentoring. Or whatever. Anyway, once you end up in bed together, it should clear up the mystery."

I loved Nina, but I was beginning to think she was incapable of viewing any man as anything other than a penis on legs. "I wasn't even talking about sex," I said irritably.

"Then what's the point? Like I said, an older man is good for one thing," Nina said. Then, abruptly, she said, "Did I tell you that I was seeing someone?"

"Seeing someone? No. You mentioned that you finally got together with that guy from your yoga class."

"His name's Josiah. We've been out a few times," Nina said. "And I even followed your stupid *Rules* book and waited to sleep with him until the second date. Well, I mean intercourse. I did blow him the first time we went out."

I laughed. "I don't think *The Rules* recommends oral sex on the first date. In fact, it pretty much rules out sex altogether until the relationship gels," I said.

"How does a relationship gel without sex? And why would you want to have a relationship with someone you haven't slept with? Why get involved if you're just going to discover he has a teeny penis, or if it feels like he's trying to hoover you out when he goes down on you? Anyway, I think that we're a little beyond that." Nina paused. "Josiah and I are thinking about moving in together!"

"What? Nina, that's so ... I mean, how long have you even known him?"

"God, you are *such* a prude. I knew that you were going to act like this."

"Act like what? I'm not trying to discourage you. It's just ... I want you to be safe. I worry about you sometimes," I said, reaching out to touch her arm.

But Nina just shrugged me off. "I can take care of myself. Besides, you should see the size of his dick," she said dreamily.

I met Ted for lunch on a Thursday at Clyde's in Georgetown. I'd been stressing over what to order ever since he'd called me at the office that morning and told me where he'd made reservations. One of my favorite meals in the world is a cheeseburger at Clyde's, and preferably joined with one of their chocolate shakes. But a greasy cheeseburger is not the most elegant food in the world to eat, and I could just see myself dripping a big glob of ketchup down the front of my baby blue cashmere shell. I'd paired the soft, fuzzy shell with my new black wool J.Crew pantsuit, and for once in my life wore sexy slingback pumps to work, rather than my usual, more sensible comfy low-heeled loafers. Mindful that Ted's mistake about my age had been caused in part by the severe bun I was wearing that night, I'd worn my hair loose about my shoulders.

Ted met me outside the restaurant, and I caught his eyes flickering over me. "You look great," he said.

I'm normally terrible at getting compliments—I tend to respond to them by saying something like "Oh, please, this outfit makes me look fat," or "No, my hair looks like a bird's nest today," but I bit back the impulse to put myself down. "Thanks," I said, feeling a little shy.

"I mean it. That shade of blue really suits you," Ted said, as he held the door open for me.

Once we were secured at our table, with our menus unfolded before us, I tried to find something—anything—that would interest me as much as a hamburger. A salad, perhaps? Maybe a light pasta dish? Ugh.

"I don't know why I'm even bothering to look at this," Ted said, decisively closing his menu shut. "I already know what I'm having."

"What's that?"

"A cheeseburger, steak fries, and a chocolate shake," he said. "I've been looking forward to it all day."

I looked at him, and felt as though the heavens had opened up and light was beaming down on us while cherubic angels played harps and sang.

"I'm having exactly the same thing," I said, also putting my menu to the side.

"You're not a salad-and-rice-cake kind of a girl?" Ted asked.

I tried to ignore his use of the word "girl"—I'm not sensitive about it, but with Ted I was more concerned that he was still viewing me as jailbait. "No, never have been. I wish I were, but I just love food too much to suffer without it."

"I'm glad." He smiled at me approvingly. "I hate it when women pick at their food and announce the fat content of every bite they take."

I shuddered. "Or when they tell you the fat content of what *you're* eating," I agreed.

After the waiter had taken our orders, and delivered us a chocolate shake each, I said, "I know we must be neighbors. Where exactly do you live? I'm on Seventeenth Street."

"I'm just a few blocks away from you. My building faces directly on Connecticut," he said.

"Have you always lived in the city, then?"

"Yes, but when I was married, my wife and I also had a house in Virginia. We'd stay at our apartment during the week, and then spend as many weekends as we could at our country house. By the time we divorced, Alice was writing more and more, and reporting less and less—she was a news reporter, used to work for CNN—and so she took the house, and I got the apartment," Ted said.

"Do you miss it?" I asked.

"Being married?" Ted's voice was wary. It was so strange—without even being asked, he was perfectly willing to dive into my life and spend all sorts of time helping me with my fledgling illustrating career, but whenever I posed a direct, personal question to him, he practically flinched. Ted's entire career was spent probing others for personal information, and yet I'd never met someone who was so uncomfortable talking about himself. It was no wonder I couldn't get a read on what was going on between us—I would need to master ESP before I'd ever divine what this man was thinking.

"Oh, no, I meant, do you miss living out in the country?" I said, flushing bright red.

Ted paused for a minute, and I couldn't tell whether he was planning to answer me or just wait for me to change the subject.

"I'm not sure," he finally responded. "It's hard to think of being at the house without Alice, and I don't know if I would have wanted to go out there on my own after the divorce. But as far as being married, the divorce wasn't really a shock. We both worked all the time, so that by the time we were in a position to start enjoying our success, cutting back on the hours, we'd grown apart. And we never had children. It seemed natural to part ways," Ted said.

I was dying to ask him who left whom, but couldn't

think of how to bring it up without seeming nosy. I've never understood that scene in *Jerry Maguire* when Renée Zellweger says, "Let's not tell each other our sad stories." Maybe that's healthier, and lets you remain mysterious and aloof, but I always want to know why the man I'm interested in ended his last relationship. I'm greedy for details about how they hated their ex-girlfriend's snorting laugh or the way her second toe was freakishly longer than the big toe. I never want to hear about the sex stuff, of course—who wants to learn that she was multiorgasmic or would give him blow jobs in the dressing rooms at Victoria's Secret?—but I was always eager for details on the breakup.

"How long were you married?" I asked, and nearly choked when he answered. "Twenty years."

"Twenty years! And it felt natural to part after all that time together?" I exclaimed, but then again seeing how uncomfortable he looked, quickly said, "I'm sorry, I didn't mean to pry."

"You apologize a lot," Ted commented.

"I'm sorry," I said automatically, and then laughed. "I know it's a terrible habit. Sorry. Damn it! I can't seem to stop."

We both laughed, and the waiter appeared with our food. After he'd laid the mouthwatering cheeseburgers before us, Ted said, "It's rare to meet an attorney who apologizes at all, much less one who apologizes compulsively."

I shrugged. "I told you that the law wasn't a very good fit for me," I said, a little defensively, as I cut my cheeseburger in half. I felt more than a little stupid for having poured out my heart to him about how much I hated my job, and whining about how I'd taken the wrong path, and all of that garbage. I've always wanted to be one of those elegant, cool-tempered women, the kind who wear their hair up in sleek chignons just to go to the grocery store and always have on polished shoes. Not a messy, blubbering whiner. I couldn't help but wonder what Ted's ex-wife was like—was she the kind whose clothes always looked as fresh and pressed at the end of the day as they did in the beginning, and who always ordered salads for dinner?

"I've been thinking about that. I have a friend who's in the art department at the *Post*. They keep cartoonists there on staff. Do you want me to talk to him, see if they're hiring? And even if they're not, I know they also use a lot of freelancers," Ted said. "It might be a good contact for you."

"That would be ... amazing," I said, surprised. Ted seemed to be taking an abnormal interest in my drawing career, if you could even call it a career. "But I don't want to impose on you."

"I wouldn't have suggested it if I didn't want to," Ted said. "I'll call him next week, and let you know what he says."

"Great," I said.

Lunch was delicious. I ate everything in sight, and by the time we left, my new black suit trousers were feeling a little snug. Everything had seemed to go well with Ted. For the first time, I'd felt really comfortable with him. I don't know if it was because he'd been more at ease with me, or if it was because I'd managed to get through the meal without obsessing too much on whether we were on a date or not. We paused outside the restaurant to say our good-byes.

"Thanks for lunch," I said.

"My pleasure," Ted said, and he glanced at his watch. "I have to get back to the office. Should I hail you a cab?"

I nodded, and wondered why I suddenly felt disappointed. We'd just gone to lunch, and both had to go back to work. What did I expect him to do, book a room at the Hilton so we could have a quickie nooner? It was ridiculous, I thought, smiling at the idea.

"What's so funny?" Ted asked. He waved at a loitering cabbie, who zipped over to the curb where we stood. Ted opened the door for me.

"Oh, nothing. Thanks again," I said. I started to duck down into the cab, when Ted touched me on my arm. I turned back toward him.

"Do you ever go hiking?" he asked.

"Sure, occasionally," I lied.

"Do you want to go out to Rock Creek Park with me this weekend? I'm taking Oscar, and I know how much he'd love to see Sally again," Ted said lightly.

And what about you? Do you want to see me again? I wanted to say, but of course didn't.

"Sounds great," I said, making a mental note to go buy a cute hiking outfit.

"I'll see you Sunday, then," Ted said, and he leaned forward and kissed me on the cheek. I blushed, and smiled nervously at him before sliding into the cab.

"K Street and Twenty-first, please," I said to the cabbie.

The whole ride back to my office I rested my hand against my cheek like a love-struck adolescent and wondered—again—what the hell was going on between Ted and me. If this went on for much longer, I was going to have to take Nina's advice after all and just jump him. At least it would end the confusion.

"What are your parents like?" Ted asked, scrambling over a small hill.

We were walking Oscar and Sally through Rock Creek Park, which was surprisingly rural, with picturesque woods broken by open, rolling fields and bubbling brooks, especially considering how close it was to the District. At least, Ted, Oscar, and I were walking. Sally, who is not big on exercise of any kind—although she will endure a short trek down to the local bakery if it pays off in a piece of my croissant—had decided she was not particularly fond of hiking. She kept dragging back behind us, flopping over in the grass at every opportunity and flailing her paws up in the air as though she were on the verge of heart failure. I didn't have much sympathy for her, particularly since at her last checkup her vet had been highly critical of the donut Sally had grown around her middle and had spoken to me quite sternly on the subject of taking her out for more exercise. Sally, immediately sensing that I wasn't buying her dying-pug routine, focused her attentions on Ted. She fixed her protruding watery eyes on him, and every time Ted glanced at her she wriggled her mushroom-shaped nose from side to side like Samantha on *Bewitched* and twitched her curled tail.

"She's remarkably communicative," Ted noted, and then—crumbling every notion I had of him as being a cool, impenetrable newsman with the steely-eyed gaze who could stare down stuttering, red-faced corporate executives until they blurted out the truth about secret slush funds or illegitimate children—he caved to the demands of the twenty-pound lap-dog dictator and picked her up, hoisting her sausage-shaped body up to his shoulder so that she could see where they were going.

I'm not much into communing with nature, but I was glad I had come. It was a gorgeous day—cool and crisp, the sun shining brightly in the blue October sky, the leaves having changed their color to lovely hues of red and orange, the trickling rivers making a soothing burbling sound. And since I was still unsure if we were dating, or just developing some kind of freaky, *Odd Couple* friendship, the idyllic surroundings were making me hopeful

Whitney Gaskell

that Ted had romance on the mind. It was so much on my mind that I was starting to worry that I was losing my modern-woman edge, and could even hear my father's voice from when I was growing up, booming about how I should worry less about whether my latest crush had called, and focus more on my studies.

"You didn't answer my question," Ted reminded me gently. "About your parents."

I had heard him, and had started to speak, opening my mouth, but then nothing had come out, so I closed it, pondering the question. What was I going to say? My father is an emotionally unavailable workaholic whose crushing expectations have been weighing me down for years? My mother has a narcissistic personality and is incapable of focusing on anything beyond the little theater stage that is her world, where she is the starring diva and the rest of us are supporting characters? Oh yeah, and they're only a few years older than you? I've always tried to hide my family from established boyfriends—I wasn't about to go exposing them to Ted.

"Mmmm, pretty normal," I said, and as was my practice when lying, I turned bright red and was unable to meet Ted's eyes. "How about yours?"

"They're both dead," he said briefly.

"Oh, I'm so sorry," I said.

"Oh, no, it was a long time ago," Ted said, and I realized that other than my maternal grandmother, the remainder of my own grandparents had been dead for years. For Ted, at his age, and at my parents' age, it was normal not to have your parents around. Other than Nina, whose father had died in a car accident when she was a teenager, all of my friends still had their parents. We took them so much for granted that the only time we talked about them was to complain about how much they'd screwed us up with their wacked-out, baby boomer ideas of child rearing.

And then a horrible thought occurred to me—Ted was a baby boomer. Maybe a young boomer, but a boomer nonetheless. Boomers were the sworn enemy of my generation—they were the selfish Me Generation, forever screwing my generation with their epidemic divorcing and nonstop selfishness. They had indulged themselves at every step of their lives—the self-indulgent, hippie war-protesting in the sixties, the tacky disco seventies, the cocaine-fueled extravagance of the eighties. Everything that was wrong with modern culture could be traced directly back to their overly padded shoulders. And here I was fraternizing with the enemy.

I gave Ted a sideways glance, wondering if this insight made me less attracted to him. But seeing him in the idyllic outdoor setting, dressed in casual chinos and a navy wool sweater, backlit by the dappled October sun, and my spoiled dog leaning on his shoulder, I found myself lusting after him more than ever. Even the knowledge that he was a hated boomer didn't stop me from stealing glances at his thin, strong lips and wondering what they would feel like pressed against my neck. And it wasn't just school-girl holding-hands-and-butterfly-kisses fantasies that I was having. I wanted to know what he tasted like, what it felt like to have him caress my body, and—brazen as it was—what it would feel like to be on top of him, straddling his long, lean body, and feeling him pulse inside of me. The thought of it made my breath catch short in my chest, and I could feel the blood rise to my face.

Just then, Ted looked at me, and when our eyes met, my heart did the Twist. I knew I wasn't imagining it—somehow he knew what I was thinking. I hoped that I hadn't been actually panting with lust, and quickly checked to make sure that my mouth was shut with my tongue secured inside. But there was no doubt that Ted knew. I could see a light flicker in his eyes, and his lips parted ever so slightly. And I couldn't look away, but just stood there, staring at him like a love-struck teenager—I wanted him to kiss me, was willing him to move closer, to wrap his arms around my waist and pull me against him. The sappy words from every paperback romance book I'd ever read about the hero and heroine being swept away by their passions on a Scottish moor or tropical island were swirling around in my head, and even all of the horrible terms those books use—like "suckling," "cock," and "man-juice"— weren't putting me off wanting Ted to sweep me off my feet and make passionate love to me in the middle of the wilderness. Okay, in the middle of the city park.

But then Ted looked away. I was still gawping at him like a lovesick guppy, and he turned his head, showing me his distinguished profile, shifted Sally to his other shoulder, and said, "Are you getting tired, or do you want to keep going up this path?"

"Sure, whatever," I said, feeling completely mortified and utterly rejected as Ted launched into a story about some congressman who'd been caught diddling the underage daughter of another congressman.

"Doesn't that happen all the time?" I asked, honestly confused.

Ted just laughed and shook his head.

Chapter 10

Harmony had a date with another tax attorney she'd met at one of those continuing-legal-education lunches, and we had to go shopping to find her something to wear.

"I can't remember the last time I bought something that wasn't a suit," Harmony said, smoothing the skirt of her lovely navy blue Ann Klein suit.

I tried to remember having seen her in something other than business clothes. "What do you wear to work out?" I asked. Harmony was almost always literal, and so I assumed she meant it when she said that she only bought work clothes.

"Well, that's true, I do buy clothes for the gym. And pajamas. But you know what I mean—clothes that you'd wear to the mall or the movies, instead of the office," she clarified.

"What do you wear to the mall?"

"I can't remember the last time I was in a mall. Do people go to the mall anymore?" she asked. "Now I just order whatever I need off the Internet. Clothes, books, makeup. Even my tampons."

I mulled this over for a minute, not sure how one

would go about ordering tampons off the Internet. Do they have online grocery stores now?

"What do you wear to the movies?" I asked, intrigued.

Harmony laughed. "I'm an associate in a D.C. law firm. I don't have time to go to the movies," she said.

I hate it when my contemporaries say things like that. It's the equivalent of e-mailing everyone in the office on the nights you work late so that they all feel insecure about the fact that you were in the office until 10 P.M. and they weren't. Actually, I never do that, because I never work that late. But I resent it when people—like Katherine, for example—do it to me. It was basically the same for Harmony to imply that she worked so much that she couldn't even take a few hours here and there for the latest Miramax flick, when I was also an associate attorney with a big D.C. law firm, and I went to the movies all the time. It had been my favorite thing to do with Eric, mainly because it was a way of spending time with him where I didn't have to hear him gush about his latest favorite sports team.

"Oh," I said, and decided to change the subject. "Where's Nina? Wasn't she going to come shopping with us?"

Harmony was eyeing a pink sweater set, and she held it up in front of her. The effect was shocking. She was right, I almost never saw her in anything other than navy or black conservative suits. Pastel cashmere was a marked change. "She said she couldn't make it. What do you think?" she asked, studying herself in the mirror.

"It's really different. I mean, it's gorgeous, but it's ... pink," I said.

"So? You're wearing pink."

She was right. I was wearing a pink T-shirt, the kind that has a little bit of spandex in it so that it hugs the body, under my gray pantsuit.

"I've just never seen you wear pink," I said.

"I know. Maybe I should soften my image a little," Harmony said vaguely.

"Why?"

"I was thinking about what you were saying at lunch the other day, about turning thirty and not being married. I hadn't ever really thought about it, but maybe I should. Maybe I should be a little less concerned with capital gains, and a little more interested in finding a nice guy to settle down with before my ovaries wither up," Harmony said. Still clutching the pink cashmere twin set, she started rooting through a rack of black matte jersey separates.

She couldn't have shocked me more if she'd pulled out a handgun from her purse and used it to rob the store clerk. This was Harmony. I had never, in all the years I had known her, heard her express any concerns about men, relationship woes, or empty-womb syndrome. She worried about the tax consequences of land sales—not dying alone. It wasn't that she didn't date—she was gorgeous, smart, and funny, so there were always men sniffing around after her. It was just that she always seemed so nonplussed about all of the relationship concerns the rest of the women our age suffered from. Well, other than Nina, of course. It suddenly struck me that my two closest friends were alike only in that one aspect—they were both totally immune to all of the social pressures to find a guy and settle down that every other thirty-something woman—or in my case, almost thirty-something—suffers from. And, ever since Beth's wedding, they were the last two of my friends still single. Sure, I knew other women who were unmarried, including lots of women attorneys. But they were mostly older than me, and either divorced or were the married-to-their-career type.

"What do you think—the pink with the black, or black with the black?" Harmony asked, juggling the sweater set with an ankle-length black jersey skirt and matching black jersey top.

"Er, the pink sweater and the skirt," I said, still trying to pull myself together after her revelation. "So, you think that turning thirty while single is something I should be worried about?"

"Well, I don't know if I would go so far as to say I'm worried, or that I think you should be. But when you were sharing your concerns with me, I dismissed them out of hand, and I think that was wrong. You know, most of the men at my firm who are my age are married. The only single men over the age of thirty-five I know are either divorced or gay. I never thought much about it before; I always figured that I would meet the right guy, and things would progress from there. But I haven't put a lot of effort into meeting Mr. Right, and I think it requires the same kind of effort I've put into my career. So that's what I'm going to do," Harmony said. "Put a little more effort into it. So, just the cardigan, not the shell?"

"No, wear a nice white T-shirt underneath instead. It will look more hip. Sweater sets can look kind of prissy . . . particularly pink ones," I said.

Harmony nodded, and spent an outrageous amount of money on the sweater and black skirt, before making me take her to Banana Republic for just the right expensively casual white T-shirt and a pair of gorgeous black mules.

"So tell me about this guy," I said as we walked back to our offices.

"Well, he seems pretty great," Harmony admitted. "He's also a tax attorney, so we have that in common, and can talk about things with each other that would bore anyone else to tears. And he's good-looking—sort of dark and swarthy. And he's only a few years older than me, which is perfect."

I knew Harmony well enough to know that she would

never be purposefully bitchy, but I couldn't help but feel a little hurt. "Uh-huh," I said, noncommittally.

Harmony suddenly realized her error, and she patted my arm. "Oh, I didn't mean to be pointy about you and Ted. I just mean that it was perfect for me," she said diplomatically.

"So you would never date someone older than you?" I asked.

"Well, I have. Remember, that guy in college? I got pretty burned in that relationship, and I decided that unless there were really compelling extenuating circumstances, I wouldn't date someone older than me again. But that's just me," she said.

"But I've been plenty burned in relationships with men my own age," I said.

"I know, I have too. I just think ..." Harmony said. And then she stopped.

"What?"

"Well ... I just think—and I'm speaking in very general terms—that the only reason most older men would want to date younger women is that they're nonthreatening. And for some men, it's very important that they retain all of the power in a relationship," Harmony said.

I absorbed this for a moment, trying to apply it to Ted and me. Not that we were in a relationship, so to speak—I had no idea what we were doing—but if we were, was he only interested in me because I didn't threaten him? I didn't think so—when we were together we spent all of our time talking, and he was always asking for my opinions on things and appeared to listen intently to my answers. True, he did laugh at many of my comments on political issues, but I couldn't really blame him—my knowledge of such things really was abysmal.

"I'm sorry, I didn't mean anything," Harmony said quickly, misjudging my silence for anger.

"Oh, no, I'm not angry. How can I be? I don't even know what's going on with Ted and me," I said.

"I thought you were dating."

"Well, we've had coffee together a few times, and lunch once, and went hiking the other day, but things haven't progressed beyond that," I said.

"You mean you haven't slept with him," Harmony said.

"I mean I haven't kissed him," I said, and she shot me a surprised look. I was lucky that I was telling this to her and not Nina, who would have started bellowing about what was I waiting for, and why didn't I just jump him. Nina was not subtle in matters of the heart, nor of the loin.

"Has he tried, or has the ... situation arisen?" Harmony asked.

"No, not really," I said, remembering how Ted had caught me making eyes at him at Rock Creek Park but had looked away and pretended not to see me.

"Oh. Well, why don't you ask him?"

"Ask him if he wants to kiss me?"

"I suppose not. Maybe you should try making a first move," she said, which was very surprising coming from Harmony, who normally applies a wait-and-see attitude to all things.

"I don't know," I sighed. "I just wish I knew what he was thinking. Ted's so ... I don't know, *self-contained*. I can't get a read on him, what he feels, what he's passionate about, what he hates. The only time he ever really opens up to me is when he's talking about his work."

"It sounds like his work *is* his passion. Some people really do love what they do for a living, Ellie," Harmony said dryly.

"I know—I know you love your job, and Ted obviously lives for his. It's more than that, though. I don't know how he feels about me, what he thinks about our seeing each other, whether he even thinks we are seeing each other. You know how you can normally read a guy, even if not by what he says, but by the way he looks at you, or the tone of voice he uses?" Harmony nodded. "Well, I can't figure Ted out at all. He was so horrified at the idea of dating someone younger than him, so why does he suddenly want to spend so much time with me? And with my cartoons, he's acting almost like a mentor—but why? And why me? If Ted was going to mentor someone, or even start a friendship up with someone twenty-five years younger, why not pick someone more like you, some-one career oriented? I can be pretty loopy sometimes."

"Maybe he's drawn to you *because* you're loopy, not to mention kind, generous, and one of the warmest, most big-hearted people I've ever known. If Ted really does have a problem expressing himself, or connecting with peo-ple, maybe he sees in you what he's missing in himself," Harmony said. She paused. "And what about you?"

"What do you mean?"

"I mean, why are you so interested in him? What at-traction does he hold?" she asked.

"I told you! He's incredibly attractive, and funny, and charming. And he's really successful, and has that whole powerful, alpha male thing going for him," I said.

"And he's almost twice your age," Harmony said dryly.

"No, he's not! He's only, well, twenty years older, or so. And anyway, I thought that you said that older men have their advantages," I said.

"Well, they do. But they also have a lot of disadvan-tages. What if you do fall in love? Would you get married? Have children? And then what? Women live longer than men do anyway, so you might end up spending half your life as a widow," Harmony said.

"But you're the one who said that I shouldn't worry

about having babies with him. You said that it was too early to think of things like that," I cried.

"When did I say that? Anyway, if I did, I was wrong. You have to think about it. Why get attached to someone you know is wrong for you? I thought you were more sensible than that, Ellie," she said.

Chapter 11

Katherine came striding into my office, dressed from head to toe in a cream wool Jil Sander suit and Manolo Blahnik pumps. I wondered how she afforded her wardrobe, immediately suspicious that her affair with Shearer might have something to do with it. Katherine and I were in the same associate class; we were supposed to be making the same salary. Unless she had a trust fund I wasn't aware of, I had a feeling that our year-end bonuses might be based on something other than our work performance. Katherine was also wearing severe, black squarish eyeglasses frames, that, I admit, looked pretty good on her, but if I tried to wear them I knew they would make me look like I belonged in the "before" picture in one of those magazine make-over articles.

"Hi, Ellie. How was your weekend?" Katherine said breezily, and stretched onto my visitor's chair with the grace of a cat. She smiled broadly, and I squinted at her, trying to figure out if she was joking. Katherine and I are not friends. We don't joke around, or visit each other's offices, or go for manicures together at lunchtime. She hated me, and I hated her. Those were the rules of our relationship.

"Fine," I said, waiting for her to get to the reason she was camping out in my office. But she just smiled benignly at me, so I said, "How about you?"

"Oh, yes, great, I worked all weekend, as usual. Anyway, I was talking to Howard—he was working over the weekend, too—and he mentioned that you might need some help on the class-action case. It's such a huge assignment, and I know you must be swamped, so I wanted to volunteer to help in any way I can," she said.

I just barely stopped myself from snorting with derision. Katherine was incredible. First pretending that she just *happened* to bump into Shearer in the office. And then making such an obvious attempt to steal the class-action case away from me. But the thing I couldn't understand was, why would she actually want it? The case had turned out to be a huge burden, keeping me at the office far past the hour when I like to be at home, firmly ensconced on my sofa with a glass of wine in hand and a pug in my lap. Was she really that worried about making partner?

"Oh, thanks, Katherine, that's so sweet of you to ask. But actually, I think I've got everything under control right now. Maybe later, when we start prepping for trial, we could use your help, but not now," I said, knowing that my answer would annoy her. Everyone hates trial prep—it was boring and, unless you're lead counsel, doesn't offer many chances for glory.

"Well, actually," she said, drawing the syllables out in the aren't-I-cute voice she used on the male office runners when she was trying to get them to bump her copy jobs in front of other attorneys', "I was thinking that I could take over the response to the defendant's Motion for Summary Judgment. I know that it would be a big load off, and it would free you to do ... well, whatever it is you do," she said, laughing.

I contemplated bouncing my tape dispenser off her forehead, but abstained. Katherine was trying to charm me as though I were some hormonally charged guy wanting to get into her pants, but she couldn't even do that without insulting me. And while it was true, our response to the defendant's Motion for Summary Judgment was going to be an impossibly large task, it was also the most visible part of the whole lawsuit. If I let Katherine take it, I knew she would make sure every partner in the litigation section knew it, painting herself as the glory girl and me as a Tom Sawyer slacker. As tempting as it was to let her shoulder the burden, if I fell for her ploy it would mark the beginning of the end of my career at Snow & Druthers.

I pasted the biggest, most disingenuous smile possible on my face. "Gee, thanks, Katherine," I said, trying to match her simpering tone as closely as I could. "But I think I've got it under control."

A flash of anger passed over her petite, pretty features before she was able to arrange her face back into a smooth, perfect mask. She stood and stretched, clearly trying to underline that this was all just a casual conversation, and that she hadn't really been attempting to do me in.

"Suit yourself," she trilled as she tripped daintily out of my office.

My pleasure at her obvious annoyance was quickly replaced with a sense of dread. The response to the Motion for Summary Judgment had been looming over me for weeks, and I knew it was going to eat up all of my time for the indefinite future. God, I hated my job. Even being able to upstage Katherine wasn't a rich enough reward.

The phone rang, and I debated whether I should just let my voice mail pick it up. But then, worried that it might be Shearer or Duffy calling to check up on me, I grabbed it just in time.

"Hello," I sighed.

"You don't sound like you're having a very good day." It was Ted! I hadn't heard from him in a week, not since our hiking expedition when he'd caught me goggling at him like a love-struck teenybopper.

"Oh, hi," I said excitedly. "No, everything is fine. How are you?"

"I'm good. I just got back into town, and I was wondering if you'd like to have dinner with me tonight. I know it's last minute, but ..."

It took me about a millisecond of debating *The Rules*, which is very specific in its advice that you should not for any reason accept last-minute date plans. But hadn't I read recently that one of the authors of *The Rules* had just gotten divorced?

"I'd love to," I breathed.

I dressed up for our dinner, wearing a two-piece black skirt and bateau top made out of a lightweight rayon knit that skimmed over my body in a sexy, but not at all sleazy way, and my favorite Nine West high-heel mules that are an almost exact knockoff of a pair made by Prada. I also spent far more than the requisite amount of pre-date time (thankfully we had a later reservation, and I sneaked out of the office early) glossing and powdering and shaving and perfuming. Sally kept me company while I dressed, curled up on the cushioned wicker chair in my bedroom, her head resting on her paws and her enormous eyes following me as I zoomed around, picking out jewelry, recovering my favorite bra from the bottom of the laundry hamper, and trying on nearly every shade of berry red lipstick I owned, which took some time since I buy lipstick compulsively and have dozens of tubes in my bathroom drawer.

When I got to the Indian restaurant on Connecticut, famous for its five-alarm curry and very romantic with crisp white linens, candlelight, and discreet waiters, I scanned the dining room, and saw Ted, who was already at a table, stand and wave to me. Luckily, I remained upright as I walked to the table—I have a tendency to take Gerald Ford–like pratfalls at the most inopportune times. I'm convinced that there's no way I'll make it up the aisle on my wedding day without tripping over the hem of my gown and ending up in a horrible, slow-motion sequence of windmilling arms, uncontrollable teetering, and finally falling ass-over-teakettle, landing on the floor in a disgraced pile of white silk. But other than having to dodge around a harried waiter loaded down with a tray of tandoori dishes, I made it to the table without incident, and even remembered to suck my stomach in and keep my chin elevated so it didn't squish down into unflattering Jabba the Hutt folds. Ted cocked an eyebrow and smiled when I reached the table, and kissed me on the cheek.

"You look lovely," he murmured into my ear in a way that gave me goose bumps all over.

"How was your trip? You said you went to Montreal, right?" I asked as we sat down, as though I hadn't been taping his show every night and hadn't seen his interview with the Canadian prime minister.

"That's right," he said. "It was just business."

"Still no sightseeing?" And then I could have kicked myself. I didn't want to remind him of our disastrous dinner that had taken a sharp, downhill turn when I asked him about whether he had taken in any of the sights on his trip to London.

"No," Ted said, smiling. "Maybe you'll have to come with me one of these days and show me how."

My heart jumped at those words, hammering inside my chest, but before Ted could say anything else on the subject, the waiter appeared. Ted ordered a bottle of pinot noir, and we chose our entrées. The waiter ran off, and then reappeared with our wine, and once Ted had gone through the ritual of tasting and approving of the vintage, we were left on our own again. Ted mentioned that he'd had the wine at a restaurant in Annapolis that he liked.

"I've never been to Annapolis," I admitted. "Two of my friends went over Labor Day weekend, but I had to go to a wedding back home."

"I can't believe you've never been! It's a great town. I've often thought of buying a house there, although the commute's a little long," Ted exclaimed.

"How far away is it?"

"About a forty-five minute drive from D.C. We should go out there some weekend, especially now that the leaves have changed," Ted said.

My heart did another little jig. Ted had now suggested we take a trip together, not once, but *twice*! He would never have done that if he was still thinking of me as someone to mentor. There was no doubt about it—this was a bona fide date.

"I'd love to do that," I said.

When our dinners came, we shifted back into the typical work talk, taking turns discussing what we were each working on, and then listening to the other person's stories. Ted was not an easy person to play this game with—his work was so much more interesting than mine, so much more important and glamorous, and I hated to bore him with the details of my dreary lawsuit. But despite my attempts to get him to tell me yet another fascinating story about some third-world uprising, or what it had been like covering the fall of the Berlin Wall, Ted insisted that I tell him about my case, and he even managed to look interested as I told him.

"Did you ever talk to your friend at the *Post* to see if they're hiring cartoonists?" I asked.

"No, I haven't had a chance, but I promise I'll call him first thing in the morning," Ted said. "And they're not the only game in town. There are other magazines and newspapers that you can contact, too. Especially once your work goes up on the Gold News website, it will be a great way to get other publications to take you seriously."

The check came, and I put up a weak protest when Ted took it. This is something that we women do—we insist that it's our turn to treat, all the while knowing full well that if the man made the faux pas of passing us the bill, it would be the death knell to the burgeoning relationship. Luckily, this is one female peccadillo that most men seemed to be clued into, and Ted slipped his platinum American Express card into the leather bill folder.

After the bill was paid, and we stood to leave, Ted smiled his sexy crooked smile. It was the end of the evening, and the big to-kiss-or-not-to-kiss moment wasn't that far away. I tried to focus on Catherine Zeta-Jones and Michael Douglas to calm myself. Ted rested his hand lightly on my back, and gestured for me to walk in front of him, and didn't drop his hand as we walked forward, but kept it steady on the small of my back, guiding me out of the restaurant.

Outside, Ted hailed a cab. This is often the time of the date that you can get a read on what the other person is thinking. If you want to get away from each other, you take separate cabs; if sex is a possibility, you try to find excuses to share one. But since Ted and I lived so close to each other, there was no question that we would share a cab home. When the cab pulled up to my building, Ted paid the driver and got out of the cab with me. My heart rate picked up, to about the speed of a jackhammer. Was he planning to come up to my apartment? I did a quick mental scramble, trying to remember if my apartment was fit for visitors—I didn't want Ted to encounter recently laundered underwear hanging on my kitchen chairs, nor a tube of mustache bleach on the bathroom sink.

We stood there for a moment, in the cool October night, facing each other. Ted looked at me as though he wanted to say something, and then frowned a little, as though he were having an internal argument with himself. Was he debating whether to kiss me? I wondered, and began to worry he might notice that I was starting to flush the color of a summer tomato. But still he didn't move toward me, but just continued to stand there, looking at me with an unreadable expression on his face. I could hear Nina broadcasting over my thoughts: "Oh, for fuck's sake, Ellie, what are you waiting for? Just do it!"

I took a deep breath, tipped my head back, and planted my lips on his. And not a chaste, thanks-for-a-nice-evening peck, but a full open-mouthed kiss. Thankfully, Ted didn't peel me off him while gently informing me that I had the wrong idea, which would have made the kiss the most humiliating moment of my life. Instead, he kissed me back. We stood there, at the bottom of the steps leading up to my building, entwined in each other's arms while kissing with open mouths and gently exploring tongues. One of his hands settled gently on the back of my neck, the other resting softly on my waist. For a moment, I hesitated—but then, somehow still channeling Nina, my hands reached inside his open coat to his hip, just below the narrow leather belt that encircled his waist, and then allowed my right hand to slide farther back and lower, until I was just barely cupping his firm, slightly rounded buttocks with my fingers. Ted made an audible noise—somewhere between a sigh and a moan—and he pulled me closer to him, so that the soft wool of his overcoat was brushing against my cheek. I could feel a rush of warmth spread through my groin as I sank into him.

A pair of college-aged boys, each dressed in the requisite uniform of backwards baseball hat, faded Levi's, and college sweatshirt, passed by us. They giggled, and one called out with beer-soaked bravado, "Hey, Gramps, get a room!" while his friend snickered and gave a long, low wolf whistle.

The interruption jarred us apart, and we broke off the kiss, although neither of us moved away. Ted's hands were still drawing me close to him, and my arms encircled his waist. I looked up at him, and his face, mere inches from mine, was unreadable.

"Do you want to come in?" I murmured, no longer caring if there was underwear and facial bleach strewn around my apartment.

"Yes," Ted said. "But ..."

I kissed his neck. I wasn't sure where this newfound boldness had come from; I seemed unable to stop nuzzling him. It's not that I'm all that virginal or prudish. It's just that in the past I'd always let the man take the lead, make the pass, suggest the next step. But here I was, dying to get him into my apartment, so that we could see where the kiss would lead to.

"But what?" I said, smiling up at him.

"I don't think it's a good idea," Ted said. He stepped back, breaking from our embrace. A burst of cold air swirled between us, more pronounced now that his body heat had been withdrawn.

I stared at him, not knowing what to say. Had I read

this wrong? No way ... I wasn't the only one who had been doing the kissing. And I had definitely felt his hand graze against my right breast when we were lip-locked. But, slowly, horror spread through me. The first time I made a pass at a man, and I was getting shot down. It was mortifying.

"Not a good idea," I repeated stupidly. "Why?"

"Because I'm more than twenty years older than you, and there's no logical reason for us to become romantically involved," he said.

Despite myself, I felt a swell of annoyance. *Logical reason*. The bloom of a new relationship, the first kiss ... it wasn't supposed to be logical. It was supposed to be emotional and romantic.

"Why does the age thing matter so much to you?" I asked irritably.

Ted looked down at me for a minute, obviously trying to figure out how to explain it to me in a way that I'd understand. "My entire career as a newsman is based on people trusting me. It's important to my audience—and to me—that I remain dignified, respectable. Trustworthy," he explained.

"And a younger girlfriend makes you undignified?"

"It makes me Larry King," Ted said, and we both laughed a little at his feeble joke, more to alleviate the tension than anything else.

"I'm not exactly a twenty-year-old cheerleader," I said softly, looking down at the dirty sidewalk.

"I know you aren't, but still, we need to think about what this step would mean for us ... whether we're willing to even take this step. I just want to have a clear head when I decide—when we decide—and," he said, as he stroked my hair back from my face, "I'm not thinking very clearly right now."

"Oh," I said, and sighed deeply.

"I'll call you," he said, and then he was kissing me again, one hand pressed against the small of my back, the other on my shoulder. It was a brief kiss, with no tongue action this time, but his lips lingered on mine before he stepped away.

"Good night," Ted said.

"Good night." I sighed again.

Ted paused and watched me while I climbed the stairs and attempted to key my door lock with a shaky hand. Once I had the door open, I waved at him. He smiled, and turned, and walked away at a fast clip. The speed of his departure just added to my humiliation—it was as though he were sprinting away from me, relieved to be spared the horrible fate of being lured into my web and subjected to my sexual overtures.

"I'll probably never hear from him again," I said to myself.

Chapter 12

Five days had passed since my failed attempt at seducing Ted, and he still hadn't called me. I was starting to suspect the worst. I checked my messages constantly, by remote access from the office, and as soon as I walked in the door I would run to my answering machine. No one called—not even Nina or Harmony or my mother. Finally, on the fifth night, the red light on my answering machine was blinking red.

"Ellie, it's Charlie. I'm going to be in D.C. this Saturday, and I was hoping you'd let me take you out to dinner. Give me a call so we can make plans." He left the phone numbers for his office and apartment.

Shit. Shit. Fucking shit. Why was it that I couldn't shake my brigade of ex-boyfriends loose, but the one man I actually wanted to call me, the one man I had practically thrown myself at, seemed to be missing in action? I kicked at the edge of the coffee table, which promptly caused me to stub my toe and hop around the apartment, cursing like a sailor on shore leave.

* * *

"Hey, kids," Nina exclaimed, as she opened the door for Charlie and me. She hugged me, and kissed Charlie—whom she'd never before met—full on the mouth. When Charlie saw Nina, who was dressed in only a sarong skirt fashioned out of a smallish silk scarf and a hot pink Wonderbra, he reminded me of one of those old Bugs Bunny cartoons where the eyeballs would actually leave the character's head and sort of bobble in the air for a few seconds.

"Charlie, this is Nina," I said.

"Hi, Charlie," Nina said. "Nice to meet you."

Charlie couldn't seem to answer her, but just swallowed and kept his eyes fastened on Nina's barely covered, perky breasts. It was actually a relief to see him openly staring at Nina—it meant that I didn't have to worry he might think this was a romantic outing (since most men, once they reach a certain age, manage to abstain from extracurricular breast ogling while on a date). I was hoping that when Charlie called to get together he didn't have any romantic aspirations, so in keeping with the platonic theme, I'd suggested we go to the party Nina was having at her apartment. To me, going to a party was not a datelike activity, and luckily Charlie apparently felt the same.

Nina was famous among our friends for her theme parties. Tonight it was "Arabian Nights," hence her skimpy costume, which was not exactly historically or culturally accurate, and I suspected that she'd fashioned it for the sole purpose of showing off her flat stomach. Her tiny, nine-hundred-square-foot apartment was strewn with silk pillows, plates of shish kabobs, and even a candle holder shaped like Aladdin's lamp. There were already a ton of people crammed into the tiny space, some wearing fezzes, others veils, although most were dressed normally, including Charlie and me.

"Thanks for inviting me," Charlie finally said. Nina, who's gorgeous and used to being stared at, just laughed.

"Where's the new guy? I can't wait to meet him," I said.

"He's right there," Nina said. I followed her gaze, but thought she must be joking. The guy she seemed to be looking at was attractive—in an overly pretty, soap-star way—but he was wearing a Eurotrash-style black and white leather jacket with zippers all over it and had his long hair tied back in a ponytail. Frankly, he looked like a pretentious poser—not the kind of guy that Nina normally went for.

"Josiah ... come here, I have someone I want you to meet," Nina called to him.

Josiah looked up from the conversation he was having with a pretty blonde, and gave Nina a small nod while holding up one finger, signaling *In a minute*.

"It's okay, I can meet him later," I said, although I was faintly annoyed that he couldn't be bothered to meet me.

Nina smiled happily and glided away, calling back over her shoulder, "Drinks are in the kitchen, and there's a ton of food on a table in my bedroom. Have fun, chickadees." And then she walked up behind Josiah, wrapped her arms around his waist, and when he turned to face her, she kissed him open-mouthed, and let her hands drop to his bottom. Josiah immediately lost interest in the blonde, which I'm sure was Nina's goal.

"Is that her boyfriend?" Charlie breathed.

"I think so, but I haven't met him," I said, laughing a little. Charlie was still staring at Nina, and looked like he might start hyperventilating and risk popping the buttons off his Brooks Brothers shirt.

"Come on, let's get a drink," I said, tugging on his sleeve to get his attention.

The kitchen was a disaster. Bottles of wine, gin, and

vodka littered the countertop, several lying on their sides and leaking onto the gummy white tile, filling the room with a foul fraternity-house stench. Crumpled paper towels and overflowing ashtrays were strewn about the counter. Someone had left the kitchen faucet on, and water was gurgling into the sink. I squeezed past a gaggle of stick-thin girls doing tequila shots, and turned the water off just seconds before it began spilling out onto the floor.

"Is this punch? Should we risk it?" Charlie nodded at an enormous bowl of dark, putrid liquid.

I sniffed at it and grimaced. "I'm going to stick to wine," I said as I reached for an opened bottle of chardonnay, and Charlie grabbed a bottle of beer from the refrigerator.

"How's work going?" I asked as we pushed our way through the crowded room. Duran Duran was on the CD player, and my voice was drowned out by "Hungry Like a Wolf," which was probably a good thing, since when had I become the kind of person that began a party conversation asking someone about their job?

"What?" Charlie yelled, leaning toward me with one hand cupped over his ear.

I nodded toward Nina's balcony, which was actually little more than a fire escape landing. "Let's go outside," I shouted into Charlie's ear.

I opened the window and stuck my head out. Two grunge youths, identically dressed in black watch-caps, huge jeans, and short-sleeve tees sporting vulgar expressions layered over long-sleeve tees, were sharing a joint. They both looked at me with startled expressions.

"What do you want?" one of the grunge youths sneered.

I had no idea where Nina found these people. Other than Nina and Charlie, I hadn't seen a single person I knew

129

at the party. Harmony had been invited, of course, but she'd been vague and hard to pin down when I asked if she was attending, so I thought that she was probably working instead. Nina and I had other friends in common, but none of them were here. It was as though Nina had just flung open her door and begun inviting up strangers on the street. Which, for all I knew, she had.

I pulled my head back through the window and shrugged at Charlie. We made our way back through the apartment, now even more jammed up with an even stranger mix of people—some looking like they should be pumping a keg at a frat party, others looking like they should be at a country club, and at least one man in overalls who seemed like he'd fit in better at a square dance. And yet they all mingled together, laughing, dancing, banging against each other with their hot, sweaty bodies, some slurping down Jell-O shots that had materialized from somewhere. I made a beeline for the bedroom, with Charlie in tow, but it was just as packed.

"This is crazy," Charlie shouted into my ear.

I nodded, and pointed toward the door. Charlie nodded back in agreement. I spotted Nina, sitting on her bed next to the ponytailed guy. He had dark hair and thick, well-chiseled features, and looked like he was pouting about something. Nina was sitting with her legs swung over his lap, and he had a hand up her sarong. She was speaking to him in a low voice, and although I couldn't hear what she was saying, it sounded like she was talking to him in the wheedling tone one might use with a small child.

"Nina, Charlie and I are going to go," I said, and as she turned toward me, the ponytailed guy pulled a face, obviously annoyed at the interruption. "This is a little too crazy for us."

"Before you go, I want you to meet Josiah. My boyfriend," Nina added shyly, patting his knee and curling her body toward his. I stared at her. I'd never seen Nina like this, all googly-eyed and cuddly. She almost seemed like she was falling in love, which is something Nina just doesn't do. She has flings, has fun, but I'd never seen her get serious about anyone. And especially not with someone who had annoying Michael Bolton hair and a unibrow. "Josiah, this is my friend Ellie."

"Oh, hey," Josiah said with a complete lack of enthusiasm.

What does she see in this guy? I wondered, immediately annoyed as I watched Nina stroke Josiah's hair and murmur soothingly into his ear. He was not at all attractive, and was acting like a spoiled brat.

I smiled at Josiah and said, a little formally, "It's nice to finally meet you."

"Yeah, you too," Josiah said, although as he spoke he kept his arms folded and his expression was sullen.

"Bye, sweetie," Nina said to me.

I leaned over to kiss her on the cheek, and as I did, I noticed that Josiah pulled her closer to him and away from me. It was a possessive gesture that was neither sweet nor romantic. I turned away, shaking my head in disgust, and decided to bring the unappealing Josiah up for discussion with Harmony. Maybe she'd have some insights into what Nina was getting herself into.

Outside, Charlie hailed a cab. "Are you tired?" he asked.

I wasn't. And I certainly didn't want to go upstairs and face an answering machine with no blinky message light, or worse, press the play button in the hopes that the machine had somehow forgotten that it had a message waiting, only to hear the creepy computer voice saying, "You. Have. No. New. Messages." A full week had passed since I made my play for Ted, and he still hadn't called. Chances were he never would.

Charlie and I decided to get a cappuccino. Our generation doesn't just get coffee—we get lattes or cappuccinos or chai tea with soy milk. The cab dropped us off in front of my apartment, and we walked down to my neighborhood Starbucks. Charlie ordered our coffee—a tall nonfat latte for me, grande café mocha for Charlie—while I staked out a pair of squishy purple armchairs. Once we were settled in, we made the kind of chitchat that old high school friends make—who we'd heard had gotten married, who had kids, how it didn't seem possible that people our age were marrying and having children, how old it made us feel. I was still feeling a little buzzed from the wine, and pleasantly warm and cozy from the coffee. Charlie was as fun and charming as he'd been at Beth's wedding reception, even if he did tend to go on about himself and how well thought of he was at his law firm. I was just wondering at his single status, considering his preppy good looks, substantial income, and bright future, all with a fond detachment and complete lack of interest on my part, when Charlie suddenly reached for my hand, entwining his fingers around mine and stroking the palm of my hand with his in a way I knew he thought was erotic, but which became very irritating, very quickly.

I guess I should have seen that coming, I thought. We had, after all, spent the night after Beth's wedding—well, what was the right term for what we'd done? Making out? Necking? Not sex, as genital never touched genital, nor mouth to genital, only mouth to mouth and very occasionally, hand ever so lightly brushing genital. The Brits call it "snogging," which, despite being a disgusting term

I associated with eating too much chocolate in one sitting, seemed to capture the activity well. Anyway, considering our last encounter was spent doing whatever it was in the front seat of his rented Camry, it was not inconceivable that Charlie had a different expectation of our evening than I did. Besides, he was away from home for the weekend, spending time with an ex-girlfriend. There's nothing men like more than travel sex, where they can swoop in, get their jollies, and then motor back home, all without being weighed down with expectations of day-after phone calls or dinner reservations.

I, on the other hand, was really hoping to keep my relationship with Charlie platonic, chalking our front-seat make-out session as nostalgia, the relationship equivalent of buying a "Best of the Eighties" CD.

"Charlie," I said, trying to extricate my hand from his.

"There's no need to say it. I know what you're thinking," Charlie said fondly.

"No, I don't think you do," I began, now tugging my hand with more force. Charlie, still attached to my hand, was pulled forward, and suddenly, while my mouth was still pursed around the word "do," he planted his lips on mine.

And in that split second, while Charlie's lips were firmly pressed against mine, Ted walked into the Starbucks. I managed to push Charlie off me, and looked up to see Ted's penetrating gaze fixed firmly on us. My heart lurched in my chest, and that sickly, I've-eaten-too-much-dessert feeling began to spread through my stomach. Ted looked right at me, and then at Charlie, and then at Charlie's hand still entwined around mine. I could actually see his face transition from soft recognition, to curious wonder, to—what? *What?* Irritation? Jealousy? Apathy?

Ted turned, and strode to the counter to place his order. He must think I was on a date. I hadn't been able to figure out if Ted was even interested in seeing me again, and now before I'd had a chance to find out, to convince him that it wasn't freakish—well, not that freakish—for us to date, he'd presume I'd started dating someone else. Ted had been looking for a reason not to get involved with me—now he had it.

"Was that Ted Langston?" Charlie asked excitedly. "I think it is! Ohmygod!"

I nodded miserably.

"Hello," Ted said, suddenly appearing in front of us, a paper cup clutched in his hand. He looked as sharp as always, wearing khaki pants and a crisply ironed oxford-cloth shirt.

Charlie dropped my hand—actually, he threw it back at me—and leapt up from his chair. He held his hand out to Ted, and gabbed, "Mr. Langston, I'm Charlie Owens. It's so great to meet you. I'm a huge, huge fan. This is . . ." Charlie stared at me as though he were trying to remember my name—the woman to whom he'd lost his virginity.

"Hello, Ellie," Ted said loudly. A little too loudly. In fact—what was he doing? Ted had begun puffing his chest out, and looked a little like a rooster getting ready to crow.

"Ellie, right. This is Ellie. But you two know each other? Ellie, you never told me that," Charlie said accusingly. He looked at me as though we were married and I'd neglected to tell him I had an evil twin sister who was locked up in an insane asylum after a failed plot to take over the world. "Please, Mr. Langston—may I call you Ted?—please, Ted, sit down and join us," Charlie tittered.

Horror of horrors, Ted sat down across from us,

crossing one elegant leg over the other. And just when I thought it couldn't get any worse, Charlie casually dropped a possessive hand on my thigh while he beamed at Ted.

Ted's eyes flickered to my thigh, and he smiled icily at me. "I didn't know you were seeing anyone," he said, skewering me with his take-no-prisoners reporter's glare.

I could only manage a surly shrug. I mean, really, how dare he? After all of the mixed signals and breaking off our kiss the other night, and then not calling me all week, he was acting the part of the wounded, jilted lover? It was a little rich.

"Ellie and I go way back," Charlie said, now rubbing my thigh. I glared at Charlie. He really couldn't have been less helpful if he'd tried. I knew Charlie was confused about what was going on, and was surely wondering how I knew Ted, and why Ted was being so stern with me, but he seemed to know just enough to suddenly become very male and proprietary of me, resisting my attempts to ditch his thigh-rubbing hand by clamping down with such a firm grip, I had to say "Ow!" and pull away, just so that he wouldn't leave a bruise.

"How have you been?" I asked Ted.

"I've been in China doing a report on their response to the new trade agreement being proposed in Congress," Ted said.

"Oh! Is that why you haven't called?" I said out loud, unfortunately, rather than in my head as I meant to.

"Yes, it is," Ted said softly and deliberately, his eyebrows arching, as he continued to gaze intently at me.

Charlie looked even more confused, and I—no longer able to bear the pressure—broke off eye contact with Ted and just stared at my feet. Ted turned to Charlie and told him in a nice enough way about the Chinese reaction to the trade bill, while Charlie peppered him with questions until he couldn't think of anything else to say, and then just stared at Ted with something approaching adoration. And there we were—Ted and Charlie sitting very tall and manly in their chairs, Charlie's hand grabbing for me, me swatting at Charlie's hand as if it were a pesky fly I was trying to chase away, Ted looking at me with thin-lipped anger, Charlie gazing at Ted as though he were a god. It was all so weird, and awkward as hell. All I seemed able to do was to look from Ted to Charlie, from Charlie to Ted, and feel like I might be sick.

"Well, I should be going. Thanks for letting me join you," Ted said suddenly. He stood and glanced down at me. "Ellie, it was good to see you. Charlie, nice meeting you."

I mumbled good-bye, and stared at Ted for a moment too long. Charlie jumped to his feet and pumped Ted's hand. And then Ted turned on his heel and strode out of the café without looking back.

After Ted departed, Charlie babbled on about how he couldn't believe he'd actually met Ted Langston, and what a big fan he'd always been, and how the guys at work weren't going to believe it, and did I think that the Gold News Network was hiring any on-air legal consultants? He barely paused for breath as we left Starbucks and walked the few short blocks to my apartment. He ceased speaking only long enough to make another lunge at me, at which I feinted and blocked, all the while smiling up at Charlie to soften the sting of rejection. After a few more unsuccessful attempts to kiss me, Charlie smiled smarmily and said, "Are you going to invite me up?"

"No, it's too late," I said.

Charlie sighed. "To tell you the truth, I could have completed my business with a phone call. I only came to D.C. to see you. I thought we rekindled something at Beth's wedding."

I nodded.

"So can I come up?"

I shook my head from side to side. "I'm sorry," I said, and suddenly realized how sick I was of repeating those two tired words.

Charlie waited a beat, looking hopeful that I might change my mind. When I didn't swoon into his arms, he shrugged and said, "You never told me you knew Ted Langston!"

I walked the rest of the way to my apartment, alone, finally having successfully shaken Charlie off. Another Nice Guy, perfect for a Good Girl like me, bites the dust. I could practically hear my mother scream "Nooooo!" all the way from Syracuse, and even I had a momentary pang of doubt. Charlie had a nice job, was pleasant looking, had a nice sense of humor. And, well, if it was easy to pick out his faults—vanity, self-centered, would-be starfucker—no one was perfect. I was still single and pushing thirty—was I really in a position to reject such a nice, straight, decent man? Was it time to stop tossing aside all of these potential matrimonial prospects? Was I a commitment phobic? What was I looking for?

The fact that I knew exactly what—or who—I was looking for didn't exactly make me feel much better. Especially when that someone was several decades older than me and not particularly keen on the prospect of throwing himself into the perils of dating someone my age. And who now thought I was ensconced in a relationship with Charlie and his octopus hands. Nor did it help when I saw the light blinking on my answering machine:

"Hi, Ellie, it's Ted. Sorry I haven't called, but I ended up going to China at the last minute. I was calling to see if you'd like to meet me for coffee tonight. If you get this message, and do want to meet me, I'll be at Starbucks at around 10 P.M." And then the machine's electronic voice bleated that the message had been recorded at 7:30 P.M.—just minutes after I'd left for Nina's party.

Chapter 13

I woke up with the horrible feeling that I'd overslept, only to have the lovely relief of remembering that it was Sunday and I didn't have to go in to the office, quickly followed by another wave of horror when I remembered the Ted/Charlie incident the night before. I stayed in bed, hoping I could blot out all memory of the hideous evening and just fall back asleep, but instead I just lay there, my eyes wide open and the scene replaying over and over in my head. Ted obviously thought Charlie was my boyfriend. Oh, God, why did Charlie have to keep pawing at me in front of Ted? I mean, really, he was acting like we were an established couple, not two old friends out for an evening. Even if he did think that we were out on a date—or, more accurately, a pseudo-date, since it's not like he took me to dinner, and he didn't pay for anything other than a latte, which hardly a date makes—groping me in public, and in front of someone I knew, was in complete violation of all accepted and well-established dating etiquette. It doesn't matter who you are or what your prior relationship is—you never, under any circumstances, engage in public displays of affection until there is a general understanding that the relationship is at least established, or better yet, presumed monogamous. The only deviation from this rule can occur (1) in a club, (2) while both parties are drunk, (3) and dancing, and (4) any public displays of affection under these conditions are under no circumstances counted toward any recognition of established couplehood.

I got up, splashed cold water on my face, snapped Sally's leash on, and wearing an overcoat over my pajamas, I dragged the recalcitrant pug out to go to the bathroom, and then returned to my apartment with bagels and coffee from the bakery down the block. I crawled back into bed to eat them, trying not to feel guilty about the extra shmear I'd smothered on my bagel, but then remembered that it was impossible to gain weight in the middle of a romantic crisis—after all, whenever you hear about someone with a broken heart, the person is inevitably described as looking pale and wan.

After I ate, I called Nina, but her machine picked up. Where would she be on a Sunday morning? Maybe she was sleeping in late, but still ... we almost always talked on Sunday mornings, particularly right after a party so that we could rehash what happened, and of all days, I needed her today. I left Nina a message to please, please, please call me as soon as possible, then called Harmony, who was of course not only up, but working in her home office. Harmony is one of those people who even works on airplanes, and not just pulling out files and pretending to read them so that she could bill out the time (like I do). She actually has a whole traveling setup so that no matter where she is, she can whip out her laptop and start plugging away at those fascinating tax cases. She's a girl who knows how to live life on the edge.

"Where were you last night? Why didn't you go to

Nina's party?" I asked her, sounding more accusatory than I meant to.

"I had a lot of work to do," Harmony said lightly, although I could hear a defensive note creep into her voice.

"Well, you didn't miss much," I said apologetically. And then, after assuring her that the party was a dud, unless of course you enjoy being mashed into nine hundred square feet with four hundred half-naked people you've never seen before in your life, I filled her in on what happened after the party, from Charlie's unwanted groping to Ted's strange, almost jealous reaction.

"Well, he probably was jealous," Harmony said sensibly. "No one wants to see the person he's seeing—no matter how casually—macking with some other guy."

"But I don't even know if we are seeing each other," I moaned, remembering the scene with fresh embarrassment.

"That doesn't mean he doesn't have feelings for you," Harmony said, and then—amazingly—I could hear the tip-tapping sound of her keyboard in the background! She was actually working, even while we were talking on the phone. I couldn't believe her! It was an affront to girlfriendhood.

"If you can't stop typing long enough to talk to me, I'll just call you later," I muttered, not really angry at her, but angry in general, and frustrated that she wasn't paying attention.

The typing stopped. "Oh, honey, I'm sorry," Harmony said so sweetly my irritation dried up immediately. "I just have this huge project due tomorrow. But once that's done, I'll be all yours. Do you want to meet up for a drink tomorrow night after work?"

"Yes, I'll call Nina to see if she wants to go, too. If she can tear herself away from her new boyfriend," I said. "Have you met him?"

"Yes," Harmony said. "Josiah, right?"

"Yeah. I met him last night, and wasn't all that impressed. What did you think of him?"

Harmony paused. "Well, actually, not too much. I ran into them at the bakery a few weeks ago, and he wasn't very friendly to me. But I suppose it's good to see Nina finally getting to know someone she's seeing. I've always thought the way she acts with men, you know, treating them as sex objects, was because she was afraid of getting hurt."

"That could be it," I said. "When we first met, she had been going out with this guy forever, and she was crazy about him. And then, out of the blue, he drove up one weekend during our sophomore year and broke up with her. Nina was devastated, didn't eat a thing for weeks and lost about fifteen pounds, and would only leave her dorm room to go to class. But then, one day, it was like she just snapped out of it. We went out to some frat party, and she ended up hooking up with one of the guys there, and basically started acting like she does today."

"I thought it might be something like that," Harmony said quietly. "You know, even if we don't like this Josiah person, I think we should try to support Nina as much as possible. It's good that she's letting herself become involved with someone."

"I guess," I said, not convinced. If Nina was going to get involved with someone, I wished she'd picked a better candidate. And then, remembering my own sticky situation, I moaned, "But what should I do about Ted?"

"Do? Don't do anything. If Ted's genuinely interested in you, then seeing Charlie kiss you won't drive him away. If anything, he'll be even more interested. All men respond well to jealousy. You know, playing hard to get and all of that."

As I hung up the phone, I thought about what she

said, and the only problem with Harmony's theory was that even if Ted was interested in me, he might think I was no longer available for pursuing. Maybe he *did* want to ask me out again, but wanted to be a gentleman and not go after what he perceived to be another man's woman. Maybe I should call him and let him know that Charlie and I weren't dating, and that I was available. I could do it in a playing-hard-to-get-but-not-really-interested sort of way.

I had a sudden flashback to my freshman year in high school when I called up Andy Baum and asked him to the winter dance, which some demented person had decided to make a Sadie Hawkins dance. As if anyone in our generation even knows who Sadie Hawkins was, or why she would be so sadistic as to tinker with the time-tested rule of men being the ones to ask women out. Andy hadn't made things very easy on me. He had hemmed and hawed, told me he'd let me know later, and then never called me back. I ended up going with Charlie—who up until then had just been a buddy of mine, and ended up launching a three-year relationship with him, while Andy appeared at the dance with Janet Coolidge, an insipid girl with blonde ringlets.

No, no, no, I thought. If there's one thing a woman should learn by the time she leaves her teens behind her, it's that you never, ever call a man. Maybe occasionally, of course, if he calls you first and you're just returning the message. But you never just out of the blue initiate a call. Of course, Ted had called me last night and left a message. So, if I called him now, it wouldn't be me *initiating* the phone call, but just returning his call.

I fished around in my purse and found the business card Ted had given me. His name and contact information were printed in black, formal letters, and the Gold News insignia was in gold foil, of course, which I normally think

PS EILING

30

143

is a bit tacky on a business card, but I suppose because of the name it could be forgiven, all on a very expensive looking linen-weave paper. On the back of the card, Ted had written down his home phone number and a number which he'd said was his direct line at the office. He hadn't written a cutesy note, like "Call anytime," but then I wouldn't have respected him if he had.

I sat there for what seemed like a long time, staring at the card and debating the pros and cons of whether I should call him, the pro being that if I did and explained about the whole Charlie thing just being a big misunderstanding, Ted would be relieved and ask me to dinner. And then there was the obvious con—rejection. REJECTION. I put the card back in my wallet and got out of bed. Lying around all morning was making me stiff, and my bedroom had a stale smell. I needed to get out.

I spent the rest of the day puttering. I went for a jog, and showered, and then once I was dressed I went to the Gap, where I bought two cute and completely impractical T-shirts that were probably meant for a younger woman, although I stubbornly decided that since I had yet to turn thirty, they were still very much appropriate for me. Then I returned home and watched *Pretty in Pink* on cable for the millionth time, falling asleep on the couch before Ducky declares he isn't going to ride his bike by Molly Ringwald's house anymore. By the time I woke up again it was late afternoon, and I started to feel grouchy that the weekend was over and I hadn't really done anything I meant to do, like going to a play or a museum or organizing my closet, so I decided to spend the evening indulging in hedonistic delights, such as watching *Moonstruck* (again) while drinking red wine and eating buttered popcorn mixed with peanut M&M's.

Sally and I piled on the sofa, wrapped ourselves in a big, cozy throw blanket, and settled in to watch Cher slap

Nicholas Cage across the face for telling her that he loves her. Sally kept batting at my knee with her little paw, tipping her head to the side and trying to make herself look as cute as possible so that I would feed her pieces of buttered popcorn, which of course I couldn't resist.

My door intercom buzzer sounded. I sighed, knowing that it was probably just a pizza delivery guy ringing the wrong bell, or one of my dippy neighbors who'd forgotten her key.

"Yes," I yelled into the intercom.

"Ellie? It's Ted."

Oh. My. God. I looked around my apartment in dismay—utter disaster. Not that my apartment is ever one of those altars to Calvin Klein minimalism, where everything is crisp and white and tailored, with black-and-white matted photos on the wall and vases of calla lilies on sleek metal and glass tables. Instead, it's a mishmash of some new pieces—a gorgeous cream chair and ottoman I snagged on sale last year, a set of nesting occasional tables from Ikea—and a wide variety of family hand-me-downs—Mark and Kate's old plaid pull-out sofa which I'd covered with a flowered Pottery Barn slipcover, the nicked kitchen table and chairs Mom gave me when she and Dad sprang for a new set. Nothing really matches, although I've always thought the apartment had a homey feel to it, particularly since I painted the walls a warm, cream color, have a ton of chenille pillows piled up everywhere, and constantly burn vanilla-scented pillar candles.

And then I caught sight of myself in the mirror. Argh! I was wearing a black sweat suit that I bought at the Gap about five years ago and had practically lived in every weekend and weeknight since, causing it to fade to a dull blackish-gray color from the repeated washings. I wasn't wearing any makeup, and my skin looked a little blotchy, although ever since Ted's ill-fated mistake about my age,

I'd been religiously applying every exfoliating/age-defying/line-erasing cream I could find on the market, so at least my skin was smooth and moisturized. But the worst was my hair, which I hadn't washed since I hadn't been planning to go anywhere that day. It was hanging limply around my face in the unattractive, given-up-on-life style favored by depressives.

"Ellie, I have to talk to you," Ted insisted, his voice sounding strangely electronic through the intercom.

"Um, okay," I said, hit the Enter button, and then ran to my bedroom, nearly wiping out as I tripped over Sally. In the course of one minute I managed to strip off my sweats, pull on my best faded Levi's and a black cashmere sweater, scrape my hair into a ponytail, slick berry lip gloss on, and spray Fracas on my neck. Considering that I normally spend more than an hour preparing for dates—a well-oiled routine starting with a facial mask, manicure, and leg shaving, and ending with twenty minutes of careful makeup application—it was a minor miracle that I managed to transform myself from Sunday night sloth to just barely acceptable in about thirty seconds. This never happens to the women on television. For some reason, even when they're hanging out alone in their apartments, television women are always wearing leather pants and stiletto-heeled boots, have their hair ironed into model-straight perfection, and are made up with the very latest in smoky kohl eyeliner. My failure to live up to this ideal, particularly my inability to relax around the house in anything other than forgiving, comfy sweats, was just one more failing I could add to my list, and I made a mental note to in the future at least try to remember to keep mascara on at all times.

And then, just as I was gathering empty boxes of Fiddle Faddle and cans of Diet Coke into my arms and throwing them into the kitchen, a knock sounded at my door. I made a final sweep of the apartment to make sure there wasn't anything embarrassing out and in view, and once satisfied it was safe, I opened the door.

Ted glowered down at me, his eyes snapping and his lips pressed in a grim line. Despite his foreboding expression and rather intimidating body language, I noted that he still looked great in well-cut gray flannel trousers, a perfectly pressed white shirt, and a camel hair overcoat.

"Is he here?" Ted asked as I stepped aside and gestured for him to enter my apartment. His eyes swept around my apartment, and I felt a stab of shame as he took in the ratty throw carpet and cheap, Ikea television stand. I had no doubt that Ted lived in some gorgeous home full of Italian leather sofas and original oil paintings, assembled by a top designer with impeccable taste.

"Who?" I asked.

"That, uh, Charlie guy," Ted said, and swung around to look at me, his arms crossed in front of him.

"No, why?" I asked, puzzled. Maybe Charlie's dream of being a legal news analyst for Gold News wasn't so far off, after all. "I can give you his number if you want to talk to him."

"I don't want to talk to *him,*" Ted snapped. "I want to know what's going on."

Was it possible ... was he actually jealous? I knew he had been annoyed last night, but since he had seemed so ambivalent about getting involved with me, I hadn't dreamed he'd actually be jealous.

"What's going on?" I repeated. Nervously, I reached up and made sure that my hair was smooth and not going into those annoying bumps that can pop up when I tie it back. Hopefully, Ted would mistake the oil for healthy shine. Aha! I suddenly remembered I had a miraculously unopened bottle of merlot in the kitchen. "Would you like a glass of wine?" I asked.

Ted nodded, and I went off to fetch the bottle and two glasses. When I came back, he was sitting on the couch, which gave me two options—one, I could sit down next to him, and risk looking foolish if he thought I was trying to seduce him again (which I wasn't planning to do, no matter what, considering the three-day stubble growth on my legs), or two, I could sit on the chair, and risk looking uninterested, when I definitely was interested. I chose the couch, but sat far away on the other end, so it didn't look like I was trying to come off as Mrs. Robinson seducing Dustin Hoffman. Only with Mrs. Robinson being the much younger woman whom the much older Dustin Hoffman has mistaken for a trollop. Whatever. I placed the bottle down on the coffee table, and as I set down the wineglasses, Ted took the bottle and the corkscrew in hand and expertly pulled the cork out. I suppose since it was my apartment I should have been offended as a feminist that he would take over the bottle opening, but actually I found it quite sexy. Ted had amazing hands, which I was able to admire as he poured out the wine—they were strong and wide, with well-tapered fingers and neatly trimmed nails. There's nothing I hate more than ugly hands on a man. I had actually broken up with one of my ex-boyfriends, Peter, in large part because he had these horrible spoon-fingered hands, where the tip of each finger was round and bulbous. It was an incredible turnoff.

Ted and I sipped at our wine, and for a moment sat quietly, neither of us daring to say anything. Well, anyway, I didn't dare. I had no idea what Ted was doing in my apartment. Was he still interested in me? I had to think so, not only because he was here and annoyed at thinking I'd been out with Charlie, but also because of that amazing kiss we'd had. But he'd also been pretty clear about not knowing what he wanted, and was having a lot of doubts about getting involved with someone so much younger than him—a dilemma that brought up all of those stereotypes about midlife crisis, and men trading in their fifty-year-old wives for two twenty-five-year-olds. I had no idea what to say to him. If Ted had decided that he didn't want to get involved with me, then I hardly wanted him to think that I was pining away for him; in fact, he should know that there were other men who wanted to go out with me. Of course, I didn't want him to think I was a kissing slut who made out with random men I met in Starbucks.

Finally, Ted put down his wineglass and said, "I'm sorry I didn't call you sooner. I hadn't planned to go to China. The reporter who had been scheduled to go got reassigned at the last minute, and I had to fill in."

"It's fine. I understand," I said in what I hoped was a calm, assured voice, but which sounded suspiciously squeaky to me.

"I didn't want you to think that I was ... well, that that was how I intended to leave things after ... after our last dinner."

"Okay," I said in a noncommittal tone of voice. *Intended to leave things.* So, he had decided he didn't want this thing between us, whatever it was, to go any further. Had he really come over here to tell me this? I wondered miserably, and glugged down the last of my wine.

I reached out to set my glass back on the coffee table. Ted suddenly reached out and took my hand. And then he pulled me to him, so that I had to scoot down the couch toward him. He wrapped an arm around me and kissed me. His lips were soft and open, and gently pressed at mine. It was a soft, gentle kiss. One of his hands held the back of my neck while the other slid down to my thigh, and I felt the same hot need plunge down through my stomach and throb between my legs that I'd felt during our last kiss. I kissed him back, more urgently than he was kissing me, although he quickly responded, until our mouths were pressing against each other, our tongues flicking and touching and dancing together, and his hand dropped from my neck to my shoulder until it was gently cupping my breast. I gasped at the touch, thrilled at how incredible he tasted and felt, and one part of me was ready to strip off all our clothes, while the other was shuddering at the knowledge of my unshaven legs and the boring, shapeless white panties I was wearing. The first time with a man—and especially this man, for whom it was crucial that he think of me as a sexy woman of substance—called for smooth skin and sexy, Victoria's Secret panties.

Ted pulled back and looked at me. His eyes had lost the anger they'd had when he first arrived, but now they were shuttered so that I couldn't tell what he was thinking.

"Ellie, I need to know what's going on," Ted said. He moved the hand that had been on my breast, so that both his hands were resting on my hips. He was sitting back on the couch, and I was facing him, one leg tucked beneath my bottom, the other sprawled out under his.

I shook my head and said, "There's nothing going on between Charlie and me. He and I used to go out—" I almost said, "in high school," but then I caught myself, knowing how that would sound to the age-sensitive Ted, so instead I said, "a long time ago. He was just in town for the day, and we were catching up on old times, and then when you came in and saw him kissing me—I don't know why he did that." Okay, a small white lie, but what was I going to do, cop to the post-wedding make-out session? "He just had the wrong idea, and sort of lunged for me, and before I could stop him, you came in, and what had just been a mistake suddenly got messy," I finished.

"But there's nothing going on between us. Charlie and me, I mean."

Ted looked at me, and I think he was trying to decide whether or not to believe me. I just kept shaking my head, wanting to get past this misunderstanding, wanting to get back to the kissing.

"I really have no right to be angry, anyway," Ted said, looking away.

What was he trying to say?

"I hadn't called you for a few days, and I'd not ... I haven't been very forthcoming about my feelings for you. About getting involved with you," he said.

He still hadn't moved his hands from my hips, but I was starting to feel an icy fear that this was some kind of a twisted breakup, starting with a to-die-for kiss and ending with that "let's just be friends" bullshit that I'd floated at Eric not too long ago. No one who's been dumped really wants to stay friends. Whenever you break up with someone, not only do you not want to be their friend, you want to have the power to obliterate their very existence from the planet. Not in a jealous-O.J. Simpson-murder-rampage kind of way, of course. More like a *Twilight Zone* episode, where you could just press a button and erase the fact that the person ever existed. Because if he never existed, then he could never have caused the awful pain that stabs you in the gut, and sits on your chest so that you can barely breathe, much less think straight.

"When I called you last night, I wanted to meet you so I could tell you that I didn't think it was a good idea for us to get involved. Not good for either of us," he began.

Here it comes, I thought, my heart giving a dreadful lurch, and, unable to look at him, I tried to focus on the neat row of buttons on the front of his shirt.

"I'm still getting over a divorce, and you'd be better off with a younger man you could start building a life with. Someone like Charlie, I guess," he continued, although now his voice sounded strangely tight.

I continued to stare at his perfectly pressed shirt. He wasn't wearing a tie, for a change, and he'd left the top two buttons on the shirt undone. I could see a few tufts of his chest hair poking through the top of the shirt. I've never liked men with smooth, hairless chests—there's something too adolescent, too boy-bandish about it. His hands were still holding me close, and I could feel their heat through my jeans, pressing against my hips. If he was going to do this, reject me, I wanted him to be gone, out of my apartment, and certainly not cupping my hips with his strong hands. But I couldn't bring myself to move away either, to slide down the couch or to the other chair safely out of his reach. And he didn't seem to be letting go.

"But then I saw you last night. With Charlie, and I felt this ..." He stopped suddenly, and then reached up, and with a finger lifted my chin so that I was forced to look at him. His eyes bore into me, but they were so dark, so unreadable, I still couldn't tell what he was thinking. "I couldn't stand seeing you with him," he finished softly.

"So, what are you saying?" I asked, completely confused. He didn't want to see me, but he didn't want me to see anyone else?

Ted nervously ran a hand through his hair, and for the first time since I'd met him, he didn't seem to be in complete control of the situation. He looked tense and nervous, not his usual buttoned-up, reserved self. "I'm not very good at this," Ted said gruffly.

"I think you're doing just fine," I said in my best jokey, sex-kitten voice.

Ted laughed. "Not *this*," he said, patting my hip for

emphasis. "I mean the ... relationship part. Talking about it. I don't do this kind of thing very well."

If I'd been startled to see Ted at my door, learn he was actually jealous of Charlie, and then have him kiss me until my legs felt like rubber bands, I was now rendered speechless with shock. This was Ted, Mr. Restraint, Mr. Stiff Upper Lip, Mr. Neutral Newsman *opening up emotionally*? I was terrified that if I made any loud noises or quick gestures, he might snap back into his shell like a frightened turtle, never to be heard from again.

"But ... you were married for such a long time. You must have some experience with it," I finally said in such a dulcet tone, he asked me to repeat myself.

When he finally heard me, Ted laughed again, but this time the sound lacked all humor. "Alice—my ex—and I are one and the same. Work always came first for both of us, and there wasn't much time for fireside chats about the meaning of Us. I think the marriage lasted as long as it did because she and I required so little of each other."

I absorbed this information, feeling another prick of unease. I decided that maybe he needed a little nudge to get it all out.

"So ... why did you come over tonight?" I asked.

Ted smiled, and I realized for the first time what a kind face he had. I'd thought all along that he was handsome, of course, and charming, and I'd seen him angry with me. But I'd never noticed how kind he looked.

"I can't seem to stay away. Against my better judgment, and all of the potential problems it could cause, I want to keep seeing you," he murmured. And then he kissed me again, which was heavenly. His arms encircled my waist, and he pulled me up against him, so that my breasts pushed against his broad chest. Suddenly he pulled back and smiled down at me.

"What do you think? About our continuing to see

each other. I don't want to assume anything, especially after Charlie seemed so intent on claiming you," he said.

I grinned back at him and managed to abstain from shrieking, "Yes, yes, yes!"

"I think we could give it a try," I said lightly, and kissed him on the nose. "Every relationship has obstacles, right?"

Ted nodded, but he looked a little more serious. "But these aren't average obstacles, Ellie. We're at different places in our lives. I know that there's obviously a strong attraction between us." At this we both laughed a little, considering I was practically sitting in his lap. "But we both have to be aware going into this that it's going to be tough."

"Mmmm," I said, and leaned toward him, closing my eyes and tipping my face up so that he could kiss me some more. But then his pants started to ring.

"Wait, I have to take this," Ted said, shifting me over so that he could dig his cell phone out of his pocket. I disentangled myself from his arms and sat back on the sofa, trying not to feel put out that he would rather take calls on his cell phone than continue to make out with me.

"Yes. I understand. All right," Ted said to the phone at intervals. His tone had changed from the soft one he had used with me, and was now clipped, almost curt. "Well, what about Mick, can't he cover it? I know, but I'm in the middle of something." Ted glanced at me and smiled his crooked smile.

Whatever his caller said next caused Ted to sigh and close his eyes. "I'll be right there," he said in a resigned voice, and then clicked his phone off.

"What's going on?" I asked, wanting to yell, *Nooo, don't goooo!*

"There's a rumor that the president has ordered air strikes on Iraq," Ted said. "There isn't an anchor at the station, and rather than have one of the weekend news readers cover it, they want me to go in."

"Oh," I said, nodding as though I completely understood the complex interworkings of the Middle East and the United States' relationship to it. Which, of course, I didn't. I didn't even know if our air strike thingamajiggy was all that unusual. Weren't we sending troops over there all the time?

Still, as I walked Ted to the door, and we kissed goodbye, I was deliriously happy. My crush liked me! Yeah! And before he left, he'd asked me if I'd like to have dinner Tuesday night, and he invited me to go to a cocktail party with him at some society-type person's house on Friday night. Now the only question was whether I had enough time to book a lunchtime facial for Tuesday or Wednesday, so that my skin would be gorgeous (and not still postfacial blotchy red) on Friday.

Chapter 14

The next day, I went to work humming with pleasure—
an absolute first for me, particularly on a Monday
morning. Usually after a day or two away from the
office, instead of feeling relaxed and recharged, I'm just
reminded of how much I hate my job and how much I
don't want to go back to it. But today was different. Part
of me could scarcely believe what had happened the night
before. It was as if my favorite daydream had come true—
the man I've been secretly lusting after swoops in, tells me
he feels the same way about me, and we fall into each
other's arms. The other part of me was smug and content, and all lit up with that gorgeous feeling you get
when you know that someone thinks you're beautiful and
interesting and charming. It actually makes you feel beautiful, interesting, and charming.

When I got into the office, surprising most of the support staff with both my beaming smile and my early
arrival, I attacked my in-box with a newfound vigor. Everything was glorious, wonderful, perfect. And tonight, I
was going out with the girls. Well, at least with Harmony,
which reminded me that Nina had never returned the
messages I left for her on Sunday. Remembering this struck

a flat note to what was an otherwise superb mood. Nina and I always talked, almost every day, and certainly every Sunday, which was spent dishing on the phone, or better yet, brunch and shopping. Either she'd just forgotten me, or worse, she'd been sitting in her apartment, all snuggled up with Josiah (he of the stupid name and unibrow) and screened my call.

Willing to forgive and forget, and also a little worried—had Nina not called because Josiah was really one of those creepy weirdos who kidnap and torture their girlfriends?—I called her just after lunch. Nina answered right away.

"Where were you yesterday?" I asked her. "I called and left a bunch of messages."

"Oh, Josiah and I went to the park and had a picnic lunch, and then just spent the day lying in the sun, holding hands," Nina said dreamily.

I nearly dropped the phone. Picnics? Holding hands? This from the woman who had once climbed off a lover before he had time to climax, because she'd already orgasmed and didn't want to be late meeting Harmony and me for dinner?

"Oh," I said uncertainly. "Harmony and I are meeting at Ozio tonight for drinks. Are you in?"

"Tonight? No, I can't. Josiah and I are having dinner," she said.

"Well, this won't be until later. I have to work late," I said.

"Maybe," Nina said, unconvincingly. "It's just Josiah really likes it when I stay home with him."

Josiah was sounding more and more like a pain in the ass. And Nina was starting to act like the pod people had taken over her body. I had never known her to turn down a night out with the girls, even if she did have a date. She'd usually make a joke about how they'd just skip dinner, go right for the dessert, and that she'd meet us out as soon as she could get him out of her apartment. I thought about what Harmony had said. Maybe it was good that Nina was settling down, maybe it did mean that she was maturing and growing. It just seemed strange that it would cause her to go through a personality transplant overnight. And why did she have to go and fall in love right now, when I needed her to listen to my dreamy news, and to help me dissect all of the nuances?

But then, feeling all warm and mushy at the memory of Ted—his arms around me, his lips on mine, the teasing slant of his smile—I forgave Nina. I knew what it was like to fall hard for someone.

As I worked late into the evening, I tried to put Ted out of my mind and concentrate on the task at hand so that I could get out of the office in time to have some fun. I spent the entire day poring over maddeningly dry depositions, reading one after another, highlighting the crucial bits and generally trying to stay awake. At around 8 P.M. I was ready to call it a day, and I stretched my arms over my head, causing the muscles in my shoulders to snap, crackle, and pop. If ever there was a sign that I'd spent too much time hunched over my desk, that was it. I could hardly wait to go home, get out of my work clothes, let Sally out, and then go have a drink. I stood, sighing, and threw my keys and sunglasses into my handbag. As I was walking out of my office, something stopped me in my tracks.

There was a light on in the War Room—a spare office furnished sparsely with a few folding tables and chairs that we'd turned into the command center for the class-action case. I'd turned the light off an hour earlier after retrieving a file, and specifically remembered flipping the switch because it had given me a static shock. So who had turned the light back on? I knew it wasn't the cleaners—they'd come and gone already. Everyone else working on the case—Duffy, a few paralegals—had long since gone home. I walked over and opened the door. And there, on her knees, bending over one of the file boxes full of depositions, rifling through the contents, was Katherine.

"Katherine?" I said, surprised to see her. There was absolutely no reason for Katherine to be in there; the only files being stored in the War Room were those for the class-action suit.

"Oh," she gasped, clutching her right hand over her chest. "Ellie, you scared me." She laughed and tossed her hair back.

"What are you looking for?" I asked.

She laughed again, dropping the femme fatale bit, and moving on to chummy, girlfriend mode. "I know how hard you've been working, and I just wanted to help out by going over some of the depositions for you. Howard thought it would be a good idea for me to be involved," she said sweetly.

"Oh ... well. Really, I have it under control," I said, not sure what else to say, and a little uneasy. We'd already had this conversation; I had already told Katherine I didn't need any help. I knew she was ambitious, but even she couldn't force her way into a case she hadn't been assigned to. "Shearer isn't involved in it anyway. I'm working mainly with Duffy."

I just stopped myself from calling him Shearer the Shit before remembering Katherine's relationship with him. I grimaced at the thought of her repeating my nickname for him over a postcoital snack of champagne and strawberries.

"I think he's planning to get more involved in the case," Katherine said.

I shrugged. "I haven't heard anything about it."

"He said he was," she insisted.

Now I knew she was lying. Only last week, I had overheard Shearer and Duffy talking about how it was a good thing that Duffy was overseeing the class action, since Shearer had a case going to trial in Baltimore next month. What's more, Katherine surely knew this; no doubt she had intimate knowledge of Shearer's schedule.

"Well, if you want, I can ask Duffy about it tomorrow morning. Maybe Shearer said something to him about wanting to get more involved in the case, and wanting you assigned to it, and they just forgot to tell me," I said.

Two pink spots appeared on Katherine's cheeks, and her mouth tightened. "No, you don't have to talk to Duffy about it," she said quickly. She dropped the file she'd been holding back into the box and slowly rose to her feet.

I knew that my instincts had been right—no one had assigned her to the case, and if I told Duffy that Katherine was snooping through the files, he'd be annoyed and might even take her to task for it. Although I couldn't imagine she'd actually get into all that much trouble over it. With her spinning technique, Katherine would just convince them that her desire to take on more work made her Super Lawyer. Still, knowing that I'd caught her in a lie, and that it was throwing her into a panic, was enormously gratifying. I couldn't stop myself from smiling a little at the thought that, for the first time since I'd met Katherine, I had one-upped her.

Unfortunately, Katherine saw my smile and wasn't amused. Her face set in a cold, hard expression that reminded me of Sharon Stone playing the psycho in *Basic Instinct*—pure malevolence with a complete absence of emotion.

"I wouldn't fuck with me if I were you, Ellie," she

said, arching her eyebrows and looking at me as though I was a cockroach who had scuttled into the room. "You should know that all I have to do is say one word to Howie, and you're history. He'll do anything I ask him to."

I stared at her, shocked by how confrontational she was being, and that she'd basically just admitted that she and Shearer were sleeping together. Not to mention that she was apparently perfectly willing to use that relationship to cause me harm. I wished I had a good comeback, but all I could do was stand there, speechless.

Katherine marched past me, her head high and haughty, and took a few steps down the hall. Then she stopped and turned back to look at me. I was amazed that I had always thought her to be such a beauty. Right now, with her eyes narrowed and her face drawn back in a sneering smile, she looked mean and ugly. "Don't get in my way," she said. "I'll make you regret it if you do."

And then she was gone, leaving behind a sickeningly musky cloud of Obsession perfume. I stared after her. Her threat had caused goose pimples to rise on my arms. Katherine and I had never really liked each other, but it had always been a pretty low-key animosity. But now, apparently, Katherine had decided we were just plain enemies.

I made it to Ozio's a few minutes early so that I could snag us a table and glug down a gin and tonic. As I felt the warmth of the alcohol spread through my stomach, the stress pinching at my neck and shoulders since my run-in with Katherine began to loosen. I ordered a second drink, and scanned the crowd to see if Harmony had arrived. Out of the corner of my eye, I saw a familiar flash of red hair near the bar, and heard a light, feminine laugh float over the crowd that reminded me of someone. I craned my neck, trying to get a glimpse of the woman. I knew it was probably just someone I worked with or had gone to school with, but these things always drive me crazy until I figure them out. An Asian man in a dark business suit moved to the side, clearing my line of vision, and I saw the redhead again, or at least the back of her. She was slim, and well-dressed in an expensive-looking sweater and slacks, and her head was bent toward a good-looking man who looked a little like Tom Cruise, whom I definitely didn't know. His hand was on her waist, and they were laughing together. Lovers, I thought. Or else strangers who are picking one another up in the bar and hoping for a night of anonymous sex. And then the woman turned to face me, and my mouth dropped open.

It was Kate. As in my brother Mark's wife. As in my sister-in-law. What was she doing here in the District? And who was the man with her? I sat there, my mouth hanging open, and Kate looked right at me. She turned pale, and a hand flew up to her mouth. She couldn't have looked more guilty if I had caught her with her panties around her ankles. She looked like she might say something to me, maybe try to spin a lie about why she was so far from home and with this man instead of my dorky brother. But instead, she just turned and fled, practically running out of Ozio, with Tom in pursuit. I stood, thinking I might go after her, but just as I did, Harmony appeared.

She plopped down on the stool. "Did you order me a drink?" Harmony asked, and when I shook my head, she called for the waiter.

I sat back down, my forehead still knit in concern. The question wasn't whether Kate was having an affair—if she wasn't actually engaging in one, she certainly seemed on the cusp of it. The question was *why*? She and Mark had the perfect marriage. They even looked perfect together, with his ruddy blond good looks and her clean-cut, preppy style. So if Kate was far from home letting a handsome stranger rub his hand on her back, where did that leave Mark?

I remembered Ted's words from last night: "We both have to be aware going into this that there are going to be obstacles we'll have to face," he had said. At the time, I had been quick to shrug it off. All relationships have their problems, don't they? So our age difference made our relationship a little unusual—was that really so different from couples who come from different religious backgrounds, but somehow manage to make things work? Or my friend Samina, an associate at my firm, who grew up in India, moved here when she was fifteen, and is now happily married to Brian, a white Irish Catholic from Boston? But now, seeing Kate in what was clearly an extramarital fling of some kind, Ted's words struck me as a little more ominous. If Mark and Kate couldn't make it—the world's most perfect couple, perfectly suited to one another in every way—then what chance did Ted and I have?

"So, what's up?" Harmony said, tucking into her pink Cosmopolitan.

"You are not going to believe who I just saw," I said, still feeling a little stunned.

"Who?"

I started to tell her, but then hesitated. I shook my head. "It's not important," I said.

Since I didn't know what was going on with Kate and Mark, it seemed crappy to gossip about it, even to Harmony. Until I knew what was behind Kate's odd behavior, I needed to put it out of my mind. Harmony looked at me, a quizzical expression on her face, but she didn't press me on it.

"So, are you still concerned about Ted and Charlie?" Harmony asked.

I smiled smugly. I filled Harmony in on the blow-by-blow account of Ted's unexpected visit, how jealous he'd been seeing me with Charlie, the amazing kissing, and how he wanted to keep seeing me. Harmony was the perfect audience—she gasped, asked questions, and sighed girlishly at all the right points.

"So, what do you think?" I asked, sipping at my gin and tonic and smiling with delight.

"It sounds amazing," Harmony admitted.

"It was," I said.

"It's just ..." Harmony began to say, and then she stopped. "No, never mind. Is Nina coming?"

As though such an obvious and awkward change of subject would work.

"No, she isn't. What were you going to say?" I asked.

"It's just ... I know that you're excited, but I just can't help wondering—do you really think getting more involved with him is smart?"

"Well ... I know he's a lot older than me, but I don't know how to describe it ... it just feels right. He feels right. Different, but right," I said.

Harmony sighed. "I don't want to be a downer, especially since you're so excited. I'm just worried about you—you're not one of those women, like Nina—or at least like Nina used to be—who can have sex with a man and not get your heart involved. You're not cut out for those sophisticated, black-lace-underwear-and-hotel-rendezvous affairs," Harmony said.

"Why would it have to be like that? He's not married, and neither am I. Why do you think we'd have to sneak around?" I asked.

"Because he's obviously not comfortable with your age difference. Do you really think he's going to take you to social functions, and treat you as a real partner?" Harmony asked.

I knew she was being sensible—Harmony is always sensible; I swear, she should write one of those Dear Abby–type columns—but I couldn't help feeling a little smug as I told her about the cocktail party Ted was taking me to that weekend.

"Well, good, I hope I am wrong," Harmony said, smiling sweetly. I knew she was just trying to look out for me and to make sure that I didn't get hurt. Harmony isn't one of those green-eyed-monster women who secretly wants her friends to fail. She leaned across the table and patted my arm. "Just be careful, that's all. Now, what's up with Nina?"

Chapter 15

By the time I got home from work Tuesday, I was starting to feel more than a little nervous about my date that night with Ted. Ted had called me earlier in the day to tell me that he had to stay after his show for a bit to tape an interview, and would I like to come over to his apartment for dinner. My stomach gave a great, nervous lurch, but I heard myself calmly agree and offer to bring Chinese take-out. So. Now we had plans for a lovely, romantic dinner (Chinese take-out is always romantic, I don't know why) in the intimate setting of his apartment, which could only mean one thing. Tonight was going to be The Night. S-E-X.

Now that the moment of truth was about to arrive, I was as jumpy and twitchy as a virgin on prom night. I hadn't even been able to eat lunch, so I rushed around my house getting ready—a laborious process involving shaved legs, tweezed brows, facial masks, curling irons, and more cosmetics than a Vegas showgirl—fueled only by nervous energy and anticipation. All along I'd been sure that things could work out with Ted, just given a chance. And while part of me was still confident, another part of me was shaken. I knew relationships were hard work, but now I wasn't so sure that my antennae were as reliable. If perfect Kate couldn't be satisfied with my perfect brother Mark, was any relationship a sure thing? And Harmony, the one person in my life whose good sense was completely sound, had expressed doubts about whether it was a good idea for me to deepen my relationship with Ted. Who was I to disagree with her? I make horrible decisions. I'm the person who hates conflict more than anything and yet made the disastrous choice to be an attorney, dooming me to a life of misery. So who was I to disregard everyone else's good judgment and all of the obvious roadblocks that awaited Ted and me, and jump into a relationship that everyone else—including Ted—seemed to think was a disaster waiting to happen?

But then, before I could spend too much time pondering this, it was time for me to go. I called in my order to Ding How (sesame chicken, Kung Pao chicken, orange beef, vegetable lo mein, fried rice, crab dumplings—enough food to feed an army, but I didn't know what Ted liked, so I wanted to get a little of everything), and checked myself in the mirror one last time. Even I, my worst critic, had to admit I looked pretty good. Since we were eating at his house, I knew I should dress casually, but not too casually, since I had never seen Ted in anything that wasn't tailored and pressed. So I opted for my black silk pants with the drawstring waist and flowing, flattering line, and my very best black cashmere sweater. Like most women, at least one-half of my wardrobe is black, which makes coordination easy, although since Sally sheds constantly, her silverish-fawn hairs always stand out. But I'd managed to keep her off the soft cashmere, and for once I was fuzz-free. It was the kind of outfit I could have dressed up with kitten-heeled mules, but looked casually elegant with the ballerina flats I'd chosen instead. My hair, which is wavy and normally leans toward frizzy puffiness, was

167

actually behaving for once and, for the most part, staying in place.

The underwear had again been a bit of a quandary. I wanted to look sexy, of course, but not too sexy—for example, the red lace push-up-bra-and-garter-belt combination Nina had given me for Christmas last year would make me look more like the Happy Hooker than a sexy sophisticate. White cotton briefs were too innocent, and too ... youthful. My favorite panties for work, the kind that don't show panty lines when you wear trousers, were too frumpy. Do men ever struggle with this? They really only have two choices—boxers or briefs (because frankly, if they're experimenting with black G-strings, it would be a deal breaker for me anyway). Maybe they put in the extra effort of making sure their briefs don't have any holes or funky stains on them, but I seriously doubt if they spend the last few minutes before a date sitting on the floor surrounded by every piece of underwear they own, wondering which would best communicate the current status of the relationship. I finally decided on my beautiful black silk camisole-and-tap-pants set, which were lovely and had the added benefit of not having bra straps for Ted to struggle with.

I hooked Sally up into her leash and halter, since she had also been invited to dinner. As usual, she thought she was going for a walk and growled at me.

"Just wait until you see where we're going, and then you'll really have something to growl about," I told her, knowing that she wasn't going to be too thrilled at spending an evening with the amorous Oscar. But then again, if she had the opportunity to steal all of Oscar's toys and bite him on the ears if he tried to join her in playing with them, then maybe she would have a good time after all. In any event, Sally perked up once we'd stopped off at Ding How. She loves their egg rolls.

Ted lived quite close to my apartment, and it was just a short walk to his building on Connecticut. But once I got to the high-rise redbrick building, complete with a uniformed doorman, I was taken aback. It was a completely different world from my shabby, yet cozy, building. The lobby was as opulent as a high-end hotel, with marble floors and lit by a giant, crystal-encrusted chandelier. I made my way to where a chubby, bespectacled man was standing behind a wooden counter and looking at me with arched eyebrows.

"Hi, I'm Ellie Winters. I'm here to see Ted Langston," I whispered. At my feet, Sally flipped on her back and waved all four paws up at him. I nudged her with my toe, trying to upright her, but she wouldn't budge.

The clerk picked up a black telephone, and after a brief pause, discreetly murmured in a crisp British accent, "Ellie Winters to see you, sir. Very good." He hung up the phone, and smiled without showing any teeth. "Mr. Langston is expecting you."

I nodded and thanked him and then dragged Sally to the elevator. We rode up to the twentieth floor. There were only four doors on the long hallway, which meant that each apartment must be palatial.

I knocked on Ted's door, number 2002, and I heard his voice, muffled through the door, "Coming!" I nervously looked down to make sure that my outfit still looked all right, and was glad it did, because if I had suddenly noticed something awful, like having put on one black shoe and one blue shoe (which I did one day when I dressed for work still half-asleep) there was nothing much I could have done about it. The door swung open, and Ted was standing there, looking gorgeous and smiling his crooked smile at me.

He had on gray wool suit pants, but had shed his coat and tie, and was wearing a pressed blue shirt with the top

169

two buttons undone and understated silver cufflinks at the sleeves. He was clean shaven and looked like he had gotten a fresh haircut. And if I wasn't mistaken, despite his casual smile, his eyes gleamed with what looked like a mixture of nervousness and anticipation.

"Hi. I brought dinner," I said, holding up the white paper bag.

"And Sally, I see," Ted said, stepping to the side so that Sally and I could come in. He closed the door behind us, took the white paper bag from me, and then, with his free hand, helped me shrug out of my black trench coat. He carefully hung my coat in his front hall closet, and then led me in to the starkly modern kitchen, with its bleached pine floors and polished chrome counters, and set out two wineglasses. It all seemed strangely formal, particularly since two short days ago his tongue had been in my mouth.

"Red or white?" Ted asked.

"What are you having?"

"Red, but I have both opened."

"Red is fine, thanks," I said, although I instantly regretted it when I saw that all of the floors in the apartment, other than the kitchen, were covered in pure white pile carpeting. I tend to revert to klutziness, particularly when I'm drinking or nervous, and I was terrified of spilling my drink. One drop of the garnet liquid would stand out like blood on the snow white carpet.

Oscar had come forward to greet Sally, as enthusiastically as he had the last two times he'd met her, spinning and twirling with happiness, although as soon as he poked his pointy little nose in the direction of her rear end, Sally snarled at him. Her teeth bared and every hair standing on end, she stared Oscar down until he crept back, alarmed at her anger. Satisfied that she'd taught him a lesson in etiquette, Sally sauntered over to Oscar's food dish, where she finished off the last of the kibble he'd left from dinner, and then slurped from his water bowl, all the while Oscar worshiped her from a safe distance across the kitchen.

"No, Sally, don't eat Oscar's food," I scolded her, and tried to no avail to shoo her away from the red plastic dog bowls.

"It's fine, he already ate all he wanted. Let's go sit down," Ted said, laughing, as he guided me to his gorgeous, posh living room.

It was like those apartments that they photograph for home design magazines, but that you don't think anyone really lives in. For one thing, it was enormous—easily three times the size of my apartment, maybe more. Windows surrounded the living room on three sides, rising from the white carpeted floor to the palatially high ceilings, giving an amazing view of Washington. I could actually see the Potomac River past the thousands of lights that made up the capital. The sofa and club chairs were upholstered in soft black leather, and the tables and bookshelves were a beautiful, dark mahogany. A fire blazed in the white stone fireplace, and I saw that he had even lit taper candles around the room. The room was modern, but not at all cold. Instead, it was the kind of room that you wanted to curl up in on a winter day, snuggled up warm and safe from the cold, biting wind, while watching old black-and-white movies on his enormous flat-screen television.

"Wow," I breathed, looking around the room, impressed and terrified, and even more embarrassed about Ted having seen my cramped little apartment, which looked like a crack house in contrast to this palace. "This is the most incredible apartment I've ever seen. I can't believe the view."

I sensed, rather than heard, Ted come up behind me,

so close that I could feel his warm breath in my ear as he murmured, "I'm glad you like it," and then he was spinning me around, catching me in his arms, and lowering his mouth to mine.

After a brief moment of panic about my wine spilling, I kissed him back, feeling the same delicious heat rising in me that had been there on Sunday. His lips were warm and soft, and lingered on mine.

"I've been looking forward to doing that all day," he said, smiling. He took my hand and led me over to the sofa, and we sat down, turning so that we were facing each other, our knees lightly touching. He leaned back, completely relaxed, and any of the fear I thought I had seen in his face when I first came in was no longer there. I, on the other hand, was even more nervous. I'd never been so aware of another person's presence. Even the slight pressure of his knee on mine felt seductive.

"How was your day?" he asked, which was lovely, since I don't think Eric asked me that the entire time we were together.

I shrugged. I didn't want to ruin the moment by bitching about my job, but it was hard to come up with anything remotely interesting about it. "Dull," I said, trying to keep my voice sounding droll. "But what else is new? How about your day?"

"Pretty routine. We had the leader of Sinn Fein on the program so I could ask him about the latest violence in London," Ted said, without a trace of irony in his voice.

I rolled my eyes. "Just another dull day," I teased him.

Sally came marching in the room, dragging a pink plush dinosaur behind her. I'd never seen the toy before, but judging from the anxious look on Oscar's face, it wasn't hard to guess who she'd nicked it from. Sally spread out on the floor, lying with her back legs extended behind her, and propped herself up on her forearms, holding the pink dinosaur in her paws, looking like a child lying on her belly to work on a coloring book. She began to gnaw on its ear. Oscar sat far enough away from Sally so that he was out of her biting range, but close enough to view the wanton carnage being unleashed on his toy.

Ted just laughed and said, "Poor Oscar. I think he's got it bad for Sally. That's his favorite toy. He doesn't let just anyone play with it."

I put my wineglass down on a cocktail table with a stunning inlaid design, and started to get up, saying, "Oh, honestly, Sally, leave poor Oscar alone."

But before I could get all the way up, I was stopped by two strong hands holding my waist and pulling me back. Ted pulled me against him, a little roughly, and then we were kissing again, only this time our mouths met with more urgency, our tongues arching and bracing against each other, our breath quickening. And then his hands started to move, and so did mine, roaming, exploring. Through the hormones and the fog of pleasure, there was a clarity and rhythm to our movements, as we each seemed to anticipate what the other wanted at exactly the right moment. We began to dispense with the clothing, layer by layer. He pulled my black sweater over my head and gave a little groan of appreciation at the sheer silky camisole. He plucked gently at the black satin straps, and then lowered his hand so he could brush his fingers against my breasts through the light layer of material. My hands shaking, I unfastened the row of white horn buttons on his shirt and untucked it from his pants so I could slide the shirt off his shoulders.

I was delighted to find that not only did Ted not have Cary Grant's soft, rounded physique, but quite to the contrary, his chest was muscled and broad, with a light scattering of hair running down his torso. Sure, there was a little wear and tear, but the effect was about as far from liver spots and adult diapers as you could get. In fact, he was in better shape than most of the men my own age I'd dated. I traced the pattern of hair on his chest, my fingers lightly running over him, and then I leaned forward and kissed the soft skin of his neck.

Ted wrapped his arms around me, holding me to him, and then with a quick flick of his hands, my camisole was lifted up over my head. His eyes glowing, he started to reach for me, but I hopped up off his lap, and standing before him, I slowly shimmied out of the silk palazzo pants. All I was wearing now were the briefest tap pants ever made. Ted's eyes never left me as I knelt before him, unlatching his belt buckle, unbuttoning his pants, and sliding them off his body. One thing was very obvious— Ted was not going to be pitching Viagra anytime soon.

Afterward, we just held each other, both of us exhausted. I finally lifted myself up off him, with the vague idea of retrieving my clothes, but Ted just pulled me back down, so that we were both lying on the sofa, my head nestled in the crook of his arm, the warmth of the fire making clothing unnecessary. Neither of us spoke, but Ted's hand stroked my hair, and occasionally he leaned down to kiss the top of my head. I felt like I was glowing. It had never been like that before. It was simply the most incredible sex I'd ever had. It's not that I've never had an orgasm before; I had, and even occasionally when a boyfriend was in the room. But before, I'd always felt that it was just playacting, pretending that my boyfriend was a super stud so that he'd finish before the chafing caused me to limp for a week. With Ted, there was no chafing, no acting, no wanting it to be over. We simply luxuriated in each other, and each other's body.

After a while, urged on by our grumbling stomachs, we managed to rouse ourselves up to go seek out the now cold Chinese food. And then we were kissing again, and suddenly the entire thing repeated itself, this time in Ted's bedroom. I can say this about older men—and perhaps I'm generalizing, since I've only been with one—they know what they're doing. They know where everything is, how it works, and how spinning their finger in a certain direction will make your toes curl. And they have nicer sheets than younger men, clean cotton ones with a high thread count.

When we were finally finished, spent from the carnal gymnastics, we just lay together in his bed, Ted snuggling me in his arms. I breathed in deeply. He smelled like skin warmed by the sun, faintly of cinnamon and good quality soap. It reminded me of something, triggering a memory so strong, the way that the mingling of coffee and lipstick always reminds me of my mother when I was a little girl. But I couldn't place this smell, this wonderful safe, warm smell. And as I drifted off all I could think of was one word—home. He smelled like home. Not my apartment, nor my parents' house where I grew up. But like the home I'd been waiting to discover my entire life.

Chapter 16

The rest of the week passed in a haze of sexual satiation. Work was routine, if not thrilling, and I was able to coast through the days by looking forward to my nights. Sally and I spent every night sleeping over at Ted's apartment, and if Sally wasn't thrilled at the prospect of spending her nights fighting Oscar for his bed, I was more than happy to share Ted's with him. If I'd had any fears that as an older man Ted was going to have an inadequate sex drive, then they were certainly laid to rest that week. We made love in every corner of his apartment, covering most of the furniture, quite a bit of the floor space, and one very memorable encounter in the bathtub, which was one of those enormous, claw-foot creations, with the faucets thoughtfully located on the side of the tub, so that two people could luxuriate in hot, scented water without either having to lean against the knobs.

For the modern, single woman there's a period in the beginning of every new relationship that's filled with anticipation and lust, but also a lurking fear that your new man is going to go do something to spoil the whole thing by trotting out some gruesome sexual peccadillo, such as needing to lick the soles of your shoes before achieving an erection or wanting to make love wearing an executioner's hood while whipping you on the bottom with a riding crop. Luckily, Ted seemed—at least, so far—fetish-free.

I was so happy that I'd forgotten to be terrified of the impending cocktail party. It wasn't until Friday morning, when Ted and I were engaging in a prework kiss, the kind that's long and soft and makes you want to shed your clothes and jump back into bed, that he pulled away long enough to remind me.

"I'll pick you up tonight at seven, okay?" he said.

"Oooo, where are we going?" I asked excitedly, irrationally hoping for a surprise trip to Paris.

"The Whiteheads' cocktail party. I told you about it, remember? They're old friends of mine."

The room seemed to close in on me, and I could swear I was having one of those vertigo moments, where everything goes fuzzy and bells start ringing in your ears. In the sexual gluttony of our foundling relationship, I had completely forgotten about the cocktail party. Meeting a new boyfriend's friends is a tricky enough business as it is, usually involving new clothes, time at the spa, and prescription drugs. But meeting Ted's friends, most of whom were surely to be a few decades older than me, and many of whom—particularly the women—were sure to fix me with a critical eye, was going to be nothing less than traumatizing. And here I was, having done no preparation at all.

"Breathe, Ellie," Ted said, laughing, and I realized I was clutching him like a security blanket.

"Okay," I said.

"Did you forget about the party?"

"Yes."

"Can you still go, or did you make other plans?"

Aha! A way out. All I had to do was tell him that I

had other plans—something with Harmony or Nina, and I was home free. But as I thought quickly, racking my brain for something I could claim to be doing that would justify ditching what was sure to be a horrible and judgmental party, Ted continued, "I hope you can go. I told Ginger Whitehead all about you, and she's so eager to meet you."

"You told her about me?" I asked. I couldn't help but be flattered. It was one thing for a man to sleep with you—that didn't signify much other than that you were easy. But once he started to tell his friends about you, now *that* was big news. Notifying friends meant that we had moved past a relationship based only on casual sex and into a more serious realm.

"Of course. I wanted to warn her that I was showing up with a hot young tomato on my arm," Ted murmured in my ear, and then began his wonderful soft, seductive kissing on the curve of my neck.

"A tomato?" I asked, puzzled. I had no idea what he was talking about.

"You know. It's a slang term meaning 'sexy woman,' " Ted said, still snuffling about in my neck area.

"Oh, right," I said, although I had never heard the term before in my life. I wondered if Ted had ever heard of Max Headroom or Bananarama, and thought he probably hadn't.

I spent my lunch hour running from store to salon, trying to squeeze a week's worth of maintenance into a scant hour. All right, two hours, although I was hoping and praying that neither Shearer nor Katherine would catch me playing hooky.

First, a new dress. Ted had told me that the party

wasn't that dressy, although once I pushed him, he admitted that it was a casual black-tie kind of affair. "But don't worry, I'm sure that whatever you have in the little-black-dress department will be perfectly appropriate," he had said soothingly, thus showing he lacked all conception of women and their wardrobes.

This was going to be a Big Night, and I needed something to strike the perfect chord between glamorous and sexy, something that would make Ted's eyes pop out of his head, all the while being careful not to play up the difference in our ages too much. That meant that everything from J. Lo sex goddess (low-cut and navel baring) to those horrid cocktail suits that middle-aged women flock to was off limits. I finally found a winning candidate at Neiman Marcus—a chic and simple black sheath, with short, capped sleeves and a gorgeous neckline that would have been definitely too low were it not for the sheer band of black chiffon making up the difference. It was definitely sexy, yet reeked of class. As with all women over the age of twenty-five, I already had a pair of black evening heels and a black evening handbag in my closet, so I had time to squeeze in a manicure and pedicure, and had all twenty digits painted dark red.

I spent most of the afternoon in my office with the "Do Not Disturb" on my phone, pretending to work, yet trying to think of witty cocktail party banter appropriate for the fifty-plus crowd. Something told me that an in-depth analysis of the latest episode of *Sex and the City* wouldn't fly, and I couldn't trot out my usual standbys— "I used to listen to R.E.M., but before they were popular," "Madonna is *so* played," or "I think Ewan McGregor is definitely the new Russell Crowe." Instead, I had to think up something more sophisticated, like knowing who had written a recent acclaimed short story in *The New*

Yorker, or knowing where the best undergraduate colleges were. I spent some time flipping around the Internet, hoping to find out who had invaded whom recently, or what person with an unpronounceable name had just won a Nobel Prize, all while being too nervous to soak in any true knowledge. And, as time always does that weird thing of passing really quickly when you're dreading doing something later, the day whizzed by far faster than it should have, and pretty soon it was time for me to go home and pretty myself up.

Lacking any truly useful sedative medication, I glugged down a few glasses of white wine while dressing, hoping it would calm my nerves, although all it did was increase the difficulty of walking in my Jimmy Choo stilettos. I cursed at my hair, which stubbornly refused to be twisted up into a classy chignon, and then rebelled at being coaxed into a sexy spill of curls, insisting only on lying heavily on my shoulders in boring, flattish waves. It took me three tries to apply liquid eyeliner, causing me to have to wipe off the wonky line after each attempt, until I ditched the liquid stuff altogether and instead settled for kohl liner, which did smudge as intended, but which also ran the risk of spreading out into raccoon circles as the night progressed on. When I was finally dressed and ready to go, I was reasonably pleased at my image in the mirror—it really was a great dress—although I was now convinced that if an Oscar nominee gets to have a whole posse of stylists and beauticians buzzing about her on the big day, then there was no reason why I shouldn't have a similar team available to me prior to meeting a new beau's friends.

Ted arrived to pick me up at 7 P.M. on the dot. He gathered me in his arms for a long, sexy kiss, and then looked me up and down and held my arms out to the sides so that he could take in the whole picture (although he seemed to be concentrating mainly on my chest area, which I had lifted and padded with a Wonderbra). Ted gave an appreciative whistle.

"You look amazing in that dress. Even better than when you're wearing one of my shirts and those skimpy underpants, and I didn't think anything could top that," he said, and then pulled me up against him, letting a hand roam over the general area of the Wonderbra. "Maybe we should stay in after all."

Honestly, I thought. Ted had a higher libido than any man I'd dated. Maybe even higher than Nina's, although that was a truly frightening thought. Don't get me wrong—it was nice he found me so desirable, and part of me wanted to go hop in his enormous, two-seater tub for another erotic bubble bath. But, at the same time, I had gone to an awful lot of effort to doll myself up for this party. I was also a little concerned that he was going to figure out that my breasts were suddenly larger, higher, and perkier than he remembered, which conjured up all sorts of adolescent angst from the time that Billy Summers took me to see *Planes, Trains & Automobiles* when I was fourteen, and spent the entire movie terrified that his roaming hands were going to discover that I'd enhanced my cup size with a few well-placed nylons I'd pinched from my mother's lingerie drawer.

"I thought you wanted me to meet your friends," I said, laughing, as I slipped out of his clutches. "You know, Bunny, Muffy, and the rest of the Peanuts gang."

"Ginger and Bingo," Ted corrected me. "I don't know any Bunnys or Muffys, although with this crowd you never know. I should warn you, though . . ."

"What?"

"Well, Alice might be there. My ex-wife."

"What?" I said, and felt a sudden case of the jelly legs come on. Ted had completely deviated from the dating rule book—you never impose exes, particularly ones you were married to for twenty years, on your new date. Similarly, it was my duty to keep my dysfunctional family away from Ted, thus protecting him from their toxic craziness until such time that he'd made a commitment to me he couldn't back out of. It was only fair.

"Alice and Ginger are best friends. They were, er, college roommates. But I had to accept Ginger's invitation to the party—she's been very kind to me. When you go through a divorce, even an amicable one, most of your friends take sides, and half of them don't talk to you ever again. Ginger was very careful not to do that with Alice and me. Please don't worry, Ellie," he said, cupping my face in his hands, and drawing my chin up so that I could look into his eyes.

"Are you sure?" I whispered, and he nodded and kissed me.

There wasn't enough chardonnay in the world to dull the anxiety that being faced with The Ex was causing me. I had no idea what she was like. All Ted had ever said about her was that she used to be a reporter for CNN and now wrote for *Newsweek,* and that the reason they had never had kids was that they'd both been too caught up in their careers to ever get around to it. I didn't know if she was thin or fat, beautiful or plain, clever or dull. I knew just enough about the news business to know that it was highly unlikely that she was stupid, and every other combination terrified the hell out of me. I was hoping for fat, plain, and clever.

The Whiteheads lived in Alexandria in a Georgian house that was just large and ornate enough to make it clear that they had a lot of money. A uniformed maid answered the door, took our coats, and led us into the gargantuan foyer complete with what appeared to my amateur eye to be real—not reproduction—Chippendale furniture. Ted took my hand and squeezed it, silently communicating to me not to worry, and I tried not to clutch at him as we walked into the ballroom. I didn't even know there still were houses that had ballrooms, and I actually gasped and staggered a little when I saw the size and opulence of it. I was starting to feel like Eliza Doolittle, and was actually worried for a minute that I might start speaking with a thick Cockney accent.

"Darling!" a voice called out, and a beautiful woman swept toward us. She was absolutely stunning, with a firm body and loose blonde hair, and clad head to toe in an Escada outfit I'd just seen featured in *Vogue*. There was a diamond the size of a small lemon on her left hand, and slightly smaller ones on each of her ears. She looked like a model, and it wasn't until she drew near that I could see by the faint lines at her eyes and subtle crepiness at the neck that she was over forty. Not that it mattered— she was exquisite, far prettier than me. In fact, I immediately felt like a tarted-up minx, and wanted to kick myself for not having sprung for something couture, not that I could have afforded it. All I could do was suck in my stomach and pray that this vision was not Alice.

"Ginger, how are you?" Ted said, and kissed the beauty on her proffered cheek.

"I'm Ginger Whitehead," she said to me, smiling sweetly and holding out her hand.

"This is Ellie Winters," Ted introduced me, and I said hello and shook her long, thin hand.

"Very nice to meet you," I said, and then she and Ted began to chitchat, catching up on mutual friends that I didn't know. I wished I had something to add to the conversation, something that would compete with Ted's dry witticisms and Ginger's tinkling laughter, but all I could do was stand there, feeling more and more homely and wondering what Ted ever saw in me if this was the sort of person he was used to socializing with.

"Alice is here, I know you'll want to see her. Where did she go? Oh, there she is," I suddenly heard Ginger say, and I perked up, looking around keenly, as though The Ex would be backlit by a spotlight so I'd know who she was.

Ginger was waving, at whom I couldn't tell, and I snuck a glance at Ted to see how he was reacting. He just had a polite smile fixed on his face, and then he looked over at me, and the smile softened enough to bolster my confidence. I wished we were still holding hands, standing as a united front when The Ex did appear. Ted had let go of my hand when he hugged Ginger, and I felt a little lost and alienated without it.

"I was just looking for you. I knew you'd want to say hello to Ted," Ginger said, and then suddenly I saw her. Alice. The Ex.

She wasn't at all what I'd expected, and yet as soon as I saw her, I couldn't imagine she would be any different. Alice was slim and pale, with enormous dark eyes and an edgy bob of stick-straight, black, glossy hair. She didn't have any of Ginger's luminous beauty, and at first glance she looked too sharp—her nose pointy, her chin a chipped V. But she'd played up her lovely eyes with lots of dark eye makeup and had perfectly applied matte red lipstick on her thin mouth, and I started to see an exotic glamour about her. She looked like she belonged in the twenties as a flapper, perhaps dressed in a silk kimono. But she was wearing nothing of the sort, instead dressed in a severely tailored yet obviously expensive cream wool suit, with only a single string of pearls on underneath. Alice Langston did not look like a particularly nice woman, but she was far more sophisticated than I could ever dream of being.

"Hello, Ted," she drawled, the words rounded in an

unmistakable Northeastern prep school accent. She leaned toward him and kissed him lightly on the lips. I can't stand women who greet another woman's boyfriend with lip kisses and thigh touches. And then I remembered— she didn't know he was my boyfriend. She probably still thought of him as hers.

"Hello, Alice," Ted said, stepping away in order to prevent her from threading a long arm through his. "I'd like you to meet Ellie Winters."

Alice turned toward me. I could see a flicker of dislike in her eyes, before she composed a creamy, cat's smile on her face. "Nice to meet you," she said, offering a limp hand for me to shake.

If I'd thought Alice looked unlikable at first, I now knew I hated her. And she me. There is a level of primitive animus that can spring up between two women who barely know each other that in prehistoric times probably ended up with one of them being stabbed in the ribs with a dino bone. Had I a bone handy, I might have done the same. I could see plainly that Alice was Trouble. It didn't matter if she and Ted were divorced—to my eyes it didn't look like she was through with him. It occurred to me that I didn't know who had left whom in the marriage, but from the proprietary gleam in Alice's eyes, I had a feeling that she had been the discarded one.

"And what do you do, Ellie?" Alice asked. "Are you one of the student interns at Ted's network?"

I glanced at Ted to see if he was reacting to the cheap shot about my age, but he seemed nonplussed.

"No, I'm an attorney," I said smugly, glad for once that I had a career that actually sounded impressive. "I'm in the litigation department at Snow & Druthers."

"Are you now?" she said, this time her voice full of amused condescension. She turned away, as though to indicate that her interview was now over and she had no further use for me. Instead she addressed Ted, her voice full of spicy suggestion. "Did you just arrive?"

"Yes. In fact, we haven't had a chance to swing by the bar, so I think we'd better head over there. Good to see you, Alice, Ginger," Ted said, and then, placing a hand on my back, smoothly guided me away. Really, he was so incredibly skilled at elegant getaways. I was going to have to learn his technique. It might come in handy when Duffy cornered me at the firm's holiday office party, as he did every year.

"Did you survive unscathed?" Ted whispered in my ear as he waved for the bartender's attention. "Two glasses of the cabernet, please," he said, and the uniformed man nodded gravely.

"Yes, but as they say, if looks could kill," I muttered. "I don't think she liked me very much."

"She's like that with everyone. When Alice started as a young reporter, the business was still pretty much an old boys' club, and she had to harden up in order to compete. So I'm not surprised you found her a little sharp."

"A little? I think she left claw marks on my hand," I said, and then regretted it. I knew that insulting his ex-wife might make Ted feel like he had to defend her.

"Well, I'm sure it was difficult for her to meet you," Ted said, rising to her defense, just as I'd feared. But then he saved it, by continuing, "Especially considering how ravishing you look tonight. You're really the most beautiful woman here."

I smiled at him, wanted to rub up against him and start purring. "I'm sure it was difficult for her," I said, finding it easy to be magnanimous when he was being so complimentary. "How long has it been since you left her?"

Ted fixed a gimlet eye on me. "You mean since she left me. We separated three years ago, and divorced eighteen months later."

His words stunned me, and I paused for a minute, considering what he'd said, and took the opportunity to finish my drink. I hadn't eaten since lunch, and with the half-bottle of wine I'd downed before Ted had picked me up, I was starting to feel a little light-headed.

"I just assumed that you left her," I said carefully. "From the way she was eyeing you."

"Nope. Other way around. Our marriage had been pretty empty for a while, what with us both working all the time. We'd grown apart, and we talked one night, and she said that she wanted to move on," Ted said, shrugging. It didn't seem to bother him all that much, I was relieved to note. "If she seemed proprietary of me, I'm sure it's just her competitive nature rearing up. She never could stand to lose anything, even a race she'd already quit. Oh, look, there's Randy, an old friend of mine from when I was at NBC. I want you to meet him."

And we were off, on a whirlwind tour of This Is Your Life, Ted Langston. In two hours, I met more of his old friends and colleagues than I would have thought possible (including a bunch of sycophantic types I could tell he didn't like at all). We got more than a few surprised looks when Ted introduced me as his date, the men normally reacting by giving Ted a wink, while the women looked as though they'd bitten into a lemon. I repeated that I was an attorney and where I worked about four hundred times, and then mainly stood by while Ted and whoever caught up on each other's life. Some nice young waiter type seemed to be trailing after me, filling my wineglass whenever it hit the half-full point, and as a result I completely lost track of how much I'd had to drink, although once I reached the point where I could no longer feel my lips, I knew that I'd had quite a lot. I tried to maneuver toward the food spread, but every time I got close, Ted was shanghaied by yet another long-lost friend, and I was forced to endure their arched eyebrows and surprised frowns and then repeat my resumé yet again.

"Perhaps next time I can just have my name, age, rank, and serial number stamped on my forehead," I grumbled to Ted during a lull. "I haven't even had a chance to eat, and I'm starving."

I didn't add that my gorgeous Jimmy Choos, which I'd purchased at Nordstrom's Rack two years ago for only fifty dollars, were killing my feet. I was beginning to think that if I didn't get a chance to sit down soon, I'd never again be able to wear anything other than what I fondly refer to as birth control shoes (i.e., shoes so ugly, no one will ever want to sleep with you again, for example those horrid Birkenstock thingies). Ted kissed me on the top of my head, and I felt his hand brush against my bottom. "Go ahead and eat. I'll catch up to you in a few minutes," he said.

I didn't need to be told twice. Feeling like I'd been paroled after a long stint in the federal pen, I hobbled to the impressive spread located at the far end of the ballroom. Despite the crushingly large number of people at the party, the food had only been picked over. Most of the revelers were those whippet-thin society-wife types who shudder in horror at the idea of letting a drop of olive oil pass their Chanel-rouged lips. The husbands were circled around the spread, eyeing the long banquet table that was practically groaning under the weight of pâtés, miniature quiches, chèvre tarts, stuffed mushrooms and grape leaves, sesame chicken brochettes, mini steak tartare served on rounds of french bread, heaping mounds of glistening black caviar, seared foie gras, crepes stuffed with crabmeat, a tree made out of steamed artichokes, and then rows and rows of decadent desserts, from towering chocolate creations to flat, fruited tartlets to an enormous cream puff baked in the shape of a swan. I attacked the buffet with all the vigor of a political zealot coming off a hunger strike. I loaded up a plate with as much seared foie gras as it could hold, and then added a few crepes and a stuffed artichoke for good measure. I thought for a minute that I should just come back for dessert, but noticed a squad of portly men who'd appeared to have shaken off their wives/keepers descending on the table, and so made a quick grab for a slice of rhubarb pie and a dish of chocolate mousse. Balancing all of the plates, along with a glass of merlot, I retreated from the ballroom. All I wanted was to find a quiet place where I could sit down, kick off my heels for a few glorious minutes, and dig into the plate of goodies.

I hung a right out of the ballroom, went down some incredibly long hallway, turned left, and then left again, and found myself in the largest pantry I'd ever seen. It was lined with shelves that were so precisely straight they could only have been hung by Nazis, and contained enough cans of Italian tomatoes, bags of pasta, and jarred olives to see the Whitehead family through a nuclear assault. Lucky for me, it also contained a steel-top table and a few stools, presumably where the vast Whitehead staff could congregate, and I slid out of my heels and climbed onto the nearest stool and tucked into my dinner. I don't know what it is about drinking that makes you ravenously hungry. Does the introduction of alcohol into your system somehow stimulate that portion of your brain that craves chocolate and cheese? Or is it that you've been so busy sucking down liquor that you've inadvertently forgotten your poor tummy for such a long time that it goes into some kind of starvation mode? Maybe it's just that the alcohol suppresses any kind of willpower you might otherwise possess, thus turning you into a gluttonous pig. In any event, I sighed with relief at finally being able to wriggle my toes, and began to scarf down the mountain of food I had gathered. I was just trying to decide if I'd made a mistake in not grabbing a few chicken brochettes when I heard a familiar voice.

"[muffled noise] doing a series on that in March," a male voice said. It was Ted! I started to call out to him, but was prevented by the slice of olive bread I had just stuffed in my mouth. The bread was dense and chewy, and other than spitting it out, I had no choice but to keep chomping on it.

"It's wonderful that you're doing so well. I know that the success of your show must have made the past few years a little easier," a woman's voice said. Who was it? Alice? No, it lacked the creamy bitchiness her voice was laced with. She continued, "Bingo and I have always hoped that you and Alice would be able to work things out . . ." she trailed off delicately.

Aha! It must be Ginger Whitehead. How many other women out there could possibly have husbands named Bingo?

"I know how you feel, Ginger," Ted said, confirming my guess.

"So," Ginger said, pausing dramatically. "Who's the girl?"

"Ellie," Ted said.

"Right, Ellie. What's the story there?"

"I don't know what you're referring to," Ted said, in his usual calm, deliberate manner.

"I'm referring to the fact that she's fourteen years old," Ginger said archedly. "And still wearing a training bra."

I nearly gave myself away by gasping with indignation. My back is turned for less than ten minutes, and Miss Skinny Escada Pants sharpens up her knife and plunges it into my back. I knew she was a friend of Alice's, but still, there was no reason for her to be so catty.

"Please don't talk about her like that," Ted said sharply. I smiled to myself. Now he'll show her what's what, I thought. But then he said, sounding a little wistful, "I know she's young."

"Too young, don't you think?" she said. "I mean, what kind of a future could you expect to have together? And what about Alice, how do you think it will make her feel?"

Ted responded, and then Ginger said something else, but I couldn't hear what they were saying, no matter how closely I inched toward the door, holding my ears up like Dumbo's. Just a lot of hushed murmuring, and the only thing I could make out was when Ginger said my name, and Ted responded, "I know, I know."

Then Ginger's voice rose to an audible tone. "I know how much you must miss Alice. It's impossible to not think of you two as a couple. You were always so perfectly suited for each other," Ginger said. Interfering trollop, I thought, hoping that Bunny, or Bingo, or whatever the hell his name was, was playing Hide the Tootsie Roll with the parlormaid.

"Well, the divorce was hard on both of us," Ted said, in a level voice. Or was he sounding wistful? It was hard to tell through my haze of champagne.

A third person, a woman with a voice like an oboe, came crashing in, warbling that Ginger was needed to settle a debate between the Indian ambassador and Bob Dole. The three of them departed together, their voices fading away as they left the room. I stayed perched on my stool, feeling drunk and stunned. What had Ginger been saying to Ted about Alice, and, more importantly, what was Ted agreeing to when he said, "I know, I know"?

Ginger had been going on about how inappropriate it was for Ted and me to date ... was *that* what Ted had been agreeing to? I knew he'd had second thoughts about getting involved with me—but now that we were lovers and had been spending every night together, surely he'd decided to put those concerns behind him. And then there was his divorce ... I had no idea that he was the dumpee, and not the dumpor. And from my admittedly biased observation, Alice had seemed set on ensnaring him back into her clutches. Was that what Ted wanted, too? Since he had been cut loose by a woman he must have once loved, would he jump at the chance of getting back together with her? So much so that he would dump his girlfriend of only a week?

I got up from my stool, leaving my plate of half-eaten food behind me, and made my way back to the ballroom. I was starting to feel a little dizzy, and putting my stilettos back on my aching feet was torturous. Before heading into the ballroom, I ducked into a powder room and peered at myself in the mirror. Oh no, I thought, despairing at my red flushed cheeks, shiny forehead, and smeared lipstick. Compared to Alice's flawless glamour, I looked like a sorority girl who'd been at an all-night keg party. I did as much damage control as I could with a powder compact, highlighting stick, and red lip gloss—the sum total of cosmetics I was able to cram into my tiny evening bag—and then reemerged, ready to find Ted and talk him into getting out of there.

Instead, the first person I saw, heading toward the powder room as I was departing, was Alice. She didn't seem to notice me at first, and I hoped for a moment to avoid having to talk to her again, but then she turned and rested her bird-of-prey eyes on me and a thin smile appeared on her sharp face.

"Ah, Ellen," she said. "It is Ellen, isn't it?"

"Ellie, actually," I said, and smiled my best so-good-to-see-you-but-I-really-must-run smile, hoping to be able to slip past her without stopping, but she somehow imperceptibly moved in front of me, blocking my way.

"So, you and Ted have been dating for, what, a few weeks or so?" Alice asked. Her eyes glittered coldly at me over the brim of her martini glass.

"Ah ... yes, I suppose," I said, hoping to sound enigmatic.

"I knew it!" Alice cackled. "Ted's incapable of anything much longer than that."

I frowned. "You were married for quite a long time," I said, trying to keep the irritation out of my voice, but failing.

"Yes, but Ted and I are so much alike, we're the only ones who could ever stand one another. Ted's simply incapable of connecting with someone who's emotionally needy. You must have noticed how, well ... *closed off* he is?"

I stared at Alice. Her tone was friendly, but the hard glint in her eyes was not. My feeling of irritation mingled with fear, tied together with a knot of insecurity. I knew Alice was trying to get under my skin, purposefully stirring things up—and knowing this made me want to accidentally-on-purpose dump my glass of blood-red merlot down the front of her cream jacket—but it didn't mean that what she was saying was without merit. Ted *was* distant, so distant sometimes, I couldn't tell if he felt anything like the rush of emotion I did for him. And *emotionally needy* ... wasn't that me in a nutshell? I was the woman who needed everyone to like her, who believed in love at first sight, who dreamed of the perfect soul mate. What did Ted see in me? Was I a novelty after the decades he spent with the chilly Alice, a novelty that would be wearing thin when we reached that relationship stage when dating either turns into something more or just stops altogether?

I shivered, and felt an overwhelming desire to get away from Alice, from the party, and even from Ted. "Excuse me," I said. "I think we're getting ready to leave."

"It was so nice to meet you," Alice purred, and as I walked away, I swear I could hear her laughing softly at my departing back, although when I turned around, I no longer saw her standing there. Intolerable woman. How had Ted been able to stand being married to her? But just as quickly as I posed the question to myself, I realized that I didn't want to know the answer, or at least not now.

I went into the ballroom and looked around for Ted. When I found him, he was still talking to Ginger, along with a stout, loud woman I assumed was the one who had interrupted their tête-à-tête in the kitchen.

"Hi there," Ted said, reaching out to me and entwining his hand in mine. He pulled me to him, so that the sides of our bodies were melded together.

"Hey, you," I said softly, delighted to see him, despite myself. I had meant to be cross with him for talking about our relationship with Ginger, although since I would have to cop to eavesdropping on them, I didn't know exactly how I was going to go about being annoyed.

"Where did you run off to? I tried to find you by the buffet earlier," he said softly in my ear, following up the words with a discreet kiss.

"Oh, here and there," I said noncommitally. "Are you about ready to go?"

"You bet," Ted said. He turned to Ginger, who was talking to the loud woman and pretending not to listen to us. "Thank you for a wonderful evening, but I'm afraid that we have to be going," he said.

"So soon?" Ginger said. And then she leaned toward Ted, pretending to whisper to him, but obviously speaking loud enough for me to hear her. "Do you want me to find Alice before you go? So you can say good-bye to her?"

"No, that's all right. Just send my regards," Ted said, and I looked up at him quickly to see if his expression was betraying the neutrality of his tone. It wasn't. I wished that everything he said wasn't in that inscrutable reporter's voice of his, so I could for once get a tiny clue as to what he was thinking. *Closed off,* Alice had said.

We took a cab back to my apartment, and Ted waited while I went up to fetch Sally and an overnight bag. There was a moment when I was sliding off the smooth leather seat of the taxi when I knew that I should thank him for the lovely evening and then make my excuses why I couldn't accompany him back to his apartment. Every night that I spent with Ted was just going to plunge me deeper into the precarious position of falling for a man who might be incapable of caring for me on a deeper level, and worse, whose heart might still belong to another woman. But as I sat on the edge of the seat, my hand on the door handle and the words "Why don't you call me" on my lips, Ted suddenly leaned over and placed a hand on my right cheek, sort of both cradling and stroking my face at the same time. And then he kissed me. One of those heady, to-die-for kisses that make me go weak in the knees, and instead of telling Ted I would see him later in a detached and sophisticated girl-about-town kind of way, I heard myself telling him I wouldn't be but a moment, and then sprang from the cab to get Sally and my overnight things.

Chapter 17

I hadn't seen Nina in weeks, not since her Arabian Nights party. I'd called her a few times, but she'd always been noncommittal about getting together, usually saying she already had plans with Josiah. I was a little miffed, but since I was spending so much time with Ted, basking in the glow of our new relationship, I had been too preoccupied to brood over Nina's absence. Still, I was happy when she called me the weekend before Thanksgiving and asked me to meet her for brunch.

We decided to go to the Ebbitt Grill, which was, as usual, teeming with tourists wearing fanny packs and cameras strung around their necks. I met Nina in the lobby, and it had been so long since we'd seen each other, we embraced; she smelled so familiar, a mixture of vanilla and plumeria. After settling into a booth, we ordered mimosas and omelettes and then settled down to the business of catching up.

Nina looked as gorgeous as usual, but different. Her curly red hair, which she normally wore wild and full, spilling down her shoulders, was instead up in a loose, messy bun. Like me, Nina was dressed casually, wearing faded jeans, a green sweater ... and a tiny diamond ring on the third finger of her left hand. It was actually the first thing I'd noticed; women are trained to immediately assess the third finger of the left hand of every woman they run into, even old friends who have been single for as long as you've known them.

"Josiah was hinting about buying me an engagement ring," she said shyly as I goggled at her. "But I thought maybe for Christmas. And then last night he surprised me with this!"

She held up her hand, to show off the tiny fleck of a diamond set on a narrow band of gold. I did what girlfriends are expected to do on these occasions—I swallowed all of my critical thoughts about her betrothed and cooed over the ring, feigning jealousy and asking if they'd made any wedding plans.

"We haven't decided yet. Josiah doesn't believe in big weddings. He wants us to go away somewhere and elope," Nina gushed.

"Oh, well, that could be really romantic," I said, fighting back my urge to ask her if after they were married, Josiah was going to insist she wear a burka and walk ten steps behind him. Since the day she'd met him, Nina had been getting more and more lost, replaced by this shell of her former self. Every time I'd asked her to do something with me, she'd responded with a "Josiah doesn't like it if . . ." or "Josiah would rather that we . . ." But for him to veto their wedding—the one thing that is universally accepted to be completely the domain of the bride—was just ridiculous. Nina had never talked much about getting married, but the few times she had mentioned it, she'd said that she wanted her wedding reception to be a huge party, and she'd invite all of her ex-lovers so that they could ogle her in a sexy white dress. Whatever she did, her wedding should be like her—loud, splashy, irrepressible. Not a demure elopement.

"So, how did he ask you?" I said, trying to be enthusiastic. "Did he get down on one knee?"

"No." Nina laughed, as though the idea was absurd. "We were sitting on the couch, watching TV, and he just sort of handed it to me."

"Oh," I said brightly, trying to think of a way that such a dull proposal could be seen as romantic, and utterly failing. To make up for my lack of enthusiasm, I overcompensated by plastering a large smile on my face and talking in an overly bright, Pollyanna way. "That's *so* wonderful. I'm *so* happy for you."

But Nina didn't seem to hear any of the insincerity in my words, and she just kept blushing and smiling, and looking at her ring as though she were a virgin bride, and not the girl who'd had more threesomes in her life than most people have actual sexual partners. She told me a little bit more about Josiah and what he was like, and I learned little about him to change my first impression, particularly after hearing that he'd bought her the tiny diamond because he was saving up to buy a new motorcycle for himself.

"So how are you doing? Are you dating that guy you brought to my party?" she asked.

I shook my head, and felt a little sad that for the first time in over a decade, my best friend was so distant and preoccupied that she didn't even know who I was dating.

"No, I've been seeing Ted. Remember? The news anchor?" I reminded her.

"Oh, right. The last time we talked about it, you didn't think it was going anywhere," she said.

I filled Nina in on everything that had happened between Ted and me, from the run-in with Charlie after her party, to the night Ted told me how he felt about me, to seeing Alice at the cocktail party. And that we'd been spending nearly every night together, cooking dinner, walking the dogs, watching videos—all activities that are routine for established couples but seem hopelessly romantic in new relationships.

"I have no idea where it's headed," I said. "And now I'm afraid that he's still hung up on his ex-wife."

"Why would you think that? Just because she still seemed interested in him doesn't mean that he wants to get back together with her," Nina said.

"Well, I guess. But I overheard him talking to one of his ex-wife's friends, and she kept saying that I was too young for him, and how perfect he and Alice were together, and how she'd always hoped they would get back together," I said.

"So?"

"Well, I couldn't hear what else she was saying, but then I heard Ted say, 'I know, I know'—what if he was agreeing with her? Agreeing that I am too young for him, and he and Alice should have stayed together?" I said.

"You said yourself that you couldn't hear everything they were saying," Nina reasoned. "So you don't really know what he was agreeing to."

"I do know that they were talking about our relationship, which everyone seems to think is so crazy and inappropriate, but it isn't. Somehow things just work between us. I've spent enough time with boyfriends that seemed like they should be so right for me, but weren't. I know that this is different. With Ted everything just fits ... and I'm terrified that it will never go anywhere," I admitted, a little nervous to say this to Nina, who in the past would have begun bellowing, "Why does it need to go anywhere? He's fucking you, you said the sex was incredible, what else do you need?"

But that was the old Nina, not this new blushing

bride-to-be. She didn't yell at me about my puritanical notions of home and hearth, husbands and babies, but just patted me on the hand and said, in an almost maternal way, "I guess time will tell."

It was so weird seeing her like this. I felt a little awkward around her, like you do when you first become friends with someone, and the conversation is a little stilted as you edit what you share, what you keep to yourself. I longed for the days of easy conversation between us, of finishing each other's sentences and laughing together until our stomachs hurt.

"So I thought we'd take the train home Wednesday. I know that means we have to spend an extra night in the nuthouse, but Mom said she wanted to have dinner early on Thursday," I said, changing the subject. Thanksgiving was only a few days away, and Nina had always, from the time we were freshmen in college, come home with me to my parents' house. Nina's dad had died when she was young, and her mother was one of those adventuring types who was always off on some kind of safari or archaeological dig somewhere, and so was never around for Turkey Day. I'd taken it for granted that the tradition would go on.

Which is why, when she looked at me with alarm and said, "Ellie, I'm not going home with you. I'm going to spend Thanksgiving with Josiah—it's our first major holiday together," I felt as though I'd been slapped in the face.

Now perhaps my reaction was immature. The simple truth was that I wanted Nina to come home with me because she always had before, and I didn't want things to change. Plus her presence turned what would otherwise just be another hellish family get-together, with sullen tempers and hurt feelings, into a fun, girly weekend, full of cooking and shopping and manicures. Grown women don't get to have sleepovers, so it was the closest thing we had to the frilly, giggly slumber parties of yesteryear.

"But you always come with me," I said, feeling utterly abandoned. Nina knew how hard it was for me to go home without her, to deal with my crazy family without a buffer. And besides, Thanksgiving wasn't a datelike holiday.

"I know, but this year is different. Now I have Josiah," she said. "How would he feel if I left him?"

"Well, doesn't he have a family to spend it with?" I asked.

Nina sighed. "He wants to be with *me*. I think that now that we're engaged, it's unfair to expect us to separate," she said.

I could feel anger bubble up inside of me. It wasn't that she didn't have a good point—it was that I didn't care if it was a good point. I was sick to death of Josiah, of hearing her gush on about him, and particularly sick of having every last trace of the old Nina, my Nina, disappear into this pliant, blushing supplicant.

"Oh, no, we wouldn't want you to separate. If you two spent one night apart, both of your heads might explode," I said nastily. And then, hearing the knife-blade sharpness to my voice, I said more carefully, "I'm sorry, I didn't mean to sound so harsh. It's just that you two are *always* together. . . . I miss you."

"I think it's normal to want to be with the person you love," Nina said defensively. "He's not just some random boyfriend. He's the person I'm going to spend the rest of my life with."

"But how do you know that already? You haven't been together that long. How can you be sure he's The One? Marriage is a really big step. And, I'm—" I paused for a minute, but then took a deep breath and plowed ahead. I knew Nina wasn't going to want to hear it, but as her friend, I felt obligated. "I'm just worried about you. Ever since you've been with Josiah, you've been so different. All of the light has gone out of you, and he just seems so controlling."

Nina looked at me and then said evenly, "My relationship with Josiah is really none of your business. I know that you haven't liked him from the beginning, even though you never made any kind of an effort to get to know him. I think that maybe you're just jealous about my engagement, particularly since you're having so many insecurities about your own relationship."

"I'm not jealous," I gasped. Jealous of that ponytailed, unibrowed control freak she had unfortunately snagged? Ha! "I'm just worried. Nina, I don't think that this guy is good for you. The way he doesn't let you go out with your friends, it's just not healthy."

Nina stood up, tucking her bag under her arm. "I love Josiah. He's going to be my husband. If you can't accept that and be happy for us, then I don't think it's healthy to have you in our lives," she said coolly. And then my oldest, dearest friend turned on her heel and walked out of the restaurant, with me gawping after her.

In all the years we had been friends, Nina and I had never had a fight—mainly because I could never tolerate the conflict. Sure, we'd had PMS-y days where we'd sniped at each other, but nothing serious. No one had ever gotten up and stormed out on the other. The pain of it, of being dumped by a friend—which is probably even more devastating than being left by a boyfriend—sliced through my chest. Why had I been so honest with her? I never tell people what I'm really thinking, especially when I know it's going to piss them off. And for good reason—when I do, they get angry and they leave.

* * *

Ted drove me to the train station late Wednesday afternoon, and after helping me with my bag, he held me close and gave me a long kiss. "I'll miss you," he murmured in my ear.

The words caused a little shiver of pleasure to run down my back. Ted was an admitted emotional phobic, but with each passing day, he seemed to be opening up to me more and more. He still worked a zillion hours a week, but when he wasn't working, he was usually with me, and when we were together we were connecting in a way that was only possible because he was dropping his defenses and letting me in. Maybe Alice was wrong after all. I kissed him on the neck, not wanting to let go, and at the same time relishing how wonderful it was to have someone who was hard to leave.

"Are you sure you're going to be all right here alone?" I asked, hoping that I didn't sound too much like a fussy hen. "What are you going to do for Thanksgiving dinner?"

Ever since Nina had backed out on me, I had half-heartedly invited Ted to my parents' house for the weekend, although I was relieved when he said he had to stay in the city and work. Our relationship was far too fragile to be subjected to my mother and her inevitable tirade on how I was dating someone closer to her age than my own. Actually, I was hoping that he would ask me to stay in D.C. and spend the holiday with him. As annoyed as I was at Nina for ditching me for Unibrow, I had to admit it did sound wonderfully cozy to spend the holiday curled up in front of a fire with Ted, watching old movies and sharing a roast turkey breast for two. But he hadn't. Ted told me that as much as he would love to meet my family, he had to work all weekend, but that I should go and have a good time without him. Obviously, he didn't know my family and how unlikely that was.

"Work. Like I told you, I'm going to cover a lot of air-time so that the anchors with kids can spend the holiday with them. I'm sure the station will have some kind of a spread for those of us working. They normally do," Ted said, smiling at me and brushing a few spare hairs off my forehead. I love it when he does that—there's something about it that's incredibly sweet but also sexy as hell.

"Are you sure you don't mind watching Sally?" I asked for the millionth time.

Ted had volunteered to keep Sally for me while I was out of town. Amazingly enough, the two of them actually got along. Ever since the day Ted had carried Sally through Rock Creek Park, he had endeared himself to the little tyrant. Every time we visited Ted at his apartment, Sally followed him around with slavish devotion, hopping up into his lap as soon as he sat down and sluttishly rolling over onto her back so that he could rub her ample belly. It was hard to imagine this was the same grumpy pug who tried to bite me every time I approached her with a pair of doggy nail clippers.

"No, we'll be fine. At least, Sally and I will be fine, although Oscar may be traumatized by our houseguest," Ted said with a laugh.

"Okay. Well," I said, hesitating. "Bye."

Ted leaned over and kissed me again, a nice, long, lingering one. Hours later, as the train chugged toward Syracuse, I was still touching my lips and remembering the kiss, smiling at my reflection in the window and into the darkness beyond.

Chapter 18

My bliss didn't last for long; my family managed to first deflate it and then stomp on the carcass of my joy-filled soul within mere hours of my arrival. As if it wasn't bad enough that Nina wasn't there, her absence a constant reminder of our estrangement, my family decided to spend the holiday making each other as miserable as possible. In fact, Thanksgiving Day that year would go down in the family annals as one of the worst holidays ever.

It started off with the food. Mother had grown bored with her earth goddess phase, and instead had begun channeling Martha Stewart. This might have been tolerable if the result was a gourmet dinner served in a house full of shimmering glitter lights and white roses blooming out of cranberry-stuffed glass vases. However, Mother had never really excelled in the homemaker department. She's an able enough cook, if she focuses on casseroles and pasta, but doesn't really have the stick-to-itiveness required for something more complicated.

"Guess what we're having for dinner," she trilled in an annoyingly chirpy voice when I dragged myself into the kitchen Thursday morning. Before engaging in any conversation, I headed to the coffeepot. I can't speak to anyone until I've had at least one, and preferably two, cups of coffee after waking up. Strangely, as I wearily grabbed a mug out of the cupboard and reached out for the carafe, my hand was grasping empty air. I looked around to see if the coffeepot had been moved from its traditional counter spot. It was nowhere to be seen.

"Coffee?" I grunted, which sounds rude, but was really all I was capable of.

"We've given it up," Mother said with an unmistakable air of moral superiority. Her hair had been blow-dried into a Martha smooth blonde shaggy bob, and she was wearing a red sweater with a Santa Claus appliqué on the front. "Guess what we're cooking for dinner."

"Given ... it ... up?" I repeated dumbly.

"Yes, dear. All that caffeine isn't *good* for you, Ellie, so Daddy and I aren't drinking it anymore."

"But what about me?"

"What about you?"

I sighed. "I need a cup of coffee, Mother, or I'm going to die. Do you have any instant or anything around?"

"No, nothing," she said. "You'll have to do without. And go get dressed. I need you to help me glue together the centerpiece, and then we'll get started with the cooking. We're going to make clam and corn fritters with cilantro dip, herb-roasted turkey with shallot pan gravy, oyster stuffing with shiitake mushrooms and leeks, candied root vegetables, butternut squash gratin with rosemary breadcrumbs, cranberry-maple sauce, homemade yeast rolls, and pumpkin pie with toffee-walnut topping." As she finished pattering out the menu, she clapped her hands together with self-satisfaction.

"Who's going to make all of that?"

"I am, of course. With your help."

Oh no. I was going to be stuck in a kitchen with my

mother all day, cooking a meal neither one of us was remotely capable of making, with her ordering me around, all on *zero* cups of coffee. It sounded like absolute hell. And then, remembering something she'd said, I started. "What do you mean gluing the centerpiece together?" I asked suspiciously.

Mother beamed at me. "We're going to make a candelabra. You drill five holes in a log for the candles, and then glue gilded pinecones and sugared plums all over it. So, I need you to go find a good log, and the drill, and start putting it together."

It was a black start to a black day. I hadn't started a day without coffee in over fifteen years, and family visits were no time to give it up. Within an hour I'd developed a splitting withdrawal headache and, slumped at the kitchen table, mangled the centerpiece that "we" were making, while Mother called Nana and her various aunts, bragging about the glorious meal she was going to make. In my caffeine-deprived haze, I found it damn near impossible to drill the holes straight, or paint the pinecones, or make sugar-dipped plums stick to anything except each other, although I did manage to sustain third-degree burns on every finger, thanks to the hot glue gun. In the end, the candles jutted out from the log at wonky angles, and only one solitary paint-smeared pinecone was glued to the log, and it was upside down. Mother's face fell when she saw it, and she began to look a lot less like the smooth Martha portrayed on television and a lot more like the insane, homicidal Martha the gossip columns were always going on about.

"The Thanksgiving Log is supposed to be the decorative element that ties together the entire event," she said sharply. Then she shook her head and rolled her eyes, and said, "Oh well, fiddle-dee-dee. When life hands you lemons, you make lemonade. We'll just put this"—she swept the log and the pinecone rubble off the table and into the trash can—"away, and go get out my good silver candlesticks."

"Fiddle-dee-dee?"

"Just do it," she said. "We have a lot of cooking to do."

Dinner came out exactly as I thought it would: disaster. The turkey was black on the outside and dangerously raw on the inside, the dressing had dissolved into mushroom mush, and the squash gratin had fallen. The candied vegetables were at least edible, if a little on the raw side, and the rolls, which I had made, were halfway decent. But on the whole, the dinner was a complete failure. It wasn't as though Mother had never cooked Thanksgiving dinner before. But in the past she'd always stuck to cooking the turkey inside one of those plastic no-fail roasting bags, throwing together some green bean casserole and mashing up some potatoes, and then finishing it all off with canned cranberry sauce and store-bought rolls and pumpkin pie. Maybe not Martha-approved, but certainly edible.

We all sat gathered around the logless table—Mom, Dad, Brian, his new girlfriend, Maria, Mark, Kate, and me—picking at the food. It was hard to eat it, much less find anything nice to say about it. Maria, a lovely, olive-skinned woman with long, blue-back hair, had started to rave about how good the fritters looked, but after biting into one her expression had turned into one of pained horror. Somehow she managed to bravely chew and swallow it, and when she'd finally downed it, she weakly murmured, "You must give me the recipe," at which point Mother glared at her, and refused to acknowledge her for the rest of the meal. Even Kate, who was normally the one redeeming person at these gatherings, was unusually quiet. I hadn't seen her since the strange episode in D.C., and although I'd glanced in her direction a few times, she refused to meet my eyes. I didn't know what to make of it, or her. I loved Kate, and wanted to hear her side of the story. At the same time, I knew it would kill Mark to find out that Kate was running around behind his back.

And just when things couldn't get much worse, Mark cleared his throat and said, "Kate and I have an announcement to make."

Mother gasped and then squealed, and she hopped up from her seat to envelope Kate in a hug. "I've been hoping, although, of course, you hadn't said you were trying. You're hardly showing, dear," she said, patting Kate's flat tummy. "I was the same way when I was carrying Brian. I didn't pop out until I was in my sixth month. Until then, no one would believe I was pregnant—everyone said there was no way I could be carrying and still have such a flat stomach."

Dad grunted, "Well done, son," and Maria cried out, "Oh, how wonderful!" I didn't know what to say. If Kate was pregnant, why was she cheating on Mark? And then a terrible thought occurred to me—could she even be sure the baby was his? I looked at Kate, and for once, she returned my gaze, although her eyes were shuttered and her face calm.

"Please, everyone, stop. I'm not pregnant," Kate said coolly.

The chattering died out, and Mother said, "Oh, but I thought . . ." and then fell quiet and returned to her seat.

"Mark, do you want to tell them, or should I?" Kate said. Mark stared at his plate, and it looked as though he were trying not to cry. He shook his head briefly, and so Kate continued. "Mark and I are separating."

I know now what they mean when they say that silence can be deafening. Although no one was saying a word, Kate's words had fallen like a giant turd of dog shit landing on the table. Everyone looked at each other. Maria was mortified, Brian looked oddly triumphant, and Father looked as uncomfortable as I'd ever seen him. Mother's face began to twitch, and I could tell she was working herself into a good cry.

"Don't say that," Mark said stiffly. "They might as well know the truth. We're not just separating, we're getting a divorce."

"But why?" Mother cried. And then the waterworks began, pouring down her cheeks while she looked from Mark to Kate and then back again to Mark.

"Things haven't been going well for a while between us, and we've been growing apart," Kate said delicately. She still looked calm, too calm, I thought, feeling myself starting to get really angry at her. Even if no one else in the family knew, I had a pretty good idea what had caused the split.

"Kate," Mark said sharply. "They're going to find out anyway, so we might as well tell them."

And this time, Kate shook her head, and her face crumpled up. She dropped her head into her hands and began to sob.

"Kate ... well, she found out ... I did something really stupid," Mark said softly. "I had ... an affair. And she hasn't been able to forgive me."

Kate stood, and ran out of the dining room, heading toward the kitchen. I hopped to my feet and ran after her. I found her in the kitchen, pulling on her overcoat. She was crying. Not sobbing anymore, but a quiet, defeated tearfulness. She looked up at me, her eyes rimmed with redness, and said, "You want to go for a walk?"

I nodded, grabbed my coat off the rack next to the back door, and we wandered out into the cold, clear night. The winters in Syracuse are very dark, the sky such a midnight blue that it seems to absorb the lights of the city. Even the streetlamps seemed strangely ineffectual, each one casting only the dimmest of light circles. Kate and I walked together, in almost total darkness, neither of us talking. She had stopped crying, at least for now, but somehow that made things seem worse. As though everything had been decided, and was over, and there was no chance of reconciliation. And I badly wanted her and Mark to reconcile. This family needed Kate in it.

"I know what you must have thought when you saw me that night at the bar. I was with that guy—his name's Michael, he was my old college boyfriend, from before I met Mark—and you looked at me like I had just run over your dog," Kate finally said.

I glanced at her, but she kept looking ahead at the road, although it didn't look like she was even seeing it. I knew that in her mind she was back at Ozio, and I was again looking at her with eyes that must have been filled with disappointment and judgment.

"I thought you were cheating on Mark," I admitted.

Kate laughed humorlessly. "You weren't far off. I was trying to cheat on him. I'd just found out that he ..." She paused, and inhaled, as though even speaking of the woman caused her physical pain. "Mark had just told me about his girlfriend. He said it was eating him up, my not knowing, and he wanted to get it off his chest. Selfish asshole." She snorted. "I wanted to get back at him. So I called Michael, and he invited me down for the weekend. And until I saw you, and started to feel guilty, if you can believe that, I was fully planning on sleeping with him."

"Oh," I said, wondering if I should apologize. Apologizing is a knee-jerk reaction of mine, but I didn't know if it was appropriate at this admission. Should I be apologetic that I somehow stopped her from cheating on my son-of-a-bitch, adulterous brother?

"But then, I didn't. I just came home. And I tried to forgive Mark, I really did. He said he did it—did *her*—when he was out of town on a business trip. He said she was just someone he met at a convention, that he was drunk and he'd never see her again. But then she called. She called my house, and told me that she and Mark had been seeing each other on and off for the past two years, at just about every convention he's gone to, and that she was glad he'd finally had the courage to tell me."

"Oh my God," I gasped, reaching for her mittened hand and holding it in my own. "I can't believe she called you. What a vindictive bitch."

Kate shrugged. "Yeah, well. I hope he does end up with her. He deserves it after what he did to me," she said. Her voice was high and thin, and I knew that maybe everything had been decided, but that didn't help her much right now. Kate's heart was broken. She had been a perfect wife to her perfect husband, and somehow they hadn't been able to make it work. He had hurt her, and she had tried to hurt him back, and in the end it had all fallen apart.

The weekend didn't improve much. Now that Mark had finally come clean to his family, Kate wanted him to move out of the house immediately, and so he moved in with Mom and Dad, into the bedroom he'd had as a kid. It had been a long time since Mom, Dad, Mark, and I had all lived under the same roof, and I can't say it's something I would want to try again. Mark spent most of the time moping in his room, and Mom vacillated between crying jags and screaming at Mark through the locked door. Dad hid in his study, and I did everything I could just to keep out of the house. I love shopping, but the day after Thanksgiving I've always avoided the mall at all costs.

Nothing saps the holiday merriment from me faster than being crushed among hundreds of harried, anxious parents intent on saving five bucks on the latest toy their child has to have lest they risk becoming the school pariah. But this weekend I was willing to endure it, if just to get away from my insane family.

I hit the Carousel Mall—so named because of the giant carousel constructed in the middle of it—with a shopping list. By five o'clock, I had completed my Christmas shopping for the year. I never make holiday shopping that complicated, usually getting books or ties for the men, earrings or necklaces for the women. This year I made a few edits, punishing Mark—whom I was so furious with that I had contemplated getting him nothing—by buying him a cheap motorized tie rack, and demoting Nina, who wasn't speaking to me, to a T-shirt. On the other hand, I splurged on a bottle of Joy perfume for Kate, since I thought she needed the lift, and then after much dithering, I shelled out two hundred dollars for a sumptuous navy cashmere sweater for Ted. I knew all of the dating rules strictly forbid buying expensive presents for new boyfriends, because if you break up, the last thing you want to see is him wearing the clothing you got him with a new woman on his arm. But still. I touched the luxuriously soft material, saw how gloriously the blue would go with Ted's eyes, and before I knew what was happening I was handing over my Visa card to the salesclerk.

When I got home from the mall, exhausted from the shopping, everyone was locked away in his or her private room, and so I made myself a turkey sandwich out of the few remaining cooked spots on the bird and watched *The Sound of Music* on television. Saturday morning the household didn't seem to be in much better spirits. I was able to escape for a few hours when I met Beth and Seth for lunch at a local Chinese restaurant, and was treated to a never-ending album of wedding pictures—including only one of me, where I was looking unattractively drunk with a prominent Scotch stain on my cream sweater—and their annoying kissy-baby talk, until I finally made up excuses about being needed at home.

I found Mom in the kitchen, throwing out leftovers. "Everything's ruined," she announced darkly. "First Brian, and then you and Eric, and now Mark and Kate. None of my children can keep a relationship together. I'm a failure as a mother."

"Well, to be fair, I wasn't married to Eric, nor did I cheat on him," I said irritably, kicking off my shoes.

"Humph," my mother said, as though my breaking up with my boyfriend of less than a year wasn't really all that different than my two moronic brothers screwing around on their wives. I opened my mouth, ready to hold forth on what an incredibly unfair comparison this was, but then I closed it. Nothing good ever came of confronting my mother. She took the smallest criticism as an ugly attack, and would view an outright confrontation as blasphemy. I would never hear the end of it. So I did what I do best in times of crisis.

"Mother," I said, "I'm taking an early train back to the city."

It's not like leaving home a day early was conflict-free. Mother cried, and talked about my deserting her in her time of trouble, and refused to drive me to the train station. Dad gave me a stiff hug and handed me some articles that he thought would be the good basis for a paper on something or other, although what I don't know, since I actually stopped listening, I was so irritated that he couldn't act like a human being for once. Instead of having to endure Dad on the trip to the train station, I dragged

Mark out of his room to drive me. His face was red and blotchy, and once we were in the confines of the car, I noticed that he'd achieved a rather ripe body odor, smelling a little like a cheese that's gone funky. I guess he didn't want to risk running into Mother in the hallway, and so had been avoiding the bathroom.

"You ever plan on taking a shower?" I asked, rather nastily.

Mark, who would have once responded by poking me so hard on the side it would leave a black and blue bruise, just sniffed and looked pitiful.

"Oh, come on. You don't really expect me to feel sorry for you, do you?" I said, actually feeling a little sorry for him despite myself.

Mark still didn't say anything. His eyes looked watery, and then a tear trickled down his unshaven cheek. I sighed and relented.

"So what happened?" I asked.

"I don't know," he said. And then he added, "It just happened. One time, when I was drunk."

"Bullshit," I said.

"What?"

"I said 'bullshit.' You don't *just happen* to cheat on your wife. That's something you decide to do. Besides, your little bimbo called Kate and told her that you'd been seeing each other for years, so don't lie about it now," I snapped.

"What? Valerie called Kate?" Mark looked at me with alarm. "When? Kate never said anything about it to me."

"Maybe she didn't need to. I think she'd already made up her mind to leave you," I said.

"Yeah, I guess," he said. An infinite sadness seemed to settle on him, and when he spoke again, it was in almost a whisper. "It's not what you think. I don't know why I did it. I don't even like Valerie that much."

"Was it the sex?"

"Well, sort of, but not really. It's that it was ... different."

"You mean she was different from Kate?" I asked, and I could hear my voice go a little shrill. Craving sexual variety was, as far as I was concerned, one of the shittiest possible reasons to cheat on your wife. Not that there was a good reason, but that certainly wasn't one.

"No, that's not what I mean. I mean when I was with Valerie, it was like getting away from myself. *I* was a different person."

"And you liked your lying, cheating self more?"

"It's just at work, and with Kate, and with Mom and Dad, and you, I always have to be a certain kind of guy. Responsible, dependable, you know, Mr. Nice Guy. I just wanted to not be like that for a while. Just for a little while," Mark said. I could hear the desperation breaking in his voice. "Kate's been talking about wanting kids, and my boss has been talking about promoting me, and it just felt like it was getting too hard to keep being me."

I knew what he was talking about. Mark was one of those guys who'd always been a golden boy. In high school he'd been at the top of his class, was the captain of both the soccer and baseball teams, and had dated a string of gorgeous cheerleader types, all while being an incredibly nice guy. He was never one of those meatheads that would tease the dorks wearing bottle-thick glasses and pocket protectors, but would talk to them as though they were not only human, but equals. Ditto the chorus nerds, the stoned Dead-heads, and the big-haired metalheads. And then when he went to college, it had just been more of the same—he'd been on the dean's list, a top athlete, and then his senior year he'd met Kate, and they'd become two halves of the Golden Couple. I couldn't even hate him for excelling at everything, since he'd always just been a great guy, even to his pesky little sister.

"Well, if you wanted to stop being a nice guy, you certainly pulled it off. In fact, like everything else you do, you were an overachiever," I said. But I leaned over and squeezed his hand. Mark didn't need me to tell him what an idiot he was. Unlike Brian, who ran about as deep as a puddle, and I'm sure never thought once about his ex-wife after he started screwing around on her, Mark was going to be feeling the effects of his actions for a long time. He was going to lose the most important thing he'd ever had in his life. There wasn't much I could say to make him feel better about that, so we spent the rest of the ride to the station in silence.

Chapter 19

When I arrived back in the District, rain was pouring down in great sheets. I could barely see more than a few inches outside of the taxi cab window, and had no idea how the driver was managing to find his way down the waterlogged streets, particularly at the breakneck speed he was driving. I decided to stop by Ted's on my way home to take Sally off his hands, and gave the driver his address. I actually missed Sally, even if she was a little dictator. I was used to the little furry butterball following me around the house, and snoring softly in my ear while I was sleeping, and it was strangely lonely to be away from her. I was also hoping that Ted had missed me so much that he would gather me into his arms and bundle me off to bed. After all of the heartbreak I had been exposed to this weekend, I needed to reconnect with him, to be given hope that all relationships don't eventually turn to crap. Kate and Mark's marriage was the only one I knew of that actually seemed to work. They had been my relationship role models. If they couldn't make it, who could? Ted and me? I knew the odds were against us, but was it even possible? I shivered, and couldn't tell if it was from fear or the fact that I'd gotten soaked with rain while leaving the station, and now the taxicab driver had the air conditioner roaring at full blast.

As we approached Ted's building, I whipped out my compact. Once I'd wiped the rain-streaked mascara off my cheeks and freshened my lip gloss and powder, I looked fine. Not great—who does after traveling?—but presentable. I paid the driver and hoisted my overnight bag to my shoulder. Ted had sweetly put me on the clearance list with his doorman, which meant that I didn't have to wait for him to call up to Ted's apartment before letting me through. It was one of those lovely relationship milestones that had let me know we weren't just temporary, but there was something solid between us, maybe even something important, and breezing past the security desk with a smile and wave made me feel smugly content.

I took the elevator up to the twentieth floor and then padded down to his apartment. I knocked on the door, and heard Sally and Oscar howling and racing down the hall, setting off the most reliable burglar alarm in the world. I waited for a few minutes, listening to the dogs bark and scratch at the door. It occurred to me that Ted might still be at the station, but then realized that the security guard would have mentioned that to me when I came in. I knocked again, and this time I heard footsteps. There was a pause, and then I heard the door being unlatched from the inside and the security chain being dragged off its track.

"Sorry to stop by so late, but I got in a day early, and wanted to pick up Sally ...," I started to explain as the door opened. Then I stopped. It wasn't Ted standing on the other side of the doorjamb, stepping aside to let me into the apartment with a sexy crooked smile, telling me he'd missed me and peppering my face with a hundred soft kisses. Instead, it was Alice. Ted's ex-wife. Wearing what looked like Ted's plush, navy robe and apparently little else. And she wasn't stepping aside, but blocking my way into the apartment, baring her teeth in a triumphant, cold smile.

"Hello again," she drawled. I looked her up and down. Her legs and feet were bare, and her smooth, dark bob was a little tousled in the back. She looked like she'd been rolling around in bed only seconds before.

"Sally?" I croaked. I felt exactly like I imagined it would feel to have someone rip open my chest, pull out my heart, shred it to bits, and then thrust the pieces back in. The pain was so intense, I actually began to feel a little light-headed, and could see fuzzy pins of light around the edges of my vision.

"No," she said, pretending to frown, but looking amused. "Alice. We met at the Whiteheads' party."

"No, I mean, I came for my dog," I said. Alice had been blocking the door, keeping me from getting in and Sally from getting out. But now, hearing her name and determined to be reunited with me, Sally stood on her hind legs and shoved at Alice's leg, hitting that tender spot on the back of the calf, causing Alice to stumble forward and mutter, "Oh, shit, that hurt." Sally took the opportunity to dodge by her and hop into my arms, and I made a mental note to buy her some of her much beloved hot dogs the next time I was at the store as a reward for her well-timed loyalty.

"Well, now you've got her," Alice said, arching her eyebrows up and moving back to take her place blocking the door.

I opened my mouth and looked over her shoulder, down at the empty hall. Where was Ted? Was he back there, listening to us at the door? Was he really such a complete coward that he wouldn't even come out and face me, and at least apologize for going behind my back and fucking his ex-wife when we were supposed to be in the happy thralls of a new relationship? Maybe we hadn't yet had that conversation, the one that usually takes place when you're lying in bed together in a haze of postcoital bliss, wrapped in each other's arms, where you promise to one another that yes, it's all going somewhere, and no, you don't want to see other people. But it had felt like that was what we were doing.

Alice followed my gaze down the hall, and a nasty smile spread across her pointy face. She was clearly enjoying the moment, which made my humiliation all the more acute. "Oh, I'd get Ted for you, but he's in the shower just now," she said, smirking.

Her words cut through me. There was only one reason why Alice would be here, wearing Ted's robe while Ted was taking a shower. I turned to leave, clutching Sally in my arms like a safety blanket. For once, the pug didn't fight me, but clung to my shoulders, and glared at Alice with her wet, bugged-out eyes.

"Ellie?"

I turned and saw Ted in the hallway, walking up behind Alice, wearing only a towel around his waist. I opened my mouth, hoping that something really cutting and fantastic would come out, but instead only a sob tore lose from my throat. Lovely, I thought, as my breathing quickened and tears burst from my eyes. I had to cry in front of *her*. Ted looked as mortified as I felt; men hate scenes, particularly ugly ones between former and current lovers. Only instead of Alice being the former lover in such a scenario, now I was. I turned and rushed for the elevator.

"Ellie, wait!" Ted called out, and I looked back to see him pushing by Alice and running after me, at least running as best he could while holding the towel up around his waist.

I hit the Down button, and luckily the elevator that had brought me up had never left the floor. The doors opened immediately, and I hopped in, pushing first the Lobby button, and then hitting the Door Close button repeatedly until the steel doors began to close. Ted closed in on me just as the space between the doors was disappearing. He looked anguished, his face a mixture of shock and irritation. For a minute, I thought about hitting the Door Open button, and giving him a chance to explain, a chance to tell me that it had all been a mistake, that Alice had somehow bewitched him into sleeping with her, and that I was the one he really loved.

But just as my hand hovered over the Door Open button, my eyes never leaving his, Ted said, "This isn't what it looks like."

I couldn't believe he would say something so trite, so pathetic, so obviously a lie. They were the exact words that Mark had used to feebly defend himself. Why should I be surprised? My brother Mark, Mr. Perfect himself, had screwed around on his wife, as had Brian on his. I shouldn't have expected any more from a boyfriend of only a few weeks, particularly one with an ex-wife who had left him, who had broken his heart, and who now obviously wanted to get back together with him.

And then the doors closed, and the floor was dropping down twenty stories. I stood in the elevator, clutching Sally to me, my tears soaking her velvety fur, and listened to the sound of my heart breaking.

I walked back to my apartment, crying freely now that there wasn't a bitchy, robe-wearing whore to smirk at me. The rain, which was still coming down in a Wrath-of-God-style storm, camouflaged my tears, so at least I didn't have to bear the pitying looks of strangers I passed on the sidewalk. When I let myself into my apartment, setting Sally and my bag—both of which had become unbearably heavy on the walk home—onto the floor, I automatically looked at the answering machine. It was a bad habit, one going back to the first days that Ted and I had spent together, when I had viewed every message as a triumph, and every day without a message as a hopeless failure. Now the answering machine just had a fat red zero in the message window. He hadn't even bothered to call me.

I burst into fresh tears. Everything seemed so bleak, so horrible. I had honestly thought that Ted was The One. Maybe it was stupid, considering our age difference, and his resistance to the relationship. But when I was with him, everything felt right. It felt the way I always thought it would be when I met The One. For the first time, I felt like I could truly hand my heart over to someone, knowing that it would be in the hands of the one person who was meant to hold it. I had never felt like this with Eric, nor with Alec, Peter, Winston, Jeremy, or Charlie.

I stripped off my rain-soaked clothing and put on my grungiest sweats, the ones that had once been black but were now a dirty dark gray and soft from years of washing. I felt like lying in bed wearing ugly but comfortable clothes, listening to heartache songs sung by Barry Manilow, Neil Diamond, and Elton John, and eating ice cream and popcorn and chocolate, and every other comfort food that makes me gain weight, retain water, or break out. I felt like crying until my eyes were so hot and tired, it would feel as though I were bursting blood vessels. I felt like drinking bottles of wine, until thoughts of Ted could only cause me to sway from side to side with a stupid smile on my face, while I crooned the words to "Somebody Done Somebody Wrong Song" in an off-key tone. I felt like dying.

My door buzzer rang. I stumbled up to the intercom and stared at it for a minute, wondering if it had actually sounded, or if I had just willed myself into believing that it had happened. As I stared at it, it buzzed again, and I jumped back in amazement.

"What?" I said into the intercom, in my surliest, litigator-kicking-ass tone of voice.

"Ellie, it's me. Please let me up so I can explain," Ted said. His voice sounded tinny transmitted through the poor electronics of the intercom.

"Go away," I said, somewhat hysterically. Why was it that when confronted with heartache and a treacherous lover, I couldn't keep it together, and ended up sounding like one of those scorned women on the Lifetime Channel's made-for-television movies?

"Please let me explain. It wasn't what it looked like," Ted said. He was using that tone of voice that people use when they're talking to a crazy person, which I did not appreciate.

"You are such a liar!"

"It's true. Please believe me. Look, just let me up and I'll explain everything," Ted said.

And for a moment I wavered. But then I remembered about ripping off the Band-Aid, and hardened my heart.

"I don't ever want to you see again," I said into the intercom. And then I went into my bedroom and turned my radio up as loud as it would go, so loud that my next-door neighbor—a freaky, myopic guy who kept a half-dozen parrots as pets—banged on the wall. Loud enough so that I could only barely hear the door buzzer ring and ring and ring. And then finally go quiet.

I eventually fell asleep. There's something about crying until your eyes hurt and you can barely breathe that allows you to escape your demons long enough to fall into an exhausted sleep. When I awoke the next morning, the sun streaming in through the slats in my venetian blinds, for a minute I felt rested, though oddly drained. And then I remembered. The pain of the previous night flooded me, stabbing at my heart, pricking at my stomach, until all I could do was curl up into a ball on my bed.

Normally, this was the point where I would call Nina, and she would come over, bully me into taking a shower, and then would escort me to the movies, not anything heavy, but something that was purely mindless pleasure. And then we would go to Bennigan's, or some other cheap restaurant, and order far more Buffalo wings and chicken tenders and nachos than we could possibly eat, and after we were so full it hurt, finish up the artery-clogging meal with a brownie à la mode. It had always been my cure for the broken heart, not that anything I had suffered in the past that I'd thought was a broken heart even came close to approaching the pain I was feeling now. Only I couldn't call Nina—she wasn't speaking to me. The painful realization cut through me, twisting in my already broken heart. Part of me was tempted to call her anyway in the hopes that our friendship was strong enough to see us through this rough patch and that we could just forgive and forget. But what if I did call her, and she used it as an opportunity to tell me that she didn't want me in her life anymore? Or, worse, what if she just hung up on me? No, Nina wouldn't do that to me, I decided. Not when I really needed her. I dialed her phone number before I could lose my nerve.

"Hello," a slightly nasal male voice said.

Oh, shit. It was Josiah. I considered hanging up on him, but then, just as my finger was closing in on the switch hook, I remembered Nina had Caller I.D. There was no turning back.

"Hi ... is Nina there?" I asked.

"Who is this?"

I was taken aback at how rude he was being. "Um ...

Ellie. I'm a friend of Nina's. We, er, met at her party that time," I said in a fake, overly friendly way.

"I remember you. Nina doesn't want to talk to you," he said.

My heart sank. "Please ... it's important," I said, fighting back my irritation with the insufferable creep. I knew that if I blew up at him, I'd never get to talk to Nina.

Josiah paused, and I could hear some muffled sounds as his hand cupped the receiver.

"She's not here right now."

He was a terrible liar. I could tell from the way he was talking that Nina was there, probably sitting about an inch away from him. Knowing this hurt—and pissed me off.

"Oh. Well. When she comes in, will you ask her to call me? And please let her know it's important."

He responded by hanging up on me. I stared at the phone, outraged at his behavior and stung by Nina's betrayal. Had I really lost my boyfriend *and* my best friend in the same week? Determined to get some female solace, I called Harmony, first at home, and then when I wasn't able to rouse her there, at her office.

"Hello," Harmony said, in her usual brisk, business tone of voice.

"Why are you at work on a Sunday morning?" I asked.

"Ellie? Hey, you! Oh, I just had a few things to clear off my desk. How was your trip to Syracuse?"

"Horrible," I said, and filled her in on Mark and Kate's breakup.

"Oh, no," Harmony said. "That just sounds awful."

"But that's not all. When I got home ... when I got back to the city ..." I stopped and restarted, and then stopped again. And then, remembering Alice cozily wrapped up in Ted's robe, and Ted's face when he saw me at the door, I burst into tears.

"What is it? What happened?"

I told Harmony the whole sordid story, breaking occasionally to hiccup or blow my nose. When I finished telling her how Ted had followed me home and tried to make excuses through the intercom, she exhaled a soft, sympathetic sigh.

"That just sounds awful. I'm so sorry you had to go through it."

I knew that she must have been thinking that she told me so, that she had warned me that going out with Ted was only likely to lead to heartache. But that's the great thing about Harmony. Maybe she did tell me so, but she would never say that aloud.

"I hate to tell you this, Ellie, but I did try to warn you that you and Ted were probably not a great match," Harmony said.

Okay, so I was wrong.

"I know that," I said, a defensive note creeping into my voice.

"I wouldn't say it, except that I don't think you should dwell too much on what happened with Ted. I know it sucks, but at least it's good that it happened now, and not later when you were really serious about him," Harmony said.

I went silent. I knew that what she was saying made sense, but it sort of missed the point, since that was just my problem—I already was serious about Ted. And as much as I wanted to tell myself that it was just a minor affair, a short fling with a guy who'd turned out to be less than I thought he'd be, it didn't do much to help the stabs of pain that shot through me every time I thought about the way his sharp eyes always softened when they rested on me, or the way it had felt to snuggle up to his naked chest and fall asleep.

"Do you want to come over? We can go see a movie, and maybe get some dinner or something," I said hopefully.

"Oh, Ellie, I'd love to, but I just can't. I'm swamped at work right now, and I went out again with Harry last night instead of working, so I really can't afford to take today off," Harmony apologized.

"Oh, okay," I said.

"Why don't we get together for lunch this week, instead. Can we do that?" she suggested.

"Tomorrow?"

"Ummm. Well, I already made plans to meet Harry for lunch tomorrow. I'd cancel, but he's going out of town for the rest of the week, so it's the last chance we'll get to see each other before he goes," Harmony said.

I felt deflated. Now that Nina had suddenly turned into the poster girl for Monogamous Weekly, Harmony had been my last single friend, and now she had found someone, too. Other than a few women I knew from work (who were definitely not the kind of friends I would call on to help me salve a broken heart), all my other friends were married, or engaged, or living with someone. I was the only one who was still alone. *Alone*.

"Who's Harry? Is he that tax attorney you were seeing?"

"Yeah. He's really sweet, I'd love for you to meet him sometime," Harmony said.

"That would be great," I said without enthusiasm. Harmony might be brilliant, but sometimes she's just clueless. No one who has just had her heart broken wants to hear about how great her friend's boyfriend is, much less make plans to meet him. "Well, I should get going. I'm going for a jog," I lied.

We made plans to meet for lunch on Tuesday, and I flopped back on my bed, staring up at the ceiling. I was going to have to spend the day alone. *Alone.* Just the thought of the long, empty day stretching before me—a metaphor for the long, lonely, single life I was destined to lead—made me curl back into the fetal position, and there I would have stayed had Sally not started to howl, vigorously protesting the brief delay in receiving her breakfast. I dragged myself out of bed and stumbled into the kitchen, where I found Sally lying prone beside her food dish, moaning pathetically. I thought about pointing out to her that the rolls of fat spreading out from her sausagelike body undermined her Poor Starving Orphan routine, but what's the point of arguing with a diva? I fed her and, now that I was up, didn't feel like going to bed. Instead, I took a shower, and then went to the store to stock up on chocolate, Kleenex, and magazines—the heartbreak essentials.

Chapter 20

I told myself that the one good part about breaking up is that it frees up a lot of time to do all of the other things in life you want to do, but have been neglecting in the gluttony of romance. So, after allowing myself a day of moping around my apartment, watching old black-and-white movies on cable and eating everything I could find in my refrigerator that wasn't growing mold, I decided I needed to shake off the entire Ted episode and reclaim my life. For starters, I was determined to throw myself into my job and become the best damned litigation associate at my firm. It didn't even matter that I hated litigation; if I was going to become an old, lonely spinster, then at least I would be a successful, career-oriented spinster. I was going to become a whole new Ellie: I was going to lose ten pounds, start working out—maybe even train for a marathon!—volunteer for animal rescue charities, travel extensively to exotic and foreign lands, and take up fascinating new hobbies, like parasailing or Brazilian jujitsu, and even learn a new language. Japanese, maybe, or Russian. One day of mourning, and then on with the rest of my life. Alone. Probably forever. Never again to lie against Ted's bare chest, and listen to the steady, soothing sound of his heartbeat . . .

No, thinking like that doesn't help things. Best not to think of Ted at all. I just had to put him out of my mind, and try not to remember the way he looked in his cashmere overcoat, or how it felt to talk to him and know that he was really listening to what I was saying. Or remember the way he smelled, that spicy, earthy fragrance that I just wanted to wrap around myself. No, better not to think of it at all. Although it wasn't helping that Ted wasn't letting me forget him. He called me all day Sunday, leaving messages on my machine at home when I didn't answer the phone. I only listened to the first message, in which he repeated his lame excuse about how my crashing in on his reunion sex party hadn't been what it looked like, blah, blah, blah. I actually said "Hah!" out loud. Not wanting to hear anything else he had to say on the matter, I erased the rest of his messages without listening to them, and when I got to work Monday morning and found he'd left more messages on my work voice mail, I erased those, too. Ted also tried e-mailing me, which I thought about reading, but then again remembered about the Band-Aid, and deleted the e-mails without opening them.

I settled in at my desk, intent on obsessing on something healthier than my now extinct relationship with Ted. I reread the final draft of my Response to the Motion for Summary Judgment for the class-action case. It was beautiful, if I did say so myself. In fact, a work of legal art. I had researched the law for days, read every page of deposition testimony, and rewritten the sucker about twenty times. It was now near perfect. Duffy had read it and raved, and even Shearer had stopped his incessant testicle-adjusting long enough to nod approvingly and concede that he didn't have any major edits to suggest.

The motion was going to go out in the mail on Wednesday, which left me just enough time Monday and Tuesday to get all of the many exhibits photocopied and organized.

I started out strong, organizing the class representatives and the medical expert testimony into two neat stacks, using sticky notes to direct the copy room on which pages I needed duplicated. It was monotonous, time-consuming work. Once I dug into it, I didn't lift my head to peer at the clock until it was nearly five o'clock. That morning, when I first got into my office, I had activated the Do Not Disturb on my phone, to avoid work-related interruptions as well as Ted. Without the constant ringing of the phone, the time actually passed without my noticing. Now my stomach was rumbling with hunger, and I was starting to feel tired. My eyes were still sore from my crying marathon, and although I had slept, it was fitful and hot and not very restful. Between my aching eyes, stiff shoulders, and general malaise, I was ready to quit for the night.

Just before packing it in, I double-checked the stack of exhibits and noticed that a couple of the key depositions were nowhere to be found—one from our medical expert, Ralph Murphy, and one from an employee of the defendant, Bobbie Curtis, who'd given some particularly damning testimony on the defendant insurance company's policies. I'd seen them as recently as last week, or maybe the week before, but now they'd apparently vanished from the file. Still, I knew they had to be around the office somewhere, since I always kept at least two paper copies of every document in the file.

But after a dozen exhaustive searches of my office and the War Room hadn't turned up the missing depositions, I was starting to feel a little panicked. I tried to calm my nerves by reminding myself that even if I couldn't find the hard copies of the depositions, it was firm protocol to obtain a computer file of the deposition from the court reporter, and keep copies of the depositions on the office computer network. So I sat down at my desk, switched on my computer, and started typing. But no matter how many times I ran computer searches, or even manually looked up and down the list of documents, the two most important depositions were nowhere to be found. I kept hoping that I was just tired, and it was one of those occasions where the documents were right in front of me and, but for the stress and strain of the past few days, would be easily found. But each time I looked and was unsuccessful in my search, my lungs tightened a bit more, so that eventually I was panting, and my heart was beating with an odd staccato pattern.

Although my motion ran to seventy-five pages of complex arguments, backed up by as much case law and witness testimony as I could throw at the court, our entire case really rested more or less on these two depositions: Murphy was the only doctor who had been able to conclude unequivocally that the defendant's careless handling of its insureds caused the worsening of their ailments, and Curtis was the only employee of the defendant willing to go on the record regarding her employer's mishandling of the claims. Without the testimony of those two witnesses—particularly at this late point—our case would crumble. And if the case fell apart, not only would our clients recover nothing, but Snow & Druthers would be out the hundreds of thousands of dollars for the expenses it had fronted to prosecute the case. It was the biggest case I had ever been entrusted with, and if I screwed it up over something like lost copies of depositions, I would be a goner. I would certainly lose my job at the firm, and even a city as big as Washington still had a small enough legal community that word of such an unforgivable blunder would get around in no time, and then no firm would hire me. If I didn't find those depositions, I was screwed.

I spent the entire night at the firm, tearing through every single file that had anything to do with the class action, not to mention as many of the unrelated files as I could get to, hoping that they had somehow been misplaced. By Tuesday morning at 8 A.M., when the secretaries began streaming into the office and the smell of freshly brewed coffee began to waft through the stale, recycled air, I knew I was sunk. The Murphy and Curtis depositions had vanished. I had one day to get the motion together, have copies made, and send it off to the court, and there was no way I was going to be able to make the deadline. I knew I was going to have to come clean and tell Duffy about the crisis. I had a last glimmer of hope that maybe he had taken the depositions home, or put them somewhere in his office that I hadn't been able to see when I ransacked it at about 2 A.M.

"Ellie, you look like you've been here all night," a mocking voice said from the vicinity of my doorway. I'd been kneeling on the floor, going through the case file boxes for the hundredth time, knowing it was hopeless and yet hoping for a miracle. I looked up from my work and saw Katherine leaning against the doorjamb. She was, of course, immaculately dressed, every hair in place, her makeup fresh. I knew just how awful I looked, as I'd caught a glimpse of myself in the ladies' room mirror earlier. I looked exactly like I'd spent the night searching through dusty files and tearing my hair out. My bob had wisped up into an unspeakably large frizz, and my eyes were bloodshot and ringed with smudged, day-old eyeliner, the only makeup remaining on my face from the day before. My black pantsuit was covered with lint, and the white shirt that had been crisply ironed twenty-four hours earlier was now wrinkled and pulled out of my waistband.

"Having trouble with the big case?" she asked, innocently raising her perfectly plucked eyebrows.

"What? No ... why?" I lied, not wanting to give her anything to gloat over.

"Well, sometimes problems can crop up at the last minute with key witnesses," Katherine said lightly.

"How did you know that?" I asked, and then, as it hit me, all I could do was stare at her in a state of anger and disbelief. Katherine and I weren't friends, but we were on the same team. She couldn't have—wouldn't have—purposefully sabotaged my case ... would she? Even if she wanted to see me go down, why take the chance? She could get caught, or if the firm lost enough money, they might end up firing more associates than just me. But then, remembering that she was sleeping with Shearer, I realized that she wouldn't have to worry about that. He would protect her job, even if every other associate in the firm was fired. And with me out of the way, she wouldn't have any competition for the big cases anymore. Her path to partnership would be as secure as could be.

"What did you do?" I asked her in a strangled whisper.

"Do? Whatever do you mean?" she asked. But the nasty smile that stretched across her face belied the words. And I knew—those depositions were gone, never to be found. Without them, the case would crash in a spectacular fiery explosion. And with it, my career at Snow & Druthers.

*   *   *

After breaking the news of the missing depositions to Duffy—a hideous experience, where instead of screaming, he just sort of went pale and clutched at his chest—I returned to my desk, staring blankly into the air before me, wondering how the hell I was going to get out of this mess, and how my life had turned to such complete shit overnight. I don't know how long I sat there before Shearer appeared at my door, looking grave.

"Ellie, we're ready to meet with you now," Shearer said. I started, and nodded mutely.

Maybe they just want to have a status meeting to go over our options for damage control, I thought, trying to be positive and trying to ignore the deafening sound of my heart, as heavy as a potato, thumping against my chest. I stood, took a deep breath, and gathered up a yellow legal pad and pen just in case it was a status meeting and I needed to take notes.

Shearer had gone ahead of me, so when I entered the conference room, with its ridiculous claw-and-ball-foot table that would have looked more at place in the dining room of a medieval king, and the enormous chandelier creepily made out of deer antlers, Shearer and Duffy were already sitting at the table, both of them silent and impassive, their arms folded in front of their chests.

I sat down, smiled nervously, and, still thinking positive thoughts, uncapped my pen so that I was ready to take notes. Maybe if I pretended this was a status meeting, they would play along.

Shearer cleared his throat. "I've been thinking for a while that you're not really that happy here. And lately, considering your handling of the Armor case, I fear that my instincts were correct. We're trying to build a top-notch commercial litigation department here, and within the next five years we want to be considered one of the top, if not *the* top plaintiffs' firm in the city. And pursuant to that goal, we want to make sure that we have the best possible team of both partners and associates possible, all of whom are willing to sacrifice their personal lives for the firm. And, Ellie, I don't think you have what it takes to be that kind of a team player," Shearer said, waving his hands occasionally in the air in a strange circular motion.

"I think what Howard is trying to say is that we both have the utmost respect for your talents as an attorney, and that on a personal level we like you very much. It's just that after watching you for the past few years, we don't think you really want to be a litigator. It's just not a field that you're happy in. And we don't want to waste any more of your career, and your time, practicing in an area that you're not truly committed to," Duffy said.

For the next hour, Shearer and Duffy took turns basically repeating these opinions over and over, occasionally throwing in baseball metaphors, while I sat there quietly. It was the employment version of the "it's not you, it's me" breakup. Every ten minutes or so they would pause, and glance at me as though I should say something, but I would just look back at them, and they would fill the silence with their "it's not you, it's us" and "you're not happy here, and we just want to help you reach your professional goals" bullshit. At one point, Duffy even said, "We're not firing you, of course. We just think it's in our mutual interest for you to move on." Right. I wasn't being fired. Except, of course, for the part where I wasn't going to work there anymore.

I wanted to say something. Something classy and composed, the kind of line that you sweep out of the room on. Maybe even explain that it was all Katherine's doing, that it was only through her evil sabotage that the depositions had gone missing. But then how would

I prove it? Shearer, who was balling Katherine, would never believe my word over hers. And besides, my mouth was suddenly dry, as though all of the saliva had been sucked out of it, and my tongue felt heavy and thick, and I didn't seem capable of forming actual words. I took a few deep breaths, and nodded mutely at points, and prayed that I wouldn't cry. *Whatever you do, just don't cry,* I told myself over and over, more of a plea than a mantra. But then my lower lip began to tremble, and my eyes welled up, and I knew that if I didn't get out of there soon, the waterworks would be turned on.

"Are you offering a severance package?" I managed to ask, cutting Shearer off as he launched into his fourth iteration of the "we want this to be the best firm" line. My voice sounded tinny and strange, and quite a long way off from the cool dignity I was so desperately seeking.

"Three months' salary," Duffy said. "And health insurance."

"Good," I croaked. "Please excuse me."

I jumped up from the table, and without pausing to shake either of their hands, I turned and scurried out of the office. My shoulders were hunched up under my ears, and my eyes fixed on the carpet before me, and I deliberately didn't look at any of my coworkers. I didn't know how many of them knew I had been fired—Duffy had claimed that no one knew, but he was either lying or completely underestimated the speed with which office gossip travels, because of course they knew, I could tell by the way their conversation faltered as I passed by, could hear the whispers exchanged in my wake. I felt like I'd had an enormous scarlet "F" burned into my forehead, marking me forever as She Who Was Fired. Terminated. Axed. Sacked.

We want to have the best people working here. And there just isn't a place for you on that team. Shearer's words rang in my head, taunting me for my inadequacies.

At least Duffy had tried to be nice, even if he was an inhuman automaton. I made it to my office just in time, slammed the door shut, and then burst into tears. I was so, so tired. All of the conflict, all of the turmoil was starting to be more than I could bear.

Once I got it together, dabbing at my eyes with a scratchy Kleenex, I looked around my office with new eyes, aware that I would never see the world from this view again. I started to pack. Somehow, I managed to fit all of my pictures, papers, coffee mugs, and various incidentals (my pink feathered gel pen, an old "Far Side" cartoon, my pug-a-day calendar) into two copy-paper boxes and tried to slink out of the office with minimal attention. I had to pass by about fifteen people—secretaries, paralegals, and attorneys—on my way to the side door. Most of them had the decency to pretend they didn't see me, although a few said, "Bye, Ellie," in dulcet tones. I tried to look calm and dignified, and smiled politely without meeting their eyes. I didn't want their sympathetic glances, their piqued curiosity. But when I passed by Katherine's door, I couldn't stop myself from looking in. She was sitting behind her desk, dressed in a glorious midnight blue Donna Karan suit, looking beautiful and composed. She glanced up at me, and actually smirked. At that moment, I would have given anything to have the strength to drop my Good Girl niceties, just so I could stalk into her office and smack her as hard as I could across her MAC painted face. But, of course, I didn't. I just looked away and kept walking, passing out through the side door, the one I sometimes used to sneak out of early on sunny Friday afternoons. Holding my two boxes before me, so that they nearly obscured my vision, I walked out of Snow & Druthers for the last time.

* * *

239

The elevator made a dinging sound to alert me—its sole occupant—that we'd reached the lobby. The doors opened, and I staggered out, struggling under my load of boxes. I dropped them on the ground to take a rest, and to see if I could spot Pete the doorman, so I could get him to hail me a cab and just maybe carry one of the boxes out for me. I don't often like to utilize the damsel-in-distress routine, but now was not the time to worry about presenting myself as a strong, capable woman, especially considering that I was grubby, sleep-deprived, and unemployed. I didn't see Harry behind his desk, but as my eyes scanned over the lobby I instead saw ...

"Oh, shit," I said as Ted and I locked eyes, and he started toward me.

I was not up to this right now. I was exhausted and drained and looked horrible, and if running into an ex-boyfriend wasn't bad enough, looking like death warmed over when you did was unbearable. Particularly when the last time you saw the boyfriend, he was basking in the glow of postcoital bliss with his ex-wife. It was like the real-life version of that anxiety dream where you show up to school naked. Only far, far worse.

But as Ted drew near, I saw that he wasn't looking much better than I was. His face was gray, and he also looked as though he hadn't slept very much. Even his clothing—normally so crisp that it looked as though it were pressed thrice daily—was rumpled.

"Ellie," Ted said. "We need to talk."

"What are you doing here?" I croaked.

"I tried calling, but you wouldn't take my calls. I thought I'd wait down here for you and intercept you when you went to lunch." He noticed my boxes for the first time. "What's all this?"

"I was fired," I said, and as the words left my mouth,

the reality of this truth suddenly became clear for the first time. My chest tightened as fear and anxiety began to well inside of me. *What was I going to do now?*

"Oh, Christ, Ellie . . . I'm so sorry. Can I do anything? Let me help you, and I'll get a car to take you home," Ted said, reaching for the boxes.

"No!" I said, surprising myself with how fierce I sounded. People walking around us on their way out to lunch—men and women dressed in their professional uniforms of buttoned-up suits—turned to look at us, their faces bright at the prospect of seeing some sort of a lovers' quarrel they could later relate to their coworkers to brighten the dreary workday afternoon. I closed my eyes for a minute, trying to collect myself. It had been a horrible enough day as it was, and the last thing I wanted to do was talk to Ted, to hear his pathetic excuses for sleeping with Alice, or worse, lies about how it wasn't what it had looked like. All I wanted to do was get the hell out of there, away from Ted, away from the firm.

After I collected myself enough to speak, I pasted a cold smile on my face and said, "No, thank you, I can get home on my own."

"Ellie, we *need* to talk," Ted insisted. He took a step closer to me and placed a hand on my shoulder. "We need to straighten things out."

"What's to straighten out? You were right about us, our ages, and how it would never work out," I said, stepping aside to allow a group of secretaries to skirt past us, and also to dislodge Ted's hand from my shoulder.

"That has nothing to do with why you're angry at me," Ted said.

"I'm *not* angry at you. I'm . . . disappointed, I guess, that you don't . . . didn't . . . care enough about us. About me," I said softly, and suddenly I was again in danger of bursting into tears. I clamped my lips tightly together as I tried to get my breathing under control.

Ted flinched a little at my last comment, but his eyes never left my face. "Is that what you think? That I don't care?" he asked.

I shrugged. "Does it matter what I think?"

"Yes," Ted said.

I felt as if I were skewered on his direct, unrelenting stare. I shifted, and looked around him, desperate for an escape route.

"Look, I told you, you were right when you said you didn't think this would work out. You need someone older, someone more like you, someone less ..." I was going to say "needy," but to keep my dignity I instead substituted "involved."

"I need to go. Don't worry about me. I'm fine with everything," I continued.

I finally spotted Pete, and leaned over to pick up my boxes. Ted tried to take them from me, but I sidestepped him with a not-so-graceful shuffle-and-duck move.

"Well, *I'm* not fine with it," Ted insisted.

"No. Just leave it," I hissed.

"I can't do that," Ted said, and it occurred to me that he seemed to be struggling to get the words out. I felt a little sorry for him, and for a brief second, I softened and almost relented. But then the memory of Alice, naked under his robe, flashed before me, and my empathy froze and then dissipated.

I looked up at Ted, my face tight and angry. "It's over, Ted. Just leave me *alone*," I said softly, but with a grim finality.

My words seemed to have a physical effect on Ted, as though the sharp edges cut through him. He stared at me, and finally nodded curtly and stepped out of my way, clearing my escape path. We didn't say good-bye, and as I marched away with as much dignity as I could under the strain of carrying two heavy boxes, I didn't look back to see if he was watching me.

Being fired, particularly when you receive a severance package, should be like a paid vacation, a time to catch up on your sleep, reading, favorite television shows, whatever. And it wasn't like I was going to miss working at Snow & Druthers. I'd hated that job, and the thought of never returning to their freezing, sterile offices with the horrid fluorescent lighting should have filled me with ecstasy. But instead of celebrating, I spent the next few weeks sinking into a deep depression. I felt like a complete and utter failure. Not even my best friend wanted to talk to me.

As if it wasn't bad enough that I was turning thirty in a month, I was turning thirty alone, unemployed, and if I kept making and eating whole trays of brownies, I'd be grossly obese as well. In fact, I was even failing at being depressed—most depressives get super skinny and sleep all of the time. I was scarfing down Reese's Peanut Butter Cups and spent entire nights awake, staring up at my ceiling. And during the day, I couldn't even get into a good funk, doing nothing but marathons of TV watching, catching up on *Law & Order* reruns, and finding out how to be a better person on *Oprah*. Instead, I was filled with nervous energy, and cleaned my apartment compulsively. I pulled everything out of my kitchen cupboards and scrubbed down the shelves, pulled all of my clothes off their hangers so I could reorganize my closets, and painted my bathroom a nice, soothing light pink.

My mantle of gloom was briefly lifted when Nick

Bloomfield called, raving about the cartoons I'd sent him (I'd completed the assignment in one of my frenzied bursts of activity) and asking me to become a regular contributor to the website, working up sketches to accompany the column. It'd be about a third of what I had earned practicing law. I had no idea how I was going to live on the paltry salary, but it was still a rush, and a much needed shred of good news in an otherwise dark period.

Thanks to my hyperactive cleaning/drawing/brownie-eating, the only time I was forced to stop and contemplate everything that had happened after Thanksgiving was during the sleepless nights. Lying in my bed, I couldn't block out thoughts of Ted and Alice and Katherine and Shearer and Duffy and Nina. They surrounded me and mocked me for my failures, until I felt as though I were falling into a deep, bottomless black hole. I found the only way to counterattack the images was to imagine all sorts of hideous revenge. I fantasized about Alice suffering from a glandular problem that caused her to suddenly gain two hundred pounds, about Duffy losing ten additional big cases in a row, forcing the partnership to kick him out, and leaving him penniless and alone, and even spent a few fun hours contemplating sending anonymous notes to Shearer's wife and everyone at the firm, letting them know about his illicit affair with Katherine. Not that I would ever do such a thing—it was against the Good Girl code—but it was fun thinking about it.

It was harder with Ted. I wanted to think up something really awful for him, something epic—despair, destruction, something that would cause him apocalyptic suffering. But every time I thought of him, and pictured the curves of his face which had been so dear to me, I had to screw my eyes shut and think of something else. The pain of our breakup was still too raw, even for cathartic revenge fantasies. Ted had called a few more times, leaving messages on my machine. In the last one, he'd said, "Ellie, please let's talk. I just want ... at least a chance to explain. You've made it clear that you want to be left alone, so I won't keep pestering you, but please ... call me when you're ready." He hadn't called since, which was a good thing ... at least, that's what I tried to tell myself.

Chapter 21

Christmas rushed up like an out-of-control train, threatening to flatten me if I stayed in its path. I'd been pretending the holidays weren't happening—I didn't send out Christmas cards or attend any of the parties I'd received invitations for. But although denial may be an effective way of protecting yourself from anticipating the inevitable shit-storm, it doesn't stop the shit-storm from striking. One day I looked up from my sketchpad, and the chirpy, blonde reporter on the Fox News Channel (I avoided watching Gold News at all costs, even if it was, in a sick twist of fate, my new employer) was announcing through her perfectly glossed mouth that there were only two shopping days left until Christmas, and then the television cut to footage of two soccer moms rolling around on the floor of a toy store, grappling like Greco-Roman wrestlers over the last Princess Foopy doll left on the shelf. Just as one mom was throwing a left hook at the other mom's nose, my answering machine clicked on—I had turned the ringer off on my phone—and my mother's voice filled the room, berating me for not having called her, asking me which train I was taking home, and pleading with me to talk Kate into coming over for Christmas dinner.

I picked up the phone. "Hi, Mom."

"You're there," she said accusingly.

"Yeah. I was, um, in the bathroom, and couldn't get to the phone."

"You were screening your calls. I can't believe you'd do that to your own mother," she sniffed.

I sighed. "Okay, I was screening my calls. But since I picked up when I heard your voice, that means I wasn't screening you."

"That doesn't make it right," she said. And then, switching into her fakey cheerful voice, she said, "So what time are you getting home tonight?"

"What?"

"Ellie, what's wrong with you? You sound strange." And then, before I could answer, she continued, "You're taking the afternoon train home, right?"

Ah. Home for the holidays. Boy, did Bing Crosby, or whoever it was that sang that stupid song, have it wrong. There was no place I would rather *not* be. Mark was still moping around after Kate, Dad was still completely inaccessible, Brian was still an ass, and who knew what kind of narcissistic melodrama Mom would be indulging herself in. And to make matters worse, I still hadn't told them—any of them—that I'd been fired. Since there was no way I would be able to get through the holidays without Mom (or more likely Dad) asking me how work was going, and since I was completely incapable of lying to them about it, I was going to have to come clean. *Quelle* nightmare.

"I'll take the first train tomorrow morning," I sighed.

"Tomorrow? No, you have to come home today. Tomorrow we're supposed to go to the Parkers' for cocktails, and you'll never make it. Plus, there won't be anyone to pick you up at the train station," Mom said.

"Mark will pick me up. There's no way he's going to let you drag him to the Parkers'," I said.

"But tomorrow is Christmas Eve! And you always run back to the city right after Christmas, which will mean you'll hardly be here at all," Mom said, sounding like she was on the verge of tears, which no longer bothered me the way it might once have. Maybe my fog of depression came with the unexpected benefit of blunting the sting of parental guilt.

And she had to be kidding about my hardly being there at all. Ha! I only wished. But then that spine-tightening note of anxiety entered into Mother's voice, and with shrill, borderline hysteria she began to launch into a hissy fit about how my coming home late would ruin everything, how selfish I was being for not being more supportive of Mark, how Dad was counting on me to come home early, and who knows how much time Nana had left, and how sorry I'll be that I didn't spend more time with her before she passes on, and . . .

"Okay, okay. I'll come home this afternoon," I sighed, not so much defeated as just not wanting to fight this battle. I had a much, much bigger one coming when I announced that I had been fired from my job and was now working as a freelance cartoonist. The parental units were not exactly going to love that little holiday surprise.

But as it turned out, I was granted a temporary reprieve from having to spring my news on them. By the time I got to my parents' house, Dad was already in bed, and Mother was too busy twittering on about how she had been so successful at counseling Mark through his separation that she was thinking of going back to school so that she could become a psychologist (at the suggestion that she was helping him, Mark pantomimed behind her back that he was ready to slash his own throat).

The next day, both Mom and Dad disappeared—the former doing some last minute shopping, the latter off to the office, of course, so I spent the day sacked out on the couch with Mark watching television. Mark flipped through the channels without much interest.

"There's nothing on," he complained. Sally came trotting into the room with her stuffed soccer ball in her mouth. She dropped it in front of Mark and barked at it until he picked it up and threw it for her. "You should rename her Mia Hamm," he said, grabbing the ball out of Sally's mouth when she had retrieved it, and throwing it again. Sally scampered off after it, growling with delight.

"So, how are things going with you?" I asked.

He looked at me, incredulously. "My wife has left me, or rather I should say, has kicked me out of our house, and I'm stuck living with Mom and Dad, in all their dysfunctional glory. I'd say it's going great."

"You seem, well, pretty normal, though. From the way Mom was talking, I thought you were one step away from being committed," I said.

"Ah. The power of antidepressants," Mark said, smiling without humor.

"Really? Oh. Well ... good. If that's what you need. I know this must be a hard time," I said. Considering the cause of his marital split, I was still having a hard time mustering up compassion for him.

Mark, probably sensing my lack of genuine sympathy, just shrugged, and kept clicking through the cable channels. "I think they're running a story on the Finicorp merger," he said, turning the volume up on a news story, filling the room with Ted's voice.

I looked up, and Ted's disembodied face on the television screen was looking back at me. For a moment, my fog of depression lifted just enough to allow stabs of pain to puncture my chest. It was so strange, and so difficult to see him again. I had studiously avoided watching Gold

News, and had even removed the channel from the scan list on my remote so that I wouldn't stumble on him while flipping through the channels. To now see his face—his intelligent eyes, dignified chin, determined lips—caused a ripple of pain to rise up from somewhere deep inside of me and course through my body. Worse, our breakup didn't seem to be affecting him at all—there were no dark circles under his eyes, no weary sadness in his voice, no wan paleness to his cheeks. He was just sitting there introducing some news story, and then joking with the correspondent, as though life was as peachy keen as ever. But, of course, he hadn't suffered, I remembered. *He'd* gone back to his wife and rekindled what was probably the great love affair of his life. I was the only one left alone and brokenhearted. Ted and Alice were probably in the middle of planning a second honeymoon.

"What?" Mark said, glancing at me. "You gasped."

"Can we watch something else?" I asked.

"In a minute, as soon as the Finicorp story comes on," Mark said. "Being exposed to a little financial news won't kill you."

"I just don't like this station. Turn it to CNN, or Fox News, or something else," I insisted.

"In a minute," Mark said.

"Turn it the hell off!" I screamed.

Mark switched the television off and looked at me. "Okay, what's going on? You've been dragging around here looking like you lost your best friend, and now you're getting hysterical about a news show. You're not pregnant, are you?"

I had been taking a sip of Diet Coke, and as I snorted with laughter and surprise, it came out of my nose, bubbling and burning. I wiped my eyes, and blew my nose, and shook my head. "God, no. Everything else in my life has turned to shit, but no, at least I'm not pregnant."

"Tell me," Mark said.

"Yeah, right," I snorted, remembering the last time I'd confided in him about my love life. I'd been a sophomore in high school, and had proudly shown Mark a hickey on my neck—my first, given to me by Charlie—and for months after, every time Charlie came over, Mark would turn up, cackling in a Dracula voice, "I vont to suck your blood," and then laugh himself sick.

"No, really, I want to know," Mark said gently.

And for some reason, maybe because I didn't have anyone else to talk to, I told him all about it—about being fired, my fight with Nina, and Ted. And finding Ted with Alice. I started to blubber as I talked, and expected Mark to heckle me for it, as he would have when we were younger, but instead he just kept nodding and listening and handing me tissues. I wondered if the divorce was mellowing him, or if maybe a depressed society is a kinder society—depressed people just don't have the energy to mock you or burst into fits of homicidal road rage.

"I can't believe you were actually dating Ted Langston," he said, a note of reverent awe in his voice. "He's such a pro. I've been watching him for years. It's just ..."

"What?"

"He doesn't seem like your type. I mean ... he's so *old,*" Mark said.

"Gee, thanks," I said, a little huffily.

"It's just that all of your boyfriends have always seemed so interchangeable," Mark said. "Preppy. Boring. Young."

"I know," I said.

"Ted Langston is a *lot* older, not to mention smarter than anyone you've ever been with," Mark said.

"Mm-hmm," I sniffled.

"And I've never seen you this upset over a breakup. You're always breaking up with guys, not that I blame you. I don't know how you could stand Eric for so long.

All that guy wanted to talk about was football," Mark said, rolling his eyes. Mark had once made an innocuous statement about liking the Philadelphia Eagles in front of Eric, and every time they had met up after that, Eric had tried to engage Mark in long, detailed discussions about the stats of various players, going back fifty years. "But you went out with him for, what, a year? And you haven't mentioned him once since you dumped him. And yet you were with Ted Langston for all of a few weeks, and I've never seen you so upset."

"Well, there's also my job. And Nina," I said defensively. "My best friend has completely abandoned me. So I'm upset about other things, too."

"You didn't give a shit about that job. You just went to law school to please Dad. It's about time you stopped living out his blueprint for your life. And you and Nina will get it together. Old friends always do. I don't think that's what's really bothering you," Mark said.

I shrugged, and could feel the tears welling up in my eyes again. "I don't have a choice about Ted. He got back together with his ex-wife. I can't make him love me," I sniffed.

"Well, still. 'The heart wants what it wants,' " Mark quoted sagely.

"Who said that? Shakespeare?"

"No, someone more your speed. An older guy who chucked it all for his much younger girlfriend."

"Who?" I asked eagerly. Even though Ted and I had broken up, I was still compulsively collecting positive-role-model stories of May-December relationships. So far the only one I had come up with other than Michael Douglas and Catherine Zeta-Jones, and Rupert Murdoch and his wife, was Bogie and Bacall, although I think he up and died on her when she was still in her thirties.

"Woody Allen," Mark said, and he laughed wickedly.

I leaned over and punched him. "That's gross. I'm not Ted's adopted daughter, or whatever Soon-Yi was to him," I cried out, swinging wildly at him.

Mark just kept laughing as he blocked my blows. And then he lunged and tackled me, tickling my sides until I was crying and laughing at the same time.

"I really am sorry you got fired. I know that must have felt like shit," Mark finally said, after our giggles had subsided.

"No, it's fine. You're right. I hated that job."

"I know. I think you'll be happier in the long run," Mark said.

"Yeah, but what's Dad going to say?" I asked.

"Well, it should be another fun holiday at the Winters house," he said. "Merry Christmas, Ellie."

"Merry Christmas," I sighed.

I talked Mark into going to the Parkers' Christmas Eve cocktail party for my sake, which he finally agreed to on the condition that we took a separate car from our parents and only put in a brief appearance. This arrangement suited me fine. I knew I couldn't get out of going—any attempts to try would just spawn another tantrum from Mother—but I was all for cutting the visit as short as possible. I had been to the Parkers' annual holiday gathering before; between the inane chitchat and constant questioning about my love life, it was boring and tiresome under the best of circumstances. With my newly unemployed status and Mark's pending divorce, it was going to be impossible to get through the evening without having to endure a thousand prying questions from the gossipy old farts. Brian, of course, managed to worm his way out of going with little commentary from Mother, which was so unfair—my brothers never get pressured to go to these family events, but if I should try to get out of it, I would never hear the end of it.

The Parkers lived in the typical suburban family home, not unlike ours—four bedrooms, three baths, a formal living room, clubby television room, a pool table in the finished basement, newish Volvos parked in the two-car garage. Mrs. Parker had an unfortunate fondness for country kitsch when it came to decorating, and on every free wall hung rustic pictures of cows and pigs, and a ruffled plaid material was draped on every window and table. She also had a collection of those loathsome little porcelain boxes, and had hundreds of the things sitting out on all of the occasional tables, which meant that you couldn't rest your wineglass without knocking over some tchotchke or another.

"Ellie! Mark! How wonderful to see you both," Mrs. Parker cried out, pressing her bright red lipsticked mouth against my cheek. I furtively tried to wipe off the mark I knew she'd left, while she turned her attention to my brother.

"Now, Mark, your mother told me all about what happened with your wife. Just terrible. You know, my niece, Annabelle, is here, and I want you to meet her," Mrs. Parker said in a confidential voice, nodding at a lumpish looking woman in the kitchen who was arguing with someone. Mark made a strangled noise and started to back away, but Mrs. Parker got a firm grip on his wrist and started to drag him down the hallway. "Oh, no, don't give me that baloney about it being too soon to get involved with someone. As I was telling your mother, the only way you can get over a broken heart is to get back on the horse and ride again," she chirped.

With my only comrade-in-arms gone, I realized that I was vulnerable to a sneak attack by another neighborhood busybody. I tried to make a quick dash for the bar, set up as always in the living room, with the Parkers' sad-sack of a son pouring drinks. Ernie Parker, who was still wearing a retainer and had acne as bad as he'd had as a teenager despite the fact that he was a few years older than me, was thankfully now married, and so I didn't have to worry about anyone trying to play Cupid when I went over to get a drink (although Mother had actually tried setting us up when I was a freshman in high school, when Ernie hadn't been able to find anyone willing to go with him to the senior prom). But before I could make it to the bar, I was intercepted by a house of a woman who was wearing a sweater with little Santa Clauses and candy canes embroidered all over it.

"Ellie Winters," Christmas Sweater boomed. "I haven't seen you for years! Your mother told me that you were engaged."

I stared at the woman, trying to place her, but came up a complete blank. "Engaged?" I repeated, dumbly, wondering where Mother could have gotten that from.

"Oh, Gladys, I *told* you that her young man was *begging* Ellie to marry him, but that she simply wouldn't have him," Mother smoothly intercepted.

"Oh, that's too bad. My Sophie just got married, and I was going to see if you'd want to borrow her dress," Gladys said smugly.

Aha! I placed her. Sophie Metzger had been a year ahead of me in high school. Back then Sophie had thighs the size of tree trunks, and had sported a head full of tight, bright red Orphan Annie curls. Oh, God, if this woman thought I could share clothes with Sophie, had I somehow put on thirty pounds and not realized it?

"No, Ellie's far too busy with her career to worry about getting married. She's a very successful D.C. attorney, you know. What was it that Sophie does again? Isn't she a flight attendant?" Mother asked sweetly, taking a sip of her Scotch and soda. I could tell from the way she was slurring her words ever so slightly that it wasn't her first.

"She's a baggage-handling manager at the airport," Gladys said gruffly. "She's up for a promotion next month."

"How nice," Mother said, smirking a little behind her glass.

"So, your father's been telling me about a big case that you've been heading up," a loud male voice boomed. It was Dr. Berry, a neighbor from down the street who had been my orthodontist when I was thirteen and sentenced me to two years of wearing braces as large and shiny as the grille plate on a new Mercedes.

"That's right. Ellie's firm has big plans for her. Of course, I'd just as soon see her back home, where she might be able to get a seat on the bench," Dad said, also appearing. He was, as usual, wearing his favorite gray flannel three-piece suit, although tonight he'd paired it with a bright green Christmas tie that was more festive than the staid, striped ones he normally wore.

"Oh, is that right? Ellie, are you about to make partner?" Marion Charles asked. She was a thin stick of a woman, who Mother swore was an anorexic.

"Any day now, right, Ellie?" Dad said proudly.

There was a lot more chattering along these lines, and all of a sudden I realized that the elders had circled me in. No matter what direction I looked in, there was an older person blocking my way, peering at me as though I were an animal on exhibit at the zoo. They were all well on their way to getting loaded, and most had some sort of Christmas ornamentation affixed to their person—

a wreath pin here, reindeer antlers there. I desperately looked around for Mark, and finally found him, in the doorway to the kitchen, where he was pinned down by the lumpish Annabelle, who was wearing red leggings and sporting combs in her mousy brown hair. He gave me a wild, cornered look, and I could tell he wasn't going to be any help to me.

"Tell them, Ellie. Tell them about your lawsuit," Mother prodded me.

"It's a major class-action suit, and Ellie is the lead attorney on it," Dad bragged.

"I wasn't the lead attorney," I muttered. "Duffy is lead on that case."

"Well, that's just the name on paper. You're the one who was in charge of prosecuting the case," Dad corrected me.

I could hardly breathe. The living room was getting smaller, and with all of the people crowded in, it had become hot and stuffy. It felt like everyone's eyes were on me, waiting for me to hold forth on my glorious career. I started to feel a little dizzy, and my skin grew wet and clammy. I looked over at Ernie, willing him to toss me a glass of something—anything—but he was reading the labels off the liquor bottles and wouldn't meet my pleading gaze.

"Ellie?"

"Ellie ..."

"So tell us, Ellie ..."

I knew that there could only be, at most, six to eight people around me, including my parents, but it felt as though I were being crushed by a mob of thousands, all of them looking at me, waiting to see what I'd do or say, all of them expecting something from me.

"I'm not working on that case anymore," I said in a strangled voice.

Instead of my words dispersing the crowd, everyone just pressed closer, hands were touching me, mouths were gaped open, questions bubbling on the dry, rouged lips of the women and the dry, pale lips of the men. There were "Whys?" and "What did she say?" and my father was frowning and my mother looking at me a little anxiously, the way a circus trainer might look at a dancing poodle who was refusing to do the cha-cha on command. It was that look, the one on my mother's face, that caused me to snap.

"I AM NOT ON THE CASE ANYMORE BECAUSE I GOT FIRED!"

And then there was silence. The crowd thankfully backed off, giving me some air, which I gasped in.

"What did you say?" Dad asked, peering at me under furrowed brow.

"Ellie," Mother said, in a sharp, reprimanding voice.

"That's right. I was fired. And now I'm working as a freelance artist for a political news website. I'm never going back to being a lawyer," I said shakily, realizing for the first time that this was true, that I really wasn't ever going to seek out another firm job. The thought was liberating, which was ironic, considering I was currently being held hostage by a mob of what looked like oversized, drunken Christmas elves.

I became vaguely aware of the murmurings of the old gossips, and of Dad muttering under his breath, and of Mother trying to float overly cheerful suggestions for my behavior.

"She's been under a tremendous amount of strain," Mother explained.

And then I felt a heavy glass of amber liquid being thrust in my hands. I looked up and saw Ernie.

"I thought you might need this," he said. And then he

winked at me. If he hadn't been married, I would have tongue-kissed him in gratitude.

Mark and I departed from the Parker party about sixty seconds after I'd made my ill-timed announcement. Just enough time for me to suck down the straight Scotch, which burned my throat and hit my empty stomach with a dangerous rumble, and for Mark to shake off Annabelle and grab my hand.

When we were safely in the car, Mark shook his head and gave a low whistle. "Well, I think that went well," he said.

"Definitely," I said. "Please pull over."

Once Mark did, I opened the door and puked the Scotch up onto the curb.

We weren't home for long before Mother and Dad arrived. Mark and I had taken up our old positions, sacked out on the couch in front of the television set, Sally on my lap, half-watching *It's a Wonderful Life* and pretending as though we weren't dreading the return of our parents, when Mom stalked into the room, Dad following silently behind her. One look at their faces, and my spirits sank. Why couldn't our parents be divorced like all the *normal* adults their age, and spare us from these intolerable holiday get-togethers?

"How could you do that to me, embarrassing me in front of all of our friends?" Mom hissed.

"Mom," Mark started, but I waved him off. This wasn't his battle to fight.

"You're right, I should have told you earlier about my job. I just didn't know how," I sighed.

"Didn't know how? So that's the way you do it? Pulling a stunt like that?" Mom shrieked.

"Why did you lose your job?" Dad asked, and I was a little startled to hear from him. I knew he was heavily invested in my following in his footsteps, but he usually wasn't one for the family drama. Normally when Mom wound herself up, her eyes going all cold and narrow, her mouth pinching up as though it were on a drawstring that had been pulled tight, Dad disappeared into his study. It wasn't like him to stick around for the fireworks.

Mom quieted down long enough for me to briefly tell them what happened, about how Katherine had sabotaged me, how the case had been destroyed, and how all of the money the firm invested in it had gone down the drain.

"Well, why didn't you tell your bosses about this woman, this Katherine person?" Mom asked.

"Because she was sleeping with one of them," I said, with a humorless laugh. "Well, at least one of them. Who knows who else she was screwing."

There was an uncomfortable silence. Mom looked at Dad, Dad looked at me, I looked at Mark, Mark looked at the television, where *It's a Wonderful Life* was still playing with the volume muted.

Finally, Dad cleared his throat and said, "I think you should go back to the firm and ask for your job back. Accept full responsibility for what happened, promise them that it will never happen again, and then work twice as hard as you were working before."

I stared at him. "I'm not going to do that," I said.

"Why not?" Mom asked.

"Because I didn't do anything wrong. My work on that case was sabotaged," I said.

"But you don't have any proof that woman took the depositions," my father said.

"No, but I know she did. How would I prove it? I'm

sure they're not sitting in her office, waiting to be discovered," I said, not sure why we were even debating this point.

"Well, if you can't prove it, then you have to accept responsibility. You seem to be forgetting that, my dear. It was your case, those files were your responsibility, so the fact that papers were taken is really your fault," Dad said.

I stared at him, aghast. "No, it wasn't. How could it be? The files were kept at the firm, and every attorney who works there could have gotten to them. What was I supposed to do, bring home forty document boxes every night?"

"You could have made a duplicate set and kept them in your apartment," Mother suggested. I stared daggers at her. "Well, you could have," she sniffed. "It would have saved us the embarrassment of having all our friends know that our daughter can't hold a job."

"Mom," Mark said, his head snapping up. "Lay off her."

"Watch your tone of voice, young man," my mother said coolly. "You've hardly been an exemplary son yourself lately."

My father ignored them both, but continued to appraise me with his expressionless, judicious eyes. "If you won't try to get your job back, your only other choice is to move back to Syracuse. I can arrange for you to get a job with a firm here, or maybe with the district attorney," he said.

I looked from one parent to the other, shaking my head. "How dare you?" I said, my voice shaky but strong. "How dare you treat me this way? And how dare you tell me what my choices are?"

"How dare *you*! Going to a function where you're

representing the family, and causing a scene. You embarrassed your father and me in front of all of our friends, acting like that," my mother shrieked.

"I can act any damned way I please. I'm your daughter, not a performing monkey! And, yes, I lost my job, and maybe if I had been less trusting, or whatever, it wouldn't have happened. But that doesn't change the fact that it did. And I'm glad it did," I said. I looked at my father, who had folded his arms and was leaning against the doorjamb. "I *hated* that job. I *hated* being an attorney. I only did it because I thought it's what you wanted."

"I do want you to be an attorney. It's a good and honorable profession," Dad said.

"But I hate it! Every single day I worked there, I felt like it was killing me a little bit at a time," I cried.

Dad just shook his head dismissively. "Your entire generation expects life to be a walk in the park," he said.

"What? I have been working my ass off my entire life! First school, then college, then law school, then the firm. And all because it's what you wanted. It never occurred to me to do what I wanted to do. But now, for the first time in my life, I'm doing exactly what I want to do. I'm drawing, and I love it. Yes, it all happened in a way that was unexpected, but it's still better," I said.

And to this, my father simply shook his head, and started to leave the room.

"Yeah, go on and leave, Dad. That's what you do best, isn't it?" I said, my voice becoming shrill.

My father paused for a minute in the doorway, his back still to me. And then he left the room without looking back. I watched him go, and tears began to stream down my face.

"Eleanor Ann Winters, how dare you talk to your father that way? And how do you think all of this makes me feel? How do you think this makes me look to have all of my children fail?" she said, going into one of those rants that always used to make me shrink away from her with fear as a child. But I wasn't afraid anymore.

"Mother, there is a world beyond you. You should check it out sometime," I said.

"Excuse me?" Mother gasped with far more melodrama than the situation called for.

"This is my life. My being fired affects exactly one person. Me. Not you. Me. I haven't asked you for money, or for anything other than to listen to me and offer support," I said. Thirty years of anger started to well up in me as I stood and faced her. Sally fell off my lap onto the floor with a dissatisfied grunt. I continued, "You are the most selfish person I have ever met. You never think of anyone other than yourself. Yes, Brian, Mark, and I have all screwed up. But instead of offering us love and support, all you do is talk about how it affects you. How it makes *you* look and how *you* feel. Do you even care about how humiliating it was for me to be fired, or how much I love the work I'm doing now? And maybe Mark did screw up, but how do you think it feels for him to always have all of that pressure on him to be the perfect Golden Boy? We're your children. Why can't you just love us?"

"I'm not going to listen to this anymore. If you can't behave yourself, then I think you should leave," Mother said. She looked up at me with a set face, her lower lip trembling, tears welling in her eyes.

I shrugged and pressed my fingers to my temples. I suddenly felt so tired and drained.

"Fine," I said. "I'll go. Mark, will you take me back to the train station? I'll just go get my things."

And a few minutes later, we were in his car and on our way. The streets were empty; it was Christmas Eve and everyone was probably at home with their families, celebrating the holiday. Many of our neighbors had lined their driveways with luminaries and had turned their outdoor Christmas lights on, giving the deserted streets a strange, beautiful glow.

"Well, *that* went well," Mark said. He jabbed at the radio, and suddenly Frank Sinatra's voice singing "Jingle Bells" filled the car.

"Shut up," I said, without much force.

"No, I think we've stumbled onto a good strategy for ending these mandatory holiday family get-togethers once and for all. At every holiday, one of us will drop some sort of a bombshell—my getting divorced, you losing your job—and pretty soon Mom and Dad will start leaving town instead of forcing us all to come over. We can get Brian in on it, too—hey, maybe he can get his girlfriend *du jour* knocked up in time for Easter."

Despite the icky black gloom that had settled on me after the run-in with my mother, I started to giggle. "You could quit your job and join the Army," I suggested.

"No, you're thinking too small—how about getting charged with federal racketeering offenses, or adulterous affairs with the members of Mom's garden club? No, on second thought, I'll leave that to Brian ... for all we know, he *is* sleeping with the membership of the garden club."

"Which one?"

"Knowing Brian, all of them."

We laughed, and when I looked over at Mark and saw his face in profile, I felt a sudden rush of kinship.

"Tell me to butt out if you want, but I think that after you drop me off, you should go home. To your home. To Kate," I said.

"Butt out," Mark said, his eyes flickering toward me, and I fell silent, turning my attention to the people streaming out of our church after having attended the evening services. My family usually went to the midnight candle-light service, where everyone sings "Silent Night" while lighting candles, and the church is so lovely, so restful, and afterwards I always feel completely at peace. I would miss that this year.

After a few minutes, Mark said, "What if she won't let me in?"

"Then you sit down on the doorstep and don't leave until she lets you in," I said. "Or has you arrested."

Mark finally looked over at me. "I love her, Ellie. I love her so much I can hardly breathe. I can't imagine living my life without her. I don't know why I cheated on her, it was so fucking stupid. But if she took me back, I would spend the rest of my life proving to her that I'd never let her down again."

"Don't tell me. Tell her," I said. "Tell that to Kate."

I arrived back at my empty apartment well after midnight. Christmas had arrived, and I was spending it alone for the first time in my life. Well, except for Sally, of course, who, after going out for a potty break, trotted into my bedroom and leapt onto the bed. She circled three times, curled up in the middle of the bed, and immediately began snoring softly. I smiled at her, envious at how easy it was for her to relax. I looked around my empty apartment, wishing that I had taken the time to put up a tree, or at least some tinsel.

My parents hadn't bothered to come down and say good-bye, or to wish me a Merry Christmas when I left. My mother had locked herself in her bedroom, crying loudly enough for me to hear down the hallway, and my father had retreated to his office. It was the worst fight I had ever had with them. Sure, we'd had spats when I was a teenager, mainly over my use of the family car or my wanting to stay out past curfew. But I'd never confronted my dad on his coldness, or my mother on her selfishness. It had always been part of my role in the family to make nice, to do whatever I could to please them. And now that I had finally faced them for the first time, they'd carried through on the unspoken threat that had always lingered between us—they'd cast me out. As soon as I stepped out of my role as the Perfect Daughter, they'd discarded me like I was the family dog that had contracted rabies. And although it was hurtful, more than anything, I felt angry.

And in that anger, the fog that I had lived in for the past month dissipated. It was awful. I had never felt lonelier. My parents were gone. Nina was gone. Ted was gone. Everything was bleak, and gray, and hopeless, and it might never get better again. I started to shake, and I quickly changed into my grungy, soft plaid flannel pajamas and then jumped into my bed, pulling the comforter around me for warmth. Still trembling, I curled into a ball. I felt a sniffle at my ear. I turned to see Sally standing on my pillow, looking down at me with round, watery eyes. She stretched her chunky neck out and sniffed my face, finally stopping to lick my nose. I lifted the blanket up for her. She trotted down, under the covers, and curled up in the crook of my legs, behind my knees. Her hot little body warmed my own, and soon I stopped shaking, and eventually fell into a dreamless sleep.

Chapter 22

A few days after Christmas, I was awakened by the sound of the phone ringing in my ear. My bedroom was dark, and it felt like it was the middle of the night, but then I saw the bright numbers on my clock glowing. It was still early, only 10:03 P.M. I had been asleep for hours, but that was only because now that I was working at home, and no one was talking to me, I had started going to bed at about eight o'clock unless there was something worth watching on television, which wasn't very often.

I fumbled for the phone, grabbing it before the answering machine could pick up.

"Hello," I said, my voice still thick with sleep. I leaned over and switched the light on.

At first no one said anything, and just as I was about to hang up, thinking it was probably a crank caller, I heard a sound. It was a moan.

"Who is this?" I asked.

"He's gone," a voice said. It was a voice that I recognized even through the hiccuping sobs. It was Nina.

"I'll be right over," I said.

Nina and I hadn't talked in over a month, which was the longest we'd ever gone without speaking over the course of our twelve-year friendship. But there are some people you can always count on, no matter what. It wouldn't have mattered if ten years had passed by—one phone call from Nina, and I would still be by her side, holding her hand, no questions asked. She was the closest thing to a sister I'd ever had.

Thirty minutes later, I was sitting on Nina's couch, handing her tissues and trying to get her to drink a glass of wine, as she wailed, tears streaming down her face. The diamond chip engagement ring was gone from her hand. When the wails trailed off to sobs and then finally to hiccups, and she wiped her face with the wet facecloth I'd been pressing on her, she was finally ready to talk.

"What happened?" I asked.

Nina didn't speak for a minute, and I couldn't tell if she was getting ready to wind back up into tears again. "It's over. I gave him back the ring, and he's gone," she said.

"But why?"

Nina looked at me, sorrow etched on her pretty face. Well, it wasn't so pretty at the moment; it was actually red and blotchy and her nose had swollen up from all the tears. "He might have given me ... herpes," she finally whispered.

I gasped. With the exception of HIV, herpes was one of the worst sexually transmitted diseases you could get. There was no cure. If she tested positive for herpes, Nina would have it for the rest of her life. It would be something she'd have to share with every lover, every doctor, every insurance company, a check mark under the "yes" column of every medical history form she ever filled out.

"How do you know?" I asked.

"I found his prescription for a medicine called Valtrex, and when I looked it up on the Internet, I found out what it was for. I went straight to the health clinic and got tested. They told me that they'll have the results back in a few days," she said ruefully.

"What did he say when you confronted him about it?" I asked, reaching out to take her ice cold hand in mine.

Nina's eyes welled with tears again, and they spilled over onto her flushed cheeks. "He was so awful. At first he tried to accuse me, to act like I gave it to him. He called me a whore, and a slut, and he ... he raised his hand like he was going to hit me," she sobbed.

Now I was angry. So angry I wanted to track the son of a bitch down and slice off his balls with a rusty bread knife. First he might have infected my best friend with a horrible disease, and then he threatens her with physical violence. He was worse than a lowlife; he was the living embodiment of a puss-filled herpes sore.

"But you know how safe I always am—except for Josiah, I've used a condom with every guy I've ever been with," she continued, talking through hiccupy sobs. "And besides, he had his prescription filled in September, which was before we'd even met. He knew he had it, and he insisted that we stopped using condoms anyway. He *knew* what he could have been doing to me." Her voice was agonized.

"So did you ask him to leave?" I asked.

"Not right away. I was upset, but Ellie, I loved him so much. I actually thought that maybe we could work things out. You know, maybe there was a good excuse for it, maybe he thought that if he wasn't having a flare-up he couldn't pass it on. Anything other than finding out that he'd intentionally hurt me. But he just went crazy. He started yelling, and breaking things. He even shredded two of my canvases," Nina said in a trembling voice.

I noticed for the first time that her apartment looked like it had been hit by a tornado. Nina's work, her bright, larger-than-life paintings, normally hung all over the apartment, but now most of them had been knocked to the floor. One of them looked as though someone had stomped on it. Plants were overturned, a chair was on its side, and there was a hole in the wall between the living room and kitchen.

Nina saw me looking at the hole. "He punched it," she explained.

She seemed to be in a daze, and she'd started to shake a little. Although I thought it was more from the shock than cold, I got up to fetch a blanket from her bedroom and I wrapped it around her.

"Once he started getting violent, I told him to leave. And he just laughed at me, and said that if he left he would go stay with his ex-girlfriend. That he was still sleeping with her anyway, and that she wanted him back. And so I handed him his ring, and told him to get out and never come back," she said, shaking her head as though confused. She reached up to push some stray hairs back from her face, and I saw a dark discoloration on her wrist.

"What's this?" I asked, reaching for her hand to look at the bruise. "What did he do to you?" I demanded.

"He just grabbed me. It was my fault, really, because I tried to pull away from him," Nina said.

"Bullshit. It wasn't your fault. Do you hear what you're saying? You sound like one of those women whose husbands beat them up and they blame themselves," I said.

And strangely, because it wasn't funny at all, Nina started to laugh. "If he had tried to really hurt me, I would have kicked him in the balls so hard, he would never be able to fuck anyone ever again," she said. Despite her strange sense of comedic timing, Nina sounded a little more normal, as though the shock were starting to wear off.

"You're better off without him," I said gently. "You know that, don't you?"

Nina didn't seem as though she heard me. She still had a strange smile on her face, and she was rocking back and forth a little on the couch. "You want to know something? Josiah wasn't even his real name."

"It wasn't? What was it?" I asked.

"Joseph. He didn't think it sounded exotic enough, so he changed it to Josiah when he was in college," she said, starting to laugh again. "He told me a while ago, and made me promise not to tell anyone."

"You knew?" I shrieked. "You knew he changed his name to a stupid, pretentious name like *Josiah* and you agreed to marry him anyway? Okay, that's it. You know what we have to do."

Nina made a face. "Aren't we getting a little old for this?" she asked.

"Never. Come on. Every last picture that you've got," I insisted.

Nina got up and went to her bedroom, where I could hear her rummaging around. A few minutes later she reappeared, holding a bottle of wine, two glasses, an ashtray, a box of matches, two Sharpie markers, and a stack of photos of the despicable Josiah/Joseph.

"This will show that poser freak," I said, and, brandishing a Sharpie, made quick work of altering a close-up photo of his face. I darkened in his unibrow, added a pretentious goatee, and drew a dialogue bubble over his head that read, "I suffer from erectile dysfunction." After showing my handiwork to Nina—who rewarded me with a fit of giggles and a glass of wine—I set the photo on fire and placed it in the ashtray. Together, we watched the orange flames and black curling edges consume the asshole's picture.

"My turn," Nina said, selecting another photo from

the stack. "Ugh. I always hated the way he smiled in pictures. Look at the way he cocks his eyebrow up, like he's James Bond or something."

We happily dove into our work, and thirty minutes later, our supply of photographs exhausted (and a black, slightly toxic-smelling cloud of smoke thickening the air), we collapsed back on the sofa.

"What now?" Nina asked.

"Well, crank calls are out, thanks to Caller I.D. Did he leave any valuables around? A favorite leather jacket? His motorcycle, maybe?" Nina shook her head. "Unless you want to break into his ex-girlfriend's apartment and toss a dead fish behind her sofa, I guess our work is done."

Nina smiled. She looked calmer than she had when I arrived—a little revenge always does the broken heart some good. "I'm glad I called you," she said, a little shyly. With her hair pulled back in a high ponytail, her vulnerable face bare of makeup, Nina looked like I imagined she must have as a little girl.

My heart twisted as I realized we hadn't yet resolved our fight. As much as I hated confrontation, I hated my estrangement from Nina even more. If I didn't say something to her about it now, our friendship might never again be the same, but slightly crooked, like a broken bone that hasn't been set properly. Besides, lately my life had dissolved into a series of fragmented relationships—it was about time that I fixed one of them.

"Me too. I'm sorry about our fight," I started to say, and then stopped. I took a nervous breath, and continued. "It's just, I felt like I was losing you, and it scared me. I should never have said anything about it though. You were right that your relationship with ... whatever his name is was none of my business."

"No, *you* were right. I was losing myself. I never saw you, or any of my friends, or did anything that I wanted to. It's like I lost myself in him. I mean I was there, and I was sort of aware of what was happening, but I didn't care. It just felt so good to love someone," she said, her voice cracking. "I won't make that mistake again."

"You can love someone and not lose yourself. I think you just have to pick someone better. Someone stronger."

Nina laughed bitterly and her face hardened, and for a moment I thought that she was still angry at me. But then she said, "Someone who deserves me, right?" and I knew her anger was aimed entirely at her asshole ex.

"Don't do that," I said sharply. "Don't give him the power to diminish you. You *do* deserve better."

Nina shook her head, and looked tired. "What kind of a person am I that I would allow a guy to convince me to turn my back on my best friend? Because that's what happened, El. When I told Josiah about the fight you and I had, he told me that you were just jealous of my relationship with him, and that's why you wanted to break us up. And I actually believed him," she said, and her eyes filled with tears. "I've always hated those women who lose themselves when they become involved with someone and just push everything else in their lives aside. And that's exactly what I did."

I hugged Nina, holding her so tightly that I could feel the warm trickle of her tears seep into my T-shirt. "Well, good girlfriends don't *let* themselves get pushed aside," I said. "So it's just as much my fault."

"Men are assholes," Nina said darkly as she sat back and picked up her glass of wine.

I couldn't disagree with her there. "Even the ones that you think are okay turn out to be jerks," I agreed, and tipped the last of the wine into my glass.

Nina heard something in my voice and looked up at me sharply. "What's going on with you? Are you still seeing Ted?"

I filled Nina in on what had happened. I didn't have to get much further than finding Alice in Ted's apartment, wearing Ted's bathrobe.

"Men are such bastards," Nina hissed. And I couldn't really disagree with her.

When Nina was tired enough to fall asleep, I tucked her in and went home to take Sally out. The next morning I returned first thing, hot coffee in hand, knowing Nina would wake up lonely. In the bright, unrelenting glare of the morning light, Nina was drained and exhausted, but I was glad to see her still angry at Josiah, and not blaming herself for his unforgivable behavior. She smashed a few of the CDs he'd mistakenly left behind, and called a locksmith to have her locks changed. There was a gleam in her eye that I'd seen before. She was tired, and a little beaten down, but I could see glimpses of the old Nina for the first time in a long while.

We went to a greasy diner for breakfast and got more pancakes than two people could possibly consume, and as we started to eat, Nina perked up a little, and announced that she didn't want to talk or think about Josiah, at least for a little while.

"So what really happened between you and Ted?" she asked. "I thought you guys were getting serious."

"I did, too. I guess he was still in love with his ex-wife," I said, trying to sound more blasé than I felt.

"But why? I mean, they were married, and it just didn't work out, right? So why would they be in such a rush to get back together?"

I shrugged. "I don't know. It wasn't like I hung around to ask questions."

"You never asked him? But you must have talked. How else did he tell you that he and Alice were back together?"

"I thought the fact that she was in his apartment and undressed was as much information as I could handle," I said. "I haven't spoken to him since. Well, except for when he ambushed me at my office, but I told him that it was over."

"But then you have no idea what happened," Nina exclaimed, nearly dropping her fork.

"He did leave a message on my machine saying 'it wasn't what it looked like.' But it sounded like such a lie," I said.

Nina just stared at me. "And he kept pursuing you?"

"Yes. He called for weeks. I screened his calls."

"If he was getting back together with his wife, why would he keep calling you?"

I shrugged again. "Guilt, maybe."

Nina shook her head. "I can't believe you. Men who go back to their wives do *not* feel guilt over leaving their girlfriend. The only guilt they have is for their wife. I know, I've slept with married men before. What they do is disappear and never call you again. They want to pretend that you never existed. Maybe he was telling the truth," she said.

"I can't believe that you of all people would think that," I said hotly. "Why would Ted be any different than Josiah, or whatever the hell his name is?"

And then I immediately wished I hadn't said it, because Nina's face grew somber, and I could tell that she was fighting back tears again. After a minute she said quietly, "Do you think that Ted is just like Josiah? Do you think he's the kind of man that would cheat on you, maybe give you a communicable disease and then trash your apartment?"

And I knew that she was right. Ted definitely wasn't anything like the horrible ponytailed Joseph/Josiah.

"Okay, maybe he wouldn't do that, but Ted's incapable of opening up, of expressing how he feels. Sometimes, I guess, when we were alone, I could feel him lowering the walls a bit, but most of the time he'd just look at me with this completely shuttered expression. Even his ex-wife—or ex-ex-wife, I should say—said something about how closed off he is."

"Oh, yeah, we should take her word for it. The jealous ex-wife desperate to get her husband back—of course she'd tell the truth. Besides, what if he is a little distant?" Nina asked. "I know you've been waiting for Mr. Perfect Soul Mate to show up, but I hate to break it to you, El—no one's perfect."

"I didn't say he had to be perfect. But it's just one more way that we're totally wrong for each other. And look what he sent me," I said, and pulled the invitation to the Gold News New Year's Eve Ball out of my purse that I'd found waiting in my mailbox upon my return from Syracuse. I'd pathetically stuck it in my bag so I could reread the note he'd penned on the back. "See, he wrote, 'I'd like to still be friends. Hope to see you there,' on the back of the invitation."

"So?"

"So, if he wasn't back together with his wife, and he still wanted to see me, why would he say he wanted to be friends?" I explained.

"Well, maybe because he was trying to get you to go to the party so that he could finally pin you down and make you listen to what he has to say, you ninny. Say," Nina said, and her eyes narrowed as she stared at me. "What's going on? I think ... you are, aren't you?"

"What?" I asked, exasperated. Why did everyone feel they had to stare at me with laser-beam eyes, as though boring through my skull?

"You're in love with him. And it scares the hell out of you," Nina said, snapping her fingers, as though she'd just discovered how to separate the atom.

I scowled down at my plate and didn't answer her.

"After dating those chinless boys you couldn't have cared less about all these years, you finally met someone you could love. Who you *do* love. And instead of being brave, and accepting that, and accepting that Ted's a real person with real flaws, and not some generic fantasy man, and facing the parts of the relationship that are a challenge, you've just run away. The way you've been running away all your life," Nina said.

"I don't run away," I muttered.

"Yes, you do. Instead of standing up to your parents, or your boss, or me for that matter, you just run off and hide. You say it's because you don't like conflict, but I don't think that's the whole story. I think you're scared of what will happen if you start living your life on your own terms. As long as you're hiding from everyone and everything, then you don't have to be bold. You don't have to be brave," Nina said. She was back in her old form, her head tossing, her eyes blazing, and talking at a volume that would have drowned out General Patton addressing his troops.

I wanted to block out her words, wanted to put my hands over my ears and say, "Nah, nah nah, I can't hear you." But it was too late. They were oozing through the thick layers of my skull, coursing through my veins, puncturing into my heart. I looked up at her, and Nina went all blurry as my eyes watered up.

"If you don't start living the life you want, if you don't start being brave, you're going to lose everything," Nina said, gently.

The tears broke over my eyelids and began to stream down my cheeks, stinging my skin with their salty warmth.

277

God, I *hated* crying, and it was all I seemed to do lately. I'd even taken to bursting into tears during Kodak commercials, episodes of *Oprah*, and, on one dark night, during a particularly moving scene on *Survivor*. I looked up at Nina and saw her smiling at me with an almost maternal empathy.

"I do love him. But he's so much older than I am and no one thinks that it will work and look at Kate and Mark, they didn't make it and they're perfect and what if I want babies and marriage and he thinks he's too old, what then?" I gushed, and although it was gibberish, Nina was nodding wisely as though she knew exactly what I was saying.

"What if the world ends tomorrow? You love a good man, a strong man, and he loves you. Are you really willing to throw that away on a few 'what ifs'?" she asked.

And I knew I wasn't. I loved Ted. I loved him so much it hurt, so much that it was hard to draw a breath. When I was with him, everything felt right. And since we'd been apart, it felt like my heart had been pushed through a food processor.

"But how? How do I get him back?" I wailed.

"Well, now *that* is an interesting question," Nina said thoughtfully as she leaned back in her seat. "So, maybe we need to give him a bit of motivation." There was a glint in her eye that both frightened and heartened me. Although fragile and still a little soggy with tears, the old Nina was definitely back.

Chapter 23

It was the day before my thirtieth birthday, and, of course, also New Year's Eve. Some people might think that a January 1st birthday could be fun, and sure, at least I've never had to go to work or school on my birthday. But I have to tell you, New Year's Day really sucks as a birthday. First of all, as all people who have a late December or early January birthday know, the presents are awful. Either people are broke after all of their Christmas excess and end up getting you chintzy gifts, or they spend an extra five dollars more than they otherwise would on one gift and announce that it's a Christmas/birthday combo present. But being born on New Year's Day is especially rotten, because friends and family always want to tack my birthday celebration onto the already omnipresent New Year's Eve celebration, which no one really likes anyway. The parties always feel desperate, where everyone overdresses and overdrinks, all while worrying that there is another hipper, more glamorous party happening somewhere else that they weren't invited to. And every year, when everyone's really sloshed and has finished a raucous, slurred version of "Auld Lang Syne," the band inevitably kicks into an off-key "Happy Birthday to

Ellie," and maybe occasionally someone remembers to have brought me a cake. No one ever takes me out, or throws me a party (who feels like going to a party on New Year's Day?), and I have to be content playing second fiddle to Baby New Year.

But for once, this year I wasn't feeling bitter about my birthday, which was really pretty amazing considering that I was turning thirty, unmarried, unemployed, and my parents weren't speaking to me. Not to mention that I had spent the last five months obsessing about the day I would leave my ingenue days behind me, trading them in for crow's-feet, gray hairs, and the increasingly deafening boom of my internal clock.

Maybe it was lucky after all that I was having a crisis of the heart so that I wasn't worrying about everything else. I knew I loved Ted, which was terrifying, but it was about the only absolute truth I had in my life. And even more frightening, I didn't know if he loved me. I didn't even know if he was available, or if he had run back to the obviously open arms of his ex-wife. And if he was still single, I didn't know if the fact that I'd been snubbing him for the past five weeks had caused any interest he might have once had in me to dissipate. Even if I did get him back, we still had all of those life issues to deal with, namely that I wanted him to marry me and father my children, and for all I knew, his only immediate plans were to retire and lead the life of a wealthy, idle bachelor. So I was faced with this daunting challenge: I had to persuade Ted to leave Alice, love me, and give me the whole white-picket-fence American dream of a diamond ring, house in the suburbs, two cars, and rosy-cheeked babies clad in Baby Gap. And I didn't have the first idea of how I was going to do it. With that kind of a mission on my mind, it was impossible to spend too much time worrying about Father Time bearing down on me.

Nina said that she had a plan to get Ted back for me, which was more than I had, but that she wasn't going to tell me what it was. I begged, pleaded, and cajoled, but she held firm, saying that if I knew, it would just make me nervous. Which, of course, made me nervous. All she told me was that we were definitely going to be attending the Gold News New Year's Eve party, and that I should look gorgeous.

I hadn't completely forgotten that it was my birthday, and even though I had to be recession-minded, considering I was now existing on a rapidly ending severance pay and my diminutive income drawing for Gold News Online, I decided to throw caution to the wind and treat myself to a New Year's Eve spa day. The spa day is to women what the one-night stand is to men—a surefire way to reclaim your self-confidence (despite, in both cases, a small amount of initial anxiety about being seen naked by a complete stranger). One whole day of lying still while tidy women in starched white coats kneaded my aching shoulders, sloughed the dead skin off my feet, and vacuumed out the pores on my face. I was steamed, had jets of water pound at my body, and was wrapped in hot towels. For the first time in what felt like a million years, I felt light and unburdened. My back had been massaged, and I had taken deep breaths of lavender-scented air, and all of the stress I'd been weighed down with for the past few months lifted. I knew it was temporary—the minute I went back to the reality of being poor, unloved, and old, my shoulders would resume their normal position of being bunched up under my ears—but for now it was nice to be free of it all.

After my body had all of the stress rubbed out of it, I was prettied up—my hair was cut and blown out, my nails and toenails were buffed, filed, and polished, and finally, as an extra treat, the makeup artist applied foundation, blush, and eyeshadow with such a deft hand, I barely recognized the Ellie that stared back at me from the mirror. She lacked my constant dark under-eye circles, and somehow had new cheekbones carved into her face. I don't normally wear very much eye makeup, but the makeup artist rimmed my eyes with black eyeliner and layered shimmering gray and pearl shadows over my lids. The effect was dramatic, and incredibly glamorous.

I left the spa feeling like a new woman, like the kind of woman who gets profiled in magazines—the dewy-faced women who start up cosmetic companies or are the vice president of whatever at Prada, and who always have impossibly slim figures and über-hip wardrobes. And there I was—toned, pampered, and dolled up, looking like I could share their ranks, and all it took was five hundred dollars and an entire day spent in a terry cloth robe. I've often wondered, after being plunged into a dark hole of self-loathing and envy in the face of the beautiful, unattainable glossy-magazine lifestyle, why the entire readership of *Vogue* doesn't pitch themselves off their rooftops the day the magazine arrives in their mailbox.

The spa was in Georgetown, an area of the city I absolutely love and always wished I could afford to live in. After I left the spa, I decided to stroll around the posh neighborhood, past the quaint colonial row houses and upscale stores. I window-shopped for shoes I couldn't afford and dared not try on, considering the fat wad of cash I had left behind at the spa. But then I passed by a charming vintage clothing store, with gorgeous beaded flapper dresses and Jackie O sheaths in the window. I hesitated for a moment, seeing from the sign on the shop door that they were closing in only thirty minutes—I hate being that last person in a store that the salesclerks are dying to shoo out so that they can close up for the day—but then I caught sight of a dress hanging on a mannequin near the front of the store that made me gasp. I pushed the door open and made my way to the gorgeous creation, reaching out to touch it as if it were a mirage.

The dress was exquisite—it was classic and charming and bursting with such retro glamour, it looked like something a starlet might wear to the Academy Awards. It had two layers. The bottom part was really a slip of black silk, cut low in the bust and high at the thigh, and was sexier than any nightgown I'd seen. But over the slip was a second layer, also of black silk, but sheer and with silver and black beading forming an elegant, shimmering pattern.

"It's my favorite, too. In fact, it's one of the prettiest dresses I've ever had in," a voice said, and I turned to see a slim woman with a silver bob and unlined face, making it impossible to place her age. She was very slight, dressed in all black, and had a kind smile. "It's from the forties, although it's not representative of the era. So many women have tried it on, but for some reason, it just hasn't suited anyone. If they're too bosomy or curvy, it ends up looking almost burlesque. But you just might have the right shape to carry it off. What size are you?"

"I wear an eight or a ten, depending on the dress," I said.

She frowned. "I would have put you at an exact eight," she said.

I hadn't been eating very much since the Christmas blowup—maybe it had balanced out the post-breakup brownie-gorging damage. "Maybe I have lost a little weight recently," I admitted.

"I think it just might fit you. Would you like to try it on?" she asked, and I nodded excitedly, feeling like a little girl about to play dress-up with her mother's clothes.

A few minutes later, I had stripped out of my jeans and gray sweater, slipped the fairy wisp of a dress over my head, and was transformed by the vintage couture. The bottom layer clung to my body, making me look far more curvy than even my Wonderbra could. The top layer ended just over my knees. The cap sleeves and the hem were scalloped and festooned with a heavier beading, and as I turned to look at myself from all directions, there was no mistake about it—it was as if the dress had been made for me. It made me look like a movie star, particularly with my dramatic makeup, and the sleek cap of hair falling to my shoulders.

"Let me see how it looks," the nice shopkeeper called out, and as I emerged somewhat shyly from the dressing room, she gasped in appreciation. "It's incredible. It looks absolutely perfect on you. Are you going somewhere tonight that you can wear it?"

"Yes," I breathed, and then feeling a girly need to confide in her, said, "There's someone I'm going to see tonight. Someone that I . . . I need to look gorgeous for."

"Well, you'll certainly pull it off in that dress," the woman said. "Shall I wrap it for you?"

I felt the agony all women do when confronted with something absolutely beautiful that they want—no, *need*— to have, and yet know that there is no way they can afford it. I couldn't believe that I was even punishing myself by trying the dress on. It's like going to a French confectionary shop and ogling all of the cakes and pastries, and then going home to a box of Snackwells.

"I'm sure there's no way I can afford it. How much is it?" I asked, not having seen a tag, and braced myself to hear a sum roughly equivalent to the price of my first car.

But the salesclerk pursed her lips and appraised me in the dress. "I'll tell you what. I think that you were meant to have this dress. There's just something special about you in it. How does two hundred sound?" she said.

I was speechless. I could tell from the quality of the

fabric and the beading alone, not to mention the prices on the other gowns in the store, that the dress should easily have fetched four times that much. I nodded, and then before the woman knew what hit her, I'd thrown my arms around her. It was like having my own fairy godmother.

At 7 P.M. I was standing in my apartment, admiring myself in the mirror. The transformation was complete. I'm the kind of woman who looks in the mirror and instantly zeros in on every last zit, frizzed hair, and bulge of fat. But even I, my own worst critic (well, apart from my mother), had to admit that I looked prettier than I ever had before. The dress looked even better now that it was paired with sheer black stockings and my beloved Jimmy Choo strappy black stilettos, helped out by a pair of gut-sucking panties and a black Wonderbra. Plus, the sparkly vintage look of the gown, along with my black-kohl-rimmed eyes, made me look like someone altogether different, someone maybe a little more dangerous and mysterious than I, the consummate Good Girl, could ever hope to be. My hair, falling to my shoulders in a straight, shiny sheet, also looked liked it belonged to someone else; the stylist had spent a good twenty minutes blowing out every last bit of curl and frizz.

My door buzzer sounded, and my heart skipped a beat. I knew it was only Nina—although I still didn't know what she was up to—but this was it. We were going to go to the Gold News Ball, Nina was my date, and somehow I was going to find Ted and convince him that I was his Happily Ever After. How I was going to go about this (particularly if Alice had managed to attach herself to him), I had no idea. Other than looking my best, and opening my heart to him, I didn't have any plans.

285

"It's me," Nina said when I pressed the intercom, and I buzzed her up.

A minute later she knocked on the door, and I opened it. And then nearly passed out from shock. Nina wasn't alone. Behind her, decked out in a well-fitted tuxedo, was Eric. As in my *ex-boyfriend* Eric, whom I hadn't seen since the night we broke up in the bar of McCormick & Schmick's.

"Eric, um ... it's good to see you," I said, glaring at Nina and gesturing for them both to come in the apartment.

Nina was looking smug and a bit vampy in a skin-tight red gown cut so low that a nipple threatened to pop out every time she moved an arm. She air-kissed me on the cheek, and then whistled with appreciation. "Ellie, you look amazing. I've never seen you look better! Turn around," she insisted.

"Thanks. What's going on?" I asked, looking from Nina to Eric and back again. Surely these two weren't dating. Not that I'd mind—actually, I'd be thrilled for them both. Eric was a sweetheart, and probably exactly what Nina needed, coming off her relationship with the odious Josiah/Joseph. But judging from the way Eric swooped in and planted his lips on mine while simultaneously copping a feel of my bottom, I thought probably not.

"Hello, Eric," I said in a tinny voice while prying his hands off me. "Um ... what are you doing here?"

"Surprise! Nina called and told me you wanted me to come but were too embarrassed to call me yourself," he said, smiling.

I looked at Nina, confused. Had she told him about Ted? Why did he look so happy about my being in love with someone else, particularly since he'd made it so clear that he wanted to get back together with me?

"I told Eric that you'd had second thoughts and maybe

wanted to get back together," Nina said slyly. "So I took it upon myself to play Cupid."

I stared at her, wondering if in her misery over her breakup with Josiah/Joseph, she'd somehow confused everything I'd told her about having fallen in love with Ted. But then, with a slow burn of horror, I suddenly realized what she was up to—Nina was planning on using Eric to make Ted jealous. I shook my head, still staring dumbfoundedly at Nina and Eric. How could she? Nina knew that Eric had feelings for me. It was cruel to bring him into this, especially telling him that I wanted to get back together with him.

"Eric, can I talk to Nina for a minute? Here, pour yourself a glass of wine if you want. We'll be right out," I said, and then clamped a hand on Nina's wrist and practically dragged her into my bedroom, closing the door behind us.

"Ow," she yelped, rubbing at the Indian burn I'd given her on her wrist. "That's a fine way to thank me for all the trouble I've gone to."

"This was your plan? How could you?" I hissed at her. "Eric is a person. He has feelings. How could you tell him that I want to get back together with him? All it's going to do is hurt him."

Nina waved her hand at me dismissively. "Men don't have feelings. Eric's probably just excited at the idea of sleeping with you again, and once he realizes that it's not going to happen, he'll toddle back to his football and beer, and never give it a second thought," she said flippantly.

"Jesus Christ. I can't believe that you'd do this to me. And to *him*." I gestured toward the closed door. "You know how important tonight is to me. This is just going to complicate everything," I exclaimed.

"You're being awfully shortsighted. You said that Ted has a jealous personality. Seeing you on the arm of another guy is going to drive him crazy! All you'll have to do is say the word and he'll be yours," Nina said, looking pleased with herself.

I could only shake my head. "When he saw me with Charlie, Ted and I were dating, and were already set to have one of those State of the Union relationship talks. Seeing me with Charlie just made him realize that he wanted to be with me enough that he wasn't going to worry about our age difference. Everything's different now. We're not seeing each other, he may or may not be reconciling with his wife, and I actually know that I ... love him. I need to be honest with him, not pull some Lucy-and-Ethel stunt like trying to make him jealous with an ex-boyfriend," I pleaded. "Please undo whatever it is you've done."

To her credit, Nina mustered up a semi-contrite look, although I could tell that it was about as genuine as Bill Clinton professing to feel my pain. From the glint in her eyes, and the mischievous pull at the corners of her mouth, I knew that she thought her little scheme would work as well as the Scooby gang's plan to uncover who was behind the haunting of the old mill.

"I don't know how I can do that," Nina said innocently. "I can't very well go and tell Eric that he's no longer invited, can I? If you're so worried about his feelings, won't standing him up now that he's already here, already dressed up, be worse than letting him down gently later, after you've reunited with Ted?" She paused, and then grinned wickedly. "And if for any reason your reunion with the newsman doesn't work out, at least you know you can get laid tonight. Just kidding," she trilled, dodging out of the way as I took a swipe at her.

Nina was right about one thing—how could I possibly tell Eric that I didn't want him to come with us? I followed her out to the living room, feeling the great weight of despair settling in on what had previously been my massaged, stress-free shoulders. The last thing I wanted tonight was complications. And seeing Eric, beaming at me with his enormous, puppy dog eyes, holding my wrap and purse with the propriety of a newly reinstated boyfriend, I knew that was exactly what Nina had pushed me into—a great big complicated mess.

Chapter 24

The Gold News New Year's Eve Ball was held at the Grand Hyatt Washington on H Street. I'd never been inside the hotel before, and was struck that it seemed better suited to the ring-a-ding-ding glitz of Las Vegas than the frumpy old District. The atrium soared several stories above us, and a pianist was tinkling away on a piano that was sitting on a lily pad floating in the middle of a miniature lagoon.

But if I'd thought the hotel lobby had been spectacular, the ballroom looked like a winter wonderland. Twenty-foot Christmas trees adorned with twinkle lights and gilded ornaments stood shoulder to shoulder, flanking the walls. More twinkle lights, twisted together with white roses and fir garlands, were wound up all of the pillars and strung across the ceiling. Above the garlands, gold and silver balloons were suspended from the ceiling by a silvery net, ready to drop at midnight. The tables were topped with snowy white tablecloths and festive topiaries of pine, roses, and poinsettias, and the chairs were dressed in white skirts. The wait staff were all wearing white satin suits trimmed with white faux fur—looking like escaped cast members from the Ice Capades—and they expertly navigated (on foot) through the glutted crowd bearing trays heavy with champagne goblets, bowls of caviar, and plates of lobster puffs, seared tuna, and truffled eggs.

After the month I'd spent watching cable news shows, I recognized quite a few famous politicians there, sleek and smarmy with attractive spouses on their arms. The Gold News broadcasters were also there in full force—I'd had to memorize their faces for the cartoons I'd drawn for the network's website, and easily picked them out of the crowd. The glossy women anchors were without exception breathtakingly gorgeous with perfect figures and flawless features, and the male reporters all had faces like game show hosts and sported little wire glasses. Standing just inside the door, I looked around, trying to catch sight of Ted. I strained up, standing on my tiptoes as best I could in the stilettos, looking for his familiar, lanky figure. But there were just too many people, especially too many tall men with graying hair dressed in tuxedos, to easily pick him out of the crowd. Where was he? Please tell me that I hadn't spent seven hundred dollars getting dolled up for the party, not to mention all the hours of obsessive worrying about what I would say to him, how I would say it, all of the possible fairy-tale endings, all of the possible hellish, mortifying, doomsday endings, only to have him not show up at the party.

"Here, Ellie," Eric said, handing me a flute of champagne he'd retrieved from a passing waiter. He slipped an arm around my waist, and smiled down at me in a frighteningly possessive, all-too-familiar way. He was acting as though we'd gone back in time to the day before we'd broken up, as though I hadn't been dodging his phone calls for the past five months.

"Oh, um, thanks," I said, trying to step away, although the sudden crush of people entering the ballroom prevented me from being able to duck his embrace. I glanced over at

Nina, and gave her an imploring look, silently pleading with her to intervene and confess her little scheme to Eric. But she just smiled at me, pretending not to notice my dilemma, and then looked back at the party.

"Would you like to dance, hon?" Eric shouted in my ear.

I shook my head and sighed. During the cab ride to the hotel, Nina had prevented me from coming clean with Eric, but now that we were at the party, I was going to tell him the truth—that I did not want to get back together with him and that I had not known what Nina was up to when she invited him—and hope that he wouldn't be too hurt by the charade. Maybe he would even laugh it off, and use the opportunity to scout around the party for someone new. I knew it was far more likely that I would either hurt or anger him, or possibly both, but a girl could hope.

"Eric, I need to talk to you," I began slowly, determined not to chicken out. "It's about why Nina invited you tonight . . ."

"Hello, Ellie," a voice said from behind me.

I spun around, dislodging Eric's arm as I turned, and found myself facing Ted. My heart leapt into my throat, and for a minute all I could do was gasp. He looked so gorgeous in his well-cut tuxedo. I've never been all that fond of men's formal wear, particularly since most of the time I'd seen men in ill-fitting rentals, with gaping collars and ugly cummerbunds. But Ted looked like Cary Grant in a black wool jacket that draped beautifully around his shoulders and nipped in at the waist. The suit had obviously been tailor-made, and it made all the difference.

I smiled up at him, feeling shy, not knowing what to say. I wanted to pour out my heart, to tell him how much I missed him, to tell him how much I hoped he wasn't with

Alice, that I wanted to believe that he had been telling the truth when he said that it wasn't what it looked like that night I found them dressed down in towels and robes. That I wanted to go back to the time when we had eaten pizza in bed, stayed up half the night talking, and made love in a way that made me blush just to think about it. And I wanted to tell him how much I loved him, and that I hoped he loved me. As I looked up at him, my eyes shining, I could swear I saw his neutral, expressionless face soften, the corners of his mouth turning up in a smile, his eyes looking down at me with tentative hope.

"You look lovely," Ted said softly.

"I was hoping you'd be here," I said, still smiling up at him. "I . . . I've been wanting to talk to you."

"Oh?" he asked.

Eric, who's always been a little slow on the uptake, suddenly realized that I had shifted my attention away from him, and he turned to find me, spinning around until he had inserted himself directly in between Ted and me.

"Aren't you going to introduce me, sweetie?" Eric asked, looking down at me. I could tell Eric didn't recognize Ted from television, which didn't surprise me—Ted was not, after all, a sports commentator.

"I'm Ted Langston," Ted replied, holding out his hand to Eric.

I quickly glanced at Ted to see if he had caught the "sweetie." He had. Ted was looking at Eric closely, and then at me, his face again unreadable. I knew I had to step in and do some damage control, or I was going to lose him before I had a chance to make my case.

"Ted, this is Eric Leahy, an old *friend* of mine," I said, hoping my emphasis would make it clear that I was not sleeping with him. "And this is Nina Renaud, also an old friend."

"So nice to meet you," Nina said. And then, turning toward me, she undid my damage control by saying, "Ellie, do you mind if I borrow Eric for a dance? I love this song."

I glared at her. "No. I don't mind. Why should I? Eric is just a *friend*." Friends only, I tried to make my tone imply. With no sex, ever again.

Nina gave a tinkly laugh, as though I'd said something hysterical, and dragged a confused Eric away. I winced when I saw Eric's face, and silently prayed that now that Ted had seen me with my faux date, Nina would be ready to come clean to Eric about why she had invited him. Ted also looked confused, and after watching Nina and Eric depart, he turned his reporter's gaze back to me. "He seems very nice," Ted said.

I nodded. "Yes, he's a sweet guy. But anyway, I really need to talk to you," I said, looking up at Ted imploringly. "Can we go somewhere private?"

"What, and miss the party?" a female voice interrupted. Out of nowhere, Alice had appeared and hooked her arm into Ted's in an overly companionable way. She was wearing a red sheath that was so understated it must have cost a fortune. With her smooth, glossy bob, creamy pale skin, and sticklike body, she looked terribly exotic, and far too cozy as she cuddled up to Ted. I tried to comfort myself with the thought that even though Alice was beautiful, she just didn't look like a nice person, but more like the kind of woman who would devour her young. Of course, considering the last time I had seen her she'd been in my boyfriend's apartment wrapped in his robe, maybe I was a little biased.

"Hello, Ellen. So nice to see you again," Alice cooed.

"It's Ellie," Ted and I both said at the same time.

Alice giggled, and shrugged. "Sorry," she said gaily. "Ellie, of course. Isn't it lovely to see Ellie again, Ted? So I guess tonight's not a school night for you?"

I stifled my impulse to kick Alice in the shin, and instead looked from Ted to Alice and then back to Ted again.

"Christ, Alice," Ted said. He looked uncomfortable—maybe even annoyed—and he stepped away from her, breaking the hold Alice had on his arm. Still, I had to assume that his discomfort came from facing me, not from Alice's touch. In fact, it was obvious from the way she was standing so close to him that they were still together. And, I had to admit, they were a handsome couple. Looking at them, this successful, cosmopolitan couple, I felt nauseated, exactly the same feeling I'd had as a girl when I'd stayed on the merry-go-round for too long after eating a strawberry-dipped soft ice cream cone, and had stumbled off the ride with wobbly legs looking for a place to puke. Feeling rather like that now, I looked around, trying to locate an escape route.

"Well, it was nice to see you both again, but I should go find my date," I said in a falsely cheerful voice, and turned away, looking frantically around for Nina and Eric. I spotted them by the bar. Eric was waving at me, and Nina was holding on to him as though he were a frisky Labrador retriever puppy trying to run off, apparently trying to keep him from coming after me. I set off toward them, determined to look cheerful and carefree on the arm of another man, if only to save face in front of the sharply clawed Alice.

Before I could get too far, though, I felt a hand on my arm, gently spinning me back around. It was Ted—he'd apparently managed to escape Alice's clutches for a minute.

"Didn't you want to talk to me about something?" he asked softly.

I studied Ted's face for some sign that he still cared, hoping to see something that would give me hope. But Ted was as inscrutable as always, and as I glanced over his shoulder, I saw Alice waiting for him to finish talking to me.

"No," I said reluctantly, turning away from them. "It wasn't important."

For the rest of the night, I drank. A lot. As soon as I reached Nina and Eric at the open bar, I ordered two champagne cocktails, which I drank, one after the other, hardly pausing between the two to take a breath. I put the empty glasses down on the bar and ordered two more.

"Come on, let's dance," I said grabbing Eric's hand and pulling him toward the dance floor. I was starting to feel giddy and loose, the pain of seeing Ted and Alice together blunted by the champagne. I danced around wildly to the band's covers of "We Are Family," "Buttercup," and "Brown Eyed Girl," wiggling my hips and swinging my arms around, dancing in the way you can only when you have enough drinks in you that you don't care what you look like. Besides, the rest of the crowd was hardly sober and sedate. I clearly saw the House whip doing a drunken version of the twist, a congressman from Rhode Island dancing with three women, twirling them each in turn, and a member of the Senate Judiciary Committee dirty-dancing with a young tart clearly not his wife. In fact, no matter where I looked, there was someone even more uninhibited than me, and the raucous mood of the crowd just seemed to grow and grow.

When the band shifted down into "It Had to Be You," Eric pulled me close to him, and we swayed from side to side, my cheek resting against his shoulder. Eric turned me around in a circle, and I saw Ted. I'd been avoiding him all night, keeping track of where he was and making sure to stay on the opposite side of the ballroom. Now he was dancing with Alice, rather formally. Ted was holding her out from him at a distance, one hand on her waist, the other gently clasping her hand. Alice was looking up at him, smiling happily and chatting about something. Ted smiled back at her, and then looked over her head, directly at me. When our eyes met, I pulled away from Eric and strode back to where Nina was flirting with a semifamous congressman at the bar.

"Vodka and tonic, please. On the rocks," I said to the bartender.

"Hon, don't you think you should slow down a little?" Eric asked.

"No, I don't," I said, taking my drink and slurping at the cold liquid. I tried not to wince as it burned my tongue.

"Ellie, what did he say?" Nina asked.

"What did who say?" Eric asked her, a confused expression on his face.

Nina ignored him, but nudged me. I drained my cocktail and shook my head at her. Thankfully, the room was already starting to get a little blurry. The blurrier, the better, I thought, and signaled to the bartender for another drink.

"Ellie," Nina nudged.

I turned toward her, trying—and failing—to focus on her face. I squinted, thinking she would look clearer, but all I managed to do was stumble toward her.

"Whoops!" I said, catching myself, and then stood, swaying from side to side. I clumsily pulled over a nearby chair.

"I think we should take her home," Eric said to Nina.

"Maybe we should. I think she's had a little too much," Nina agreed.

Humph, I thought foggily. They were talking about

me as though I weren't sitting right there, as if I weren't a fully grown adult capable of handling a few drinks at a New Year's party.

"Don't talk to me as if I'm not here," I said, and then realized that it hadn't come out quite right. "Mmmm, I mean, don't talk to *him* if I'm not here."

I paused, and hiccuped, and looked down at my feet.

"What did Ted say?" Nina hissed, kneeling in front of me. "Are he and his wife back together?"

I nodded miserably, and tears began to well up in my eyes. My head kept bobbing up and down, yes yes yes, while tears slipped down my cheeks. I waved at a passing waiter, and despite Eric's best efforts to intercept the flute of champagne, I soon had the glass in hand, and drank it, the tears still streaming down my cheeks.

"They were holding hands, and dancing, and are going to get remarried, and be together forever and ever, and I'm not ever going to marry anyone ever," I said.

As I slurred the words aloud, the blackness of this thought enveloped me like a thick, vile fog, filling my chest, lungs, throat, and nose, until I could hardly breathe. I had finally met my one true love, and I'd lost him. Forever. And now I was going to have to choose between a loveless life with Eric, or someone just like him, someone bland and boring who didn't challenge me or inspire me or encourage me to do something as crazy as leaving behind the law to pursue a career of cartooning, or else be alone for the rest of my life. And that wasn't a choice at all, because either way, I would be alone. Alone, alone, alone. Alone. Forever.

A sound gurgled in my throat, somewhere between a howl and a gasp, and I jumped to my feet and hurried from the room, out a side door and down a hall. I wanted to reach fresh air, to breathe in and out and make the blackness go away. But it followed me, shadowing my every step, cloaking me with a sticky film of misery. I couldn't outrun it, or hide from it, so finally I just slumped down on the flat plaid carpet, leaning back against the wall. I looked around me, blinking at the bright overhead lights, so startling a contrast from the candlelit glow of the ballroom. I was in a hallway, although not one that had hotel rooms on it. I could hear the whir of an ice machine, and the strong smell of chlorine permeated the air. Aha. I was near the pool. The thought of jumping into the cold, tranquil waters of a swimming pool sounded like a wonderful idea, the perfect way of clearing my head, of washing away the pain of having lost Ted.

I rose shakily to my feet and, leaning on the wall for support, began to inch my way down the hallway.

"Ellie!"

I turned, and there was Eric, his tie undone, frowning at me. I turned away from him, and tried to speed up, which wasn't easy to do on heels and which must have looked like I was doing a strange, teeter-tottering hopping. It wasn't helping that the hallway wouldn't remain steady, but kept spinning around me, so that it was near impossible to keep straight.

I looked back, and gave a little shriek when I saw that Eric had closed the space between us in no time at all, and was now looking quite irritated. He grabbed my arm, holding me steady, and said, "Come on, I'm taking you home."

"No you're not," I said hotly, trying to grab my arm back from him, but I only succeeded in giving myself a rub burn. "Ow, lemme go! I'm gonna swim."

"What has gotten into you? I've never seen you act like this," Eric said, staring at me.

I shrugged and stopped fighting him, and he released my arm. I rubbed at the spot where he'd been holding me.

Eric sighed. "Come on," he said. "I guess we can talk

about … things in the morning, when you've had a chance to sober up."

"What things?" I asked.

"I don't think we should talk about it now," Eric said. He nodded his head back toward the ballroom, the last place I wanted to go. For all I knew, as soon as I walked back in there I'd be faced with Ted nuzzling Alice's neck, or the two of them cooing to everyone that they'd just gotten reengaged. I sat down on the carpet again, wrapping my arms around my knees. Thankfully, the world stopped spinning, except of course when I leaned my head too far back or closed my eyes, at which point everything would start spiraling so quickly I felt as though I were on the Tilt-A-Whirl ride at an amusement park. And not in a good way.

"I want to know what you're talking about," I said crossly.

"Fine," Eric sighed, and sat down next to me. He tried to take my hand in his, but I grabbed it back from him, and crossed my arms in front of me. "God, Ellie, what is going on with you? Nina said that you wanted to get back together with me, but all night you've been acting like you can't wait to get rid of me."

I closed my eyes and shook my head. In my vodka-soaked state, I had completely forgotten to tell Eric that Nina had lied to him. How could I have neglected to tell him that I had no intention of getting back together with him? It was downright cruel to use him this way, and I'm never cruel. If I ever sobered up and regained my motor skill coordination, I planned to kick myself, hard, and Nina, too. I could throttle her for setting Eric up to get hurt, as well as for putting me in a position where I would have to hurt him. I had already broken up with him once, and through no fault of my own the entire thing had been undone, and I was stuck having to start from the beginning. I knew I should have done it in the ripping-off-a-Band-Aid style in the first place, so I guess it served me right.

"Eric, you know I'm fond of you, but Nina shouldn't have called you and invited you here tonight," I said. I closed my eyes, trying to control the carnival ride effect.

"Oh?" Eric said. I opened my eyes to look at him, to see if my words had angered or hurt him, but he had adopted Ted's neutral, impossible-to-read expression. Is every man capable of this? I wondered, irritated at the thought, but then felt guilty because it was hardly Eric's fault that we were having this conversation.

"Yes," I continued. "She asked you for her own reasons. I had nothing to do with it."

"So you're not interested in getting back together with me?" Eric said.

I shook my head. "No. I'm so sorry. I wanted to tell you earlier, but then ... well ... I'm just sorry," I finished stupidly.

"I see," Eric said, and then fell silent for a minute. "Do you know why Nina told me that you were?"

This time I nodded, not wanting to tell him that he'd been used, and I'd been first too chicken and then too drunk to tell him.

"Why?" he asked.

I sighed, and bit my lower lip. Suddenly I felt sober, although I knew from the buzzing in my head that I really wasn't.

"Because there's someone else that I'm ... interested in, and Nina thought that if he saw me with you, it would make him more interested in me," I said, aware of how awful the excuse sounded. "I'm so sorry, Eric."

He didn't say a word, and I dared to sneak a peak at

him. But his face was still blank, his eyes shuttered, as he digested my pathetic story.

Finally, still looking straight in front of him, he said, "So you were just using me?"

"No," I said. "Absolutely not. Well, maybe, but I didn't mean to. I didn't know what Nina was doing until she showed up with you at my door tonight. And then I tried to tell you, but I got distracted and . . ." My voice trailed off. My excuses sounded pathetic to my own ears, so I could only imagine what they sounded like to Eric.

Eric exhaled audibly, and when I glanced up at him this time, a shadow had fallen across his face, and his normally jovial blue eyes were dark and angry. He shook his head from side to side, as though disbelieving what was happening.

"I'm so sorry," I said, and reached for his hand, but this time he pulled away from me.

"You know how I feel about you. I can't imagine I've left you in any doubt over it, considering how many times I've called, how many messages I've left you that you never bothered returning. And you and your little friend in there"—Eric jerked his head toward the ballroom—"think nothing of lying to me, of, of . . . *using* me so you can make some other guy jealous?"

I looped my arms around my bent knees, and bent my head forward in contrition, tears streaming down my face.

"I'm sorry," I whispered. "I didn't mean for this to happen."

"Yeah, I bet." Eric spit out the words as he jumped to his feet. He stood over me, a formidable, towering figure. "You know, Ellie, I really loved you. And the main reason was that I always thought you were a really good person. At least that's how you always acted. But now, knowing how I felt about you, knowing what you meant to me, you didn't think twice about using me in your sick little game."

"No," I said, appalled. "No, I didn't want to do it. I didn't want to involve you in any of this. I just didn't know how ..."

"To tell me the truth?"

I nodded. "Please believe me, I never meant to hurt you."

"Too fucking late," Eric snarled. He turned to leave me, but then glanced back. "You know what, Ellie? You're not the nice girl I always thought you were. You're a manipulative, scheming bitch, and I'm glad to be rid of you."

And then he left. And I stayed on the floor, my arms wrapped around my legs, crying until I didn't think there were any more tears left in me. After what seemed like hours, I struggled to my feet, and limped back into the party to search for more alcohol.

Chapter 25

When my eyes opened, I immediately felt like retching. The nausea lapped over me in waves, and I lay as still as I could, breathing in and out through my cotton-dry mouth, until the impulse had passed. The room was no longer spinning, thank God, but there was a larger problem.

I sat up and looked around. Everything was white—white walls, white ceilings, white bedding on the modern steel bed. The modern theme was repeated throughout the room—sleek black bedside tables and dressers, steel-toned lamps, black-and-white photos in well-matted frames, a long flat planter of grass by the window. It was the kind of room they showcase in magazines, everything very expensive and minimalist. But that wasn't the problem. The problem was that it was a room I'd never seen before. I had no idea where I was.

I looked down at myself, praying that I wouldn't be naked, or sporting some kind of a leather-and-chain bondage ensemble. Thankfully, I was wearing blue cotton men's pajamas, although they were far too large for me and definitely not mine. Then I noticed that my dress and stockings were neatly folded on a black steel chair by the wall, with my purse and shoes stacked on top of them. Obviously, someone had undressed me, and then redressed me in the foreign pajamas. The idea that I had been so drunk I had somehow ended up in a strange place, and that someone—or some people—had dressed me and seen me naked, was terrifying, and I wrapped my arms in front of me, feeling violated but thankful that I was waking up safely, and not bloody and bruised in a street alley. Wonderful way to turn thirty, I thought, suddenly remembering that it was indeed my birthday. If I had been conscious at midnight, when the Gold News revelers were sure to have been ringing in the New Year by throwing confetti and blowing those obnoxious paper horns while balloons and glitter fell from the ceiling, I had absolutely no memory of it. This—waking up in a strange place, wearing strange clothes, with the worst hangover of my life—would be my first memory of my fourth decade of life. Lovely.

Trying to ignore my pounding head, I slid out of the bed, landing on the floor with a soft thud, and padded to the door, which I opened and peeked out of. The hallway was much more familiar than the bedroom. I instantly recognized the toffee-colored walls and white carpeting, and at the end of the hallway I caught a glimpse of a familiar blonde wooden floor that I knew led into a sleek kitchen stocked with stainless steel appliances. It was Ted's apartment. A cold dread settled on me, and all I could think was, *Shit, shit, shit, fucking shit.* Ted must have brought me back home with him last night, and I could only imagine how I had behaved while so drunk I couldn't remember what had happened the next day. I took some comfort in knowing that I hadn't been kidnapped by a gang of sexual sadists, and that the person who had likely undressed me and then redressed me in the blue pajamas—which I now recognized, they were Ted's favorite pair—had at least seen me naked before. I fervently hoped that I hadn't made any drunken confessions to him.

With my head still poking out the door, I listened intently, trying to hear if he was also in the apartment. Or, nightmare of nightmares, if he and Alice were both in the apartment, snuggled up in his enormous bed, maybe indulging in a little early morning nookie. With this dark thought, I retreated back into what I now knew was the guest room—just how big was this apartment, anyway?—closing the door behind me with a click. I wanted to think things through, remember how I'd ended up here, but all my head could produce was the dull, steady ache of a hangover. Try as I might, I couldn't remember anything about last night after the point that Eric had told me off. I shuddered with embarrassment, horrified that I had hurt Eric, ashamed that he now thought so poorly of me. The last clear memory I had was of grasping the ice cold drink in my hand and then throwing my head back as the ice cubes rattled against my teeth, impatient to have the effects of the alcohol seep through my body.

Well, at least one wish had come true, I thought. The alcohol had certainly hit me hard and fast.

I began to assess my options. I needed to get out of the apartment as soon as possible, and preferably before Ted and Alice began to stir. I didn't want to have a discussion with them about how loaded I'd been the night before, since it was obviously bad enough that they felt the need to bring me here rather than back to my own apartment. I briefly wondered what had happened to Nina and why I hadn't woken up on her sofa, but put that question aside for the moment.

I opened and closed a few drawers, hoping I'd find some sweats and running shoes in just my size, but they were all empty. Which left me with two options—either I'd have to get redressed in my cocktail dress and heels, or go home in Ted's pajamas. Neither option was all that appealing. I didn't want to be seen running around in oversized nightclothes, but on the other hand, in college everyone had always made fun of the girls who walked home in the morning dressed in formal wear from the night before, usually with hickies on their neck and carrying their stockings in their purses. The Walk of Shame, we'd called it, and it advertised to everyone you ran into that you'd fallen victim to the drunken hook-up.

Still, I didn't see a better solution. Besides, now that I was a grown-up, at least in theory, who cared if anyone knew I'd spent the night away from home? And what were the chances that I'd run into anyone I knew, anyway? All I had to do was get past Ted's doorman with my head held high, and I'd be fine.

I've got to get out of here, I thought. As I tried to both pull down my pajama bottoms and walk across the room at the same time, I stumbled over my own feet and fell to the ground with a resounding thud.

"Shit," I swore, and started scrambling to my feet, my heart pounding. *Please don't let them hear me,* I prayed. *Please don't come and ask me if I'm all right.*

There was a knock at the door.

I froze, the pajama pants still bunched up around my ankles. *Shit. Shit. Shit.*

"Ellie?" Ted's voice was muffled through the door. "Are you okay?"

"Um, uh-huh, fine," I said.

"May I come in?"

"Um," I said, stalling. I reached down and hurriedly pulled up the pants. I looked around to see if there was a mirror, wanting to see just how terrible I looked—if you're going to face the love of your life who dumped you for his ex-wife, and it's the morning after he hauled you home drunk and stumbling from a party, you don't want to face him with blotchy skin, bloodshot eyes, and breath that smells like you've been licking the floor of the subway station clean. But there was no mirror to be seen. I ran my hands through my hair, but it was all sticking up on top of my head. I remembered how much dark eyeshadow I'd been wearing the night before. It was probably bleeding around my eyes, no doubt making me look like a wonky raccoon.

"Ellie?" Ted said, and turned the door handle, cracking the door open. "Are you okay?"

I looked around, hoping to find a place to hide, perfectly aware that I was being ridiculous. And then I remembered once hearing someone say that the measure of a person is not what she is when everything is peachy, but what she does when the shit hits the fan, so to speak. So I sighed, and straightened up as much as I could, squaring my shoulders, lifting my head, and said, "Come in."

The door opened, and Ted stepped in the room. He was in pajamas, too, although he was also wearing his navy wool robe and leather slippers. For a minute, neither of us said anything, but just stood there, looking at each other. I was all too aware of how ragged I must have looked, but I loved the rumpled, almost vulnerable way Ted looked when he first woke up. It was the time when he was all mine. Or had been mine, I thought, remembering his ex-wife, and how she was likely in the next room.

"How are you feeling?" Ted asked.

"Never been better," I said crisply, but as his look turned incredulous, I grinned sheepishly. "Well, maybe a little rough around the edges."

"Happy birthday," he said softly.

He remembered. "Thanks," I said. "So, um, I'm afraid

to ask—and please don't feel the need to fill me in on every last embarrassing detail—but how did I end up here last night?"

"You don't remember?" He seemed surprised.

I shook my head.

"Any of it?"

"No," I said, feeling the color start to rise on my cheeks, now feeling quite sure that I didn't want to know.

"Oh. Well, I . . . I don't want to overstep my bounds," Ted said a little stiffly.

"What? Oh my God, what happened?" I asked, starting to feel a little panicky. Whatever had happened was so bad that Ted didn't even want to tell me. That must mean that it exceeded just normal drunken debauchery, or even stupidity. What had I done? I remembered my job with Gold News Online—had I done something to offend Nick Bloomfield, or one of the other higher-ups who had been at the ball? Were they going to fire me? And what if they did? My severance from Snow & Druthers was going to be over in a few short months. What would I do then? Go back to being a lawyer? The thought of going back to the litigation coal mines was unbearable.

"Well. Maybe you should sit down," Ted said, still standing across the room, and looking as though he would rather be anywhere else.

"Just tell me!"

"Okay, okay." Ted sighed. "I'm sorry to have to be the one to tell you this, but you and your . . . boyfriend broke up last night. And after he left, you became very upset, and had too much to drink, and I was worried about you, so I brought you here," he said. He thrust his balled-up hands in the pockets of his robe, and stared hard at the framed black-and-white prints hanging on the wall over the bed.

"Eric? He isn't—wasn't—my boyfriend. I mean he was, 309

before, but not last night. We broke up ages ago. Nina asked him to come with us last night because ... ah ... well, it's not important why, and he sort of got the wrong idea of why she asked him, and I had to tell him that he was mistaken in thinking that we were getting back together, but we certainly didn't break up. Not last night, anyway," I explained.

"But you said ..." Ted began, and then stopped. He'd stopped staring at the wall, and now looked at me, his face unreadable.

"What did I say?" I asked.

"You said that ... that he was the love of your life, and that now that he'd gone back to her you were going to be alone for the rest of your life. I was under the impression that he had broken it off with you for another woman," Ted said.

I blushed so furiously, it felt as though my skin had caught fire. Stupid ass that I was, I had obviously been so blotto I'd not realized I was talking to Ted when I started to go on and on about how heartbroken I was now that Ted had gotten back together with Alice. I had no doubt that I was verbose, since I've always been a Chatty Cathy when drunk. Thank God Ted hadn't known I was talking about him. That would have turned what was an incredibly embarrassing situation into the kind of unbearable mortification that would prevent me from ever going out in public again.

"Ah," I said, struggling to regain my composure. "Well. I'm so sorry that I was such a bother. If you'll give me a minute, I'll get dressed and be on my way. I don't want to take up your whole day."

Ted looked as though he wanted to say something else, but then he just nodded, and left the room, closing the door behind him. Once alone, I quickly stripped out of the pajamas, neatly folding them on the bed, and pulled on my dress and shoes. I stuffed my pantyhose into my tiny, bejeweled evening bag (a near magical feat, since it looked like it was only big enough to hold a lipstick). While doing so, I found the powder compact I had stuffed in there, and now eagerly opened it so that I could see if I looked as bad as I suspected. But when I peered into the small round mirror, I was surprised to see not a speck of black eyeliner, dark gray eyeshadow, thick mascara, or blood red lipstick anywhere on my face. Instead, the face I was looking at had been freshly scrubbed at some point, and other than my skin being a little puffy from the evening's excesses and my eyes more than a little bloodshot, I looked about as I normally do in the morning. My hair wasn't even that bad, other than being a little frizzy.

I snapped the compact closed, and stuck it back in the bag, wondering if I had washed up and been just too drunk to remember it . . . or if Ted had not only gotten me out of my dress and into the pajamas, but had also washed off all of my makeup. But then I shook my head and decided that, for all I knew, Alice had been the one to do it. She was probably worried that I would get makeup stains on their clean white sheets.

I walked to the kitchen, thinking that Ted would be there—I could smell the coffee from down the hall, and could have killed for a cup—but the kitchen was empty. I could hear him talking to someone, probably Alice, in the other room. I steeled myself for the unpleasant and inevitable meeting with her. I took a deep breath and followed Ted's low baritone voice to the living room.

But once I got there, Alice was nowhere to be seen. Ted was alone, talking on the phone. I looked around, expecting her to pop out from somewhere. But there were no telltale signs of her presence, like the running of water or the smell of her perfume. Other than Oscar stretched out on his Orvis bed, happily chewing on a piece of raw-hide, Ted and I seemed to be alone. Ted was sitting on the couch—the same one we had first made love on, I remembered. When Oscar saw me, he gave a happy, throaty bark and raced over, his wiry body wriggling happily around my feet, and I leaned over to pet his fuzzy head. Ted turned to look at me. I saw a flicker of emotion cross his face, but it was quickly replaced with the shuttered, distant expression I was starting to get used to seeing on him. He was still talking on the phone, mainly saying "Yes" and "All right" to whoever was on the other end, but he held up a hand to me, signaling that he didn't want me to go until he'd gotten off the line.

"That's fine. Put it on my desk and I'll go over it in the morning. I have to go now, I have someone here. That's fine. Bye," Ted said, and then hung up the phone.

"Working on New Year's Day? That's dedication," I said, trying to keep my voice light.

"That's the news business. It doesn't stop for holidays," he said. "Would you like a cup of coffee before you go?"

I wanted one more than I could say—Ted has one of those high-tech cappuccino machines. But I glanced back down the hall, to where the closed door of the master bedroom was just in view.

"Don't you think I should just go? I don't think she'd really want me to stay," I said quietly.

It was Ted's turn to look confused. He frowned. "Who, Sally?"

"Oh, God, Sally. I forgot all about her. I'd better get home and let her out," I said. The thought of my poor baby at home, probably totally freaked out that I hadn't come home the night before and about to wet her pants—that is, if she wore pants—flooded me with guilt. "Thanks for everything. I'm . . . I'm sorry if I intruded."

I turned to go, still motivated by the need to get home to Sally, but also thankful for a reason to scoot out so quickly. I wanted not to have to talk to Ted about his rekindled relationship with Alice, to hear things I didn't want to know, to face him and have him tell me that no, he didn't love me after all. All I wanted was to get out of this apartment, away from Ted, from Alice, from all of the pain just being there caused me. All of my hopes and plans for reconciling with Ted had vanished; it truly was over. Even if Ted had been telling the truth about the night I found Alice in his apartment, it was obvious that they were together now. I had seen the way they stood together at the ball, her arm looped possessively through his. Maybe it was my own fault—if I had taken the time to listen to Ted's explanation that night, if I hadn't run away like a scared little mouse, then maybe it would have been me dancing with Ted and celebrating the arrival of the New Year with a midnight kiss. But I had run away, the way I always did at the first hint of conflict.

And then I remembered what Nina had said to me about taking off every time anything unpleasant cropped up. She'd been right—it was what I'd done all my life. I never stuck around and faced the conflict, I never argued for my position. Anytime there was the least amount of conflict, I tucked my tail between my legs and fled. It was what I wanted to do now.

But, at the same time ... something in me didn't want to run. I was tired of fleeing, much the same way I was tired of always hearing myself apologize about everything. What had all of this running done for me? Had spending my life avoiding the conflict actually gained me anything?

I thought about the day that Shearer and Duffy had fired me, and how I'd just sat there, not saying a word. Why hadn't I told them what Katherine had done? Maybe they wouldn't have believed me ... but maybe they would have. And even if the outcome had been the same, even if they had still decided to fire me, wouldn't I have felt better standing up for myself? Instead, I'd just slunk from the office, ashamed and defeated. I didn't even say anything to Katherine, the woman who had purposely sabotaged my career. And maybe I was happier out of the job, better off where I was now, but shouldn't that have been *my* decision to make?

And I thought about my parents, and how they had confronted me on Christmas Eve. True, I had stood up for myself then ... at least at first. But just when my Mother intensified the fight, I ran, bolting from the house without resolving anything. And I hadn't called her since, hadn't forced her to listen to me. Maybe she wouldn't see my side; in fact, chances were she would react in the same way she always had. But I *let* her do it. I did exactly what I'd criticized my father for ... at the first sign of conflict, he hid in his office. I'd learned from his example.

And I even thought about my little Sally, and how despite the fact that she was a tiny lapdog (well, okay, a fat, butterball lapdog), she had no qualms about making her wishes known and standing up for what she wanted. I never had any doubt about her feelings on taking walks (bad), going to the vet (very bad), and having her toenails clipped (would rather shred the hands of her beloved mistress than allow it to happen). And yet, despite her bossy, dictatorial personality, I still adored her, and loved having her sit in my lap while I stroked her silky forehead or round belly.

The last thing I wanted to do at that minute was to face Ted and confront him about Alice. And, knowing Alice was in the next room, the idea of her overhearing such a messy scene was unbearable. The easiest thing in the world would be for me to say my polite good-byes and walk away. But I had been doing the easy thing all my life ... and look where it had gotten me. I had allowed Alice to chase me away; I'd let everyone talk me out of a relationship that I had believed in; I'd thrown away what might have been my one chance for true love.

I turned around slowly, feeling truly sick at what I was about to do. I faced Ted, holding his gaze with my own, and taking a deep breath, I said, "Do you remember last night when I said there was something I wanted to tell you?"

Ted nodded. "Yes. You said it wasn't important."

"It is important. At least, it is to me. What I was going to say is ... that I should have said something to you that night. The night that I found Alice here in your apartment wearing your robe. I still don't understand why she was here, or why you were in a towel ... but I should have at least told you how I felt. I shouldn't have run away."

Ted's eyes didn't leave mine. "I know how it must have looked to you. But really, she just stopped by to talk. We're in the process of selling a vacation house we used to have in Maine. It wasn't dealt with during the divorce, and we needed to go over the details of the sale. Alice was soaked to the bone when she got here. On her way over, she'd been splashed by a truck hitting a puddle, and she was wearing my robe while waiting for her clothes to dry. We decided to go out to eat, and discuss our business over dinner. Since we had to wait for her clothes to dry anyway, I decided to take a quick shower, since I'd just gotten home from the gym. I know what you thought, but it wasn't that. I would never have done that to you."

This was harder than I thought. I actually believed what he was telling me ... it all sounded perfectly reasonable. Maybe if I had listened to him that night, Alice

315

wouldn't be in his bedroom now, waiting for me to leave. I wanted to cry.

"I believe you ... I'm sorry I didn't before. But maybe things worked out for the best for you," I said softly. "I know it must mean a lot for you to be back together with Alice."

This time Ted frowned, and looked confused. "What do you mean? Alice and I haven't reconciled."

"But ... isn't she here?" I said quietly, pointing down the hall to his bedroom.

"Here in the apartment?"

I nodded, feeling miserable.

But Ted shook his head. "Ellie, Alice isn't here."

I felt like I'd been granted a stay of execution. *Thank God,* I thought, breathing freely for the first time since I'd woken up. *Thank God she isn't here.*

"She's not?" I asked, trying to sound casually indifferent.

"Why did you think she was?" Ted asked. He was still frowning, his forehead knit with confusion, as though trying to piece together a complicated puzzle.

"Well, I ... I mean, I just assumed that since you were at the party together, that you'd ... well, I mean isn't it ..." I paused, not knowing what else to say.

"I didn't go to the party with Alice. The network sent out invitations to most of the newspeople in town, including Alice, but we didn't go together. Is that what you thought?"

I nodded. A tiny glimmer of hope found its way into my heart, and all I could do was look at him. Even if Alice wasn't actually in the apartment with us, for all I knew they could still be seeing each other. After all, I had seen the cozy way they were acting together the night before. Maybe they were keeping the whole reconciliation thing a secret, and in a minute he'd ask me not to tell anyone about it.

"No, Ellie. Last night Alice told me that she'd thought the divorce had been a mistake, and that she wanted to give it another try. But I told her no. I've moved on, and don't want to go back," Ted said.

"Oh," I said, happily. "Oh."

I realized that it had been Ted who had put me to bed the night before. He had changed me, and washed my face, and it suddenly struck me what a tender, romantic thing that was for him to do. I was suddenly filled with such a burst of joy, I wanted to kick off my heels and dance around the room.

But Ted didn't start dancing, nor did he run across the room and sweep me into his arms. He just kept standing there, looking at me with that same unreadable expression.

"But none of this really matters, does it?" Ted said. "Even if I haven't moved on, you certainly have. It was obvious last night that you're in love with another man."

I was a little startled by how angry he sounded. For a minute, I just stared at him, increasingly aware of my flight instinct beginning to kick in again. But I continued to steel myself against the discomfort, particularly when it occurred to me that this was as hard for Ted as it was for me. He hated discussing his feelings just as much as I hated conflict. And yet, we were both still there—I hadn't run off, he hadn't shut down. The thought gave me strength, and I pushed on.

"I told you. Eric was someone I used to date, a while back. I wasn't there with him. Well, I was, but we weren't on a date. Nina brought him along without telling me," I said.

"You told me that you loved him. In fact, you were

317

quite insistent about it last night. You went on and on about how he was your one true love, and that you'd never be happy with anyone else," Ted said.

"When you heard me say that my heart had been broken, I was telling the truth. But I wasn't talking about Eric last night. That wasn't about him," I said.

"Is there someone else that you've been seeing?" Ted asked, crossing his arms in front of his body.

"No. I haven't seen anyone since you," I said pointedly, but he just kept looking at me, now with that frown on his face again. "When I said that … about my heart being broken … about losing the man that I loved …"

I paused, and took a shaky breath. I didn't know if I was going to be able to say it. But then I looked up at Ted, and despite the hurt and anger etched on his face, I knew I had to continue. Even if Ted didn't love me anymore, I had to be brave and tell him the truth.

"I was talking about you," I said softly.

"You were?" Ted said, and the frown disappeared, to be replaced by a look of astonishment. "But I thought you … I didn't think you wanted to see me anymore."

"I thought that you were in love with your ex-wife," I said.

"I'm not. I'm in love with you," Ted said.

"Well, I'm in love with you, too."

And then we smiled at each other. Big, goofy, falling-in-love smiles. I jumped up from the ottoman and into his waiting arms, curled up in the one place I wanted to stay for the rest of my life. He squeezed me so hard, I had to gasp for him to loosen his grip, which he did while laughing into my hair. I took a deep breath and inhaled his familiar, spicy scent—and felt just like Cinderella must have felt when the slipper fit.

"I've missed this. I've missed you," I said, nuzzling the soft, warm area of his throat.

"Me too. I've been such an idiot. I should have planted myself on your doorstep and stayed there until you listened to me," Ted said.

"No, it was my fault. I was scared and confused, but I should have listened," I said smiling.

"I was scared, too. Mainly about being too much of an old fogey for you," Ted said quietly. "But then I learned what it was to lose you, and that was worse than anything else."

We began to kiss, and shortly thereafter we put the couch back to the test. And once again, it didn't disappoint.

Chapter 26

When Ted and I had finally disentangled ourselves from the couch, and after a protracted search discovered my bra wedged under a cushion, we dressed and went to my apartment, so that I could take a very disgruntled Sally out. While Ted was over, I also gave him the cashmere sweater I'd bought for him for Christmas, and in return he gave me a thousand kisses, which, all in all, seemed like a fair trade. Then he left for the office, giving me a final kiss and a promise that he'd take me out to dinner that night. I checked to see if I had any messages, and was delighted to see the light on my answering machine was blinking.

The first message was from Nina: "Ellie! Where are you? I saw you leave with Ted last night, and I want to hear everything. I stayed at the party until three, and had a great time. I left with such a hottie. I'm back in the saddle, girl! Talk to you soon. Oh, and happy birthday, by the way! You're a grown-up now!"

The second message: "Hi, Ellie, it's Harmony. Happy birthday! I hope I get a chance to talk to you, so I can tell you in person. Also, I have some big—*big*—news. It's about Harry ... oh, I can't wait to tell you. He proposed! Last night, at the stroke of midnight! I'm so excited, I can't wait to tell you all about it. Call me as soon as you get this. Bye!"

The third message was from Mark and Kate. They started it off by singing "Happy Birthday" in a horrible, off-key tone, and then Kate blew some kisses into the phone, and Mark said, "Talk to you soon, frog face," and sounded much happier than he had at Christmas.

Then there was another message from Nina: "Where are you? It's me again. Guess what? I called the clinic this morning, and they said the test is negative! Oh my God, I am *so* relieved! Call me as soon as you get in."

My parents hadn't called, and I knew that I was going to have to call them, to face them the same way I'd faced Ted. But I'd had enough conflict and confrontation for one morning. Today Ted, tomorrow the parents.

After I returned Nina's and Harmony's calls, and we all squealed girlishly about all of the big news we had, Sally and I crawled into bed and slept most of the day away.

Ted took me to Melrose in the Park Hyatt Hotel for dinner, where we ate in the glass-walled dining room. Ted had the Dover sole with roasted peppers and mushrooms; I selected the crab cakes accompanied by a rémoulade sauce. After many hours of sleep, a handful of Tylenol, and two gallons of water, I'd shaken off enough of my hangover to accept a glass of chilled sauvignon blanc, although it would be a long time before I'd indulge in vodka again—just the thought of it made me shudder.

"What's wrong?" Ted asked, noticing me wince.

"Post-traumatic stress disorder," I said darkly.

"Are you up to being out? We don't have to stay if you're not feeling well," Ted said. He leaned forward and touched my hand.

I laced my fingers with his. "No, really, I'm fine. This is all so wonderful," I said.

Ted lifted his glass to me, and I followed suit. "To the future," he toasted, and then we clinked glasses and sipped the wine, which was wonderfully crisp. "And happy birthday."

"Thanks ... I didn't quite expect to be spending it this way," I said, smiling at Ted. I was still holding his hand, and I squeezed it softly. "How have you been?"

"Work has been busy, as usual. We're launching a legal commentary show next week in the nine o'clock spot. It's going to highlight a major trial each night, not just the ones that are in the national spotlight already, but also smaller cases with really interesting facts or players," Ted said.

Our appetizers arrived—grilled squid for Ted, vegetable terrine for me. "Mmm, this is delicious. Want a bite?" I spooned a piece of the terrine onto Ted's plate. "I know someone who would kill or die to get on your show," I said.

"You?" Ted asked, sounding a little surprised. "But I thought you were out of the legal game for good."

"No, not me. Charlie Owens." Ted looked puzzled. "Cute guy, very smart, quite a bit younger than you," I said playfully. "Don't you remember? He was kissing me at Starbucks ..."

"Ah, yes, *Charlie*. Hmmm ... no, I don't think there's a place for Charlie at Gold News. At least, not while I'm still in charge," Ted said. He offered me some of his squid, but I declined. There are just some things you cannot inflict on a delicate stomach.

"Anyway, that's not what I meant. I mean, I do want to hear about everything you've been up to at work, but I wanted to know how *you* are," I said.

A familiar look of discomfort crossed Ted's face. If I had to start standing up for myself, then Ted had to start opening up. It was only fair.

"December was ... difficult. I thought I'd lost you," he said quietly.

I waited for a minute, while our appetizers were whisked away with a deft efficiency and replaced with plates of tossed greens and Parmesan shavings, thinking that he was going to go on, but Ted didn't say anything else.

"I know. Me too. Good thing you stopped running away from me every time I tried to talk to you, or else we might never have gotten it together," I teased.

"Yes, good thing. And you? How have you been? I talked to Bloomfield, and he tells me that you're going to be a regular contributor to the website," Ted said.

I knew he was changing the subject, but I didn't have the heart to keep prodding him to open up his deepest, darkest feelings to me. No one was perfect, after all, and if it took him a while to open up, then I was willing to wait. He was worth it. I was suddenly reminded of what I'd thought when I first met Ted—I'd thought he was attractive in a perfectly imperfect sort of a way. Perfect for me, anyway.

"Yup. I'm now a full-time political cartoonist," I said, shaking my head in amazement. "Which is pretty incredible, since I don't know a damn thing about politics—I don't even vote. I draw all of my work as a complete outsider."

"But that gives you a fresh perspective. Being neutral in such a partisan town will make you truly unique, and will make your work stand out. I'd be amazed if you

POSEING 30

aren't being chased around by every newspaper in town soon. Are you enjoying the work?"

"It's incredible. I absolutely love it. Of course, my father is darkening my face out of all the family pictures, but that's the price of happiness," I said wryly.

"Everyone's a critic," Ted said.

My crab cakes were incredible—it was the best meal I'd ever had. It was hard to say if it was just that the food tasted heavenly, or if it was the combination of it all—the lovely restaurant, the coolness of the wine, Ted sitting across from me. It was the most perfect birthday I'd ever had, even including the fact that I hadn't known where I was when I'd woken up that morning.

"Thank you," I said, reaching over again to pat Ted's hand.

"For what? I haven't even given you your present yet," Ted said.

"Oooo, what did you get me?" I asked excitedly. I hadn't expected anything, since it was a holiday and most of the shops were closed. Surely he hadn't had something secreted away just in case we reconciled . . . had he?

"I'll give it to you later," Ted said, but then, seeing my disappointed face, he laughed and relented. "All right, stop sulking."

He reached into his inside jacket pocket and withdrew a plain white business envelope. I frowned a little as he handed it to me, truly hoping he hadn't written me out a check . . . not that I couldn't use the money, it's just that it would be so impersonal, so tacky. But the envelope was thick and a little stiff.

"What is it?" I asked.

"Open it and see," Ted said. He'd tried to adopt his impassive, newsman expression, but for once, he was betrayed by his eyes, which were dancing with excitement.

I took a deep breath, tore open the envelope ... and withdrew a British Air ticket holder. I gasped, opened the holder, and pulled out the itinerary that had been thoughtfully tucked into the front pocket. It was two round-trip first-class tickets to London for a two-week stay later on in the month—one had my name on it, and the other Ted's.

"We're staying at the Meridien Waldorf Hotel. And I promise, it will be all play and no work. We'll sightsee to your heart's content."

All I could do was stare, openmouthed, at the paper in my hands. I barely noticed it when the waiter removed our plates. "How did you plan this?" I finally managed to say.

"Let's just say I may be my travel agent's least favorite client right now. I had to twist her arm to go into the office on New Year's Day, and I think she spent the entire time cursing my name. But I wanted to make sure I could give it to you tonight," Ted said. He looked a little worried. "Don't you like it? I know that you wanted to go on your birthday, but ... well, it wasn't logistically possible."

I realized that I hadn't yet thanked him, or told him that it was the nicest thing anyone had ever done for me. It wasn't just the expense of the present—which was considerable. It was that I had told Ted it was my dream to celebrate my thirtieth birthday in London, and he had made that dream come true. I looked up at him, his face becoming blurry through my tears.

"Thank you," I said hoarsely. "I just didn't think ... it didn't seem possible ... that this day could get any more perfect."

And then it did.

"I love you," Ted said.

"I love you, too."

We were sitting there, holding hands across the table, when our waiter reappeared with a slice of dark chocolate cake with a single birthday candle in it, and placed it in front of me.

"I'm not going to sing to you," Ted said, cocking an eyebrow. "I have a dismal voice."

"That's okay," I said, laughing. I closed my eyes, tried to think of a wish that hadn't come true, and then blew out my candle.

"Want to share?" I asked, pushing the plate between us so that he could reach it with his fork.

"Yes," Ted said. "Yes, I do."

About the Author

Whitney Gaskell grew up in Syracuse, New York. A graduate of Tulane Law School, she worked for several years as a reluctant lawyer before writing her first novel, *Pushing 30*. She lives outside of Washington, D.C., with her husband and two spoiled dogs.

You can visit her website at www.whitneygaskell.com.

Don't you love hot new novels like

Pushing 30?

It's fun.
It's fashionable.
And it's completely fat-free!

And now, here's something totally indulgent:
two exciting sneak-peek excerpts from two novels
sure to hit the "must-read A list" upon release.

Turn the page to sample

Kim Green's

Is That a Moose
in Your Pocket?

and

Sue Margolis's

NeUroTica

A Novel of Dating, Mating,
and Other Animal Instincts

Is
That
a Moose
in Your
Pocket?

KIM GREEN

Is That a Moose in Your Pocket?

BY KIM GREEN

On sale November 2003

Prologue

January 2001, San Francisco

It started with an e-mail, as things often do these days.

You see, I never intended to move to Montana. Or fall in love with a guy who thinks crème brûlée is men's hair gel. Or get caught in flagrante delicto with my ex-boyfriend by, of all people, my parents. Or commit industrial espionage. (Okay, that one had crossed my mind on occasion.)

In fact, the spring of my thirtieth year, getting away from it all was the last thing on my mind. My job as a Website editor was going well. I had lots of friends and a nice apartment, and, having been raised in Miami, where the unceasing sunny days and rows of scorched backsides tend to give one a permanent headache, I was looking forward to a typically bracing, fog-shrouded, tourist-lamenting San Francisco summer.

My stats: Name: Jennifer Maya Brenner. Born: Miami. Live: San Francisco. Surrendered virginity: Fort Lauderdale (embarrassing, but true). Provenance: Eastern European Jewish-American with a dash of French Catholic—just enough to cause me to turn up my nose at a youngish Brie, but not sufficient to know how to tie a scarf with panache. Family: Quite mad. Siblings: Karen, 38, and Benjamin, 34. Parents: See *Family*. Age: As I said, 30. State: Relatively, if inconsistently, well preserved. On my best days, I've been known to get carded for buying cigarettes. (Yes, I used to smoke, back when it was socially acceptable in California.) On my worst days, I can sometimes score a senior discount at the movie theater. Therapy: Most definitely. Light therapy: Probably not. Massage therapy: Whenever and wherever. Exes: Too many for sainthood; too few for a memoir. Interests: Writing, editing, drinking red wine, drinking white wine, killing green plants, extracting twenty-dollar bills from ATMs, stalking attractive fellow gym-goers, buying red shoes, yoga, and feeding the poor (okay, once, but I intend to repeat the act next Christmas, so I'm claiming hobby status in advance). Things I would never say in a personal ad, even though I enjoy them: walking on beach, seeing movies, cruising to Mexico, dining at fancy restaurants, watching sunsets, and doing it in hot tubs.

So there I was, in a nutshell.

If not perfect, my life was at least bearable and, on paper, even a little impressive. Okay, I cried on the stair-climber once in a while and ate whole pints of Ben & Jerry's New York Super Fudge Chunk in one sitting and dreamed about chucking it all and having tantric sex with my Indian ob-gyn, but basically, life was tolerable.

Then I got the e-mail and everything changed in a heartbeat. Sure, it all worked out great in the end, but it took a lot to get there.

Ex Marks the Spot

Six Months Earlier

The e-mail arrived in my in-box as I was killing time adding books and CDs to my Amazon wish list that I would never buy. *Starting a Dialogue with Your Inner*

Child's Child and *The Best Latin Dance Party Hits of 1980–1990* ring any bells?

To: Carl Hanson
From: Nancy Teason
Subject: Department Changes

C,
I've been giving the changes we talked about some thought, and the topline is, Jen's just not ready for this kind of responsibility. She has tons of talent, and with the right kind of mentoring, I think she could be a managing editor in a year or two. Irregardless [sic] of the current budget freeze, I think we need to look out of house on this one. We can talk about it more but this is really my gut call.

p.s. Steve and I have tickets to the Giants game on Sunday. Interested in making it a foursome?

Nance

Nancy Teason, Director of Product Development
Technology Standard / TechStandard.com

I read it through several more times, heart pounding. My college roommate, who is now a practicing personal coach with two homes (Laguna Beach, California, and Old Saybrook, Connecticut) and two ex-husbands (both in L.A.), says that the important thing in times of stress is to isolate the thought attack and put it away in your "negativity closet." I have tried this method several times and have found that it is nowhere near as satisfying as imagining backing an SUV slowly over the backstabbing turncoat who has wronged you.

    For about six weeks now, I've been going through the humiliating process of applying for my own job. Why do I think it's mine? Well, for one, my former boss, Jem Abbott Pierce (yes, that's really her name—Mayflower forebears) had the temerity to go have a baby and leave me stranded with her work. Not that I mind, since her job is infinitely more interesting than my own, what with the trips to L.A. in spring, New York in fall, and free shwag up the wazoo.

It just stands to reason that I, Jem's Fully Anointed Protégée, am supposed to take her place when she invariably decides that darning pashmina shawls, painting landscapes of rotting barns, and nurturing her blue-blooded progeny are more important than covering high-tech news in Silicon Valley.

One Internet hiccup, and a message I was never intended to see found its way to my in-box. This happens, what, once every five years or so? Twenty? As there was something omenlike about this, I grabbed my spongy carpal-tunnel wrist ball and squeezed obsessively while staring out at the parking lot, hoping for a divine or at least everyday revelation. I considered my options: Forward dreaded message to Carl and cc Nancy Teason (Treason?) with a kind *fyi* at the top, and pretend ongoing ignorance while conducting a quietly dignified job search, which would hopefully offer me 387,000 instantly vesting stock options and an all-straight-male staff? Delete dreaded message and sublimate my rage into therapeutic massage and book club? Reply to dreaded message using colorful expletives, stomp over to Carl's office, urinate on the copier, and fling my meager belongings in a box?

In the end, I did what I always do when I'm panicked—I called Robert.

He answered before the first ring.

"O'Hanlon." Robert always sounds incredibly butch on the phone.

"It's me. You are not going to believe this."

"Try me." Keyboarding clacking.

"Somehow an e-mail from Nancy to Carl was misrouted to me. They're not going to consider me for Jem's job." Tears at the back of my throat threatened to choke me. This only happens with Robert and my mother.

"Holy shit."

"Yes," I whispered.

"Hang on."

I can hear Robert ordering his minions around in a charming, drill sergeant–esque kind of way. Robert is creative director at a trendy advertising agency in The City, and that, in addition to his brilliant wit, ridiculously handsome black Irish looks, and ambiguous sexual orientation, has everyone from junior copywriters to VPs in a constant dither to get his attention.

"Okay, I'm back. What are you going to do, lovey?"

"I don't know. I've worked hard for this, and I deserve it! It sucks, it just sucks . . ." Then I ranted a little more.

"Okay, what time is it?" he asked when I was done. I held my tongue on this one because most of Robert's non sequitur remarks end up somewhere good.

"Three forty-five."

"Leave. Leave right now and meet me at work."

"I can't. I have to finish editing this week's bullpen and call some of the freelancers and—"

"No. Drop everything. It is absolutely essential that you leave immediately and take the special O'Hanlon job-fuck treatment."

Treatment?

Which is how I ended up puking in a gutter at three A.M., the *Meredith Gazette* editor's business card crumpled in the back pocket of my favorite jeans.

The next few weeks passed in a holding pattern. I struggled with how to act around Nancy and Carl, who, presumably, weren't aware that their betrayal had been discovered. In the meantime, I hung out with Robert, went to the movies, and spent one wrenching nuclear familial afternoon with Jem and her husband Micah, watching their adorable baby Milo systematically destroy their living room.

As always, Jem's view of my situation was illuminating.

"Why don't you just take that job in Montana with that friend of Robert's?"

"Montana? Jem, are you kidding? I live here, I have a *life* here. I can't just go off half-cocked to the boondocks for the first half-baked offer I get." I stroked Jem's old lab's auburn back.

Jem put her latte down and looked at me. "How do you think I ended up in San Francisco, Jennifer? Do you think the Abbotts and the Pierces grow up thinking of the West Coast as a civilized place with cities and culture and decent marital prospects? Hell, no," she snorted. "I'm not saying Montana is the panacea for everything you feel is wrong with your life, but you need to look at what is really keeping you here. You came out because of Damon, and I wonder if you're still here because of him. If I were your age, I'd definitely consider it. You're like me. We like everything scripted and deliberate and guaranteed. And that's fine, but it would be a shame for you to miss out on some really interesting opportunities just because you still hold out hope that Damon—who has his own baggage, mind you—will realize what he gave up and come back to you."

I doodled happy faces on the corner of the *New York Times* crossword. I knew she was right. I had rationalized my solitude over the past two years as a kind of break between relationships and a day didn't go by that I didn't bemoan my lack of a partner to experience life with. It was interfering with . . . oh, just living, and I knew it.

"I suppose it wouldn't hurt to send him my résumé," I said slowly.

Jem gave me her serene, patrician smile.

"I've always wanted to see Glacier National Park." My voice quickened. "I could sublet my apartment, maybe even take a leave of absence at the Tech Standard. It's not like it has to be a permanent thing—more like a vacation, really. A chance to do some beat reporting, see the country, get away from here for a while. If I don't like it, I can come home anytime."

Now I was getting excited. I could reinvent myself in the great outdoors, the Wild West, home of the free and survivalistic. A vision of me slinging a battered four-wheel-drive truck into a snowy parking lot crystallized. I would live in a cabin à la the Unabomber and order all my clothes from L. L. Bean. I would get to know people who gutted fish, shot moose, and maintained stern silences when confronted with the sissified behavior of city folk. I would eat steak for breakfast. I would be automatically skinny, a fortunate side effect of extreme cold and daily tussles with bears. If I didn't rope steer and barrel-race horses myself, I would at least drink beer with those who did.

I was going to Montana.

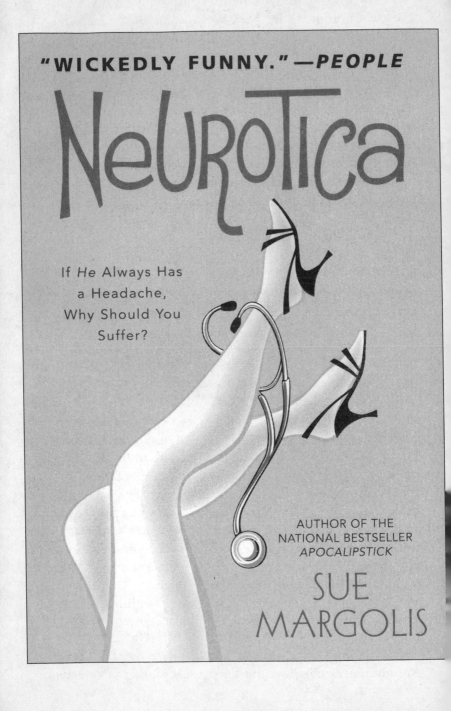

"WICKEDLY FUNNY." —PEOPLE

NeuroTica

If *He* Always Has
a Headache,
Why Should You
Suffer?

AUTHOR OF THE
NATIONAL BESTSELLER
APOCALIPSTICK

SUE
MARGOLIS

NeuroTica

BY SUE MARGOLIS

On sale in trade paperback
September 2003

Chapter One

Dan Bloomfield stood in front of the full-length bathroom mirror, dropped his boxers to his ankles, moved his penis to one side to get a better look and stared hard at the sagging, wrinkled flesh which housed his testicles. Whenever Dan examined his testicles—and as a hypochondriac he did this several times a week—he thought of two things: the likelihood of his imminent demise; and the cupboard under the stairs in his mother's house in Finchley.

It was a consequence of the lamentable amount of storage space in her unmodernized fifties kitchenette that Mrs. Bloomfield had always kept hanging in the hall cupboard, alongside the overcoats, macs and umbrellas, one of those long string shopping bags made pendulous by the weight of her overflow Brussels sprouts. From the age of thirteen, Dan referred to this as his mother's scrotal sac.

These days Dan reckoned his own scrotal sac was a dead ringer for his mother's. His bollocks couldn't get any lower. Dan supposed lower was OK at forty; death on the other hand was not.

By bending his knees ever so slightly, shuffling a little closer to the mirror and pulling up on his scrotum he could get a better view of its underside. It looked perfectly normal. In fact the whole apparatus looked perfectly normal. There was nothing he could see, no sinister lumps, bumps or skin puckering which suggested impending uni-bollockdom, or that his wife should start bulk-buying herrings for his funeral. Then, suddenly, as he squeezed his right testicle gently between his thumb and forefinger, it was there again, the excruciating stabbing pain he had felt as he crossed his legs that morning in the editors' daily conference.

Anna Shapiro, Dan's wife, needed to pee right away. She knew because she had just been woken up by one of those dreams in which she had been sitting on the loo about to let go when suddenly something in her brain kicked in to remind her that this would not be a good idea, since she was, in reality, sprawled across the brand-new pocket-sprung divan on which they hadn't even made the first payment. Looking like one of those mad women on the first day of the Debenhams sale, she bolted towards the bathroom. Here she discovered Dan rolling naked on the floor, clutching his testicles in one hand and his penis in the other with a look of agony on his face which she immediately took for sublime pleasure.

As someone who'd been reading "So you think your husband is a sexual deviant"–type advice columns in women's magazines since she was twelve, Anna knew a calm, caring opening would be best.

"Dan, what the fuck are you up to?" she shrieked. "I mean it, if you've turned into some kind of weirdo, I'm putting my hat and coat on now. I'll tell the whole family and you'll never see the children again and I'll take you for every penny. I can't keep up with you. One minute you're off sex and the next minute I find you wanking yourself stupid at three o'clock in the morning on the bathroom floor. How could you do it on the bathroom floor? What if Amy or Josh had decided to come in here for a wee and caught you?"

"Will you just stop ranting for one second, you stupid fat bitch. Look."

Dan directed Anna's eyes towards his penis, which she had failed to notice was completely flaccid.

"I am not wanking. I think I've got bollock cancer. Anna, I'm really scared."

"Relieved? You bet I was bloody relieved. God, I mean for a moment there last night, when I found him, I actually thought Dan had turned into one of those nutters the police find dead on the kitchen floor with a plastic bag over their head and a ginger tom halfway up their arse. Of course, it was no use reminding him that testicular cancer doesn't hurt. . . . What are you going to have?"

As usual, the Harpo was full of crushed-linen, telly-media types talking Channel 4 proposals, sipping mineral water and swooning over the baked polenta and fashionable bits of offal. Anna was deeply suspicious of trendy food. Take polenta, for example: an Italian au pair who had worked for Dan and Anna a few years ago had said she couldn't understand why it had become so fashionable in England. It was, she said, the Italian equivalent of semolina and that the only time an Italian ate it was when he was in school, hospital or a mental institution.

Neither was Anna, who had cellulite and a crinkly post-childbirth tummy flap which spilled over her bikini briefs when she sat down, overly keen on going for lunch with Gucci-ed and Armani-ed spindle-legged journos like Alison O'Farrell, who always ordered a green salad with no dressing and then self-righteously declared she was too full for pudding.

But as a freelance journalist, Anna knew the importance of sharing these frugal lunches with women's-page editors. These days, she was flogging Alison at least two lengthy pieces a month for the *Daily Mercury*'s "Lifestyles" page, which was boosting her earnings considerably. In fact her last dead-baby story, in which a recovering post-natally depressed mum (who also just happened to be a leggy 38 DD) described in full tabloid gruesomeness how she drowned her three-month-old in the bath, had almost paid for the sundeck Anna was having built on the back of her kitchen.

Dan, of course, as the cerebral financial editor of *The Vanguard,* Dan, who was probably more suited to academia than Fleet Street, called her stuff prurient, ghoulish voyeurism and carried on like some lefty sociology student from the seventies about those sorts of stories being the modern opiate of the masses. Anna couldn't be bothered to argue. She knew perfectly well he was right, but, like a lot of lefties who had not so much lapsed as collapsed into the risotto-breathed embrace of New Labour, she had decided that the equal distribution of wealth starting with herself had its merits. She suspected he was just pissed off that her tabloid opiates earned her double what he brought home in a month.

"But what about Dan's cancer?" Alison asked, shoving a huge mouthful of undressed radicchio into her mouth and pretending to enjoy it.

"Alison, I've been married to Dan for twelve years. He's been like this for yonks. Every week it's something different. First it's weakness in his legs and he diagnoses multiple sclerosis, then he feels dizzy and it's a brain tumor. Last week he decided he had some disease which, it turns out, you only get from fondling sheep. Alison, I can't tell you the extent to which no Jewish man fondles sheep. He's a hypochondriac. He needs therapy. I've been telling him to get help for ages, but he won't. He just sits for hours with his head in the *Home Doctor.*"

"Must be doing wonders for your sex life."

"Practically nonexistent. He's too frightened to come in case the strain of it gives him a heart attack, and then if he does manage it he takes off the condom afterwards, looks to see how much semen he has produced—in case he has a blockage somewhere—then examines it for traces of blood."

As a smooth method of changing the subject, Alison got up to go to the loo. Anna suspected she was going to chuck up her salad. When she returned, Anna sniffed for vomit, but only got L'Eau d'Issy. "Listen, Anna," Alison began the instant her bony bottom made contact with the hard Phillipe Starck chair. "I've had an idea for a story I think just might be up your street."

Dan bought the first round of drinks in the pub and then went to the can to feel his testicle. It was less than an hour before his appointment with the specialist. The pain was still there.

Almost passing out with anxiety, he sat on the lavatory, put his head between his knees and did what he always did when he thought he was terminally ill: he began to pray. Of course it wasn't real prayer, it was more like some kind of sacred trade-union negotiation in which the earthly official, Dan, set out his position—i.e., dying—and demanded that celestial management, God, put an acceptable offer on the table—i.e., cure him. By way of compromise, Dan agreed that he would start going to synagogue again—or church, or Quaker meeting house, if God preferred—as soon as he had confirmation he wasn't dying anymore.

Mr. Andrew Goodall, the ruddy-complexioned former rugby fly-half testicle doctor, leaned back in his leather Harley Street swivel chair, plonked both feet on top of his desk and looked at Dan over half-moon specs.

"Perfectly healthy set of bollocks, old boy," he declared.

Kissed him? Dan could have tongue-wrestled the old bugger.

"But what about all this pain I've been getting?"

"You seemed perfectly all right when I examined you. I strongly suspect this is all psychosomatic, Mr. Bloomfield. I mean, I could chop the little blighter orf if you really want me to, but I suspect that if I did, in six months you'd be back in this office with phantom ball pain. My advice to you would be to have a break. Why not book a few days away in the sun with your good lady? Alternatively, I can prescribe you something to calm you down."

Dan had stopped listening round about "psychosomatic." The next thing he knew he was punching the air and skipping like an overgrown four-year-old down Harley Street towards Cavendish Square. He, Dan Bloomfield, was not dying. He, Dan Bloomfield, was going to live.

With thoughts of going to synagogue entirely forgotten, he went into John Lewis and bought Anna a new blender to celebrate. One can only imagine that God sighed and wondered why he had created a world full of such ungrateful bleeders.

Anna got home just after four. Denise, her babysitter, had taken Josh and Amy swimming after school, so she would be bratless for at least a couple of hours—more if Denise got them sausages and chips at the pool. Anna decided to have a bath and a quick de-fuzz. All through the lunch she had been aware that she was having a bad pubic hair day. The sideburns on her inner thighs were reaching a density that would have done a woolly mammoth proud.

As she turned over Dan's knicker drawer looking for his razor, which he always tried to hide because whenever she used it she left it blunt and clogged up with leg hairs, Anna realized she was getting quite enthused by Alison's feature idea.

She'd said to Alison she wasn't sure if she had time to do it, which was a lie she always told features editors just in case they started taking her for granted. But she thought she probably would. She could never say no to work, in case the Alison O'Farrells of this world forgot who she was and never used her again. But more than that, while Alison was explaining the idea to her, she began to feel rather horny.

Alison had just received a preview copy of Rachel Stern's new book, *The Clitoris-Centered Woman*. Alison despised Rachel Stern almost as much as she despised polenta-eaters. Stern, an American, was one of a gaggle of beautiful Harvard-educated feminist writers, barely old enough to menstruate, who with their pert bosoms, firm arses and live-in personal trainers had the audacity to lecture the sagging, stretch-marked masses on how anti-wrinkle creams, Wonderbras and cosmetic Polyfillas were a form of treachery against the sisterhood, or some such rot.

In her last book, *Dermis,* Stern had railed against cosmetic surgery. On the day of publication she had led a massive protest rally outside an LA clinic to launch her "Get a Life Not the Knife" campaign. Hundreds of East and West Coast academics, "educators" and writers—mainly svelte Stern look-alikes, but with a smattering of token uglies—turned up to yell abuse at the women going into the clinic. According to the *LA Times* the protestors even dunked one woman's head in a vat of liposucted fat, thoughtfully provided by a mole at the clinic who was sympathetic to the cause.

"Look, I know you can't stand the bitch," Alison had said, "but I reckon *The Clitoris-Centered Woman* is actually quite sensible. It's about infidelity and why women are more reluctant to be unfaithful than men. She says women don't go in for extramarital shagging because they feel they can only do it if they are actually in love with the guy, and being in love with two men seriously does your brain in, so not doing it in the first place saves all the hassle of whose heart you're going to end up breaking. Anyway, Stern says that all this needing to be in love in order to have an affair is crap and women are just as capable as men of having affairs purely for the sexual pleasure—hence the title. So affairs become no more than a bit of glorified pampering—like going for a manicure or a facial except you get an orgasm instead of your blackheads squeezed. Of course, the most difficult part is keeping it secret and not blurting it out to hubby."

"And don't tell me, she reckons we should all be into extracurricular rutting because it can really zap up your marriage . . . and what you want me to do is to go out and interview three slappers who make a habit of being unfaithful just for the sex."

"You got it. Two thousand words if you can. You've got loads of time—she's not due over here to launch the book until mid-July, which gives you about eight weeks."

Anna realized she had got so carried away replaying in her mind all this talk of adultery that she had been absentmindedly shaving her pubes for at least ten minutes and had left herself with little more than a Hitler mustache between her legs. As she rinsed Dan's razor in the bathwater and watched her hairs float on top of the white scum, it began to dawn on her that if anybody needed to become a clitoris-centered woman, it was her.

Neurotica
Copyright © 1998 by Sue Margolis